*How do you evaluate books when you haven't
readers' reviews for my last five books from U!
— so thank you, readers!*

iews

CROCODILES ‚

Anna S (from the UK)	Hurrah for the _ ... .ciuivie wriuing tnat really gets you inside the head of Lady Bag, and tugs at your heart along the way. Brilliant!
Ann Dettmar (from Germany)	Liza Cody somehow understands the world of a paranoid, alcoholic homeless old woman as if she had been one, once... These two books... entertained me, hurt me, woke me, soothed me. I know how true to reality Cody's account is.
Holly B. (from Australia)	So glad I found these books. I enjoyed Liza Cody's books from years ago and recently came across Lady Bag, which I loved. And this sequel rounds off the story beautifully. A rare treat.
Kent E. Schroder (from the US)	Liza Cody has a sharp eye for both character and setting. This is clearly London, but a London as it is perceived by the homeless... Read every Liza Cody you can find and be as frustrated as I am, that there are not more.

LADY BAG

Joannaon	Cody at her best. If there were a possible six stars — or even ten — I'd choose that in a minute...
Virginia Ann Garbowski	Just don't pick it up when you have anything else to do before you finish.
Kirsten Johnstonon	I love the dog.

MISS TERRY

Julie Greeman	Loved this book!
Kathleen O'toole	Brilliant.

BALLAD OF A DEAD NOBODY

iChas	A gripping story very well told...
Hilde	Another great Liza Cody
A. B. King	What a writer!

GIMME MORE

A Customer	I loved this book/Leading the field again (*bought 2 copies — yay!*)
Mrs L C Harvey	The Truth About Rock and Roll
Ed "ramblingsyd"	The music biz, the seventies, born again rock chicks...

Other books by Liza Cody

Anna Lee series

DUPE
BAD COMPANY
STALKER
HEADCASE
BACKHAND
UNDER CONTRACT

Bucket Nut Trilogy

BUCKET NUT
MONKEY WRENCH
MUSCLEBOUND

Other novels

RIFT
GIMME MORE
BALLAD OF A DEAD NOBODY
MISS TERRY
LADY BAG
CROCODILES AND GOOD INTENTIONS

Short stories

LUCKY DIP and Other Stories

for Lisa — with love —

GIFT
OR
THEFT

Liza Cody

Liza Cody

iUniverse

GIFT OR THEFT

Copyright © 2020 Liza Cody.

Cover design by Olivia Rhodes.

iUniverse books may be ordered through booksellers or by contacting:

iUniverse
1663 Liberty Drive
Bloomington, IN 47403
www.iuniverse.com
844-349-9409

Because of the dynamic nature of the Internet, any web addresses or links contained in this book may have changed since publication and may no longer be valid. The views expressed in this work are solely those of the author and do not necessarily reflect the views of the publisher, and the publisher hereby disclaims any responsibility for them.

ISBN: 978-1-6632-0502-5 (sc)
ISBN: 978-1-6632-0503-2 (e)

Print information available on the last page.

iUniverse rev. date: 08/20/2020

For Mike and Delia Nassim, Chas and Jon Foulds,
Kate Butler, Sam Camden Smith, Rosie Cooper,
and Michael Z. Lewin.

And in loving memory of Felicity Bryan.

GIFT
OR
THEFT

ONE

My flatmate Amy left the Italian Bar and Grill before midnight. In a hurried whisper she told me she'd hooked up with a cousin of her second cousin by marriage. Even for Amy this was quick work. She'd only gone for a loo-break ten minutes ago.

'It's getting desperate, Seema,' she hissed as she snatched her coat and bag. 'I'm reduced to dating distant relatives now cos the only suitable guys I meet are at the funerals my mother forces me to go to. I'm sorry to leave you like this, but you know how it is – Noah's waiting.'

I looked for a Noah but I couldn't see one in the crowd around the bar. I suspected he'd be standard issue: dark thinning hair, needy eyes, medium size. Ten years ago Amy wouldn't have noticed him. Ten years ago she was trying to cop off with a tall blond singer in a goy band.

So that's why I was sitting alone in the Italian Bar and Grill round the corner from the Hoop Lane cemetery in Golders Green at midnight, looking like fair game to the elderly stranger who appeared at my side offering me another vodka and a packet of pork scratchings.

I accepted the vodka – I'd already drunk enough to zap out my cautious instincts. But I refused the pork scratchings.

He sat and said, 'Forgive me. The ancient laws pertaining to diet forbid pork, do they not?'

I smiled vaguely. I wasn't going to discuss my attitude to

religious practices with a stranger, however beautiful his suit. Peering through the gloomy lighting I revised my opinion of him. He looked as I imagined Mediterranean aristocrats to look – silver hair, fabulous suit, perfect shoes. Good taste seemed to float around him like the faintest hint of expensive cologne. And he'd probably had some extremely subtle surgery – his tanned skin was nearly unlined and was strikingly enhanced by the shining white hair.

I began to be dazzled. But I also thought he must be up to no good. Surely his natural stalking ground should be Mayfair, Paris or Monte Carlo – certainly not Golders Green. And wouldn't his natural prey be a leggy eighteen-year-old blonde of good breeding? Which I surely was not.

As the vodka worked its mojo, I said, 'You, my friend, look like a thoroughbred racehorse among run-down ponies.'

His teeth, when he laughed, were as perfect as the rest of him. He said, 'And you, my friend, look like an angel among the damned.' Which I thought was a pretty weird thing to say.

Strangely, following his notion of the damned, we talked about Hieronymus Bosch. He asked if I was an art student – which was flattering – and I asked him if he was an art historian because he knew so much more about the Garden of Earthly Delights than I did.

'I am a restorer,' he said.

And I am a gardener of sorts. I specialise in window boxes, patios and small London spaces. We went on to talk about gardens.

'A miniaturist?' He had a lilting trace of an accent which I couldn't place.

'That's a kind way of putting it. My mother calls it lazy. But the variety is wonderful: I've made Japanese moss gardens and desert cactus gardens. I've even made a Jurassic Park populated by plastic dinosaurs in a window box, and a vegetable patch on a patio.' I was showing off. Not many people take an intelligent interest in my work, and when they do I respond with too many words.

In turn he began to tell me about his Moonlight Garden in – yes – Italy. Apparently there were fountains and statuary. Scented white flowers with silver leaves filled the formal beds. There was a reflecting eternity pool, a white waterfall and a black pond fringed by white narcissi. The wild area was home to nightingales, owls, bats, silver foxes and glow worms.

'I wish I could see it,' I said dreamily, although part of me thought he was making it up as he went along. He sounded like a character from an old Fellini film.

'I wish I could see you there,' he replied. 'All women are at their most beautiful by moonlight.'

Then the barman called time and I struggled out of the dream and into my winter coat. It was only then that I remembered to introduce myself.

'Seema Dahami,' I told him, searching for my gloves. He didn't look like the kind of guy who'd engage in a hearty handshake.

He replied with the single word, 'Lazaro'. This, at the time, didn't strike me as odd.

We were the last to leave, and as we walked onto the empty street all the lights went out and the doorman bowed and kissed his hand. That *did* strike me as odd: hand-kissing isn't at all common in Golders Green. I wondered, with a sudden jolt, if my companion, far from being a romantic bull-shitter, was a Mafia don.

Then two things happened: it began to snow heavily – unusual in March – and a huge black limousine pulled up to the kerb in front of us. The driver, a young man of breathtaking beauty, opened the door and I peeked into an interior of complete luxury. There were black silk pillows, black sable throws and white ermine hangings. If Lazaro hadn't been following so close behind me I would have backed out fast: the limo didn't even *begin* to register on my normality meter. But he said, 'I will take you wherever you want to go.' So I told him my address and relaxed into cushions that held me like loving arms. I was tired and I'd drunk too much,

3

but I was in the company of a man with perfect manners. What could possibly go wrong?

Before setting off, the driver presented Lazaro with a long-stemmed ivory pipe into which he dropped a small black ball of a liquorice-like substance. He lit it with a taper before closing the door and walking through the snow to the front of the car.

Lazaro inhaled and an odd, lightly spiced smell filled the air. He leaned back and inhaled again.

'Opium,' he said gently, and handed me the pipe.

I'll try to explain why I took it. If he'd said, 'Heroin – share my needle,' of course I'd have jumped out and run for home. But he handed me something exotic in a gorgeously carved artefact. How could anything dangerous come in such a beautiful package?

After all, he was offering me the Romantics: Coleridge, Shelley, Byron, Keats and the dreams of Endymion, maybe even Mary Shelley and the nightmare of Frankenstein.

And he was offering me my own family history. My great, great grandfather, his sons, his brothers and cousins, made and lost fortunes trading in opium – the black gold they bought in India and sold in China. Yes, they traded in Arabic, Hindi and Chinese, but they prayed in Hebrew. Meanwhile their wives, aping the ladies of the British Raj, read English literature, including Keats, Coleridge, Byron and Shelley. Maybe they shivered with delicious fear at Mary Shelley's Frankenstein. Even though it's nothing to be proud of, my cousins keep our ancestors' opium weights on display as heirlooms.

Could Lazaro have offered me anything more seductive?

I took the pipe, placed my lips where his had been and tasted eternity.

His cool dry hand slid under my hair and slowly stroked the back of my neck. His touch started a tremor that spread all the way down my back.

'How did you know?' I asked.

TWO

'Get up you lazy cow,' Amy screeched. 'It's after nine. I've missed my bus and you've got to drive me to work.'

'For god's sake leave me alone,' I moaned.

'God won't help you when I get fired and can't make the rent and you have to find another sucker to put up with you.' She stripped my duvet back and flung jeans and a sweater at me. 'Come *on!*' Then, 'Is that a hickey? Seema, you dirty girl – what's Jake going to say? You were supposed to be on an innocent girls' night.'

I touched my neck and found a tender place.

'Tell me in the van,' she cried. 'Now *hurry!*'

Hurry? I could hardly struggle out of the deepest sleep I'd had in months. But Amy fed me the dregs of her morning coffee and I drove her across town to her office where she is someone importent's assistant. She is a completely different woman at work: a neat, confident, efficient dynamo.

'How was Noah?' I asked to head off questions.

'Good steady earner, imports shoes. Saving up for a house, flat, garage, whatever. Meanwhile lives with his mother.' We looked at each other. She said, 'Oy veh.' And I said, 'Standard issue.' We both laughed.

'Seeing him again?' I asked.

'Oh yeah,' she said, which ended that portion of the conversation.

'Did you get caught in the snow?' I asked – another diversion.

'What snow?' Maybe Noah hadn't been as boring as she implied.

She was fuming at our slow progress. There's no escaping London traffic. And there's no escaping Amy's curiosity either. 'Hickey,' she said. 'Spill.'

'Mosquito bite.'

'Bollocks.'

'Dog bite then. I don't know, Amy, it was there when I woke up.'

'No, no, no. Spill for true. Who did you cop off with after I left?'

'Nothing like that. An old guy gave me a lift home. I was a bit over-voddied.'

'Rat-arsed, you mean. How old?'

'Dunno. Over sixty at least.'

'Rich?'

'For crap's sake, Amy, I don't know.'

'Well, what was the car like?'

'You're sounding just like my mother,' I said, because that's what usually shuts her up. I saw the limo in my mind's eye and it raised more questions than answers.

I went on the attack. '*You're* the one who left *me*. *You're* the one who copped off. What's *Noah's* car like?'

'That thing on your neck is so definitely a hickey.'

'Is so not.'

'Jakey's going to notice.'

'Jacob Silver can kiss my rosy round rump.'

But my hair is long, I wore a scarf and Jake didn't notice a thing. He complained about the soil under my fingernails, he complained about his boss, he complained because Amy hadn't gone out so we weren't alone, but he didn't complain about a hickey.

I cooked scrambled eggs with avocado. I hadn't been hungry

all day so I couldn't finish mine. He emptied my plate onto his own and didn't complain about that either.

'Still hung over?' Amy asked innocently.

'You're a bad influence,' he said. They both laughed. He liked Amy because she was daffy enough to laugh at but not daffy enough to be annoying.

We watched 'The Misfits' because Jake liked Marilyn Monroe, Amy liked Clark Gable, and I liked old movies. After an hour though I was so tired I went to bed and left them to it.

Whatever had happened the night before was a dream of long ago, barely seen through a snowstorm.

I wanted it to happen again.

I had several jobs the next day. Mrs Seinfeld, upset, wanted me to replace her beautiful white camellia shrub which had been stolen, along with its faux Greek urn, from outside her front door. A retired couple in Finchley wanted me to set up four boxes at the front of their house with an English country garden theme that would be in full bloom for their granddaughter's wedding in late July. Then there were three maintenance visits.

Lastly, I went to see Hannah David who is eighty-seven, lives alone and was my very first client. She is more than capable of weeding and picking the moss out of her riotous show of scarlet and gold tulips, but she isn't strong enough anymore to open her sash windows. After she'd attended to one box and I'd tidied the others I closed the windows. She turned the heat up and brought out the tray loaded with a decanter of dry sherry, two glasses and a plateful of madeleines. This is why I always make Hannah the last job of the day.

'You look tired, dear,' she said, allowing me to pour the sherry. 'Too many late nights with that young man of yours? Your mother thinks you can do better, you know. But that's the song she's been singing since you were three years old. Silly woman.'

I grinned at her fondly. Hannah says she's too old to waste time on tact. She went on, 'I remember you saying that you and Jacob "got along". It isn't grand passion, but it's not to be sneezed at in such an impermanent age. It's better than loneliness. Oh don't look at me like that – *I'm* not lonely, and I wish I could reclaim the time I've spent on false friends and lovers. One thing I *can* tell you is that work won't let you down – unlike lovers, friends or family. Save passion for your work.'

I loved Hannah when she spoke like this. She contradicted everything everyone else said and made more sense. I began to tell her a little about the weird meeting at the Italian Bar and Grill.

She interrupted. 'Lazaro? Not Lazarus who was supposedly raised from the dead? How very strange.' She thought for a minute. Then she said, 'I wouldn't put much faith in a man who pays more attention to his appearance than you do. It upsets the balance.'

'What balance?'

'Such an obsession with youthful appearance in an old man means that he will always be more interested in himself than he'll be in anyone else. That's the case to some extent or other with everyone. But taken to extremes it means that unless he has a use for you, you will always be invisible or non-existent to him. You are very natural, my dear.' She nodded to my pony tail, my grubby sweater, worn old jeans and work boots.

'Another thing my mother thinks I should do better.'

'Yes, dear – dress in smart clothes, wear stockings with high heels, have a manicure, cut your hair and you'll snag a dentist for sure.'

I laughed. Her sarcasm made me feel supported. I went on with my story.

At the end she stared at me gravely for so long that I began to feel uneasily that I'd misjudged her – maybe she wasn't as free with her support and approval as I'd thought. She would now give me a lecture about drugs and risk-taking like any other elderly lady.

Instead she said, 'It did *not* snow at midnight on Thursday night. I think I'll Google this Lazaro.'

The thought of Hannah Googling made me smile. Her adventures on the internet often led her into territory not intended for eighty-seven year old women.

She glared at me stonily through her bifocals. She had, until recently, been a consultant psychiatrist at an important teaching hospital. She still saw a few private patients, almost as old as herself, who couldn't bear to let her retire completely. Her capabilities defied the prejudices even I held about old women.

'I won't see Lazaro again,' I told her. 'It wasn't like that.' And so we parted friends.

But an hour later she rang me at home and said, 'Urban Dictionary explains that a Lazaro is a bad-ass Mexican or Cuban man with huge man-parts with whom you would not wish to tangle because he would most certainly kick your butt.'

'I didn't know that,' I said, almost crying with the effort not to crack up. She must've heard it in my voice though because she ended the call quite huffily.

I was tired, but I couldn't sleep. Amy was missing, and when I rang Jake I was sent straight to voice mail. This was a pity because I wanted him to come out to see our plot. By day he's an office manager for a power company, but he has a Green conscience and we'd met in a local Guerrilla Gardening group. He had enthusiasm but hardly any know-how so we teamed up. Our private plot was on a traffic island in the middle of a main road almost exactly halfway between our two homes. It was where we planted the left-over seeds, bulbs and dwarf shrubs from my paying clients' window boxes. It attracted quite a lot of notice, and last spring the local online magazine sent a photographer to take its picture. It looked lovely.

I turned my phone off and tried to sleep, I really did. I even

Liza Cody

took a couple of Amy's antihistamines to help. But in the end, in spite of the cold, I got dressed, went out and drove to the traffic island. My garden shed is in the back of my van so all the tools I need are available at a moment's notice.

THREE

It was a clear, starry night and a half moon showed over the rooftops. I could see my breath billowing white as I stood looking at the snowdrops and crocuses that were flowering among the shoots of daffodils and tulips. I was clearing the week's accumulation of urban rubbish into a plastic bag when I found an unopened packet of *Papaver somniferum* seeds. I happen to know what *P. somniferum* is, because while Hannah was Googling Lazaro I was looking up the opium poppy.

Amazed, I picked it up. It is only in dreams that the very thing you're thinking about turns up in front of you. I put it in my pocket and finished clearing the ground. Then I loosened the soil between the clusters of spring bulbs, and added some compost.

'I'm not *really* going to do this,' I said out loud. 'I'm pretty sure it's illegal.' But so is appropriating small plots of land you don't own to plant flowers and veg on.

I looked down at the innocent snow drops. I looked up at the chilly moon. I looked for the instructions on the back of the seed packet. They were there, but in a script I took to be Greek. In spite of street lighting it was almost too dark to see.

'What the hell,' I said, and slit the packet open with my thumbnail.

Just as I was covering the seeds and gently tamping down the earth a motorcycle pulled up beside me. The rider, still sitting astride his machine, pulled off his helmet and there was Lazaro's beautiful driver. He said, 'Mr Lazaro has sent me to fetch you.'

I looked at my watch. It was two-twenty. I said, 'What for? It's very late,' like any rational woman would. But this was suddenly not a rational situation. 'How did you find me?'

'I looked for you,' he said simply. 'And here you are.' This was accompanied by a dazzling smile made charming and quirky by two slightly overlapping front teeth. Try as I might, I couldn't help smiling back.

'Mr Lazaro wants to speak to you on a professional matter. He has sent this as a gesture of good faith.' He reached inside his leather jacket and handed me an envelope, warm from his body.

As I opened it I noticed the black half moon of soil under my thumbnail and the smear of earth dirtying the white envelope. Inside was a cheque. Lazaro was paying me *two thousand pounds* for a professional matter as yet unspecified.

'Two *thousand* pounds?' I looked at the amount again and then at the driver.

'Hop on,' he said, indicating the seat behind him.

'Can't,' I said. 'This is a main road and I'm parked illegally. Even if this is real…' I waved the cheque at him. 'I can't afford to have my van towed.'

For a moment he looked flummoxed. Then, 'I'll follow you back to your apartment. We'll go from there.'

I dumped the bag of rubbish in the bin outside the Airbrush Ladies Hair Salon, and returned to my van. Now that I couldn't see the beautiful guy and he no longer had his gorgeous eyes on me, I found myself saying out loud, 'Are you bat-shit crazy, Seema?' Then I drove home and parked in the same spot I'd left over an hour earlier.

This time he merely raised his visor and patted the seat behind him.

'I need to shower and change,' I said, taking my front door keys out of my pocket.

He plucked them from my hand. 'It's impolitic to keep an employer waiting – believe me. If you need clean clothes, the household will provide.'

This is where the real me would yell, 'Fuck you and the Hog you rode in on.' Then I'd swipe him off his bike with my trusty spade and walk away in a righteous snit.

Instead I was overwhelmed by fear and longing – longing for something different, something outside my ordinary, everyday life, my lack of a 'grand passion'. I spent hours each day searching for a place to park my van where I wouldn't get a ticket or have to walk miles carrying bags of compost. I fight with Amy about potting up seedlings in the kitchen. I'm so scared of being alone that I haven't told Jake how much football bores me. I'm depressed by being such a constant disappointment to my mother. My nails are always grimy and my dreams never come true.

I feared that my dreams never would come true, and that when something mysterious happened to me and a beautiful man wanted me to ride behind him, I would miss the chance because of fear. I'd lose my one shot at beauty and a secret life because I was too sensible to reach out and grab it.

I was pulled towards the bike like a kid to chocolate.

The half moon was hidden by low clouds and it was snowing again by the time we arrived at a wrought-iron gate that closed a Belgravia mews off from the rest of the world. The gate was watched over by two winking, blinking security cameras. My rider tapped a 5 digit code into a keypad and the gates glided open.

What I'd taken as a single mews turned out to be a maze of mewses. We turned right, right again, then left. And whichever way we turned the snow was driven straight into my face, so I had to keep my eyes shut and shelter as best I could behind the rider's back. He had not provided me with a helmet so I was blinded and bedraggled.

We stopped. 'Get off,' he said. 'Ring the bell. Someone will come.'

'Aren't you coming in?' I began, but was drowned out by the Hog clearing its throat and rolling away.

The door was opened by a redhead with film star looks.

This was no ordinary mews house: the cute countrified front door led into a grand hall. It looked as if behind the folksy exteriors, at least six houses had been knocked together to form a city centre mansion.

'Come with me,' the redhead said, turning to a passage leading off the hallway.

It was time to show my claws. I stood still and said, 'Wait – who are you?'

'Gemma,' she said, looking over her shoulder at me. She took in my soaked hair and clothes. She almost smiled. 'I am your hostess for tonight. I will provide whatever you need for your comfort and well-being. This way.'

'Stop, Gemma,' I said, 'Why do I need a hostess? If someone takes me from my work, he should expect work clothes.'

She smiled sweetly. 'If you accept his invitation you must allow your host to feel responsible for your comfort. Please don't tell me you're comfortable – wet through as you are. And I'm sure you don't want to tramp snow and dirt through Mr Lazaro's house.'

There was only one civilised answer to that. I followed Gemma down the passage to a bedroom so deep inside the house that I began to doubt my perception of the size of the whole mews.

The room she took me to was furnished like a good hotel bedroom. There was a white-on-white colour scheme. Over the bed was a print of one of Georgia O'Keefe's huge Calla lilies – a cliché in a white a room, to be sure, but O'Keefe flowers always strike me as threatening. It's as if they are saying, One day, pal, it will be payback time, one day we will cut *your* head off and stick it in a vase – see how *you* like it.

The bathroom was white and intimidating too. Gemma had to show me how to operate the high-tech shower.

Lastly she opened a built-in wardrobe and pointed to a rack of clothes – all white, of course.

'Maybe you should've taken me to the blue room,' I said.

But sarcasm didn't work on Gemma. She smiled her perfect smile and said, 'When you're ready, ring this bell.' She pointed to a button near the door. 'I'll come and fetch you. Please don't attempt to find your own way – you won't succeed, and besides, the dogs are loose.' She glided away leaving me with my mouth hanging open and a sinking feeling in the pit of my stomach.

But I pulled myself together and searched the room for hidden cameras. Behind the white satin curtains, to my dismay, I found a white wall but no window. It was only then that I decided to get the hell out of this weird house and, if necessary, to walk home in the snow. I wasn't afraid of dogs. I like them and they like me.

But I couldn't open the door. I tried my phone. There was no signal.

'Gemma,' I yelled in rising fury, 'you've locked me in, you superior cow! Let me out!' I jabbed the bell-push again and again. No one came.

Suddenly I was freezing. It seemed that the only heating was in the bathroom. And then, after a few more minutes of punching the call button, the bedroom lights flickered and went out.

I sat on the bed, stubborn and shivering in the dark. The room itself was coercing me.

The bathroom however had bright lights, under-floor heating and mirrors that made me look slim. Who could resist that? I showered, washed my sodden hair and dried on fluffy white towels. Everything needed to control problem hair had been provided: conditioners, holding gel, hairspray, hot tongs, and a four-speed hairdryer.

I didn't bother with any of it. My hair had a mind and a life of its own. Taming it has always proved impossible. Of course I wasted fruitless hours of utter frustration when I was a teenager who wanted to look like a silver blonde actress with hair like ironed satin. I couldn't quite believe that my ethnic origins were completely beyond my control, and I would sit in front of mirrors and weep.

'Oh give it up,' teenage Amy would say. 'I've tried and tried. Even *I* can't argue with curls like these. Shave it all off. Buy a wig. I can do no more.' She threw the tongs dramatically onto the bed and ran her fingers through her own golden highlights, adding, 'God, I'm so glad I'm not Mizrahi like you.' It's a tribute to affection that our friendship survived our teens.

Back in the bedroom I found that light and heat had been restored but my own clothes and shoes had vanished.

'You're a fascist!' I shouted. 'Comfort? Don't make me laugh. What the hell do you want?' I was angry and alarmed. I don't take well to coercion.

The lights flickered. I was being threatened again. With only a towel for protection.

I went to the wardrobe. The room approved and the lights stayed on.

I searched through the clothes on the rack. Gardeners don't wear white for obvious reasons, and I don't wear gowns. I am not a gown kind of woman. I looked in vain for a pair of white slacks and a plain white shirt.

Finally I found something that in 1930s movies would've been called lounging pyjamas: loose-legged with a long slim-cut tunic. It was made of silk with satin facings and piping, and it hung so flatteringly and felt so light and smooth I wondered if I would ever want to take it off. The suit also had the advantage of not showing bare skin. My Amazonian arms and shoulders remained my own secret. The trousers were not split from ankle to hip; there were no sexy straps or cleavage. And yet, looking in the full-length mirror, I thought I had never looked more appealing.

I picked a pair of ballerina style flatties for practicality, checked the beautiful dishonest mirror one last time and pressed the bell to call Gemma.

She came immediately and nodded as she looked me over. She started to comment but I didn't let her.

'Where are my own clothes?' I asked. 'You had no right...'

'Washed and in the dryer,' she said cheerfully. 'Come on.' She turned and walked away so briskly that I had to trot to keep up.

When we reached the hall she made straight for the staircase at the other side, but I turned right and trotted towards the front door.

That was where I met two gigantic wolfhounds.

They appeared out of nowhere and intercepted me, standing between me and my goal. I kept going until they snarled and showed long, sharp, white fangs. Then I stopped and held out a hand to each. They lowered and stretched their necks to sniff me. Their hackles were up. I knelt down and remained perfectly still.

'Seema,' Gemma said in a no-nonsense tone, 'come with me. You're putting yourself at risk.' I noticed that she didn't move any closer.

'Shut up,' I replied in a quiet, friendly voice.

I really do like dogs, and this pair, while challenging, were remarkable examples of their breed. They were extremely tall and strong, gracefully built with thick, rough coats. We looked at each other. At last they approached, heads still lowered, back hair erect, but hiding their teeth. I sat back on my heels and waited until one of them stuck his nose under my chin. He could've torn my throat out. Instead he swiped my neck with his tongue.

'Hello, beautiful boys,' I said. I felt privileged and almost teary as I often do when close to natural perfection.

Both of them now stood over me, tails waving, ears eager, asking for attention.

Dogs are not like people. You know where you are with dogs. I gave them all the attention they wanted trusting absolutely that they wouldn't take advantage of my love.

Even so I got up slowly. These two were sight hounds – sudden motion excites them. They came with me to the front door. I opened it and they bounded joyfully out into the snow. But Lazaro's driver barred my way.

'Go back inside,' he said. 'You'll ruin your shoes.'

'Take me home,' I said. 'This deal stinks.'

'I'm sorry you should think so,' someone said behind me.

I turned and saw Lazaro. He held out his hand.

'I feel as if I've been abducted,' I said. 'I don't like it.' But for some reason I felt compelled to accept his hand. 'You shouldn't take a person's clothes away and force her to wear what *you* want.'

'You look lovely,' he said, drawing me towards him. 'But I must insist you tell me what you have done to my guard dogs. No one touches them but their handler.'

The dogs were playing in a deep drift of snow as if it were water. There's nothing happier than the sight of dogs playing. Even enormous hounds like a bit of fun. 'Where's the handler now?' I asked.

'Gemma!' he called and she appeared from where she was hiding behind the front door. 'Where's Grigori?'

'I don't know, sir.' Gemma did not look pleased with me. 'Those creatures are now wet and filthy.'

'Go and look for him.'

'And bring me some towels,' I added to her departing back. 'Two for the dogs, and one for my feet. And see if my proper clothes are dry yet. I want to leave.' Lazaro was still holding my hand, but in spite of the cold I was reluctant to leave the open door. He seemed quite content to stand beside me watching the dogs. Gemma returned with the towels saying, 'I can't find Grigori anywhere.'

'Page him,' Lazaro said impatiently. She threw me a withering look but took out her phone.

'What are your dogs called?' I asked.

'I have absolutely no idea,' he said. 'Why don't *you* give them names?'

'You don't know your own dogs' names?'

'You haven't told me them yet.' His smile was mischievous. I didn't get him at all.

But I gave a short whistle and when I had their attention I called, 'Here boys.' They galloped over from the other end of the mews shaking snow off their shaggy fur. Lazaro let go of my hand and stood well back.

'Sit down,' I told them when they reached the doormat. And they sat, grinning, their red tongues lolling.

'You're both called Beau,' I said loud enough for Lazaro to hear. Then I towelled them dry and they enjoyed it, even rolling on their backs to let me rub their bellies and paws. I ran my fingers through their coats. Of course nothing can make wolfhounds look sleek but I liked touching them.

When I could delay no longer I stood up. I was expecting to be covered in dog hair and city slush, but to my amazement the silk lounging pyjamas were as clean and white as when I'd put them on. It was a miracle I had no time to ponder because Lazaro signalled me to follow him. I did, and the two Beaus followed me. Lazaro and Gemma looked displeased, but neither of them interfered.

The reception room was at the top of the first flight of stairs. It was huge. Again there were the white on white furnishings, but the paintings and sculpture made me feel I was in a gallery. I toured the walls, the Beaus trailing behind me. Lazaro, when I first met him, told me he was a restorer, and the art on the walls seemed to me to be museum quality.

I only spent a couple of years at art school so I don't know a good copy from an original; all I can say is that everything, from a case of Etruscan votive terracottas to the Degas pastels and the Paula Rego prints looked like the real deal. There was a scattering of small Rodin and Brancusi figures on tables and mantle shelves, even a bronze Marino Marini horseman facing a Liz Frink helmet head. There were three Tang horses as well. Under glass, on a small plinth between two windows was a trio of Cycladic, white marble figurines of women. They were barely a foot high. But there was something primitive and powerful in the way they stood so straight, arms folded, faces raised to the sky. Staring at what – the moon?

'You are struck by my Three Graces?' Lazaro asked.

'Not Graces,' I murmured almost to myself. 'Goddesses. Or at least priestesses to goddesses.'

He laughed.

I turned and saw three people watching: Lazaro, Gemma and a large guy dressed like a hunting-shooting-fishing country gentleman. He looked as out of place as a trophy stag's head if it were mounted among pictures in the National Gallery.

'This is Garth Harding,' Lazaro told me. I would've shaken hands but oddly for a man who looked like a hunter he didn't seem keen on the dogs either.

The Beaus stood beside me nuzzling my hands, asking me to play with their ears. They gave me confidence.

Lazaro signalled Gemma to open a bottle of champagne. Then he turned to me. 'Now, Seema, please tell me what you've done to my dogs.'

'Nothing,' I said. 'Why have you brought me here?'

'They are trained guard and attack dogs. As you can see, there's a lot to protect here. I need them to intimidate strangers.'

'And keep people who want to leave from leaving?'

'That sometimes happens, yes.'

'Well, I like dogs and I'm not afraid of them. What's more, dogs are naturally sociable. They've evolved to live companionably with humans. Training them into aggressive behaviour is an insult to their friendly natures.'

'Wolfhounds were originally bred as fighting dogs.'

'In prehistoric times, maybe. But they were also bred to guard humans from predators. I'm not a predator. These dogs know that. So they've reverted to their true natures. And they're enjoying themselves. Can't you see that?'

He stared at the dogs with dislike. I was suddenly afraid of him.

He said coldly, 'They are not doing their job. I can see *that.*'

'They would appear to be protecting *her* rather than you,' Garth Harding said. He seemed to take some malicious satisfaction from that. Maybe, in spite of drinking Lazaro's champagne, he was not his friend.

'Why would you need protection from me?' I asked. Then I paused, laying my hands on the Beaus' heads. 'Wrong question – why do *I* need protection from *you?*'

Gemma's phone purred. 'What?' she said, turning away.

Lazaro pointed to the full champagne glass waiting for me on a side table. He said, 'You are perfectly safe here, my dear. Forgive an old man his paranoia. I have lived through wars and lost many precious people and possessions.'

That was why I consented to drink his champagne. I could've said, 'So what?' or 'That doesn't give you the right to kidnap me,' or 'You don't look as if you've suffered much.' But if my own family history has taught me anything it's that survivors sometimes react in very strange ways.

My father, when he was still alive, told me about two very rich, very old women, his great aunts. They had been interned by the Japanese in the Second World War. Even as prisoners they had been consigned to a tiny ghetto in the camp. They were not quite white enough or European enough for the other prisoners to accept.

To begin with they tried extremely hard to keep kosher but it was impossible on starvation rations. When eventually they were rescued by the American Red Cross at the end of the war in the East they looked like the skeletons of two tiny birds.

But, even while starving, sick and ragged they'd remained very rich, so when they left Hong Kong they settled in Europe. Just to make a point, my father thought. They spent nine months of every year living in a special suite at the Georges Cinque Hotel in Paris and three months at the Grosvenor House Hotel on Park Lane in London.

My father told me that as a child he was made to visit them when they came to England. They were still tiny and thin with hands like the claws of dead birds. Their skin was the texture of fallen rose petals but they smelled of violets. They always wore black. Their names were Ramah and Moselle and they told my little boy father that they were in perpetual mourning for the dead. His mother tried to shut him up but on one of their last visits, he asked them about the camp. It was the kind of direct, rude question no one in his family ever asked. But Ramah and Moselle were quite willing to talk to him. In the end, Ramah said, 'Do you want to know a secret? Come and look.' The two sisters took him into the bedroom they shared and showed him a large fridge hidden in a vast cupboard.

'Everywhere we go,' she said, 'we keep a refrigerator full of food. Look, look.'

He looked and saw that it was packed with an assortment of rice dishes, a roast chicken, slices of lamb, mountains of spiced couscous, breads of all sorts, chocolate mousse, a large variety of gateaux – too much to comprehend.

'We like to go to bed hungry,' Moselle whispered.

'We like to wake up in the middle of the night, starving,' Ramah breathed into his ear. 'We get up and open the fridge to look at all the food.'

'Sometimes,' Moselle said, 'we fill our plates and eat. But sometimes, little boy, the sight of all the food we *could* eat fills our bellies, so we go back to bed and sleep peacefully.'

'That's a war story,' my father told me years and years later. 'A survivors' tale. There are many strange tales.'

I took the glass Lazaro offered and thought how natural it would be for a man who had survived wars and losses to become a collector with an overwhelming need to protect his possessions.

Gemma looked up from her phone and said, 'Supper's ready.'

I was astonished and looked at my watch. Or rather, I looked at my wrist where my watch ought to be. Of course I'd taken it off for the shower. Now it and my phone were gone.

Garth Harding rubbed his hands in anticipation.

Gemma said, 'I'm afraid the dogs aren't allowed in the dining room.'

I said, 'I'm not hungry. It's way too late for supper, and much too early for breakfast. Please give me my watch, phone, clothes and shoes. I want to go home.'

'You accepted Mr Lazaro's cheque,' she said.

'And you've taken it away, along with everything else I came in with. I'm under no obligation to stay.'

'Please my dear,' Lazaro said, 'take no notice of Gemma. Everything will be returned to you. Gemma, fetch Seema's possessions. I know you didn't intend to make our guest uncomfortable.'

I meant to say, 'I'm not your guest.' But somehow, to my dismay, the words stayed trapped behind my tongue.

This time, ignoring the dogs, he took my hand again and drew me into a dining room. It was candlelit and the walls were covered with paintings of fruit and flowers – brilliant super-realism. I thought of Jan Brueghel the Elder because there was always a dead flower or a rotting fruit somewhere in each picture: a reminder of the death and decay hiding like a time bomb in all nature.

The room was dark and oppressive, quite unlike the whiteness of the living room. There was an oval mahogany table covered by a dark red cloth which seemed to eat the candle-light and make the massive amount of food almost invisible. The dogs followed me closely, their heads lowered and ears flattened.

'Ah, Pasqual,' Lazaro said, as the pale driver came in. 'Drinks for our guests.'

Garth Harding was already pouring himself a large glassful of red wine.

Pasqual stopped short in the doorway. 'Why are there dogs?'

He was now elegant in a black suit with a snowy white shirt, unbuttoned at the throat. He looked as if he'd never seen a motorbike in his life.

'Unfortunately,' Garth Harding said, seating himself at the table and tipping a large gulp of wine into his mouth, 'the damned dogs and our little friend here have a mutual passion.'

'Are you *all* allergic to dogs?' I asked. 'Or is it the other way round?' I decided to ignore the adjective: only someone as big as Garth would describe me as little.

Lazaro pulled out a chair for me. 'Would you ask your Beaus to sit quietly out of sight under the table,' he said. 'Otherwise Pasqual will retire to the library and no one will be fed.'

Without asking, I took a fork and picked out two fat slices of cold pink beef from a gold serving dish and fed them to the Beaus before settling them out of sight by my feet. I would not normally say that love gives a person possession, but as every one except me hated them, for now the dogs were mine. Their warm damp breath on my absurd white slippers felt familiar and comfortable.

Gemma appeared beside my chair holding a bulky Yves Saint Laurent carrier bag. She slid it under my chair, but I didn't have time to check the contents because Lazaro came and sat next to me.

While this was happening several other people entered. Two of them, a man and a woman dressed in expensive but countrified clothes, went to sit on either side of Garth Harding. His children? His retinue? I was becoming more and more confused.

As if designed to bewilder, an extremely tall woman dressed in an evening suit plus bow tie strode to the other side of the table flanked by two young men both of whom were wearing accountancy spectacles and grey suits.

The champagne was no help at all. I stifled a giggle.

'You are amused?' Lazaro said, smiling.

'It's like everyone is in fancy dress.' I looked first at Garth

Harding and then at the new woman. 'The country gentleman, the power broker and you – the aesthete – you're all dressed to type.'

'Gracious me,' Lazaro said. 'I never noticed. But how rude of me: let me introduce Lesley Sharpe and her two assistants, Julian and Duncan.'

Hearing their names all three of them looked at me and nodded their heads. I nodded back. Gemma took her place next to Lazaro; Pasqual sat beside me. Ten of us at table together, but the groups, it seemed, weren't expected to mix. I hardly had time to wonder what a gardener was doing in this company when servers came in with platters of hot meat.

There were rare steaks, pink beef, pork with crackling, lamb with rosemary, roast chicken, gammon and slabs of venison. I refused all of them. I was astounded: the cold dishes already on the table had not yet been removed and the sheer weight of the meat was overwhelming.

I was about to ask Lazaro which army he was cooking for when he turned to me and said, 'Is it an issue of the dietary laws, or do you not eat any meat?'

I stared at him. The dining room fell silent and I could feel nine pairs of curious eyes on me. Blushing, I said, 'I told you I wasn't hungry. But, this is the second time you've mentioned kosher practice so the best answer I can give is that the part of dietary law which concerns me is the bit that forbids mixing milk with blood. Milk is the gift, blood is the theft. That's all that makes sense to me in the modern world. And so I will not steal. In other words, yes, you're right, I don't eat meat.'

'This is a religious principle?'

'It's a personal principle. The only reason I've framed my answer in the way I have is because of the way you asked your question.'

'In terms of religious belief rather than secular principle. I see. When we met it was in a non-kosher setting. But you refused pork scratchings.'

'Who wouldn't?' Lesley Sharpe said, looking down her nose at me. 'But you *are* a Jew?'

'I'm a very bad Jew according to my mother and her rabbi.'

'But,' Lazaro said, frowning at Lesley, 'You observe the law about milk and meat as written in Exodus and Deuteronomy? And your mother, presumably, keeps kosher.'

'My mother doesn't have to make a living in the real world or try to have a social life not limited to only a handful of families – *if* it's any of your business.'

'Perhaps you are merely a vegetarian,' Garth Harding said. 'And not religious at all.' The word vegetarian came out like an obscenity. He was waving a fork loaded with bloody steak in my direction. 'But you fed meat to those damn dogs.'

'The dogs are carnivores – they have no choice.' I turned to Lazaro. 'Why have you brought me here? What have my so-called principles got to do with you – with any of you? And why did Pasqual give me two grand?'

He put his hand on my arm to prevent me rising. It was a tanned, shapely hand. The fingernails were oval and buffed smooth. He wore a pale gold signet ring on the middle finger of his right hand. The stone was a carnelian with a half moon deeply etched into its surface. The phase of this moon matched exactly the phase of the moon I'd looked at above my guerrilla garden on a neglected traffic island on a main road in north London.

I was a long way from home.

Lazaro said, 'I sent you a retainer – a gesture of good faith. We…' he waved a hand around the table '… have a small clubhouse. We'd like you to design a roof garden for us.'

'Oh.' I had been about to shake free and flounce out. Now I felt, and probably looked, stupid. 'You could've just rung me up.'

'Are you sure about this?' Lesley Sharpe asked.

'She's both difficult and a vegetarian,' Garth Harding concurred.

'We are not asking her to design a *kitchen* garden,' Lazaro said patiently. Everyone laughed.

I didn't get the joke although I had a queasy feeling it might be me. But perhaps the queasiness was caused by being close to so much meat.

'You're taking a big risk.' Garth stuffed a great gob of dripping meat into his mouth.

One of the accountants passed Sharpe a memo as if it were a board meeting and not dinner. She nodded. 'Have you calculated the odds?' she asked Lazaro.

'Excuse me?' I looked at Lazaro. 'What odds?'

He got to his feet. 'Speculation is premature. I suggest that as our guest doesn't wish to eat I will take her to the library to see the photographs. Her opinion matters. Meanwhile, please continue to enjoy all that my kitchen has to offer.'

I got up too, careful to remember the bag under my chair, and, followed by the Beaus, we left the dining room.

A man was waiting outside, leaning against a wall and smoking a black cigarette. His hair was uncut, he wore a baggy brown tracksuit with grey trainers and his face was scarred with past acne. I should've been relieved to see someone normal except he was carrying two choke-chain leashes.

'Grigori,' Lazaro snapped. 'Please ensure that when there are guests in the house and the dogs are loose, you remain within calling distance.'

'Doesn't look like they hurt anyone,' Grigori said, eyeing the dogs coldly. They eyed him back. 'I think if *you* had to choose between your gas boiler blowing up and a couple of dogs on the prowl you'd choose your boiler. Like *I* did.'

'Very well,' Lazaro said. 'But take them and feed them now, and do *not* crush your cigarette out on the floor.'

The Beaus submitted stoically to Grigori's chains and walked away at his side. I promised myself that if it was humanly possible

I'd come back and save them. But I said nothing – you don't share your plans if you have larceny in mind.

I was bone-weary but I had to wonder if the person responsible for interior design was a film buff. The library was so typical of the way libraries in great houses are depicted in movies that I felt I knew every inch of it. There was an oak table with green-shaded reading lamps and copies of The Times and Financial Times placed at regular intervals down its length. Lazaro pulled out a hardwood chair for me and placed a leather folder in front of me. I sighed and opened it. The five photographs were aerial views of a house – identical except for the shadows.

'Which way is North?' I asked.

'Excellent question.' He stroked my arm, an approving caress. The back of my brain said, 'This is bizarre, and I don't like your friends.' It was a small, cold voice. But my skin said, 'Love me do.'

He pointed to North and I arranged the photos from dawn to dusk noting the shadows cast by neighbouring buildings. 'Inner city,' I murmured. 'But even so, quite a lot of sunshine. What's the size?'

'Perhaps forty by sixty metres.'

It was a flat roof of course. At one end there was a structure that hid the air conditioning and water tank. I said, 'Do you have architects' drawings or plans from a structural engineer? Because the load-bearing capacity will be crucial. And do you have council permission?'

'All in hand,' he said.

'Access?' I pointed to a trapdoor. 'That won't be adequate, either for making a garden or maintaining it.'

I was trying to sound experienced, practical and impressive but my mind was full of dreams. Roses trailed over the coping stones around the edge and hung down, curtaining the front of the house. Or wisteria. Golden ghosts of carp lolled lazily just beneath the surface of a pool lined with blue irises. Camellias for January, Japanese maples for autumn – I could see it all.

Only a hundred and sixty square metres, I thought mournfully, after lopping off space for amenities and access. And then I began to think about terracing and clever ways to expand. I even imagined a miniature grassy hill with a tiny grove of dwarf trees at the top.

'You are beginning to dream,' Lazaro said gently. 'Time to share a pipe or two. Then I'll send you home. Tomorrow you'll make rare and wonderful drawings. Then we'll have something to discuss. This work could be the beginning of a beautiful new life. You'll see.'

FOUR

I woke the next morning heart-heavy with the weight of a dream: Lazaro was walking down a stony hillside. Behind him was an empty tomb cut into a wall of rock. In his hands he carried a pair of jewelled white slippers which he handed to me, saying, 'Dance for me, my dearest young love.' I began to put them on, knowing that they would teach me to dance as I'd never danced before. But I woke up without ever hearing any music. I was bereft and almost in tears.

It was nearly midday. I'd lost the whole morning. I leaped up in panic, afraid I'd missed appointments. But I saw in my diary that I'd left the morning open for a trip to my garden suppliers.

My only voicemail was from Hannah, who said, 'A Lazarus is also the name given to a beggar. Oh yes, and a leper. Do be careful my dear.'

I wished I hadn't confided in her. She was a very old woman who sometimes became obsessed by trivia. I resolved not to visit her till she'd got over her fixation about Lazaro.

I looked at my list. As well as plants and seeds I had to buy compost, sharp sand and gravel. I couldn't bear even to think about lugging that lot into the van. Instead I went to my cupboard and saw the white lounging pyjamas hanging neatly beside the rest of my clothes, which looked cheap and tawdry by comparison. A beautiful new life.

I went to my desk and found my drawing book, pencils and

watercolours. Then I made a list beginning with angel's trumpets and aurelia, jotting down all the flowers I could remember that released their perfume at night. But I found my mind meandering around tobacco plants, specifically *Nicotiana alata*, with a scent so sweet… And then, when I looked down at my pad I saw that I'd drawn a stem bearing three small white flowers shaped like trumpets. Hovering over it was a Death's Head Hawk Moth. Yes, I remembered now, a scent so sweet it attracts the nocturnal Death's Head Hawk moth.

The phone rang and Jake said, 'Where were you last night? You rang but you'd gone when I called back.'

'I couldn't sleep so I went to, you know, our garden.' For some reason I was hesitant about calling it ours. But it was. Whatever promise of a beautiful future Lazaro was offering, the here and now was with Jake, window boxes and a traffic island.

'You sound tired.

'Do I?'

'What's the matter, babe? Usually you sleep like a bear in winter. Money worries?'

'Always,' I said, relieved that he'd answered his own question. There was a moment's silence. Then he shattered my relief by asking, 'Who's the old man Amy was telling me about?'

At first I didn't associate Lazaro with the words 'old man'. Jake filled the pause. 'She said you met an old guy. The night that was supposed to be girls only but she copped off with Noah.'

'Oh yes,' I began warily. 'We got talking. He's a picture restorer. He might have a job for me.'

'She said you've been weird and secretive ever since. I wouldn't know – I haven't seen you.'

'You could've seen me last night, but you weren't in.'

'Shabbat,' he said sounding surprised. 'I was with my parents. I told you. Weren't you supposed to go to your mother?'

'Shit!' I was horrified. I never observed Shabbat when left to

31

myself but every now and then my mother twisted my arm and I had to go to her house.

'And,' he went on, his voice sounding stonier, 'Amy said you were sporting a ginormous hickey.'

'She's winding you up. It was an insect bite of some sort. I must've scratched it in the night and made it bleed.'

'Surely *Amy* knows a hickey when she sees one.'

'Surely *you* know a wind-up when you hear one,' I said tartly. 'What's going on with you, Jake?'

'What's going on with *you*, Seema?' He hung up.

I stared at my phone. What *was* going on? Why was he so aggressive? Why was Amy so intrusive? Why was I so defensive?

And why hadn't my mother rung?

Then I saw Amy's writing on a large piece of paper attached to the fridge by a scowling emoji magnet. It began, 'The landline's down. Your phone's turned off. Your mother has rung ME 17, yes, 17 times and I hate you. Amy xxx. Ps, I couldn't wake you this morning. You must've been slaughtered.'

I'd rung Jake last night. Jake rang me last night and this morning on my mobile. Hannah had left a message. There was no signal in the Belgravia house. I picked up the house phone. There was a dial tone. I began to punch in my mother's number but stopped halfway. My sluggish brain was tussling with excuses ranging from terminal illness to abduction by aliens. But I knew from experience that nothing would be good enough. And the truth was that I'd forgotten so completely that I hadn't even been aware that yesterday had been Friday, and that I'd had a date with my mother or even that I had a mother.

I needed a shower. Then I remembered I'd showered last night in a room with under-floor heating. I'd washed my hair with luxury shampoo, dried myself on warm clean towels and dressed like a film star.

I stood in the bath. The shower curtain clung, clammy, to my legs. Amy had used all the towels. The mirror was steamy, which was probably just as well as I felt lethargic and heavy. I was sure I had dark rings under my eyes.

I noticed blood on the towel when I folded it over the rail, so I used it to wipe the mirror before dumping it in the laundry hamper. Yes, there were the panda eyes, and there was a trickle of blood from the sore spot on my neck. I must have picked at the bite again in my sleep. I covered it with a sticky plaster from the medicine cabinet. Then I dressed in jeans and a sweatshirt and went back to my desk.

The drawing, to my surprise, looked quite good. I can draw. But my style has a pedantic, architectural efficiency which my clients like but which I mourn over. This time I'd managed to give the moth and tobacco plant a spooky Aubrey Beardsley look. I was pleased.

I began to work the way I usually do, rationally, using graph paper so I can clearly see what size and proportion I'm dealing with. But I was tired and my wayward mind reverted to the spicy scent of opium, the warmth of a library, the depth of the silk cushions on the daybed.

Wait a minute! Daybed? There hadn't been a daybed in the library. And then I caught at the edge of a dream as frail as a cloud of smoke. There was a cherry tree heavy with white blossom. It was so tall the petals were tickling the stars. The stars were laughing. The picture was so enchanting I began to cry.

It was an opium fantasy. I shouldn't think about it or remember it with longing. I held my head in my hands sobbing, saying out loud. 'Drugs are bad for you. Bad, bad, *bad.*' I did my best to believe myself but the other, silent, voice was saying, 'How can anything that beautiful be bad?'

Strong coffee helped. I drew for an hour, then went to the suppliers. After that I made six quick maintenance visits. Nobody bawled me out for lateness or working on a Saturday. I kept my mobile switched off.

Then it was dusk. I hadn't eaten all day and now I was hungry. Street lights came on and the city took on its evening personality.

I was walking slowly back to my car when a gaunt, shaggy man and his lurcher stopped me. Addict eyes gazed at me from behind coiled ropes of hair. He said, 'I need a bed for the night. Help me out?' His dog looked better fed than he did, but I tore a lump off my burger and the lurcher made it disappear in the blink of an eye. She even licked the grease off my fingers. I gave the man a pound coin from my pocket. It disappeared almost as quickly. I expected him to move aside to let me pass but he stood staring at me, frowning. Then he said, 'There's something wrong here,' in a puzzled tone of voice.

I felt cold. I stepped around him and walked on, stuffing the rest of the burger in my mouth. I wiped my hands on the paper napkin, balled up the wrapping and threw it in a bin.

It wasn't until I found my van and unlocked it that I realised what I'd done. But, licking my lips, I greeted the taste of meat on my tongue. It was like welcoming back an old friend.

I drove slowly home through clotted traffic thinking about nothing at all and found Amy and Jake waiting for me in the kitchen.

'You smell like bacon,' Amy said.

I walked past both of them without a word and took my coat off in the bedroom. Amy was right, the coat smelled of the bacon cheeseburger. In fact the whole room stank of unclean meat. I opened the window and saw that it was snowing. I looked down, and there was Pasqual waiting, bareheaded, under a street light.

As soon as I leaned out he looked up. Our eyes met and he beckoned.

'Who's that?' Amy asked. She'd pushed in beside me at the window.

'*What?*' Jake elbowed me out of the way. 'It's snowing,' he said, surprised.

'That guy,' Amy said. 'He didn't expect to see anyone but Seema. Look, he's walking away.'

'Shit,' I cried. I was trying to collect my drawings into the leather folder and scramble into my coat at the same time.

With my coat half on and half off I raced downstairs and out into the snow. All that remained were Pasqual's footprints, and they were disappearing rapidly. The snow was melting as fast as it had appeared and soon his footprints vanished altogether. I walked slowly back home, teary, feeling like an abandoned child.

My so-called friends were waiting for me.

'Well,' I said before they could start with the criticism I could see on their faces. 'You've probably lost me the best job I've ever been offered.'

'Rubbish,' Amy said. 'What job? You never mentioned a new job.'

'I told Jake.'

'No you didn't,' Jake said. 'You just said this weird old geezer *might* have something, *maybe*.'

'Let's look then.' Amy snatched the folder out of my hands and slid my drawings onto the kitchen table. I had to move quickly to save them from a blob of marmalade she'd failed to wipe up after breakfast.

'Wow,' Amy said, taking a deep breath.

The doorbell rang.

I reached for the entry phone but Amy got there first. 'Yes?' she said brusquely.

Jake continued, 'You never said a single word about a young biker in totally sharp leathers.'

'For God's sake, Jacob Silver,' I began. But he wasn't listening. He'd stooped to pick up a piece of paper which had fallen when Amy snatched my folder.

'Come in,' Amy said and went to open the door.

'What's this?' He was holding the cheque I hadn't had time to bank. I made a grab for it but he snatched it out of my reach.

I was wondering whether to kick him in the knee or the balls when Amy ushered Hannah into the kitchen.

'What're you doing here?' I asked Hannah.

'What have you done to earn two thousand quid?' Jake asked me.

'As you haven't answered any of my emails, texts or phone calls I came to invite you to dinner.' Hannah regarded me with raisin eyes over the top of her bifocals.

'Let me see that.' Amy took my cheque from Jake's hand and retreated to the far side of the kitchen table.

'I've already eaten,' I told Hannah.

'She smells like a bacon burger,' Jake said.

'What is Lazaro Restoration?' Amy asked, waving the cheque.

'Gracious!' Hannah exclaimed, bending over the table and examining one page of my drawings. 'Where did you find these? *Fleurs du Mal* – there's no other description.'

'They're mine.' I looked over her shoulder. And then I said, 'I did them.' I sounded uncertain, even to myself.

'They look really weird,' Amy said.

'Like snakes and devils,' Jake said.

'Those two are just orchids,' I said, keeping my voice level although suddenly I could see what Jake meant. It hadn't occurred to me before. I'd thought them beautiful.

'What sort of orchids?' Hannah asked quietly. She had her smart phone out and took a picture of the drawings.

'I don't know,' I said. I was lying. 'But everybody knows that snap dragon seedpods look like skulls.'

'I didn't,' Amy said.

Hannah was fiddling with her phone, not attending.

'You're not gardeners,' I said to everyone. 'Maybe the guy I'm pitching to has rather odd taste, but so what? I do what a client asks me to do. And by the way, that cheque you're waving around is a retainer, so give it back.'

Amy gave it a last envious look and handed it to me.

'A two grand retainer?' Jake asked. 'So we aren't talking window boxes.'

'A roof garden.' My heart rate was returning to normal so I said, 'Has anyone got any objection to me designing a roof garden?'

Jake and Amy looked a little embarrassed, but shook their heads.

Hannah's phone chirruped. She looked at it and back at my drawings. Then she pointed to each one and said, 'That's a snakemouth orchid, that's a monkey face orchid, that's a corpse lily, and that one's a devil's hand. My friend Judith at the Royal Horticultural Society has just told me. She thinks the drawings are French from the Nineteenth Century.' She stared at me, her black eyes impenetrable. 'Something's wrong, Seema. This isn't like you at all.'

'She ate a *bacon* burger,' Amy said.

It was worse than that. I'd eaten a bacon *cheese*burger; violating my own principal about mixing blood and milk, theft and gift. Worse on top of worse – I wasn't sorry.

Jake was staring at me. I could read anger on his face, and that look he gets when he wants sex. Was it jealousy because he'd seen Pasqual and jumped to a wrong assumption?

It was time to smother the flames. I said, 'Look, I'm pitching for a job to an old guy who seems to have dosh to burn. He's a very private person. The man you saw out of the window is his driver. I wasn't expecting him; there was no formal appointment, but I do want to show the drawings as soon as possible. I don't want to waste my time if I've got the wrong end of the stick.'

'At eight in the evening?' Amy asked.

Hannah said 'The "old guy" is Lazaro, I presume; the "old guy" with whom you told me you smoked a pipe of opium in the back of his black limousine?'

'The *old* guy gave you the hickey?' Amy breathed, astonished.

'Show me,' Jake demanded, advancing on me.

I batted his hand away.

'Opium?' Amy was catching up. 'But Seema doesn't do drugs. She's the boringest, cleanest-living person of my acquaintance. Now it's opium and bacon burgers. What's going on?'

'*Where's the hickey?*' Jake exploded.

'Stop it,' I yelled back at him. 'Shut up and get out! I never want to see you again. We're over. You're dumped.'

There was a moment's silence. Then Amy said, 'Your mother will be so totally thrilled and then you'll want to kill yourself.' She was laughing. I could've throttled her.

Jake said, 'If that's what you want, I'm out of here.'

'No,' Amy said. 'You're *my* guest now. You can't leave; you're part of this. Seema's a druggie – who'da thunkit?'

Maybe Hannah could see I was about to say something I'd never be able to take back. She took my hand and said, 'Let's all remember we're friends. We want the best for Seema. Nothing can be gained and everything will be lost if we start shaming and blaming. Seema, where can we talk privately?'

I stamped away to my bedroom, Hannah following more sedately. I shut the door and turned on her. 'Why did you blurt out that stuff about the opium? I only did it because of the family history in the Far East. And I told you it was a secret and that it was just the one time.'

'But it wasn't, was it?' She took my hand again and sat me down on the bed. She turned my desk chair and sat opposite me. Our knees were almost touching. She said, 'I've known you since you were born. If I had been a religious man and you'd been a boy in need of circumcision I might have been your sandek. But I am a woman and a rationalist, and you were a girl. Your mother fulfilled what I consider to be the least useful of the three obligations: she made sure you had a strict Jewish education. After your father died, I took over the other two. I made sure you were qualified in an occupation that would feed and clothe you. And I also taught you to swim – a wonderfully irrational obligation for a desert people to insist upon. Your mother was quite happy for me to take you to the seaside, but she thought that if you married well you would have no need of qualifications. It was only one of the subjects we quarrelled about. The worst, of course, was that she blamed me for your atheism.'

'That wasn't your fault.' I said. 'I have a mind of my own.'

'And I thank God for that.'

We both started laughing. Suddenly we were connected again. She said, 'Let me take a look at your neck.'

I pulled my hair aside and removed the plaster. She put on her reading glasses. Then she rummaged in her handbag and pulled out a magnifying glass.

She said, 'This needs explanation, my dear. It is neither a hickey nor an insect bite.'

My bedroom door flew open and Amy appeared, Jake at her shoulder. 'Then what is it?' she shouted.

'You were eavesdropping!' I yelled back at her. 'How *could* you? And you Jake – you're as bad as she is. I *told* you it wasn't a hickey, but would you believe me? Oh no. You've just *got* to think the worst of me.'

'Actually,' Hannah said calmly, holding her hand up for silence, 'a hickey might not be the worst thing in the world.'

We all stared at her.

'What is it then?' Jake asked, quite humbly. 'Is it infectious?'

'It's a little inflamed. But let's look at this rationally before we jump to conclusions.'

'Look at what?' Jake looked jittery. 'Inflamed? Infected?' He's paranoid about infections.

'Let's not go there just yet.' Hannah turned and took a pad and pencil from my desk. She drew two small, jagged circles about an inch and a half apart. 'These appear to be puncture wounds,' she said, 'not properly scabbed. There's bruising around them and, as I said, inflammation, so it wasn't easy to see.'

'Let's have a look,' Amy said eagerly.

'Sod off!' My hand flew to my neck. The place felt swollen, tender and a little hot. I could feel my pulse beat through it.

'Yes,' Hannah said, watching me. 'Over your jugular vein.'

Jake was staring at the marks she'd made on the pad. 'Two puncture wounds? Over Seema's jugular vein? I hate to say this Ms David, but have you been watching Dracula movies lately?'

'Not *vampires*, Jacob,' she said. 'That isn't at all rational. But, tell me, what do you know about vampirism?'

'Goths? Vampire wannabes?' Amy said promptly.

Hannah smiled. 'Succinctly put. But there might be a bit more to it. For instance, some murderers have confessed to drinking their victim's blood.'

'Hold on,' I said. 'Are you telling me... ?'

But Hannah was in full flight. 'Vampirism is sometimes referred to as Renfield's Syndrome, although the man who invented the term did so as a sort of spoof – Renfield was a character in the novel, Dracula. Officially the syndrome doesn't exist – is not recognised by the arbiters of the psychiatric profession. But there *is* forensic evidence that an obsession with drinking blood was noticed as far back as Kraft Ebbing in the late nineteenth century. Nowadays, of course, it's a matter of lifestyle choices. A sub-perversion related to Sado-masochism, associated with a blood fetish and, of course, with sexual pleasure.'

'*Excuse me?*' I broke in, as soon as she paused for breath.

'Sexual pleasure?' Jake yelled at exactly the same time. 'Sado-masochism?'

'Well,' Hannah began, too involved in her subject to realise her mistake, 'only in the sense that there is one who drinks and one who submits to being drunk from, and it is very rare for the two to exchange roles.'

'What have you done?' Jake roared. His normally placid face was dark with blood and suspicion. 'You aren't dumping me, I'm dumping you!'

'Fine!' I yelled back. 'Now get out of my bedroom – you aren't welcome here anymore.'

He slammed out of my room, but a second later threw the door open again shouting, 'And if that's how you're getting your jollies you'd better get tested for Aids and all the other STDs.'

'You too,' I said nastily, and with satisfaction watched the blood drain from his face.

'He's concerned for you,' Amy said. 'Why're you being such a bitch?'

'If that's the way he expresses concern he can stick it,' I told her.

She gave me one of her sanctimonious reproachful looks and followed Jake out. I hate that look. My mother looks at me like that too. I wanted to go after her and slap her, but Hannah stopped me.

She said, 'Wait. Better he leaves – for the moment. Testosterone interferes with rational thought. Always has, always will. Now tell me what has happened between you and Lazaro.'

Amy put her head around the door and said, 'If that old geezer bit Seema without her consent it's assault and she should call the police. If it was *with* her consent Jake's right – he *should* walk away. He didn't sign up for a relationship with a pervert. And nor did I.'

I stared at her in disbelief.

Hannah said, 'Thank you, Amy – very helpful. Neither reporting a crime nor testing for communicable diseases will be ruled out.'

Amy humphed sceptically and withdrew her head.

Hannah said, 'Talk to me, Seema.'

I got up and went to the door. No one was outside with her ear to the panel but I could hear mumbling voices from the kitchen. I went back to my place on the bed and said, 'Either I dumped my boyfriend or he dumped me.'

'Pish, is that what you want to talk about?' Hannah asked. When I didn't answer she went on, 'Alright. Is he normally so jealous?'

'Why would he be jealous of me?'

'I don't know,' she said patiently. 'Why? You always said you "got along".'

'Well, maybe that's not enough for him. Maybe he wants to inject more drama into his life.'

'I see.' She sighed. 'We could carry on pretending we're talking about Jake or you could tell me about *your* need for drama and what Lazaro means to you.'

I sighed too. 'It's all so mysterious and exciting,' I said. 'I was out at the traffic island, clearing rubbish from the guerrilla patch when Pasqual turned up on a motor bike. I asked him how he'd found me and he just said, "I looked for you". No one's ever searched for me and found me before. I've never been worth that kind of effort for anyone.'

For a split second she looked as though she was going to say 'bullshit'. And I remembered a time when Hannah, worried, had tracked me down at art school in my first term in an alien city. She found me, fed me, let me talk and cry, offered to bring me home, and finally allowed me to find my own backbone and make my own decisions.

I hurried on. 'Lazaro sent him to give me a cheque as a gesture of good faith, and an invitation to dinner.' I showed her the cheque.

'Invited you to dinner?' Hannah asked. 'What time was this?'

'I can't remember,' I said, not meeting her eyes. My face felt hot.

She waited. Then she said, 'Before or after midnight? I'm asking because your mother called me last night when you didn't go to her house as expected. And Pasqual was sent to fetch you at a rather odd time for a business meeting.'

When I said nothing, she repeated, 'Before or after midnight?'

'After,' I admitted. I knew her: she wasn't going to let it go.

'Does that seem a little unusual to you?'

She has a technique of presenting a fact mildly, as if it's a question, and then waiting for my reaction. She was watching me steadily over the top of her bifocals which had slid down her elegant nose. I always felt I was telling her something she already knew. That was why I wanted to keep secrets from her. Worst of all, she has a memory like a black hole – everything I've ever done or said is trapped forever in there.

I said, 'I want you to let this go, Hannah. It's all very strange and absorbing, and that's why I want to carry on with it. I may never have an experience like this again.'

'True,' she agreed with a hint of warning. And then, 'Is being bitten an experience you want to repeat?'

'Hannah,' I said, 'I don't remember being bitten. I can't explain the mark on my neck.'

'You smoked opium again with Lazaro. What then?'

'I can't remember, I really can't.'

Absently she took a pencil from my desk and scratched her scalp with its point. 'Are you sure it's opium you're smoking? Is there a way a drug like rohypnol could be powdered and mixed with, say, tar heroin?'

'What do you know about tar heroin?'

'Nothing but that the innocent can be persuaded it's opium. Oh, I know –' she held up one gnarly finger – 'your father's family traded in the stuff, but I'd bet a pound to a penny *you* wouldn't know opium from fuller's earth, or tar heroin from asphalt.'

'Lazaro wouldn't do that.'

'Your amnesia should tell you otherwise. Ask yourself why a man his age would be smoking pipes of illegal substances with someone your age.'

'Oh the gloves are coming off now,' I said, shocking myself with words I hadn't even thought before I heard them in my mouth.

'Does this have to be antagonistic?' She looked as surprised as I felt.

'You don't understand,' I began. 'I've been to Lazaro's house. He's the most cultivated, sophisticated man I've ever met. He's a man of wealth and superb taste. He owns Paula Rego prints, Tang horses and Cycladic figurines. He has a whole library in his house. You're talking about him as if he's a cheap sleaze-bag. Some people spend a fortune on wine or Armagnac; he likes a little opium after dinner. So what?'

'Tell me about the dinner,' she said.

She sounded so placatory that I fell into our normal way of trusting talk, and I told her about the dark dining room, the paintings, the company and the food.

'No salad or vegetables at all?' she asked. 'Totally carnivorous?' When I nodded, she said, 'You went to a dinner party which was served at three in the morning and found you couldn't eat so much as a mouthful?' She smiled as if at the irony.

I smiled back. 'How to feel *totally* out of place.'

'Your host must have been mortified.'

'I hadn't told him I was a vegetarian.'

'But now?' she said. 'Or were Amy and Jake wrong about the bacon burger?' She raised an elegant white eyebrow. She didn't give a damn about dietary laws, so I told her about the added cheese.

'Oh my!' she said, almost laughing. 'So many major prohibitions in one go; including your own philosophical ones. How did that happen?'

'I don't know,' I said wearily. 'I didn't make a decision. I haven't changed my mind. I just found myself eating the effing thing in the street, wolfing it down, loving it.'

I was suddenly overwhelmed by a toxic coupling of fatigue and anxiety. I had to stop talking. I closed my eyes and saw Lazaro looking at me with grave attention. I turned sideways and pulled my feet up onto the bed dragging my pillow down to meet my weary head. As I did so I caught a glimpse of a small smear of blood on the otherwise clean pillow slip.

Hannah could not have noticed it because she made no comment, only saying, 'Alright dear, get some rest. We'll talk again tomorrow.'

Over my dead body, I thought, but had the sense to keep my eyes and mouth shut. I heard her close the door quietly behind her.

FIVE

I woke groggily and found Amy on the bed beside me with a blanket pulled over us. I was still in yesterday's work clothes. Feeling stoned, clatty, and as if swamp moss was growing on my teeth I staggered to the bathroom and was violently sick. After cleaning the toilet bowl I threw all my clothes into the laundry hamper and climbed shakily into the shower.

I scrubbed every inch of myself under water almost too hot to bear. And then, wrapped in a towel, wet hair trailing down my back, I returned to the bedroom.

Amy was awake. I said, 'What're you doing in my room?' She was breaking the unwritten privacy rule.

Yawning so widely I was afraid she'd dislocate her jaw, she said, 'Your friend Hannah slept in mine. I heard you barfing. You're not up the duff as well, are you?'

I couldn't bring myself even to answer but as I walked out I wondered if I could evict her without the required month's notice.

I'd almost crossed the sitting room before I registered that the body on the sofa, bundled in Amy's fluffy TV rug, was Jake. I couldn't cope. I went back to the kitchen and when I could drink cold water without wanting to heave I put the kettle on.

My drawings had been carefully placed back in their folder, but the aerial photographs of Lazaro's house were stacked next to Jake's laptop. Why?

I heard Amy come out of the bathroom, and in a minute she

appeared in the kitchen, also wrapped in a towel, her clothes in her arms. She stalked across the sitting room to her bedroom. We didn't exchange a glance or a word. The kitchen clock said it was ten forty-five. If she thought I'd phone her office and call her in sick she could whistle 'Get Lucky' and dance on tiptoe. Then I remembered it was Sunday. None of us had to go to work. The memory did nothing for my state of mind – which was rancid.

The next to use the bathroom was Hannah, almost unrecognisable in Amy's inappropriate bath robe, hair sticking out like ruffled feathers. Jake slumbered on, oblivious.

The house phone rang. It was my mother. That made it a perfect morning. She said, 'Where were you on Friday night? Where were you *last* night? Why didn't you answer your phone? Do you think you're too grown up and important for your own mother? How did you get to be so big for your britches?'

'Excuse me, Mother,' I said. 'I'm only just out of the shower. I'll call you back.'

'At this time of day?' she began. 'Lying in bed with that loser, I expect... '

It was all I heard because I cut her off and went to my room to dress and dry my hair. I made sure my mobile was switched off, and then I turned on the hair dryer. I didn't want to hear the phone or my mother or Amy or anyone. I hung upside down to dry the underside of my hair, the part that can stay damp all day if I let it. The rush of blood to my head made me dizzy. I wondered if I was coming down with flu.

Outside the window the sky was quite white, and I imagined the garden I would make for Lazaro as hanging in thin air, or somehow perched on the side of a mountain like a mad Bavarian castle. But when, dressed in a boring warm-up suit, I went back to the kitchen, I saw the black and white photos of a mundane city-centre flat roof. My dreams were outstripping reality. But isn't that what dreams are supposed to do?

Jake was making coffee, stretching and yawning. I squeezed

all the six oranges which were supposed to be my supply for a week. I poured the juice into four glasses quickly because if I didn't Jake would snaffle the lot. He exchanged a mug of coffee for a glass of juice. He'd slept in his clothes and hadn't brushed his teeth, but he was as confident as only the one man in a flatful of women can be – cock of the walk, my mother would've said. For once she'd be right. I disliked him for it. We didn't speak.

Amy blew in, perfume first, wearing mascara, lipstick and blusher – not her normal Sunday face. She thanked Jake for the coffee but accepted the orange juice as her due. I disliked her for that too.

Last to arrive was Hannah, looking tidy and tired. She thanked everyone.

The house phone rang. Amy picked up. She listened for a moment, then mouthed, 'Your mother', and handed me the receiver. I passed it straight to Hannah, who said, 'Hello, Ivy dear,' sounding as tired as she looked. I offered her a mug of black coffee and she sipped gratefully before saying, 'I'm here, Ivy, because Seema's unwell... I don't know, it looks like a rather nasty bug... yes, I know anaemia is prevalent among vegetarians... no, I'm sure it's not that... or that... yes, I'll take her myself... don't worry.' She was silent for a few more minutes.

I passed her the orange juice. Amy, Jake and I were breathing as quietly as falling leaves and pretending we were somewhere else. In the end she said, 'How very odd. I'm sure it's nothing, but I'll tell her when she's feeling a little better.' She hung up and I put my palms together in the universal gesture of heartfelt thanks.

She said, 'Is Lazaro Restorations anything to do with a firm of developers called Sharpe-Harding Associates?'

'Possibly.' I was surprised. 'Lesley Sharpe and Garth Harding were both at the dinner I told you about. Why?'

'Your mother just told me that a representative from Sharpe-Harding went to her house last night to check references or something. She wasn't very clear. She thought you might be in some sort of trouble. She described the enquiry as "official". She thought the man might be a debt collector.'

'Are you in debt?' Jake asked coldly. 'You said you were worried about money.'

'I'm self-employed – I always worry about money.' I was feeling criticised. 'That's why I'm *never* in debt. You should know that by now. My mother should know it too.'

'Have you bought a big-ticket item recently?' Amy asked hopefully. 'Like a new washer-dryer? Something that might need a credit check?'

'The old one's fine,' I said.

'And why would a credit check include your mother?' Hannah said. 'No, clearly it's something to do with the potential new job and your new acquaintances. Seema, what's the name of the gated mews you were taken to?'

'I don't know,' I said sullenly.

'Might it be Palatine Mews Estate?'

'It was somewhere in Belgravia. I couldn't see. It was snowing.' I felt stupid.

Hannah and Amy looked at Jake who clicked away on his lap top and then turned the screen to face me.

'Google Earth,' Hannah informed me proudly. Jake smiled his superior technological smile. I wanted to slap him.

He said, 'That's your roof top, isn't it?'

It certainly looked like it, but I was too angry to speak.

'Watch.' The camera pulled away so that the roof top was not much more than a dot on a bird's-eye view of part of London that included Belgravia and a chunk of Hyde Park. Jake zoomed in slowly till I could see a huddle of mewses which would once have served the carriage trade of Belgrave Square and Grosvenor Crescent. It was hidden away behind the elegant facades of the grand terraces on two sides, a huge hotel on another, and to the north the shops, flats and offices that fronted Knightsbridge.

'The Palatine Estate,' Amy said.

I could see the wrought iron gates and another entrance on the Knightsbridge side, equally well-guarded.

'See this central block,' Jake pointed. 'It looks as if it's five small houses backing on to another five houses. Well, if what you told Hannah is true, someone has converted ten mews houses into one really large one without altering the exteriors at all.'

'One wonders how they got planning permission,' Hannah said. 'But Seema, your rooftop isn't on that block. It's way over here.' She pointed. 'So that implies that Lazaro owns more than the house you were invited to.'

'So?' I snarled. 'What're you getting at? Is it against the law to be rich and own property? Does it offend your left wing sensibilities if I work for a rich man? Is it illegal for him to like night-scented plants? Okay, so some of them are poisonous. Well, so are sweet little bluebells. And every part of a pretty springtime daffodil is absolutely toxic. Everyone goes on about deadly nightshade, but when were you ever warned about the innocent, joyful daf? Eh?'

'I didn't know that,' Amy admitted. 'But Seema, the man gave you drugs and assaulted you. There's something wrong.'

'I smoked a little opium,' I said. 'It was my own choice. You don't *know* he assaulted me. I don't either. So don't you go bandying accusations around without proof.'

'Why are you defending him?' Jake burst out. 'Is he Mr Perfect? You haven't a single doubt about him, have you?'

'Yes I have,' I said, stung. 'He doesn't like dogs. So shoot him.'

'I don't like dogs much either,' Amy said, thoughtfully.

'So shoot Amy too,' I added meanly.

'Children, children,' Hannah interrupted. 'Let's not lose sight of the big picture – which is that we all love Seema. You may have acted incautiously, dear, but you haven't done anything wrong.'

'Illegal drugs,' righteous Amy pointed out.

'Lying to me,' Jake said.

'I have not lied to you,' I said.

'Well, you haven't told the whole truth either,' Jake said, with justification. 'The old guy has some sort of hold over you. Is this because your dad died when you were eight?'

'Please, Jake.' Hannah intercepted a cutting remark I had on the tip of my tongue which would have reminded him forcibly that I'd dumped him last night. 'Can we keep personal quarrels out of this? Seema has done nothing wrong, but there *is* something worrying here. Just on practical points – how did Pasqual know where to find Seema on Friday night? How did the Sharpe-Harding representative track down her mother so quickly? Ivy couldn't remember exactly what he asked her but she thought he was a debt collector so it must've been intrusive. How did Seema get home on Saturday morning? What does the injury on her neck mean? What have I left out?'

'Why did she eat a bacon burger without a moment's thought?' Amy supplied. 'Why did she throw up in the bathroom this morning? And why has the weather gone crazy?'

'What has she got that a rich old pervert wants?' Jake said. 'I'm pretty sure that most of your questions, Ms David, mean that she's been stalked. I don't know if it's electronic or not. Did you let your phone or your personal ID, credit cards, et cetera, out of your possession while you were in the old guy's company?'

'Um,' I said, a cold tingle starting at the base of my spine.

'You did, didn't you?' Jake seemed half fearful, half triumphant. 'Check your bank balance. Right now.'

I reached for my phone and switched it on. There were twenty-nine missed calls. I ignored them and began the tedious business of remembering the sequence of clicks, security information and password that allowed me to see my own account. I was horribly conscious that all the information was written on a card I kept in my wallet, and that my wallet had been removed by Gemma along with everything else. But I didn't want Jake to know that. He has a separate, meaningless, complicated password for each of his accounts – all of which he can remember without difficulty. I have one damn password: *Bai Shao Yao*, the Chinese name for the white peony, interspersed with a couple of numbers. Even that won't stick in my memory.

My bank balance looked normal. I sighed with relief. It wasn't fat enough for me to feel safe but nor was it thin enough to make me panic.

'Is your phone password protected?' Jake asked. He knew the answer; he just wanted me to look careless and gormless in front of Hannah and Amy. I glared at him.

'So your contact list is compromised too? That's how the old pervert found your mother so easily.'

Something detonated in my head. I felt a rage that later I didn't think was mine. 'What gives any of you the right to interfere with my life? I have plans and purposes that are my own. Who are you to thwart me?' I was standing now, feeling weirdly as if I was looking down from a great height.

'*Thwart?*' said Amy. 'Where did that come from?'

I didn't know. I swept my drawings and photos into a pile and rushed out of the room. Without even thinking I found myself in coat and boots, bag in hand, folder under my arm running down the road towards my van.

A gardener's van will always smell like a potting shed, and after a while the scent of earth, compost and garden waste calmed me down. I stopped shaking with fury. There was no plan, but I pulled away from the kerb and turned the van towards the West End.

SIX

The iron gates to the Palatine Estate were locked. I couldn't see Lazaro's house from where I stood but the place looked deserted. There was a button under the keypad and I pressed it. Nothing happened for a long time and then, with a hiss and a crackle, the microphone next to the button came to life.

'What?' said a tinny voice almost drowned by crackle.

'I'd like to see Mr Lazaro,' I said.

'No one here,' said the voice.

'I'm doing a job for him,' I said, hoping I didn't sound pitiful.

The voice creaked and squeaked something I couldn't catch. Then the microphone went dead.

I pressed the bell push again. Again nothing happened. Now I didn't know what to do. So I stayed where I was, dithering.

After a while I heard barking, and the Beaus came racing round the corner in full attack mode. They skidded to a halt when they saw me, at first uncertain and then delighted.

I could've stayed petting them through the bars but a people carrier with The Mighty Maid Service painted in pink and cream on the side pulled up behind my van and a large woman asked me to move so that she and her 'girls' could come in. They had work to do she told me.

Reluctantly I climbed into my van and reversed out of her way. Watching her key in a code and wait for the gates to open

I had a mad idea that I could accelerate in behind her before the gates shut.

And then what? I hadn't been invited. Well, I thought rebelliously, did I have to be invited? After all, Pasqual showed up whenever it suited Lazaro to summon me. But he was demonstrating quite clearly that while the rich were entitled, the poor were not. So I sat, resentfully watching the Mighty Maid Service drive into the secret secluded maze of mewses. I felt excluded and humiliated.

But as the gates began to close an amazing thing happened: just before they clanged shut the Beaus came trotting out to find me.

At first I was thrilled. But then, halfway to my van, they yelped, stopped short and crumpled as though they'd been shot.

Horrified, I leaped down from the driver's seat and ran to them. Both huge beasts seemed to be in the throes of some sort of fit, spasming, teeth bared. The hair on their backs was erect. Their muscles had contorted to such an extent I was afraid their backs would break.

Not knowing what to do, I knelt beside them. Cradling the nearest Beau in my arms I suddenly noticed the thick collar half hidden by his shaggy ruff.

'No!' I exclaimed. 'Shit, shit, shit!'

With shaking fingers I unbuckled the collar and threw it at the gate. Then I did the same for the other Beau. Although the spasms relaxed, both dogs lay shivering on the ground unwilling or unable to stand.

It was the collars. They were the sort that people too lazy to train their dogs use. Lazy, cruel people could simply press a button and send a jolt of electricity into a dog that disobeyed or didn't respond fast enough to a command. Someone, presumably Grigori, had given the Beaus massive, sustained shocks when he noticed they'd left the Palatine Estate.

I was furious and terrified. Had the bastard killed them rather them let them go?

I placed my hand on one dog's chest. He was breathing shallow panting breaths. So was the other. I lifted one eyelid. Both dogs' eyes were rolled up, giving them a gruesome deathly look. I got to my feet and went to the van. I turned it and reversed close to the Beaus. I opened the back doors and lowered the ramp. There's a small trolley I use when transporting large bags of compost, manicure, sand or gravel. It isn't designed for enormous limp dogs that are not conveniently packaged in plastic. I struggled to lift one of them. I couldn't. I'm strong but not strong enough. And I had to hurry. How long would it be before Grigori came to the gate to retrieve his horribly punished hounds?

Help came in the form of a Norse god on a shiny multi-speed road bike. He had red-gold hair, a neat designer beard and a lot of tasteful body art.

'Can I help you?' he asked in an accent that owed a lot to expensive education. 'What's wrong with those dogs?' In spite of the cold he was only wearing shorts and a tank top. The tattoos were dense enough to look like long sleeves.

'Someone zapped them almost to death with electronic collars,' I said, and was pleased to see a disgusted expression on his face. 'I'm trying to get them into my van before anything worse happens to them. But as you can see...' My voice trailed off in the face of the Beaus' huge size and unmanageable shape.

'There's some tough plastic sheeting in the van,' I went on. 'If you're willing to help, we could roll them onto it and lift them.'

'Good plan,' he said. 'Let's get on with it. I don't really want to be within reach of those teeth when the dogs come round – if they ever come round. They don't look too well at the moment, do they?'

So that's what we did: we rolled them, one at a time, onto the plastic sheeting, heaved them up the ramp and laid them as comfortably as we could on the floor of the van. I covered them with my coat.

'What're you going to do now?' the Norse god asked.

'I don't know,' I admitted. 'I hadn't thought any further than saving them.'

'Okay,' he said. 'Find somewhere to park on the Serpentine Bridge road and I'll catch up with you.'

In fact he was much quicker on his bike than I was. He was even guarding a space just large enough for me to pull into. He leaned his bike against the van and I let him into the seat beside me. There was a temporary wire-mesh barrier between the cab and the back which was meant save me from being beheaded by flying tools if I was forced to brake suddenly, but dogs as big and strong as the Beaus would make short work of it. They were beginning to wake up. The Norse god said, 'Normally, I love dogs – especially hunting dogs – but those two are awesomely hostile.'

I stared at him in surprise. 'You know them?'

'Yes,' he said, looking equally surprised. 'They belong to Garth Harding. You know, the rich guy who lives in the big house behind the gates you just came out of.'

'Doesn't the house belong to Lazaro?' I asked, bewildered.

'The arty one with the gorgeous PA? I don't think so. Isn't he just the interior decorator?'

'I'm sure he's a lot more than that. How do you know Garth Harding?'

'He's sponsoring me. My team supports a small charity in Uganda. He's putting up – well, quite a lot of money if I complete a Tuareg Trek within a week. I'm pretty fit, obviously, but it'll be gruelling.'

'Your team?'

'I play professional rugby,' he said as modestly as he could. 'London Scorpions, Premier League. We were promoted last season.'

'Congratulations,' I said, thinking that Jake, as a sports fan, would probably be better equipped to say the right thing. But other questions were crowding my mind.

He got in first. 'How come you are rescuing the dogs? How do you know them? And what's your name? I'm Mark Kirkby.' The hand he stuck out was not tattooed. If he was wearing a jacket no one would know about the body art.

'Seema Dahami.' I shook the hand.

'Where are you from?'

'Finchley,' I said flatly, knowing that wasn't the answer he was looking for. 'I was a guest at the Palatine Estate on Friday night, and *I* thought Mr *Lazaro* owned the house and the dogs and all the amazingly wonderful art.'

'Art?' said Mark Kirkby looking bewildered. 'There was art?'

In fact in the past three years the only man I'd had a conversation about the things I hold sacred was Lazaro. And what a conversation! It had been a tapestry of dreams, gardens, painting and poets, all enveloped in the gauze of opium smoke – a cloud in which fantasies were not fantastic. I knew, absolutely knew, I could make his garden for him, and that we would be of one mind. It wouldn't be big or grand. How could it be? Where gardens are concerned I am a miniaturist. But it would be what our two minds could make possible – a place of mystery, romance, secrets, innocence and transgression.

I realised I'd given up on conversations about anything that engaged my soul in favour of listening to whatever interested my friends. In the past three years I'd forgotten how lonely I felt.

And now, here I was with a Norse god of an athlete who hadn't so much as glanced at the Cycladic priestess figurines and was afraid of the dogs I'd saved. Despicably I wanted to ask him what I should do next.

Instead I said, 'I'm a gardener. The Palatine Estate is thinking of making a roof garden.' How practical and down-to-earth a statement is that? I watched Mark re-evaluate my clothes, my van and my relationship with two sad dogs. Maybe I seemed now, in spite of my weird name and un-English looks, to be a known quantity.

I got out of the van and opened the back to see to the Beaus.

They could both stand but staggered when they tried to walk. There wasn't room to use the ramp this time, but they managed to wobble towards me. It was a lot easier to lift them down to the ground than it had been to hoist them up.

'Help me walk them into the park,' I said. 'They won't hurt you. They aren't guarding their territory any more. And you're with me.' But even so he was uneasy because there were no collars or chains. So I showed him how to hold the loose skin at the back of their necks firmly but gently, the way their mother would have carried them when they were pups.

Feeling, perhaps, that it was un-macho to be afraid of the Beaus he put his bike into the back of the van and together we guided our shaky charges into green grass and trees where, to my relief, they seemed to revive. They drank from the lake, then slept on the grass behind the bench Mark and I sat on.

He stretched his arms along the back of the bench, seeming oblivious to the cold, taking up space the way very fit, confident men do. I sat beside him, dowdy as a hen, while he seemed to glow like a young lion. I could see the Sunday walkers and joggers all glance at him as they hurried past in thick jackets, ear muffs and gloves. He looked like someone they felt they ought to recognise.

He said, 'What're you going to do about the dogs? Will you take them back when they're fully recovered? Does Mr Harding know you have them?'

He was assuming Garth Harding owned the Beaus. I knew Lazaro did. He'd called them 'my dogs' and charged me with naming them. I was sure he didn't know Grigori was mistreating them. Even if he didn't like them I was positive he wouldn't tolerate cruelty to animals.

But I had no way of getting in touch with him other than waiting for Pasqual to show up. That was why I'd rushed in person to Belgravia. Then I wondered if Mark routinely cycled past the Palatine Estate.

'Have you got Mr Harding's phone number?' I asked.

'He's a busy guy,' Mark said vaguely. 'His agent's in touch with my agent. There's going to be a TV program about the Tuareg Trek, of course. It's quite complicated.'

'Could you get his number off your agent for me?'

'Not on a Sunday.' Mark grinned ruefully. 'I'm not that big a star player yet. But I'm working on it. Besides, Mr Harding's away this week.'

'He was at dinner on Friday night,' I said.

'Was he? I must've misunderstood.' He looked puzzled.

'Is cycling round here part of your normal training routine?'

'Usually, on a Sunday, I need something tougher, like Haverstock Hill and Hampstead Heath. But I was wondering if Mr Harding had left a package for me at the gate.'

I waited for him to elaborate, wondering why I always seemed to be waiting for more from a guy when there was no more to be had. 'Is this all there is?' seemed to be the ruling question of my life where men are concerned.

'A package?' I prompted eventually.

'Mr Harding imports some special dietary supplements from Germany,' he said. 'Not steroids. Don't worry.'

I hadn't worried till he told me not to. 'Is Sharpe-Harding Associates into health foods?' I asked.

'I don't know,' he said. 'Mr Harding's company imports mainly surgical equipment and I think he takes an interest in sporting sponsorships. His company gets appeals from charities all over the country. But he likes sports so that's what he concentrates on.'

'That's very generous.'

'It helps me, you see, if people at the club notice that I'm drawing in sponsorship. Being a professional athlete can be quite insecure.'

'You only have to get ill or injured?'

'And then I could lose my place on the first team. Yes,' he said. 'I'm twenty-four now. If I'm lucky I might have seven or eight more years playing at this level. And then what?'

'So when opportunity knocks…?'

'Yeah, open the door and grab it with both hands. That's what I like about Mr Harding – he gets how chancy and unglamorous professional sport can be. He *gets* me.'

'So, this supplement,' I began.

'It's something refined from the sap of baobab trees with added vitamins and minerals. Baobabs have amazing properties if you know how to extract the right components. I'm not supposed to talk about it – the formula's still a secret. But you can put it on your skin as well. Did you happen to meet a woman called Lesley Sharpe?'

'Yes, she was at the dinner too.'

'How old do you think she is?'

I tried to recall the tall, austere women in the mannish suit. 'About thirty-five? Forty tops.'

'Sixty-three,' Mark said triumphantly. 'She's been using the supplement as a moisturiser for five years now – guinea-pigging it. They're going to get a license after the clinical trial ends.'

'Wow,' I said, genuinely amazed. 'They'll make a fortune when they start marketing it.'

'You mustn't say anything about it to anyone.' He looked suddenly alarmed. 'It's still a big secret.'

'But you're putting it in your mouth and swallowing it. Are you sure it's safe?'

'Absolutely. Mr Harding told me I might feel a little lethargic for a couple of days and then there'd be a gradual surge of energy. He was right. But I'm running out. I need more.'

We were silent for a moment. Then I said, 'I wonder why it's so hard to get in touch with anyone.'

At that moment one of the Beaus yawned, got up and stretched. He laid his head on my knee and looked up at me with forlorn, betrayed eyes. 'It's okay, baby,' I said, stroking his head.

'Baby?' Mark watched, astonished. But when the second Beau got up he reached out his hand and made friends with both dogs.

'They have to be taught to be ferocious,' I said. 'I don't know why anyone would do that – given all the security cameras, CCTV and electronic locks they have at that house. I suppose I'll have to take them back, but I need to talk to Lazaro first and I don't know how to do that.'

'Don't tell him I was involved. I really don't want to piss Mr Harding off.'

I didn't want to piss Lazaro off either. But it was too late. By driving off with his dogs I'd messed up one of his security arrangements. I said, 'Unfortunately, they'll know it was me, but with any luck you were shielded from the cameras by the van.'

'There are cameras?'

Mark Kirkby was not a guy who noticed much. I looked at his Michelangelo muscles and beautiful tattoos and wondered if, like most athletes, he was almost exclusively focussed on his own body and its health and fitness.

'They may not even know you were there.' I said. 'And if they do you can tell them truthfully it was my fault. I just wish I had some way I could explain. Meanwhile I think I'll have to take the dogs home with me and wait for Pasqual.'

We sat watching the joggers slogging past our bench and the hopeful water birds on the Serpentine. Then Mark said cautiously, 'It's a complicated set-up they've got in that house.'

'Did any of it strike you as weird?' I asked, equally cautious.

'I guess I'm just not used to that sort of company,' he said.

'Me neither.' We weren't looking at each other. I couldn't think why he was still sitting beside me, but neither of us got up to leave. Then his phone buzzed. He looked at it and said, 'My girlfriend wants to know where I am.' Even now he didn't get up. I realised my phone was still turned off. The missed calls from my mother would be in the hundreds by now. I wondered if Jake was worried.

'Okay,' he said, stirring at last. 'I suppose I'd better shift. Listen, can I have your phone number? I'll give you mine. Maybe I can help if you get into trouble.'

I thumbed my number into his phone and he put his in mine. I didn't know why. It just felt more comfortable than simply parting. In the same spirit, we hugged each other as if we'd been through an intense experience together. Which, of course, we hadn't, although it was not an ordinary day.

◆━━━━━━◆━━━━━◆

I took the dogs to Hampstead Heath, stopping at a supermarket on the way to buy dog food and paper plates. They ate ravenously and then ran off exploring. Always together, they communicated magically – turning as one, galloping, stopping as if there'd been a silent command – like trained circus animals. They were so similar that I realised I would have to know them a lot better if I was to tell them apart. But running free, they were a joy to watch, and I watched until my hands turned blue with cold and I couldn't feel my feet. Then I called them and we drove home.

The flat was empty and silent. I filled the bath with hot water and soaked until I was warm again. There was nothing to be done until Pasqual came for me again, so I dressed in a clean warm-up suit and lay on the sofa watching junk TV. The Beaus climbed onto the sofa with me, lying across my legs like giant bony blankets. We all went to sleep.

It was dark when the phone woke me. I reached for it groggily. Hannah's voice said, 'Seema? Seema, wake up. Are you alright?'

I mumbled something. I could hardly open my eyes, and my tongue seemed paralysed.

'Seema, dear,' Hannah said. 'I've been trying to find you for hours. Something terrible has happened:

Suddenly I knew without a doubt that Pasqual was waiting outside. I extricated myself from the dogs and got up.

'I'll call you back,' I said.

'No!' Hannah shouted. 'Listen! It's your mother. She's dead...'

I heard her but even so I had to go to the window. I didn't

ring off. I laid the phone gently on the arm of the sofa, went to the window and opened it. An icy blast of wind and snow hit my face. I looked down and Pasqual, black against the crystal pavement, beckoned.

'Pasqual,' I called, 'wait. Something bad's happened.'

I walked back to the phone. 'What?' I asked.

'Your mother was found... I'm sorry, there's no way to soften this. She was found dead on her doorstep.'

I felt nothing but a sense of urgency.

She said, 'Seema. You have to come. The police want to talk to you.'

'Where are you?' I said at last.

'With Ivy's neighbour, Mira Joseph, you know, one of your mother's Mahjong four. Come now.'

'What about the dogs?' I said. Sensing my distress, the Beaus were pressing anxiously against my legs.

'What dogs? Seema, have you been dreaming? I've been ringing for hours. The police knocked on your door but no one answered. You have to come right now.'

'What time is it?'

'Nearly two o'clock.'

I was stunned. I'd been asleep for hours. Amy hadn't come home to bed. Maybe I could leave the dogs here.

'What's the matter with you?' Hannah cried.

'I don't know,' I said, and rang off.

At the window I called down to Pasqual, telling him to wait. I fed the dogs again, filled bowls with fresh water and patted them with tenderness; I'd never felt more connection with any other living, loving creatures than the Beaus. 'Stay,' I said. 'Wait for me.' And they licked my face and neck which I took as agreement.

Then I snatched up my keys and went out to Pasqual.

I said, 'My mother's just been found dead. I can't go with you.' Even to me, my voice sound flat and empty. I turned away towards where the van was parked.

There were tears in my eyes, but not for my mother. I wanted to go with Pasqual. I might be missing my last chance. Last chance for what? I couldn't put words to it

'Wait.' Pasqual lifted a finger as if he were interrupting a long boring speech.

Everything felt base over apex. I knew it was wrong, but I waited while he turned away to make a phone call. When he turned back he said, 'I am to take you wherever you ought to be.'

I climbed onto the Harley behind him and we pulled away with a cough and a roar.

It was a journey that should have taken less than ten minutes but, clinging like a monkey to Pasqual's slim body, eons seemed to pass before we came to a stop in front of the gates to the Palestine Estate.

'No!' I said. 'No, no, no.'

'Yes,' he said firmly. 'My master ordered me to bring you where you ought to be and you agreed.'

'I did not.'

'Then why did you not give me a different address?'

I realised with a shock that he was right. I'd silently assumed he knew where my mother lived.

'Silence is consent,' Lazaro said, appearing in the doorway of a sort of gatehouse. 'As ignorance is no defence. You wanted to come here. You could not say so because it would not have been proper. You hid your head and let Pasqual decide where you "ought to be". Your passivity is your downfall. This is a lesson.' His voice was as cold as the wind. Tears filled my eyes and froze like crystal on my lashes.

'I want my dogs back,' Grigori snapped, appearing at Lazaro's shoulder.

'So you can torture then again?' I snapped back, suddenly feeling I was waking from a dream. 'You nearly killed them. You should not be in charge of valuable animals like the Beaus if you don't know how to treat them.' Although I was staring with accusing eyes at Grigori my last words were aimed at Lazaro.

'They've been trained never to bugger off out of the Estate,' Grigori said, and then added jeeringly, 'It was a lesson.'

'Enough!' Lazaro said. 'Go away, Grigori.' To me he said, 'Are the dogs all right now?'

'Yes,' I said, melting. He cared. I knew he wouldn't tolerate cruelty to animals.

'I'm glad,' he said simply. 'Now, my dear, you must tell me why you are here after receiving such distressing news about your mother.'

Of course I didn't know, but I said, 'I so badly wanted to show you my drawings. I don't think the news has sunk in. I can't seem to feel anything. But I know I should be there and not here.'

'Ah yes,' he said. 'You have been torn away from your duty by your heart's desire. Don't worry. I will take you there myself. Pasqual, bring the car round.' When Pasqual left he said, 'I'm afraid Pasqual is very responsive to the unspoken needs of others. You mustn't judge him.'

'I don't,' I said, although privately I thought Pasqual was pretty high-handed.

'He's a very handsome young man,' Lazaro said almost to himself. He sounded sad. Then he added, even more sadly, 'And you, dear Seema, have such a sensitive eye for beauty.'

'No!' I protested instantly. 'I mean yes… ' but I didn't know what to say. Idiotically I wanted to comfort Lazaro for being old. I couldn't say it, but his maturity and experience were part of the attraction. 'What catches the eye,' I began, faltering, 'isn't necessarily the genuine article. Maybe it won't stand the test of time. I didn't come here because I wanted to be with Pasqual.'

I'd said the right thing. His smile was so sweet and sad I began to feel comfortable with him again. Hannah was quite wrong: it wasn't vanity that made him care so much about his appearance; it was insecurity – something I could easily understand.

As if reading my mind, he said, 'My dear, what about your clothes? Your mother has tragically died: should you not show a more proper respect?'

I looked down at myself. I was wearing a clean but ancient warm-up suit. It was wet with snow. I was shivering because I'd forgotten my coat and I'd ridden through the wind and snow on the back of a bike. I was a sorry sight.

'Come into the gatehouse,' he said. 'You're freezing. I'll call Gemma. She'll find you something better. Dressed suitably you'll cope with more dignity.'

'The police want to talk to me,' I said through chattering teeth.

'Of course,' he said. 'But they will respect you more if you show proper grief for the dead.' He led me through the gate into the small house next to it, and five minutes later Gemma appeared carrying an armful of dress bags.

It took only twenty minutes but when I stepped into the limousine my hair was dry and I was wearing a long black skirt, a cloud-grey high necked sweater, knee length black boots and a fur-lined velvet jacket.

'Most suitable,' Lazaro murmured. 'And if I may say so, subtly beautiful.'

I glowed – almost forgetting I'd dressed for my dead mother rather then for his approval.

He waited till the car was moving before he lit his opium pipe. 'For courage and calm,' he said, handing it to me. 'Only a little, my dear – you may need to keep your wits about you.'

There must've been some hellish traffic accident on the Edgware Road because it was almost two hours later that I stepped out of the limousine in front of Mrs Joseph's house. I think I slept through it all.

Lazaro said, 'I won't come with you. I'm afraid your friends think badly of me.' I wanted to deny it, but I couldn't, and he placed a kiss on my forehead as a farewell and a blessing. Pasqual pulled away immediately and I turned to face my mother's house.

SEVEN

The small front garden was festooned with blue and white police tape and guarded by a very young policeman. All the lights were on inside. I could see shadows of figures moving about between badly closed curtains. My mother's careful house had been invaded.

It's true, I thought muzzily. It happened. It isn't a lie or a dream or a fantasy. I have no mother; the thorn in my flesh has been wrenched violently out.

And yet there was no sign of violence. The door had not been smashed open. There was no blood on the doorstep or the paving in front of it. Someone had politely rung the doorbell and my mother, hearing the doorbell, had politely opened the door. Good manners killed her.

I stood there in my finery staring at the house I'd been brought up in, the prison it had become after my dad died, the prison I'd escaped when I went to art school.

The cop scratched his acne and stared back at me until Mrs Joseph's front door opened and Hannah bustled out to collect me. She looked emaciated and ravaged. 'I've been up all night,' she explained, 'waiting for you. Your mother died at seven in the evening. It's nearly dawn now. Where the hell have you been? Mira gave up and went to bed. And Amy's been ringing and ringing. She can't get into the flat. Why aren't you answering your phone?'

I looked down. I was carrying a black shoulder bag made of real leather instead of my canvas backpack. I never buy real leather bags or shoes. What's the point of excluding meat from your diet and then wearing it? Of course the boots Gemma had provided were of the softest Italian leather too.

'I dropped my phone,' I said. 'I think it's broken.'

'Aren't you going to ask what happened?' Hannah led me into Mira Joseph's over-stuffed front room. It was the mirror image of my mother's: full of inherited pieces from generations of dead Josephs. Except my mother's house was full of *her* family's bequests, not my father's. The Dahami family were immigrants from the east who had pitched up in England after the war without any furniture at all.

All Mother's family history of bad taste would now be mine, I thought with a sharp stab of dismay. It was the first real feeling I'd had, and it was inappropriate.

'What happened?' I asked Hannah dully.

But she was already on to something else – the way very tired people surf topics.

'The rabbi's coming this morning. We can't bury her. The police have the body. They do what they've got to do in their own good time. They don't give a fig for tradition. Maybe the rabbi's been in touch with them already. Jews and autopsies aren't a good fit. We're just a pain in their procedural backsides. And, Seema, why are you keeping guard dogs in your flat? Amy couldn't get in or go to bed. I've no idea where she slept. *If* she slept. God knows I haven't.' She sank down in a sofa. She looked so small and frail the cushions seemed to eat her up. My strong, clear-thinking champion was withering into a dried husk of herself.

I went to the kitchen and made a pot of black tea for both of us. What was I thinking? Crazily, in Mira Joseph's kosher kitchen, I was thinking about Mary Shelley's most famous work. Why had she given the doctor a Jewish name and then made his monstrous assemblage of body parts as un-kosher as it could possibly be? And did Shakespeare know anything at *all* about Jews? What about all the blood prohibitions he violated when he got Shylock to insist on a pound of flesh in the Merchant of Venice? Worse, he gave the Christian, Portia, the lines that allowed him the flesh but forbade the shedding of a single drop of blood – which put the whammy on the Jew's evil plan. Not only was he a Jew, but Shakespeare made him a bad, ignorant Jew. A worse Jew than I am. But at least Shylock never ate a bacon cheeseburger.

Hannah was asleep in the carnivorous chair. I put her cup down on the table beside her and took mine to the window. I drank and watched dawn break over Golders Green.

Now, all I could think about was the dogs. They'd need food and water and a run on Hampstead Heath. I'd left them alone too long.

In spite of last night's snow the sky promised a clear morning. I pictured slanting dawn sunlight on the heath and two dogs racing and playing. I saw them plunging into the pond, scattering the naked men who swam there. I thought of David Hockney's Californian swimming pools, the sunlight, the underwater men.

And then my tea was cold and a tired rumpled man was walking towards Mrs Joseph's front door. Not wanting to wake Hannah I went to the door and opened it before he could ring the bell.

Almost too weary to speak he flipped open his wallet and showed me that he was a detective sergeant and his name was Edward Richardson. His greying hair stuck up like coarse grass and his left shoe was split. In between, everything was creased, especially his face.

He looked me up and down in a way that made me feel my respectful finery might have been a mistake. 'Are you the daughter?' Even his voice sounded creased and cracked. 'The next of kin?'

'Yes,' I said quietly.

'There are questions,' he began.

'Yes,' I said. 'Have you got a car we can sit in? Mrs Joseph's asleep and Ms David only just dropped off. They're old. This has been a huge shock.'

His car, an equally rumpled SUV, smelled of boiled sweets and nicotine. He started the motor and cranked the heating up before he said, 'Where have you been all night?'

'Wait a minute,' I said. 'I don't even know what happened yet. And I'm worried about my dogs.'

'Your dogs?' he croaked, temper making him straighten and swivel in his seat to scowl at me. 'Your mother had her throat cut. She exsanguinated all over the living room, the kitchen and the hall. That's what happened. And you're worried about your dogs?'

'The kitchen?' I said horrified. 'But my mother kept kosher.'

'When your throat's cut,' the detective said viciously, 'you don't have a lot of choice what rooms you bleed out in.'

I pictured my mother racing from room to room like a headless chicken. I began to shake. 'Throat? She ran around?' My voice quavered. 'Hannah said she was found on the doorstep. But there was no blood on the doorstep.'

'How do you know?' he shot back.

'I looked. When I arrived. There was no trace.'

'That is one of the puzzles,' he admitted. Then he toughened up again. 'Okay, so now you know. Now tell me where you were yesterday evening and last night. From, say, five-thirty on.'

'Nowhere particular.' I was still shaking. 'I took the dogs for a long walk on Hampstead Heath. It was dark when we got home. I was really tired and so were they, so we all went to sleep in front of the telly. I didn't wake up till Hannah phoned me.'

'But we sent someone. No one was home.'

'I was. Maybe he got the wrong flat buzzer.' That was a mistake. It sounded critical.

'And maybe you're lying. Everyone phoned you for hours. You're saying even your friends got the wrong number? Your flatmate has keys. These two famous dogs, dogs she didn't know you had – kept her out of her own home. You were not there, Ms Darma.'

'Dahami,' I said flatly. No one ever gets my name right. 'My name is Seema Dahami. My mother, the woman whose murder you're investigating, is, I mean was, Ivy Dahami.' I was sounding super snotty. I couldn't seem to stop myself. But he should've known my mother's name. He really should. I started to cry.

'Sorry,' he said, looking away.

I searched in the real leather bag and discovered that Gemma had failed to provide me with any tissues.

The detective nudged me aside and found a packet in the glove compartment. Gracelessly he dropped them in my lap.

When I'd mopped my face and blown my nose, I said, 'Thanks. Do a lot of women cry in your car?'

'Hundreds,' he said. 'And once, every ten years or so, I catch a cold. Once in a blue moon I catch a murderer too.' He sounded friendlier and even more tired.

'Good,' I said. 'Is this a hate crime?'

'It's crossed my mind. Why do you ask?'

'Bleeding out in a kosher house.'

'Are you ready to answer my questions now?' he said, ignoring me.

'Will you drive me home? I apologise for thinking about the dogs but they're living, loving creatures and I'm responsible for them. None of this is their fault.'

'Gawd save us from animal lovers.' He sighed and put his car in gear.

On the way I told him as anodyne a story as I could. I said I'd been sleeping very badly and was trying a new sleeping pill, an over-the-counter remedy, and that stupidly I'd combined it with an antihistamine known for its drowsy effects. Well, what was I going to say? That I'd been smoking opium with an extremely rich employer for several days and I couldn't account for huge chunks of time? Was I going to tell him that the clothes I was wearing were not my own, and the dogs I was putting ahead of my mother's death had been taken without their owner's consent? Above all, how could I send the cops to Lazaro to corroborate any story without ballsing up my already fragile relationship with him?

I kept it as simple as I could. He was interested in a murder, not my sleep problems. And it wasn't as if I was exactly lying. As far as I was concerned I was simply cutting out what I considered irrelevant. As I went on I was committing everything I said to memory. It helped. It distracted me from the gruesome facts of my mother's death, and the even weirder fact that I couldn't seem to feel anything about it. My heart had gone numb.

I tried to galvanise it by saying, 'She was angry with me. I was supposed to spend the Sabbath with her but I forgot. I should've seen her. And now it's too late.'

'Do you think, if you'd been there, you could've saved her?'

'I'm not talking about your Sabbath on Sunday,' I said. 'I'm talking about Friday night and Saturday.'

'I knew that,' he said, embarrassed.

'If she'd had her way I'd have been there till Saturday night,' I went on. 'She was a very strict observer.'

'And you aren't?'

'Being a good Jew can be a full-time job. And it's predicated on belief in god. I tried to please her when I could, but she was awfully disappointed in me.'

We'd arrived at my block and were sitting outside. I knew he was going to ask how I could be a Jew if I didn't believe in god – a tiresome question I often have to think about – so I said, 'Thanks very much for the lift.' And I leaped out of the car.

'Wait,' he said catching up with me on the doorstep. 'I haven't finished. Can you spare a cup of coffee for a tired old copper?'

'Okay,' I said as I let us into the communal hall. 'Stand behind me when I open my door. The Beaus may not react well to a stranger.'

But when I got to the door of my flat I found it wide open. The lock was smashed. The Beaus were gone.

My heart broke. Now I could cry – for love I'd never had, for approval I'd never been given, for the welcome I'd never received. I cried for everything the Beaus gave me; for all that I'd missed when my dad died. I cried for what my mother couldn't or wouldn't give me. I cried for all the loves I thought I'd found. I cried for all the loves I'd lost. I cried for all the love I hadn't *given*.

Dogs are that important.

Detective Sergeant Edward Richardson made the coffee while I washed my face, calmed down and changed into jeans and a sloppy sweater.

He said, 'Now this is a kitchen I understand. Your mother's was the biggest room in the whole house. It looked like a hotel kitchen.'

'Yep,' I said, grateful to him for giving me a chance to collect my tattered emotions. 'Two kitchens: one for meat, one for dairy, and a third, a secret Passover kitchenette, is concealed behind a cupboard door. She wasn't that strict when my father was still alive. After he died she remodelled the ground floor. There used to be a dining room and a study. The living-room was bigger. Religion takes up enormous time and space.'

'So this was a bone of contention between you and your mother?'

'It was an argument that rumbled on for years. It was what we talked about. It kept us together and at the same time tore us apart.'

For a moment we sipped hot coffee in silence. Then he said, 'I should call this burglary in.' He looked at me keenly.

'The dogs didn't belong to me,' I said looking back at him

steadily. 'I'm pretty sure the owners came to collect them while I was out and got impatient. I'm not making a complaint.'

He looked down at the large water bowl still on the floor, and the two food dishes licked almost dish-washer clean. I got up, collected them and put them in the sink. I could feel my mouth tremble and was afraid I might cry again.

'You should get a dog of your own,' he said. 'I had a couple of Labrador crosses. Then I got divorced and the worst thing was losing those dogs. But I couldn't have kept them – not with this job.'

'I know what you mean,' I said, picking up my coffee again. 'These two are giant wolfhounds.'

'No wonder they scared your flatmate off.'

'Yes, but she isn't crazy about dogs anyway.'

'I'd say "change your flatmate", but it isn't very practical, is it – giant hounds, small flat, no garden?'

'Yes. But… I don't know how to say this without sounding soppy, it's like, although they aren't human, they're the best part of humanity. And I feel I'm a better human being when I'm with them.'

'I'm sort of agreeing with you but I don't know what you mean.'

'Well, take love,' I said, beginning to sniff again. 'I could fall in love with the Beaus at first sight. I could love them without having to defend myself against them, or pretending I liked football. I could stroke them without having to stroke their egos. I didn't have to watch what I said. I wasn't constantly afraid they'd leave me for someone younger or prettier.'

'Don't cry.' He passed me a not very clean dishtowel. 'I do know what you mean but I'd never have put it like that.'

'Too soppy?'

'By about twenty miles. Look,' he said, 'I'm here to do a job, and I'd like to look at your phone. It's to check if your mother

73

called you about someone she might've been expecting, or any helpful information at all about what happened.'

'It's broken,' I said.

'Show it to me anyway.'

So I went to the bedroom and took my phone out of Gemma's bag. But before taking it to Detective Sergeant Richardson I whacked it hard against the corner of my desk – hard enough to crack the screen. I knew there would still be a gazillion missed calls and texts, but reluctantly I handed it to him.

He studied it. 'It's switched off,' he said. He switched it on and watched the provider identification logo swirling around on the damaged screen. 'No sound,' he commented, waiting for the screen to settle before going to the settings page. 'Why did you turn your sound off?'

'I didn't,' I said truthfully. Was this why I'd managed to sleep through so many calls? 'Could the sound have gone when I dropped the phone?'

'Don't ask me.' He looked tired and belligerent again. 'I only know the basics about these little bastards.' He touched the screen to turn the sound back on and as he did so there was a sudden shriek of feedback that made us both jump.

'What the fuck!' he said as the screen went black.

'What did you do?' I asked, devious but relieved.

'Fucked if I know.' He was furious with himself, with me, and with mobile phones. He got to his feet. 'I'll have to take it to the lab. Maybe the smart-arses there can retrieve the bleeding memory. You'll have to sign for it. Just one more effing extra I have to deal with before going home to my kip.'

And no dogs to welcome him home, I thought after he finally left. But first he'd followed me into the two bedrooms to make sure nothing had been vandalised or stolen. And he was nice enough to give me the number of an emergency locksmith who wouldn't beggar me.

I had to call from the landline. A woman said she'd be with me in about an hour. There was nothing to do but wait.

Surprisingly, given that everyone and their grandpa claimed to have rung me, there were no messages on voicemail. I thought about the way my mobile had packed up just as Ed Richardson started to turn the sound back on. Why was I so relieved? I made another cup of coffee and remembered how I'd been avoiding my mother's calls – avoiding the critical, lonely whine in her voice as, undoubtedly, she would've flayed the skin off me for forgetting Shabbat. I was guilty of neglecting my mother! I had good excuses, but now that she was dead they were pathetic and cruel.

My inner bitch told me she'd been using guilt and shame to keep me in line for years and now she was succeeding. At the same time I remembered how Amy had mouthed, 'Your mother', as she passed me the phone and how I'd handed it straight to Hannah. I wondered how Hannah felt now about lying to her for the dual purpose of getting me off the hook and continuing a line of enquiry she thought more important. All of us treated my mother as the overbearing, joke Jewish matriarch. Whose fault was that, I asked myself, knowing that the harder she pushed me the more I avoided her. And the more I avoided her the harder she pushed.

'It takes two to tango,' I said out loud. Could I have interrupted the dance, talked straight to my mother, found a compromise with some dignity for both of us? And why hadn't I thought of that while there was still time to try? Now I couldn't even hear her complaints on voicemail, and the bitch in me was glad.

I phoned Amy.

'*What?*' she said aggressively.

'It's me.' I was startled by the aggression. Thinking about the Beaus I couldn't exactly blame her. But, after all, I was an orphan now whereas she still had two parents. I'd thought she'd give me a little more leeway. All the same, expecting sympathy for a grief I didn't feel was unworthy. I said, 'I'm sorry to bother you at work, but the police have just left. We were broken into sometime last night. The dogs are gone, but nothing's been stolen or damaged. I'm waiting in for the locksmith. I don't know what else to do. I'm sure there's masses of stuff I ought to be doing but I can't think properly.'

'Like arranging a funeral? Have you even been to the house?'

'A detective just brought me home. That's when we found the flat had been broken into,' I said, feeling I was using Ed as a sort of character reference. 'I can't arrange anything. The police took Mother away and they won't let me into the house.'

There was a moment's silence before she said in a more friendly voice, 'I wouldn't know what to do about that either – if it was me in your shoes.'

'Besides,' I said, suddenly remembering conversations only half listened to. 'I think she planned to have a strictly Sephardic ritual – really, really traditional. She said she had to do it herself because she couldn't trust me to do the right thing. I think she said I'd have her cremated, wipe up the ashes in kitchen paper and dump them on a compost heap.'

'OMG, yes,' Amy said wonderingly. 'She never missed an opportunity to make you feel like the worst daughter ever.'

'Which of course made me behave like one.'

'She did have the knack,' Amy admitted.

'Hey,' I said suddenly, 'she keeps a Dead Box in the top of her wardrobe: powers of attorney, wills, insurance et cetera. I bet she has written funeral instructions in there.'

'I bet she's already paid for it.' Amy was sounding more like my oldest friend. 'And I bet she's put in something really sarcastic about preventing her gardener daughter from breaking the no flowers rule. You're off the hook, Seema.'

'Amy,' I said, 'the police have taken my phone away. It's broken, but they want to retrieve any messages Mother left on it. All I've got at the moment is the landline. But there are no messages there whatsoever, which really surprises me. Did you wipe the voicemail?'

'Of course not. None at all? But she rang scads of times and in the past she always spoke. Like I said, she never missed an opportunity. Hey!' she exclaimed suddenly. 'Suppose whoever broke in listened to all the messages and deleted them?'

'Why?' I was astounded. Because surely it was Grigori who'd broken in and taken the Beaus away. 'Nothing else was touched. Wait.' I took the phone to the kitchen. Everything looked normal so I went to my bedroom. I looked at my desk. And saw with horror that the folder of drawings I'd done for Lazaro plus the aerial photographs he'd given me were gone.

Then I remembered storming out of the flat yesterday morning. Surely the folder would be in my van. I breathed again.

'What?' Amy's voice sounded small and faraway. I put the phone to my ear again.

I said, 'I just wanted to find my old phone. I thought I could take it down to TruPhone to see if the geniuses there could at least resurrect my contact list.'

'Good idea,' she said.

I had another thought: 'Did Jake take his laptop when he left? Sometimes he leaves it here but I don't see it.'

'How should I know?' Amy said. 'Look, I've got to go. Some of us have to work.' She rang off.

I added her to the list of problems I couldn't solve right now. Instead I concentrated on a problem I might be able to solve. I dug out my old phone. It wasn't all that old – I'd only upgraded a few weeks ago so the contact list wouldn't have changed much.

But I couldn't go out until after the locksmith had mended the door. So I made as complete a list as I could from my old address book. I had to ring everyone my mother knew, friends, relations, no matter how distant.

The task should've made my mother's death real to me, but

it didn't. I felt like an actor in a drama. I coped with everyone's shock and distress but my own.

The locksmith rescued me after about an hour. She smelled comfortably of 3 In One oil and nicotine. Also she had upper body strength to rival mine. I liked her.

'Good lord,' she said, staring at the damage. 'Someone lost his rag! You can jimmy locks without mangling them. These look like they were chewed up and spat out. I'm afraid you'll need two new ones.'

'Can you do the job today?' I asked anxiously.

'Yep,' she said. 'Looking at this level of damage I think you qualify as a security risk.'

I made her a mug of coffee and a cheese and pickle sandwich before leaving her to work. I took my old phone to TruPhone where they fixed me up using my usual telephone number. But they did warn me that it might affect the phone the cops took. That, I figured, was the cops' problem. My problem was the expanded list of my mother's friends and relatives.

Everyone wanted to talk. There were so many questions and I had so little information. Everyone wanted to know when the funeral would be and of course I couldn't tell them. The necessary delay and the post mortem added to everyone's horror and of course I couldn't answer any questions about those either. Everyone had an opinion – some had as many as five – so it was mid-afternoon before I managed to get off the phone.

By then the locksmith had finished a good sturdy job. The door would need repainting but we were safe. I called Amy to tell her about the new keys. She didn't pick up so I left a message.

Alone in the flat I turned on the TV hoping to find an old movie to keep me company. Or anything that wasn't a quiz, crime or reality. I couldn't stomach reality. I felt as unconnected to anything or anyone real as a helium balloon when a child lets go of the string.

I hadn't rung Jake and he hadn't rung me. I didn't know where we stood or even if he'd heard the news.

The only one I wanted to talk to was Lazaro. Somehow he seemed to be the possessor of all calm and wisdom. He was surrounded by an aura of certainty and authority. I thought he could even explain the meaning of life. I was sure he could calm my jittery nerves. There would be nothing I couldn't face if only he would take me by the hand and lead me. I wanted to be his child – metaphorically of course.

But he didn't ring, and he didn't send Pasqual. I was heartbroken. He knew what had happened but he didn't reach out and touch me.

In the end, like the orphan I was, I rang Hannah.

EIGHT

'I'm coming over,' Hannah said after I explained I couldn't leave the flat until I'd given Amy her new keys.

She'd had a few hours sleep and a hot bath, so although she still looked tired she was more like her old self.

I made coffee although by then I felt I was swimming in caffeine – my heart was racing and my hands trembled.

'You shouldn't be alone,' Hannah said. 'Where's Jake?'

'I don't know,' I said. 'Maybe he doesn't know what's happened.'

'He knows. I rang him when I couldn't find you. I thought you might be with him. Where were you?'

'I was here.'

'You can't have been,' Hannah said, giving me her no-bullshit look. 'I never stopped ringing you – on both phones. Amy went home at about nine-thirty but couldn't get in because of wild dogs. She ended up ringing and shouting but you didn't answer. The police visited you and knocked at your door around eleven. You were not here.'

'But I *was*. I took a sleeping pill. I told the Detective Sergeant – you know, Ed Richardson? I only woke up the last time you rang.'

'At about three in the morning.' It sounded like an accusation. 'By which time your mother had been dead nearly nine hours. And even then you didn't turn up till over three hours later. The man Jacob and Amy spoke about, "the hot guy", as she described him – which annoyed Jake so deeply –he was there, wasn't he? I heard you speaking to him.'

'He isn't a hot guy,' I protested. 'He's Lazaro's driver. There was a mistake: I thought he was going to take me straight to Mother's house but he took me to Belgravia instead. English isn't his first language.' I was almost awed at the half-truths that were dripping so easily off my tongue. I hurried on, 'Lazaro encouraged me to change into more suitable clothes and then took me himself to Mrs Joseph's house.'

Hannah stared at me in silence. I'd already said too much. A week ago I'd have jumped in with further explanation. Not any more. Hannah wouldn't understand, I thought. And then, Hannah is not your friend. I was shocked. Where did that come from?

At last she said, 'Lazaro just happened to possess suitable clothes, boots and jackets in exactly your size?'

'Not *him*,' I said impatiently, 'his assistant, Gemma.'

'Who is the same size as you in all respects?'

I let that one pass. There was no way on earth I could claim any similarity to sleek, slender, sexy Gemma. Instead I said, 'I don't understand. Just for once I wanted to look the way Mother would've liked.'

Hannah's eyebrows shot up and her bifocals slipped off her nose. 'So another three missing hours are accounted for by you choosing, trying on, titivating clothes and make-up?' When I didn't reply she added, 'Or are you failing to factor in some more opium smoking with your benefactor?'

Stung, I said, 'There was an accident on the Edgware Road.'

'Will you let me look at your throat?' she asked, deceptively mild.

'*No!*' I snapped much too loudly.

'Then I will assume that beneath your strategically placed scarf the two puncture wounds over your jugular vein are larger and more painful than they were yesterday.' She glared at me narrowly.

Why had I never noticed how witchy she looked with her high-bridged nose and her deep-set hooded eyes?

She went on sweetly, 'And you won't mind if I mention to the police, with whom I have a meeting soon, the strangely intrusive visit from the representatives of Sharpe-Harding Associates – only a day before your mother's murder – or the licence plate of the limousine that deposited you outside Mira Joseph's house this morning?'

Something lurched in my chest. I said, 'Why don't you keep your ugly hooked nose out of my business?'

She stared at me. Appalled, I watched her sharp, beady eyes fill with tears – her lovely, intelligent, kindly eyes. The tears ran down beside her beautiful, sculpted nose.

Suddenly I felt as if my head would explode with pain. I clutched at my ears and my knees gave way. I fell.

When I opened my eyes I was lying on the sofa covered by Amy's TV rug. The memory of the pain was almost as acute as the pain itself. I moaned and held my temples.

Hannah said, 'Can you remember Jabberwocky?'

'Yes,' I said, teeth clenched against the phantom pain.

'Recite,' she instructed, like a teacher.

Not knowing why, I began, "'Twas brillig, and the slithy... ' but after a couple of lines she stopped me. 'Say, The Leith police dismisseth us,' she ordered.

'Wasn't that what the cops forced drunks to say before the breathalyzer was invented?'

'Say it,' she insisted.

I said it.

'There's an ambulance on its way,' she said calmly. 'You seem to have had some sort of cerebral accident, but it can't be too serious.'

The doorbell rang.

'Send them away,' I said. But she disappeared out of my field of vision. The pain was receding. All I could think of was how the Beaus had collapsed after the huge shock they'd been given by their electric collars. I touched my neck. My scarf had been removed, and my hand, when I looked at it, was bloody.

I started to cry, but hearing Hannah coming back, I wiped my eyes on my sleeve. My sleeve was bloody too.

'Not the ambulance,' Hannah said as she came over to the sofa with Amy behind her.

'Poop on a pinkie!' Amy looked aghast. 'Has someone tried to cut her throat too? What's the matter with her eyes?'

'I don't know,' Hannah said. 'I thought it might've been some sort of stroke. I'm not so sure now.'

'I'm right here,' I said. 'You can talk to *me*, you know.' But the light was hurting my eyes and I was thinking, Dusk is falling – I'll feel better after dark.

NINE

At the Royal Free Hospital, ignoring me completely, they took blood to test, injected dye into my arm and gave me a CT scan.

The scan told them that my brain was undamaged. The blood test proved that I was anaemic. The professionals wanted to keep me in overnight. I refused. Hannah insisted. Hannah won. She was satisfied. I was furious. There was somewhere I needed to be.

She took my clothes away. She said it was because they were blood-stained. I didn't believe her. She promised she'd bring me clean clothes in the morning when I would be released.

While she was talking to a doctor I asked Amy why Jake hadn't called me.

'But you dumped him,' she said, surprised.

'Did I?' I was just as surprised. 'I must have lost my temper, that's all.'

'Seema, you never lose your temper,' she said. 'Not like that. You were scary. What's going on? It's like you've had personality surgery. Maybe you really did have some sort of stroke and the scan just can't see it.'

'Don't say that,' I was shuddering in spite of the sedative the last nurse had given me. 'But my mother died ... you'd think Jake could just pick up the phone.'

'Now you're sounding like her.' Amy almost giggled. I didn't.

It was well after midnight when the nurse shooed Hannah and Amy out. They were both tired, and I was nodding off. There were four other patients in the ward – all of them seemingly comatose, all of them looking very old, possibly in their eighties. I could see that Hannah was upset; she didn't want to look at them.

My last thought, before sedation finally kicked in, was that there was no one at the flat to take all the follow-up calls from Mother's friends and rellies – I knew there would be dozens. There would be no one there when the police came for a formal interview. And Pasqual wouldn't know where to find me.

I dreamed that Lazaro brought me a plateful of roast chicken, mashed potato and gravy which was one of my favourites when I was a child, before Mother became a religious obsessive and I became a rebellious vegetarian. He looked at me, his dark eyes loving, and said, 'You look good enough to eat, Seema.' And I felt warm, appreciated and *chosen*. Then Pasqual leaned over me and said, 'She smells wrong, master. Her blood is bad. She comes from bad blood.' And before I could take a single bite of the lovely food Lazaro picked up the plate and walked away.

I woke up broken-hearted. A nurse's aid was putting a bowl of soggy cereal in front of me. She said, 'Go on, you cry, child – do you good. I lost me mam a few years back. It's a tough one.' She shoved a mug of nearly hot, too sweet tea at me and I was grateful. I didn't have to explain my tears.

The ward was busy. Two of the old women had died in the night: unexpectedly, a cleaner told me. He was mopping the floor and changing the curtains round the empty beds. I had slept through two deaths and dreamed of roast chicken. If you counted my mother I had slept through three deaths in two days. I didn't know what to make of it. I just wanted to go home.

But I couldn't leave till after the doctor made his rounds, and besides I had to wait for Hannah to bring me something to wear. To my annoyance, they turned up at the same time – about twenty past eleven.

I used to be proud of the fact that Hannah was respected everywhere she went. Now it was a serious irritation that Doctor

West assumed that she had a right to listen to what we said. Worse than that, he preferred to talk to her rather than me. He said, 'The good news is that there is no evidence of stroke. But she is anaemic. It's up to you, but I'd be happier keeping her here for a few hours more – her potassium and sodium levels need adjustment, nothing radical: a few hours on a drip should do the trick. But I have to tell you, your young friend's blood tested positive for opioids. Again, nothing drastic, but... ' he turned to me, 'you really should consider changing your lifestyle, young lady.'

'Opioids?' Hannah said sharply. 'Not opium?'

Doctor West consulted his clipboard. 'Opioids,' he repeated.

Hannah turned to me and said curtly. 'It's as I suspected. Tar heroin, as just one example, is an opioid; opium is not. Doctor, please would you examine the small wounds on Ms Dahami's neck.'

'No!' I said, covering the place with my hand.

'Seema,' Hannah said sternly. 'You have been lied to. If any of your new acquaintances have been injecting illegal substances into your jugular vein, don't you think you should know about it?'

'What a very dangerous thing to do!' Doctor West exclaimed. 'Please, Ms Dahami, would you let me take a look?'

'Oh, alright,' I muttered gracelessly. It was either that or make a scene in public.

Dr West examined my neck, and said, 'They look like some sort of bites to me. Although that would disguise track marks perfectly. How did you come by them Ms Dahami?'

'I don't know,' I said. 'I've said this before – over and over: I really don't know. I thought it was an insect bite I'd scratched and opened in the night, I have never, ever injected drugs. I'm a blood donor.'

'Well, I cannot emphasise too strongly,' he said, 'you must not, under any circumstances, give blood again until you are free of illegal substances and, even more importantly, the possibility of infection from dirty needles. Your blood could be dangerous to others.'

'I never thought of that,' Hannah said sounding interested.

'Further,' the doctor went on, 'I would suggest, for your own health and safety, that you sort out your anaemia and blood salts before making another donation.'

'Amen,' Hannah said piously. She was enjoying herself. I could've kicked her. 'When did you last give blood?' she added as an after thought.

'A couple of months ago.'

'Obviously there was no sign of anaemia then, or they would have sent you away.'

'I'm a vegetarian,' I told the doctor before she could begin to hint at what was really on her mind. 'My friends and family worry about iron. But I take supplements. I'm not stupid. And I don't want to stay here.'

'Well, both your stored and blood iron are depleted.' Dr West made a couple of notes on his chart. 'I'll be writing to your GP to recommend that he or she books you in for some more tests. But if you insist on leaving I don't see any *urgent* reason to keep you. You might want to re-evaluate some of your lifestyle choices, but that really isn't my business.' He made another note, shook Hannah's hand and left the ward.

Hannah sat on the end of my bed and just looked at me.

I said, 'We can't talk here.'

She said, 'And I suppose I can't persuade you to stay?'

'No. I hate it here. Two of the old ladies died in the night. It smells.' I gestured to the menus someone had left by the bed. 'There's no vegetarian option for lunch except a baked potato. If I stay I really will get ill. Besides, there's Mother. Everyone wants to talk to me but I can't tell them anything.'

'Unfortunately there's nothing to say. The police have your mother's body. The rabbi can do nothing about that. No one can clean the house, even, until the police finish their investigation.

They have no ideas. Someone cut poor Ivy's throat. Nobody knows why. Nobody saw a thing. All the neighbours are scared to death because, as the murder seems so motiveless, they're all convinced it's the start of a wave of anti-Semitism.'

'Why would anyone want to kill my mother?' I closed my eyes. I felt as stupid as my mother always told me I was. I wished Hannah would just give me my clothes. Hospital gowns are not an aid to competence or intelligence. I opened my eyes again to find her regarding me expressionlessly. I said, 'What do you think?'

She thought for a minute before saying, 'Sadly, no Jew can rule anti-Semitism out completely – however irrational it may seem, the absence of safety seems to be bred in the bone.' She paused as if about to step onto untrustworthy ice, 'But I can't help feeling that your mother's death is in some way connected to the mysterious events in your life.'

'I *knew* you were going to say that.'

'I felt sure you would.' She handed me a carrier bag containing jeans, a sweat shirt, underwear, socks and sneakers.

'Bless you,' I said, forcing the words out from between clenched teeth.

'Hypocrite,' she answered dryly. She pulled the curtains around my bed and withdrew while I dressed.

Half an hour later we were eating crushed avocado on toast in a corner café on Pond Street, and Hannah was saying, 'Of *course* I have no evidence. I am not the police, nor am I a lawyer. It's a question of co-incidence and proximity. It's a cluster of occurrences. I don't trust clusters to be meaningless. I don't know what's happening to you. But whatever it is, it is not proving to be benign. I'm afraid for you, Seema, truly afraid.'

I found, rising to the tip of my tongue, a remark about Hannah as offensive and unforgivable as what I'd said last night. It was as if I were a ventriloquist's dummy. I clamped my hand over my mouth.

'What?' she said alarmed.

'I don't know.' I was shaking now, and sweating. My heart raced. I was terrified there'd be a recurrence of yesterday's pain in my head. I said, 'Am I having a panic attack?'

'Look at me,' she said. 'Look into my eyes and breathe slowly. Breathe out as far as you can. Your in-breath will take care of itself. You're safe here. Just breathe.'

I did what she said and gradually everything I'd so suddenly experienced as ugly and frightening about her appearance settled into Hannah's familiar, quirky face.

I said, 'I dreamed that my blood smelled bad.' Usually I'm on safe ground with Hannah if I tell her a dream; she likes dreams. Then I wondered how much of a distraction this particular dream would be. Because the feeling associated with it, far from dealing with the mystery surrounding my mother's death, was the fear of losing Lazaro. I felt choked, suffocated, by the terror that I was disgusting to him; that he didn't want me anymore. He had rejected me in the dream. He'd abandoned me in a hospital bed. He'd taken away his gift of food. He'd revoked his gift of love and acceptance. I would now be alone forever.

Hannah stared at me as if she could see the brain behind my eyes. 'Go on,' she said quietly.

'Nothing,' I said. And then, because I felt so unwanted, 'There was a man who brought me food, who then left me because of the smell.'

'Who is he?'

'I don't know. Dad?' I was lying and sort of not lying at the same time. My mind was tearing into two parts.

Hannah said, 'Your father died of meningitis. You were in no way responsible. I know your mother told you he caught the disease because he took you swimming, but that was completely untrue. You already know that – we've worked on it.'

'Yes, but now what if you're right and Mother was killed because I want to design a roof garden for some very rich people in Belgravia?'

'Your mother did not die because of a roof garden. Your father did not die because he took you swimming. You did not dream that a man left you because your *feet* smelled. It was your blood, Seema. Your *blood*.'

'Because I'm a Jew?'

She stared at me. 'But it was *your* dream,' she said. 'Is this internalised anti-Semitism? So ask yourself, why now? You're hiding something – maybe even from yourself. And now you are looking at me as if it is *my* blood that smells.'

I was feeling such hatred for this woman I had loved since childhood that I thought I would explode with septic bile. I covered my mouth with both hands and shut my eyes tight.

I heard her get up from the table and walk away.

Gradually the vile feelings released me and when I opened my eyes and saw her empty chair at the other side of the table I was flooded by loss and remorse so intense I thought *she'd* died.

I looked for her. There were old men with newspapers, a gang of the young and beautiful with two tables pushed together who took selfies and talked loudly, a couple of tired women with prams who fed grizzling babies, but Hannah was gone.

I phoned Amy; no reply. I phoned Jake; no reply. I wanted to call the tattooed Norse god but his number was not in my old phone. I even wanted to phone Detective Sergeant Ed Richardson. Anyone would do. So, taking my courage in both hands, I called Hannah.

Her phone rang so close to me that I could feel the vibration through my sneakers. I looked down and saw her handbag under the table. I ended the call feeling stupid, and went to the counter to order us a fresh pot of tea.

She emerged from a door at the back of the café smelling of soap and air freshener. As soon as she sat down I said, 'I'm so sorry, Hannah. I don't know what I'm doing. I'm sort of at war with myself all the time. I'm not sensible any more, and I don't know why.'

'Don't hate me,' she replied simply.

'Never.'

'No, *not* never. I've heard your words and watched your expressions when we talk. But I don't think you're responsible. In fact, I'm wondering if it's possible for you to have become addicted to whatever strange substance your new friend is giving you to smoke. It's only been a few days but your personality seems to have changed so quickly and so completely.'

I started to protest hotly but she held up her hand with such authority that I shut up.

'Allow me to voice all my concerns. Try to listen with your rational mind – the mind that knows I have always loved you and tried to protect you.' She didn't wait for me to respond but went on, 'I believe, whether you know it consciously or not, you are allowing someone to drink your blood. Wait!' She held her hand up again. I'd half risen, but she made me sit.

'Let me ask you this, dear: would you allow a strange man to tie you up, gag you, blindfold you and then beat you with a whip?'

I gasped with indignation, but she went on, 'I thought not. But it seems that you *do* allow a man you hardly know to give you a drug which apparently renders you just as helpless. Whatever he does to you after that leaves you with wounds on your neck, anaemia and exhaustion. Also you defend this strange man and deny that anything damaging is happening to you at all.

'Surely you must see that this requires an explanation.'

She stopped. Flashing through my mind like a news headline came the thought: This is all true. Then instantly, lancing through my head with a spasm like an electric shock came the shriek: this is a damned lie. Don't listen to the witch!

Hannah stooped quickly and grabbed a packet of tissues from her bag. She tore it open and gave me all the tissues, saying, 'Your nose is bleeding.'

From behind a fistful of tissues and paper napkins I said, 'Don't make me go to hospital again.'

Hannah went back to the washroom and returned with wet paper towels. But the nosebleed was already slowing to a sluggish drip which very soon dried altogether. We mopped up the mess I'd made of the table and Hannah took me home in a cab. She gave me two cans of alcohol-free lager from the fridge – one to drink, one to cool my nose in case it started bleeding again. She took my scarf off and showed me that my neck had bled too. Then she said, 'When this happened yesterday can you remember what we were talking about?'

'No,' I said, gripping the cold lager tightly.

'I can.' She sat at the other end of the sofa I was lying on. 'I was telling you that I would be interviewed by the police soon and I was threatening to tell them about Ivy being harassed by representatives of Sharpe-Harding Associates. Today I was trying to convince you that Lazaro was doing you harm. On both occasions your emotional response was extreme enough to set off an intense physical reaction: a migraine-like headache and local rupture of small blood vessels.'

'You don't understand,' I began, and then stopped.

'Exactly,' Hannah said patiently. 'Please, Seema, explain what's happening. Why would the notion of my telling the police of a visit which upset Ivy cause you such emotional distress?'

I found myself looking over my shoulder as if I was afraid of being overheard. In fact I *was* afraid of being overheard. I said, in a whisper, 'If you're right, one half of my brain is punishing me for what the other half is thinking or hearing. That doesn't sound exactly rational.'

'Put like that,' she said, 'no, it doesn't. But you can't fool your own mind by whispering.'

'Okay.' I raised my voice to normal levels. 'I wish you wouldn't involve the police with Sharpe-Harding. I'm afraid they'll think I'm a danger to their privacy. I'm afraid, if my life seems messy or dramatic Lazaro won't employ me on a job I really want. And Hannah, the horrible thing is that I can't seem to care. I care more about the roof garden and the Palatine Estate dogs than I do about Mother. I try to care, but I can barely even think about it.'

'It will come in time,' she said calmly.

I wasn't so sure. I said, 'I can see that the police will ask everyone if Mother had enemies or whether she'd been upset recently, but you know, Hannah, she was always quarrelling with someone; she was always upset about something; she was upset with me – I forgot Shabbat.'

'I agree. But I still have to answer questions honestly. And we don't know who else she talked to about her visitors. This is not just down to me.'

She was right. After a pause she went back to a previous topic: 'Opium or opioids – let's not discuss that question at the moment. What I want to ask you is what does it do for you? What do you feel when you've taken it?'

I was trying very hard to love and trust Hannah again so I said, 'It's impossible to describe. But it's like total relaxation, warmth and, well, *confidence*. My mind opens and I dream. But it isn't just that: when I dream I feel that even the extraordinary is possible. When I wake up I go back to being a speck of dust in an uncaring universe – someone without the talent and ability to make or change anything.'

'Can you remember a dream?'

I told her about the cherry tree whose blossoming branches tickled the stars and made them laugh.

'How lovely,' she said, smiling. 'And then?'

'I was actually thinking about the roof garden, and planning a hillock topped by dwarf cherry trees, imagining how beautiful it would look by moonlight. Although the next day I was faced again by the knowledge that what passes for dwarf cherry trees at a garden centre actually grows far too big for a roof garden, and I'd never get council planning permission for landscaping a hill on a rooftop. But while I was dreaming I felt capable of making something impossibly beautiful.' I sighed.

'And how would you feel about never having a dream like that again?'

I was aghast. I wanted to weep.

She was reading my expression as if I were texting emoticons to her. She went on, 'And how would you feel about someone who prevented you from having those feelings?'

Fear and hatred rose up in me like sewage from a blocked waste pipe.

'I see,' Hannah said sadly.

'You don't understand,' I cried.

'Maybe not.' She sighed in her turn. 'Well, tell me this: how do you feel about the man who offers you your heart's desire?'

'That's a ridiculous way of putting it.'

'Humour me.'

'I feel he has taken my hand and shown me my own talent and power.' I didn't know where the words were coming from but I ploughed on. 'He's shown me how I can live in a world that loves and admires me.'

'Instead of?'

'Instead of a world that barely puts up with me.'

'How many times have you met him? Three times?'

When I didn't answer she went on, 'I'm talking about someone who, without your consent, is taking blood from you and probably playing a weird game of dominance and submission.'

'Lazaro isn't like that.'

'I'm so very sorry, Seema, but I think he is.' She looked absolutely straight into my eyes when she said this. 'Have you looked at yourself in the mirror lately? You have no colour in your cheeks.'

'Mother always said my skin was too dark.'

She ignored me. 'And you've noticeably lost weight.'

'She complained I was too heavy.'

She rounded on me. 'So this Lazaro is turning you into

someone your mother would have approved of – a pale, skinny, well-dressed woman with a rich boyfriend? Is that okay with you?'

I was almost speechless with rage. It was on the tip of my tongue to say something blistering but she interrupted. 'Are you about to criticise my hooked nose again, or my unwanted assertiveness, my stridency, my interference, my belief that I know best? What about my fat ankles? All Jewish women have fat hairy ankles and dark bags under their eyes. Haven't you heard that, Seema?'

'What are you saying?' I shouted.

'That you are showing signs of turning against yourself and me. Previously I discounted the bacon cheeseburger as an aberration but I'm more inclined now to see it as significant.'

'Lazaro made me eat a bacon cheeseburger?'

'I think, through the agency of addictive substances and, possibly, sex games, that he has a damaging influence over you.'

'Now you sound like Jake.'

'Jake was driven by jealousy and testosterone,' she said quietly. 'Not my particular problems.'

I was going to say, Fuck off out of my life you nosey old sow when my phone rang.

'*What?*' I snapped, answering it.

A strong man's voice said, 'This is Mark Kirkby. Am I interrupting something? I could call later.'

I went blank for a few seconds, and he said, 'We rescued a couple of dogs together.'

'Yes, of course,' I said. 'I couldn't have done it without you. How are you?'

'I'm fine,' he said sounding as wonderful as he'd looked with the sun shining on his red-gold hair. 'I gather you took those dogs back. In fact I saw them last night. They looked fine too – not half as fierce as they seemed the first time I saw them. They remembered me and came up for a pat.'

'That's nice,' I said cautiously. I was very conscious of Hannah's presence and I was wondering why Mark was calling me.

'Well, it would have been.' He began to sound cautious too. 'Except that their friendliness seemed to cause some sort of…'

'What?' I asked.

'Ruction,' he said. 'I was invited for dinner and when I got there the door was opened by their… handyman?'

'Grigori,' I supplied.

'Yeah, probably. Anyway he was totally pissed off with the dogs and he said to Mr Harding, who was right behind him in the hall, "See? They're about as much use as a pair of guinea pigs." Mr Harding said, "We'll talk about that later." The good thing was that no one seemed to realise that the dogs were friendly to me because I'd helped rescue them. So I guess I'm off the hook.'

'I'm glad about that,' I said. 'I really didn't want to get you into trouble.'

'There's more. After supper, I went to the bathroom and I was just about to come out cos everyone was going upstairs again for coffee and liqueurs, when I heard Ms Sharpe say, "Grigori wants a raise. He says he needs to budget for more security. Your protégé has corrupted the wolfhounds. That was not supposed to happen." And then, I think it was Mr Lazaro who said, "It will not happen again. She has been punished."'

'Punished? Are you sure you heard right?"

'Pretty sure. Of course they didn't have to be talking about you. But I was worried. Are you okay?'

'I'm fine,' I said. 'What about you?'

'Fit as a fiddle.' He laughed suddenly. 'Except a fiddle wouldn't last very long on a rugby field. No, I'm really, really fine.'

'So you're not worried about the dietary supplement anymore?'

'Sorted.' His voice sounded robust and I remembered the way he glowed with warmth and fitness, wearing only a tank top in a cold March wind.

'I'm so glad,' I said. 'Keeping your place in the first team?'

'It's a cert,' he said, and I could hear the smile in his voice. 'Barring injury of course. But at the moment I feel could run through a brick wall without a scratch.'

'The baobab must be some tree,' I said wistfully.

'I train hard too,' he said. 'Listen, you haven't told anyone about the supplement or the cream, have you?'

'Not a soul. And I won't. But tell me something – when you're there, at Lazaro's house I mean, do you ever have a lapse of memory, time you can't account for?' I could feel Hannah coming to attention like a pointer dog. I was thinking, I'll show you, you suspicious cow, that nothing weird's happening.

'Of course not,' Mark said. 'Well, Mr Harding gives me a top-up dose. We go to his office – he has a chair, like a dentist's, you lie back in. It's something to do with having your feet at the same level as your heart so your blood circulates more easily without your heart having to do so much work.'

'Why?' I was beginning to feel a touch uneasy.

'Well, the injection includes a vasodilator. All it does is make sure the supplement reaches all parts of my body equally. Mr Harding says I might feel a little faint if I get up too quickly so I just doze for a few minutes before leaving. It's quite nice actually. The others drink a lot and I don't, so the time after dinner, while they're all necking liqueurs and coffee, is a bit of a pain in the arse. It's a relief to be quiet for a while. Then I can use early training as an excuse and leave without offending anyone.'

I didn't know how to frame my next question, but Mark filled the pause by saying, 'I know it sounds iffy, but athletes are tested for drugs all the time and if there was anything wrong with the supplement I'd be off the team in no time flat. So don't worry.'

'I won't,' I said. 'Just out of curiosity though, where does the needle go in?' I was fingering my scarf.

'Into my neck,' he said and then laughed. 'Nothing shows because of the tattoos; not that I'm hiding anything.'

'Of course not,' I agreed. But I was looking at Hannah and feeling cold. I changed the subject. 'Do you really never drink?'

'Embarrassing, isn't it?' I could hear the smile in his voice. 'Jock culture's supposed to be seriously into beer. But, well, don't tell anyone this either, but my dad was one of those guys who couldn't have just one drink. He had to go on till he got nasty. My brother's the same. I'm afraid I might've inherited the gene. Besides I don't want to compromise my fitness. *Ever.*'

'I can understand that,' I said. 'They do drink a lot at the Palatine Estate. They seem to be into fine wines.'

'Yeah – you should've seen their faces when I asked for a Diet Coke. It's like they never heard of it. Maybe it's an age thing.'

'Or a culture thing.' I changed the subject again. 'How did the dogs look?'

'Same old dirty great wolfhounds but a lot friendlier.' He laughed again. 'I guess those electronic collars couldn't have done much harm.'

After a few more minutes we said our goodbyes and rang off.

Hannah had a face full of questions so I got up and went to the kitchen to make tea. She didn't follow me so I had time to collect my thoughts and figure out what to say. I was feeling wobbly. My brain was acting like a wasp trying to climb out of a jam jar – angry, panicky and almost paralysed.

I took the tea in to Hannah but before she could start with the questions my phone rang again. It was Amy.

She said, 'Just so's you know, I won't be home tonight.'

'Okay. Lucky Noah.' I said, puzzled. She didn't often bother to tell me her plans.'

'Not lucky Noah,' she said stiffly. 'Lucky Jake.'

'*What?*'

'He doesn't want me to tell you. But I think you ought to know. You want to know the truth, don't you?'

'What truth?' The ground shifted under my feet and I sat down heavily.

'It isn't Jake and you any more. You cheated on him. Now it's Jake and me.'

'I *never* cheated,' I shouted. 'Is he there?'

'Yes.'

'Put him on.'

'No,' Amy said coldly and hung up.

TEN

My mother was dead. My boyfriend had dumped me for my oldest friend. My oldest friend had betrayed me. Lazaro was absent and silent. Only Hannah remained.

'Tell me,' she said, concern creasing her face.

I leaned my bewildered aching head against her shoulder and told her. It had been a brutally short conversation so there wasn't much to tell. When I'd finished she said, 'I'm so, so sorry. I'd never have thought it of Amy.'

'What about *Jake*?'

'I never knew Jake that well,' she said. 'And anyway, a few years ago someone did a study about cheating. It seems that while women reported all sorts of complex reasons for cheating on their partners, men, when asked, overwhelmingly said it was because an opportunity presented itself – it's as simple and boring as that.'

'What're you saying? That Amy, my best friend since kindergarten, presented herself to Jake, my boyfriend of three years, as an opportunity and he just took it? But it didn't sound like simple cheating – Amy was implying they were already in a relationship.'

'Maybe they are. They've known each other for as long as you've been seeing Jake. And Seema, Amy's always been jealous of you.'

This was simply not true. If anything I was jealous of Amy:

of her family life, her European good looks and her outgoing personality.

'Yes, but you're creative and imaginative,' Hannah said. 'She isn't. And when your father died he left you enough money to buy this flat. She may have a good job but owning a flat in London is still beyond her. She's dependent on you. She can't like that.'

'She won't have to any more. She can't live here, can she?'

'No. But where will she go? Do you care?'

'She can move back in with her parents. Or stay with Jake,' I said meanly. 'He lives in the converted garage attached to his mother's house. We're the homeless generation, remember?' I felt hard and spiteful. I wouldn't cry, I promised myself. Let Amy deal with his gluten intolerance and football mania.

'I didn't cheat on him,' I added lamely.

'Did you not?' Hannah said. 'Well, we won't argue about technicalities now.' Then seeing I was going to protest, she went on, 'But you certainly made him jealous. You showed him that he'd been superseded in importance by Lazaro. And so quickly. Oh, I know – the job – yes, yes. But you became so enraged about his interference you broke up with him. Yes, I agree, he probably knew you didn't mean it but possibly it was excuse enough.'

'Only if he didn't love me.'

'You didn't love him either.'

'I was very fond of him,' I said, wondering if even that was true. 'We got along.'

'Or were you marking time until something better came along?'

'I don't know,' I said, because Hannah always demanded my best shot at honesty. 'Maybe he was too. But is that the point? Even if it wasn't passion or obsessive love, didn't he owe me some kind of loyalty? But he didn't even ring me about my mother. Doesn't sex count for something?'

'Shared intimacy should count for quite a lot,' she said sadly.

'But unfortunately when a fresh opportunity presents itself loyalty sneaks out of the back door.' She gave me a sympathetic look.

We drank our cooling tea in silence for a while. Then I said, 'And Amy?'

'Friendship's a different matter,' she said thoughtfully. Then she laughed. 'Amy has behaved like a bitch. We mustn't blame the woman solely because it always takes two. But she's behaved like the greedy child who points at another and cries, saying, "I want what she's got," and then takes it. But Amy isn't a child. She's a grown woman who's been your friend for over twenty years and she should know better.'

From a rationalist like Hannah that counted as support.

'Would you like a drink?' I asked. She nodded.

Dusk was falling as I went to the fridge and took out Amy's unopened bottle of Prosecco.

'Let her help me drown my sorrows,' I said as I poured for Hannah. 'She caused them.' But I caught Hannah's raised eyebrow, and backed down. She was too fair and rational to indulge in unqualified solidarity, so we sipped our drinks quietly for a few minutes. The room grew darker and I turned on a couple of lamps. I was tired but tense. I was waiting for something.

Then she put her glass down on the low table in front of her and said, 'I'm quite stunned by the way events have piled up around you. I cannot get to grips with one thing before another overtakes it. Who rang before Amy dropped her bombshell?'

'A professional rugby player called Mark Kirkby. He helped me rescue the Beaus.' Then I had to tell her what was significant about *them*. She was right: so much had happened in such a short time I hadn't had time to catch up with myself, let alone keep Hannah informed. But now, after Mark's disclosure about Garth Harding administering top-up shots into his neck and how he needed to 'rest' afterwards, I felt I should tell her everything even though I'd promised Mark I wouldn't.

But all the time I was talking, I was watching the window and waiting. After a while, annoyed, Hannah got up and closed the curtains. I pretended not to notice, but ten minutes later, when I heard a couple of dogs howling nearby, I jumped up and looked out of the window. I saw nothing. Later still, I thought I heard the slap of sleet against the glass but when I looked out again there was no snow and no one on the street outside. I was being as frank as I possibly could with Hannah but I was not absolutely in good faith with her.

'So,' she said when I finished, 'something strange is happening to Mark.'

'Is it so strange?'

'He's taking a supplement which is secret from his team-mates and club officials. That alone is odd, surely. He is a member of a team so group loyalty must be strong in him. He's taking untested medication and yet his fitness is paramount. He seems to be a naturally open, trusting guy, but he has been persuaded to keep secrets. These are contradictions that might need explanation. And when you talk about this chap, I observe that you yourself sound a little concerned and protective.'

'That's because Garth Harding is so gross. He puts me down and he seems to despise Lazaro while accepting his hospitality.'

'That too is interesting – who *is* the host? When you were the guest it was Lazaro. But Mark is just as convinced that he is Harding's guest.'

'But it is clearly Lazaro's house.'

'Because of the paintings and sculpture? Those alone give Lazaro great credibility in your mind. But what would Mark think?'

I laughed. 'He thought Lazaro was the interior decorator.'

Hannah laughed too. 'Well that's one thing surely even we can find out. We don't need Jake's computer.'

So we looked up the Palatine Estate on my clunky laptop and discovered that it was owned by Lazaro Restoration *and* Sharpe-Harding Associates.

'Neither one is the senior partner that I can see,' Hannah said. 'And two Sharpe-Harding representatives were the ones who upset your mother.'

'But if they were going to employ me to do a major piece of work on their property I suppose they had a right to check my references.'

'Did you give your mother as a reference?'

'You must be joking.' But even as I said that I realised I hadn't been asked for references.

Hannah caught my flicker of doubt and asked, 'Who did you give as references?'

'No one – it didn't go that far. All Lazaro wanted was for me to do some drawings.' And he hadn't seen the drawings. They should be in my van if I still had a van. If my van hadn't been broken into like my flat. I got up. Hannah got up too.

'It's okay,' I said. 'I need to see if my van's okay. And collect my drawings.'

'I'll come too.'

'You don't have to. Stay in the warm and finish your drink. I won't be long.'

'Mmm,' she murmured noncommittally, and picked up her handbag.

Frustration swept over me like tide on a beach. She just waited with an innocent querying look in her bright button eyes.

I said, 'I could just drop the drawings off at the gatehouse and be back in forty minutes.'

'I'll come too,' she repeated.

'No,' I said. We stared at each other.

'What do you want?' she said at last. '*Really* want?'

I couldn't speak.

'Right now,' she began, 'there are many things that should be clamouring for your attention. Most people would say that your mother's murder would be at the top of the list.

'There are quite a few reasons to mistrust Lazaro. I would say that dosing you with a dreadfully addictive opiod which he falsely claims is opium might top another list.

'And yet you've been jumping around like a frog in a frying pan, waiting for his call or his driver.'

'I can't leave my drawings in the van,' I said sulkily.

'Let's go then.' She slipped her coat on.

If I'd been a cat I would've hissed at her. Instead I followed her to the front door and out onto the street. We walked slowly round the corner to where the van was parked because that's how Hannah walks these days. She took my arm to steady herself and held on tightly.

'A hip fracture at my time of life would be a disaster,' she said apologetically.

I found myself wondering if I could push her over and make it look like an accident. Horrified, I said, 'What does addiction feel like?'

'As if there's nothing more important than what you're addicted to. It becomes your *raison d'etre*.'

'Then I'm not addicted,' I said stoutly. But there was no doubt in my mind about who I might be addicted to.

The van seemed to be intact. I took the folder out and plodded back home with Hannah. It was cold enough for snow, but the sky was clear. The moon was swelling and time was passing. I checked the street, the traffic and the parked cars. There were no black limousines or Harley Davidsons. How many nights was it since I last saw Lazaro? It felt like eternity. Last night's horrible dream had remained with me. The whole day seemed to have been about loss and betrayal. Lazaro's nightmare rejection of me felt like a foretelling.

Hannah was drooping with fatigue. Maybe, I thought, I could put her in a taxi and send her home. Then I'd be able to go to the Palatine Estate without her knowing. She knew far too much about my business as it was. I should guard my tongue more.

Guard my tongue? Why on earth was I thinking in Victorian sentences?

But Hannah settled herself on the sofa again. And we ordered a huge Vegetarian Hot pizza, eating it with our fingers. She was not my enemy. Sometimes she'd been my only friend in a cold lonely world.

I was on my own again. Amy would not be coming home full of gossip. She would never cook lasagne or offer to put my laundry in with hers. Jake would never cuddle up in bed smelling of toothpaste. He would never scratch the itch I couldn't reach or remind me to renew my TV licence. And those nagging, unwelcome pokes and prods from my mother had gone forever. There was a void even where irritation should be. The little stitches that darned the everyday fabric of my days were coming unpicked.

Was this grief? It didn't feel like grief. It was more like longing for something I could never have. Maybe it was how I'd experienced the months and years after the shock of losing my dad: the months and years when Hannah had become embedded as a crucial part of my life. But now I thought, yes, she used to be crucial, but she was never your father. She did her best, but you needed a *man* to take you by the hand and show you how to face life without fear. You still need one.

'I'm twenty-seven years old,' I said softly. 'Why am I not yet strong and independent? Why am I still such a wuss?'

But when I turned to Hannah for an answer I saw that she'd fallen back into the corner of the sofa, fast asleep. Slumped there, bright eyes closed, face unanimated, she looked like a corpse. I shuddered. But her chest rose and fell steadily. Her hands, veiny and skeletal, were clasped loosely over her stomach. Her ring was loose on her finger. I knew she'd never married but she wore the thin gold band where a wedding ring should be. One day I would ask her what it meant. Before she dies, I thought, but not now.

Getting up, careful not to jostle her, I covered her with Amy's blanket and took our glasses to the kitchen to rinse. Then I brushed my hair and swiped on a little lip gloss and mascara. I put on my padded coat and best boots.

It was well past midnight, but I decided that if Lazaro wouldn't come for me I would go to him. A dog started howling at the moon as I crept past sleeping Hannah to the front door. Just as I stretched out my hand out to turn the knob the door opened. I jumped back in surprise and saw Amy, on tiptoe stepping over the doormat. She stopped abruptly and Jake barged into her, shoving her unceremoniously into me.

'Oops, sorry,' Jake said.

'What the fuck?' I said.

'I'm paid up till the end of the month,' Amy said flushing salmon pink. 'You weren't supposed to be awake.'

'Who's there?' Hannah mumbled sleepily from the sitting room.

I dropped my coat onto the hall floor before following the others.

'Unwelcome guests,' I told Hannah.

'I'm not a guest,' Amy said. 'I'm a legitimate resident at this address. I have a legal right to be here.' It was a prepared speech.

I was about to tell her where to shove her legal right when Hannah said sweetly, 'Of course you do, *dear*. No one would dream of arguing about legalities, but your chutzpah does rather take my breath away, as does your lack of loyalty, kindness and friendship. Now, Jake, *dear*, perhaps you'd go to the kitchen and make us all a pot of strong tea. You are surplus to requirements just now. If your ears burn while you're out there, rest assured it will not be because anyone has said anything complimentary about you.'

She might've looked like an exhausted old woman, but she'd come straight out of sleep and into the ring, both fists up and punching. The word 'dear' dripped enough acid to burn the skin off Jake's and Amy's backs.

'I didn't want to do this,' Jake muttered, slouching away without meeting my eyes.

'I know you're not Einstein,' I shouted after him. 'But if you don't want to do a thing *don't effing do it.* That's simple enough even for you.'

'No need to be so bitchy,' Amy said. She sat on the coffee table in front of the sofa and addressed herself to Hannah, ignoring me completely. 'There's nowhere else for us to go. My sister and her two boys are down from Whitby so there's no room at my parents' house. Mrs Silver cut off the electricity and water to the garage. Then she locked Jake out of the main house. So we can't stay there.'

'Now why would Jake's mother do a thing like that?' Hannah asked.

'Because she's a mean, priggish cow.' Suddenly it looked as if Amy was going to cry. 'She doesn't want Jakey to grow up and make his own decisions.'

'Then maybe "Jakey" *should* grow up and stop living in her garage,' I said.

'If you ask me,' she shot back, 'I think she wanted Jake to marry you so that by law he'd own half this flat and then she could get her sodding car off the road again.'

'Stay in a hotel,' Hannah said. 'Do not come here and parade your conquest and the destruction of Seema's relationship under her nose. This is so shabby.'

'She dumped him,' Amy shouted.

'Don't pretend to be opaque,' Hannah snapped. 'You know what Seema's been going through in the past few days. She says silly things under stress. You *know* that. A true friend would cut her a little slack and smooth things over for her. She would not, as you have done, take advantage of her mistakes and profit from her loss.'

'This didn't happen overnight,' I put in. 'How long have you been putting the moves on him?'

'As long as he has been putting the moves on me,' she said, without looking at me. 'Why am I the only one being blamed?'

'Because of twenty-three years of friendship,' Hannah said.

'And the fact that Seema shared her flat with you when you left college and didn't want to go back to your parents.'

'I pay her rent.'

To my amazement, Hannah replied, 'You pay enough to cover half the rates and utilities. Have you checked to see what other people your age are paying to share flats in areas far worse then this? Seema's been subsidising you for years.'

'She had her inheritance,' Amy said. 'She's been lucky. She didn't earn it.'

'Amy!' I whispered. Hannah's memory of my deal with Amy was a surprise, but Amy's clear bitterness shook me to my bones.

'Again,' Hannah interrupted coldly, 'You've been profiting from Seema's loss and, adding insult to injury, you're telling her how lucky she is. Are you about to congratulate her on the murder and calculate how much her *mother's* estate is worth?'

'I thought you were my friend,' I said. It sounded so pathetic that I cringed.

Just then Jake came in with a tray which he put on the coffee table before going to stand by the door as if he would run at the first opportunity.

I got up and stood in front of him. 'How long?' I asked. 'Straight up, Jacob Silver, how long?'

'I've always liked Amy,' he said. 'And, remember, you *wanted* me to like her.'

'She was my best friend and my flatmate. Of *course* I wanted you to get along.'

'*You* were the one who kept pointing out how pretty she is, how smart, funny and well-dressed.'

I was speechless with mortification.

Hannah stepped in. 'Jake, *dear*, are you saying that your girlfriend's admiration of and generosity to her best friend is responsible for turning you into a treacherous, cheating insect?'

'She cheated on me with the old bloke. And she dumped me.'

'Even if that were true, are you saying that deserting her for her best friend on the night her mother died was a justifiable act of revenge?'

He shrugged his shoulders and muttered, 'You can win any argument, can't you Ms David? You're much better with words than I am.'

'I should hope so,' Hannah said, turning her back on him. 'Seema, ignore him if you can. He's beneath your contempt.'

'How long, Jake?' I repeated wearily. I'd been so wrong. My life was not what I thought it was. All certainty was gone. I just wanted one piece of information, one clear fact I could rely on.

'This wasn't my idea,' Jake said sullenly.

'Oh bollocks, Jakey,' Amy said impatiently. 'Jake and I have been meeting secretly for nearly a year only you were too stupid and self-centred to notice. He was just looking for an excuse to ditch you and you gave it to him.'

'A year?' My mouth hung open, making me look as foolish as in fact I was.

Hannah said, 'I hope blaming Seema's trust for your double-dealing makes you feel better, Amy. But you should stop talking now.'

'If you fancied Amy more than me you should've told me straight,' I said to him. 'If you weren't happy with me you should've said. I thought we agreed we wanted to be together. If you changed your mind you should've just left. Why the deception, Jake? Why a whole year of bad faith?'

'We didn't want to upset you,' he mumbled.

I gaped at him. Hannah snorted disgustedly. Amy actually blushed.

'Aha!' Hannah said as if she'd discovered the secret of the universe. 'It was the low rent. Amy can't afford to pay the market rate for a flat-share in a good area while still dressing like the princess she thinks she is. Wait a few minutes, Seema, and they'll find a way to blame their duplicity on your generosity. *You* made them do it.'

'It wasn't like that,' Jake said.

Hannah considered him. 'Maybe not for you,' she admitted. 'Maybe you just wanted to continue bedding two women. Maybe the secrecy added a *frisson*. Who knows? Given three people, it's unwise to expect fewer than three motives.'

She was showing off, I decided suddenly. And then, without warning, like a gunshot, came the thought: 'We killed the wrong old woman.'

I crumpled and sat on the floor in a thump. I felt as if I'd fallen down a lift shaft.

'What's wrong with you?' Jake exclaimed.

'Another nosebleed,' Hannah said, struggling to her feet. 'Amy, wet a clean towel and bring it here. Jake, get frozen peas or anything cold from the fridge. Hurry!' She crouched beside me.

My head was full of live locusts feeding on my thoughts. 'We?' I said. 'Am I included? Did I help kill her? But I was asleep.' The blood in my mouth tasted as if I'd been sucking dirty pennies.

'Seema doesn't get nosebleeds,' Jake said. He held a packet of frozen something to the back of my neck.

'She spent last night in hospital after a collapse like this,' Hannah said. 'Didn't Amy tell you?' She was doing wonderful things with a wet towel. 'Who do you think you helped kill, Seema?'

I wasn't going to tell her, but then something very strange happened. The blood running from the back of my nose down my throat suddenly started to taste like champagne. It had a fizz and a buzz that was delightful. I wanted more. I touched the wound on my neck with my thumb, put my thumb to my lips and sucked it.

'Oh *gak!*' Amy said. 'That's disgusting!'

She was right. I was still sucking blood off my thumb but all at once I was absolutely terrified. I managed to stammer, 'There was a voice in my head. It said, "We killed the wrong old woman."'

Then I passed out.

ELEVEN

I woke to hear Hannah saying, 'I am simply too old to go another night without sleep. Also the police have just texted asking me to make a statement at nine in the morning. If either of you has an ounce of affection left you will make sure that Seema remains in bed. For reasons I have already explained she must not leave this flat. I cannot stress this too strongly.'

I was lying on the floor, covered by a blanket. My head was comfortably cushioned.

Jake said, 'You really think the old bastard is using drugs to control her mind?'

'I would be criminally negligent to ignore the possibility,' Hannah replied. 'And so would the two of you. Do something right for a change.'

'Maybe he's inserted a chip or barcode subcutaneously.' Jake was getting interested. I could tell.

I thought, 'Hannah's leaving. Good.'

She said, 'I hadn't thought of that.' She sounded interested too.

'I think both the US and Russian military have perfected the technology.' Jake went on. 'They can certainly do it with monkeys. I read a blog in...'

Amy sighed loudly and said, 'Oh do shut up, both of you. I'm not crazy about this any more than Jake is. But it's late and we've nowhere else to go. So we'll make sure she stays put. But I'm telling you right now; if she starts a row I'll deck her. And

112

if there's any sort of collapse we'll get an ambulance to cart her off. Then we'll call you – I don't give a flying fart how late it is or how tired you are. I'm fed up of your sarcasm, and I'm fed up of dancing round her. It's all out in the open now – a done deal. Get over it. And don't give me any more of the poor Seema, dead mother routine. I'm fed up of that too. She hated her mother. We all did. Big boohoo.'

'I hope you're pretending to be callous and emotionally stupid,' Hannah said mildly. 'Because if you aren't it'll be a poor outlook for Jake and any children you might have with him.'

'Zinger!' I thought. I heard her moving towards the front door. She was finally leaving. But, however hard I tried, at the last moment I couldn't let her go. I opened my eyes and sat up.

'Hannah,' I called out. 'Be careful.'

'There's a taxi waiting,' Amy said, impatient.

But Hannah came back and knelt down. 'Go to bed. You'll be alright now.'

'Jake,' I said urgently, 'go with her. Make sure the taxi's really a taxi. See she's safely in her flat. You should stay with her.'

'No!' all three of them protested almost as one. Then Jake said, 'I'll make sure she's locked herself in then I'll come back.'

'Thank you,' I said although it made me want to barf.

Hannah gave me two very small pills with a drink of water. She told me she thought the nosebleeds were a reaction to emotional trauma and the pills would help me stay calm. 'And don't forget: diaphragmatic breathing,' she said as she and Jake made their way to the front door.

That left me alone with Amy. I pretended she wasn't there as I went to the bathroom and got ready for bed.

I put on my old soft nightgown over my underwear, left my boots by the bedroom door and renewed the mascara and lip-gloss. I thought I'd have about half an hour before Jake came back.

But Amy didn't leave the living room. She sat on the sofa with what Hannah and I had left of her bottle of Prosecco and turned on the TV. My bedroom door was ajar so I could hear if she went to bed or Jake arrived and they both went to bed. My rage with her was beginning to subside a little. Then I realised she was watching an old episode of 'Friends'. Infuriated, I got up and went to the living room. I said, 'Stop taking the piss, Amy!' and I pulled the TV plug out of its socket.

Without even looking at me she picked up her phone and began to search for the same episode. I stormed back to the bedroom and flung myself on the bed. Diaphragmatic breathing be arsed, I told myself. And went straight to sleep.

◆————◆————◆

I dreamed I was in an underground garden, a cave of ice and shining black boulders worn smooth by rivulets of dripping, falling water. Ferns and night orchids grew between the cracks, and plants I didn't recognise, that looked like seaweeds, fringed small pools like eyelashes. I was cold.

Pasqual said, 'You were not sent for.'

I wanted to say that I had drawings and information that Lazaro would want to see, but my tongue was so thick and slow I could only moan out his name. Even to myself I sounded hopeless and helpless: 'La-a-az-arrr-o-o' – horrible, slobbery, slow, echoey.

He must know how I felt about him – that I would die if I couldn't see him now. My heart was breaking, I would curl up small and live in his pocket, I would lie like a dog at his feet, I would...

Pasqual said, 'Go away. Sir is busy.'

'I'll do whatever he wants,' I slurred.

Pasqual disappeared.

Then I was in a red room. Lazaro said, 'Is she ready?'

A dog barked. I almost woke up. 'No!' I cried and closed my eyes, willing the dream to continue.

'Damn dogs,' Gemma said. 'Be careful. I think it's temporary.'

'Try,' Pasqual said from a long way away.

Gemma lifted my nightgown and slid her hand up my leg, under my panties. It only took one touch. I came with the painful violence of a seizure.

The dog howled.

I ran barefoot down the road, more frightened than I'd been in my life. Shadows with claws pursued me.

<hr>

I woke to broad daylight, half suffocated by a tangled heap of bedding. Amy had kicked my door open and was walking towards me with a mug of tea in one hand and a slice of toast on a plate in the other.

She said, 'Breakfast. You're to stay in bed. I'm going to the office and Jake's driving me, so don't think you can work on him while I'm out.'

'After he's been with you?' I said. 'I *really* don't think so.'

'It wouldn't be the first time,' she sneered and left before I could think of an answer. It was war.

She knew that, like her, I drank coffee first thing in the morning. Tea was an insult. But my mouth was claggy so I sipped it with pleasure. I'll change to tea, I thought, I don't want anything Amy wants.

I needed to wash away the taste of my dream. It wasn't the only time I'd experienced an erotic dream with an unlikely partner – once, to my acute embarrassment, it had been with a cartoon rabbit. At least Gemma was human, but I didn't like her. It had been Lazaro I'd wanted to be with. Most galling of all, Lazaro and probably Pasqual had been watching. This, I thought, would surely *not* be a dream I'd share with Hannah.

I finished the tea but couldn't face the toast. Only then did I look at the clock. It was ten-thirty. Half the morning had gone but I was still too tired to move. All the same, I dragged myself to the bathroom. Amy had left wet towels on the floor which she knew would drive me crazy. I ignored them and brushed my teeth, rinsing my mouth with mouthwash. Then I got into the shower. There were remnants of last night's nosebleed on my skin and in my hair. I scrubbed them off and shampooed vigorously. My neck was still sore. I washed it carefully with lots of soap. It was only as I was about to step out of the shower that I noticed how dirty my feet were. They were scratched and bruised too. I sat on the rim of the bath and washed them, puzzled. The only thing I could think of was the last part of the dream when, barefoot, I'd run away from shadows down an empty street.

This reminded me to check on Hannah. I'd relied on Jake to keep her safe last night, but I still had to remind myself that I couldn't trust him anymore; I couldn't think of him as a basically decent guy. Without much question, I'd taken him to be someone with whom I could share a few interests, like guerrilla gardening, old movies and bed. It wasn't a forever love; we simply got along. But now he was a stranger I'd never known at all.

I could hardly bear to think about Amy, my friend since infancy. We'd fallen over at ballet class together. Our mothers had tried to force us to learn the violin by the Suzuki method until we'd rebelled together. Together. There was no one I could use that word about now – except, with many reservations, Hannah. I picked up my phone and switched it on. It was full of messages. I must've turned it off after Mark called and then forgotten. Someone had switched the landline to silent, but the message light was flashing.

I called Hannah's number and was sent straight to voicemail. I left a message.

Then, with a pad and pencil I made a list of everyone who'd called. Mostly they were Mother's friends and relatives wanting news and saying how sorry they were. Two were from Detective Sergeant Ed Richardson asking me to call back.

Before doing that I wanted to know what Hannah had said

to the police. I rang her number again and again was sent to voicemail.

Dutifully I started going down the list of sympathisers but very soon discovered that Hannah had been in touch with one of them explaining that I'd been ill and not to worry if she didn't hear from me until there was something to tell. Cleverly she gave this information to Mother's cousin Bella who was the family social networker. Bella had networked so widely that I could turn my attention to my clients.

I'm self-employed. I can't claim sick pay. I couldn't break appointments with impunity. Some of my clients had heard the news; some hadn't. Everyone sympathised. But it was March: everyone was expecting me to be thinking about preparations for spring and summer. This was when I showed them catalogues and shared ideas. It was when I should be pruning Mr Sorkin's myrtles or the blueberry bushes on Mr Lewin's patio. It was what I wanted to do. There's no certainty of outcome in gardening because no one can predict weather or disease. Some things will succeed; some will fail. It's an art form but I don't have the control of a painter or sculptor. I'm always surprised, and, unlike a painting or sculpture, a garden or even a window box is always on the move – never finished.

Sadly, with my clients, I realised that I was pretending almost as much as I had been with my relations. It was as if I was working from a script someone else had written: I was 'the bereaved'. I was accepting sympathy for a grief I couldn't feel. I was expressing sympathy for everyone else's loss too – an unexpected duty. I was better at giving sympathy than receiving it. My heart was stone frozen. All I could think was, If only this was Lazaro I was talking to. And then I didn't want to think about him either because of the humiliating dream.

Finally I called Ed Richardson. He answered but I could tell he was in the car. 'Can't talk long,' he said. 'Look, your rabbi's hassling us but I don't think we can sign off on the body till at least next week so can you get him off my back?'

I didn't have an ice-cream on the equator's chance of persuading Mother's rabbi to do anything at all, so I changed the subject. 'Have you talked to Hannah David yet?'

'Not on my list,' he said. '*You're* on my list. But I'll have to call you later. Oops, the light's changed. Just talk to the rabbi, eh?' And he rang off.

My mother's rabbi had not called me. I remembered the adage – Never trouble trouble till trouble troubles you – and returned the favour. He got all his information about me from my mother so he had a terrible opinion of me.

Thinking of bad opinions, and having failed once more to reach Hannah, I brushed my teeth again, made a cup of coffee, drank half of it, screwed up my courage and finally rang Jake. To my astonishment, he answered.

I was very moderate and asked him politely how he'd left Hannah.

He said, 'I took her to her door. I went inside with her. I checked every room, every door and every window. She was fine – exhausted but safe. Why?'

'Because I haven't talked to her this morning and she hasn't rung me.'

'She was fine last night.' He sounded defensive. 'You think I should've stayed with her, don't you?'

'No, Jake,' I said wearily. 'I think *I* should have.'

'Oh,' he said, sounding mollified. 'Well, she told me in the cab about your anaemia et cetera, so I don't think you'd have been much protection.'

'Okay. I'll go over there now.' I was about to ring off, when he coughed and said, 'Seema?'

'What?'

'I just want to say, er, sorry?' He made it sound like he was asking my permission.

'Then say it,' I said, annoyed. 'Are you going to apologise to Noah too?'

'Noah?' He hesitated. Then he took an audible breath and said, 'Seema haven't you wondered why you never met Noah? Or any of Amy's so-called boyfriends recently? There *is* no Noah.'

Stunned, I said stupidly, 'Are you sure?' And then, when he didn't reply, I went on, 'Of course you are – she left the Italian Bar early to meet you, didn't she? Why are you telling me this?'

'I didn't want you to put all the blame on me – you being a feminist and all.' Perhaps, for once, he heard for himself how he sounded because he hurried on, 'I just wanted to say sorry. I didn't mean this to happen. I was happy with you. It was just one of those things – we'd been to Johnny and Frannie's wedding, remember? We all had too much to drink, and you went to bed early. It was like a drunken fumble I could hardly remember in the morning. I didn't see it as the start of anything, I promise you.'

'But you're saying that Amy did?'

'You'll have to ask her,' he said. 'I'm just telling you what happened.'

'*Nothing* would've happened unless you wanted it to.'

'Well, you should know a thing or two about that, Seema.' He sounded as bitter as I felt. 'What about taking drugs with an old fart you only just met?'

'Okay,' I snapped. 'But that doesn't compare with you and my best friend cheating on me for a year.'

There was a minute while we listened to each other breathing. Then he said, 'Look, do you want me to meet you at Hannah's? You aren't well; I can hear it in your voice. And you're anxious. I can hear that too.'

I said weakly, 'No… well maybe. But are you going to ring Amy to tell her where you'll be?'

He was silent for so long that I cut in, saying sadly, 'You're a piece of crap, Jake.' I rang off and cried like the lonely abandoned child I felt myself to be.

It took nearly half an hour before I could function or even begin to feel like the grownup, capable woman I knew I was. Or used to be. Then I put on my coat and boots and drove, like a sensible adult to Hannah's house.

Hannah was my father's friend. They met on an East End project designed to counsel and to teach English, or anything at all, to Holocaust survivors and their children. The war had been over for quite a long time but the damage remained. Even now Hannah was working with trauma that had lasted for seventy or more years. Two children, whose lives had been torn apart: parents lost, siblings dead, forced to scrabble for food among the dead and dying, were now older than Hannah herself. But still they clung to her and still she wouldn't let them go. 'I promised,' she told me once. 'They lost everything. They were born into a world where strangers coldly killed their whole families in front of them. They survived in a world where strangers wanted to kill them too. They were born terrified and betrayed. How could I break a promise to such people?'

My father, still a schoolboy and himself somewhat frightened by his own family's fate in the Far East, taught conversational English to children whose parents only spoke Yiddish. Even more usefully he learned and then taught double-entry bookkeeping to anyone who wanted to know. The Settlement was a hotbed of distress and disturbing behaviour so Hannah took him under her wing. Their friendship lasted until his death. She was his most important gift to me. I used to think of her as family.

I was going to her house now because I was afraid she might have died in the night. I was terrified that whoever killed my mother had slaughtered her too. She, in other words, might be the old woman they'd mistaken my mother for.

In the van, outside her house, staring at her boxes of joyous scarlet and yellow tulips, I could not understand what had happened in the last few days to make me wish for... Wish for what? Her absence? Surely not her death? Surely not that.

Suddenly, with absolute clarity, I knew that I believed two absolutely contradictory premises. The first was that Lazaro was my mentor, my teacher, my saviour, the object of my longing and desire. I would never know a moment's happiness without him. The second was that Hannah, my oldest, dearest friend and trusted mentor had never put me wrong. If she was as right this time as she had always been, then one object of my love was trying to destroy the other. Not only that, but one of them was trying to harm me.

It was, simultaneously, reality and insanity. I thought, in the end, it must be insanity. Every message, every voice I heard, must be generated by my own mind. That was surely madness. And yet the alternative – that an outside agency had invaded my brain – was madness too.

I needed help. Heart in mouth, I rang Hannah's doorbell.

TWELVE

No one came. I rang again. I stood leaning my back against the door, longing to be at the Palatine Estate, imagining myself there. But if I were there, I knew I would be worrying myself to death about Hannah. A circular gust of cold wind made the tulips curtsy and nod their heads.

I went back to the van. Hannah's spare keys were in the glove compartment along with a tin of boiled sweets, tissues and a cloth for my misty windscreen. I took the key and the boiled sweets. Hannah sometimes became dizzy from low blood sugar.

The door was double locked but not bolted from the inside. That was a good sign, wasn't it? Or was it?

'Hannah,' I called from her hallway. 'Hannah?'

The ground floor was empty and secure. There was no blood in the kitchen, but I was sweating.

'Hannah?' I almost screeched from the bottom of stairs too steep for old women. There was no blood on the bathroom landing. I went on up. 'Use it or lose it,' Hannah always said when I got anxious about her ability to climb steep, narrow stairs. 'What would I do in a suburban bungalow? There are worse ways to die than from a broken neck.'

'What about a broken hip?' I warned her darkly.

'I won't ask you to look after me.' Hannah laughed. 'In fact, should I find myself bed-bound you have my permission to shoot me.'

I found Hannah, fully clothed on her bed, covered by an old-fashioned satin eiderdown. With her eyes closed she said, 'Would you make a pot of coffee, Seema? Three lumps of sugar for me.'

I knew what that meant and opened the tin of sweets. She favoured the darkest purple ones in the Fruit of the Forest selection. I picked one and popped it straight into her mouth. She smiled at me. I left the open tin within her reach and went downstairs to her tiny non-kosher kitchen to brew the strong, sweet Greek coffee she adored. I was panting and my eyes burned with unshed tears.

I'd just put everything on a tray to take up to her when she came down. She was wearing soft black slacks and a long moss green sweater. Her crazy white hair looked like lambs wool but she was pale and shaky. I put my arms around her. She used to be taller than I was; now she was a couple of inches shorter. But I still wanted to lean on her. Instead I found some frozen winter vegetable soup in her freezer and put it in the microwave while she drank her coffee and we talked about nothing at all. I was biding my time till her blood sugar was stable enough to answer my questions and hear what I had to say. I was pretty sure she was doing something similar.

There was enough soup for two and we ate companionably without talking. I washed up.

When we were sitting comfortably in her living room she said. 'I talked to a policewoman this morning. Afterwards I was so tired I turned the phones off and went to lie down. I'm sorry you were worried.'

'And I'm sorry I've disrupted your life.'

'I told the constable about Sharpe-Harding. But, Seema, I wasn't the only one. Ivy had talked to her neighbours, Bella and heaven knows who else. Everyone knew about her visitors and the fact that you had shamed her and were probably in debt because you don't know how to run your own business and you should've studied accountancy and IT as she advised instead of art and gardening. Then you could've had a nice steady job and met a nice steady man to marry. But oh, no, you wouldn't listen and now look at you: a credit company is tracking you down and your hands are always dirty.' She said all this in my mother's anxious complaining rush of words, but with her own wry, dry smile. I smiled back. She couldn't help sounding affectionate in spite of the familiar complaints. And I couldn't help feeling irritated and attacked *because* of the familiar complaints.

'So,' I said, 'the cops know about the Palatine Estate.'

'They'll just consult a search engine like we did.' Hannah said. 'They probably already have. But I didn't give them the address and postcode.'

'Good,' I said, relieved. 'Then there'll be no need for anyone to try to stop you.'

She looked at me strangely.

I said, 'I have to tell you about something. Last night, when you were so cleverly demolishing Jake and Amy, a voice in my head said, "We killed the wrong old woman." I think it meant *you* should've had your throat cut instead of Mother. I think you're in danger. I think I'm a threat to you.'

'When you say, "a voice in my head",' Hannah asked gently, 'what exactly do you mean? Man's voice or woman's?'

I tried to explain: 'It isn't either. It was like my *own* thought, but it's not what I think.' I leaned forward with my elbows on my knees and my head in my hands. I was doing the wrong thing in the wrong way. I was doing the only thing I could. Hannah would diagnose me as having schizoid tendencies. She wouldn't believe me. But I'd have done my best. I'd be off the hook with her and with Lazaro.

'You know I've said some grotesque things to you?'

She nodded.

'And you've been suggesting that someone – ' I couldn't allow myself to use Lazaro's name. 'You said maybe someone *might* be controlling my mind with drugs. What did you mean?'

'You were saying anti-Semitic things.' She began slowly.

124

'Things you can't possibly mean unless someone or something is stimulating your internalised self-doubt and self-hatred.

'Being a Jew is hard. There are so many negative views and messages that are horribly normal in ordinary British society. We deny them and fight them, but it's like we all have message boards in our heads crammed with reminders on post-its. We never clean it up entirely – we don't take down and throw away all the post-its we don't want.

'All minority groups face similar problems. But we're Jews so I'm talking about you and me. Anti-Semitism isn't just the Holocaust – it's also the drip, drip, drip of normal, everyday prejudice. So normal, so ubiquitous, that it clings to our minds and hearts like tattoos. We wonder what's wrong with us. Isn't that outrageous? In the face of blatant prejudice we wonder what *we* did to deserve it.

'If someone has been dripping poison into your ear maybe it's finding a receptive place in your mind.

'I was thinking, given the opioids and your subsequent amnesia, that someone could be pitching some very malicious ideas into your sub consciousness. Like post-hypnotic suggestions.'

'But,' I began, hardly knowing how to go on. 'Why would anyone want to do that?'

'I don't know,' she said. 'Conjecture? Remember, right at the beginning I wondered about vampirism and games of dominance and submission? Well, if a man wants a woman to be properly submissive, it's a good tactic first to isolate her from her family and friends. It's also useful to pick someone who already lacks confidence, and then to chip away at what little she has by playing on her low self-esteem; also by turning her against those who support her.'

'And now,' I said, 'you are chipping away at my relationship with Lazaro.'

'Yes.' She nodded cheerfully. 'Only I would say I'm trying

to persuade you to think clearly about him and what he's doing to you.'

'And I'm trying to get you to think clearly about what *I* might be doing to *you*. Did you hear what I said? "We killed the wrong old woman." *We.* Who is "we"? Am I part of "we"? Did I help kill my mother? Am I a threat to you too?'

We stared at each other in silence for a minute. Then she said, 'You know, I think you're right – I'm too pedagogic. I'm always so busy thinking about how to explain something or what I'm going to say next that I sometimes fail to listen properly. And often I dismiss out of hand what I consider to be irrational. Not the most helpful characteristic in my profession.'

Hannah did not have a lot to be humble about. But I watched her quite humbly re-ordering her thoughts. Then she almost laughed. 'All right,' she said. 'If I'm correct in suspecting Lazaro, we're dealing with drugs, vampirism, sex games, assault, mind control and murder.'

'And if I'm right and you're wrong,' I said miserably, 'you're maligning a charismatic old guy who wants to employ me on the best job of my life. And Hannah, mightn't he just *like* me?'

'If he just liked you, he wouldn't be doing you harm. Fact, Seema: you've only just had a blood test in a hospital. Opioids and anaemia were found and noted by *professionals*. Fact: you have an unexplained wound on your neck. Fact: you look ill and exhausted. Fact: your flat was broken into. Fact: your mother was murdered. Question: what was a representative of Sharpe-Harding doing at her house anyway? Second question: if you think this cluster of abnormalities is unconnected with those who live in the Palatine Estate why are you concerned for my safety?'

As Hannah's list progressed my anxiety level rose until I was sweating, panting and beginning to feel faint. Suddenly there was the tell-tale wetness dripping from my nose and I was terrified the blinding headache would follow. I got up and almost sprinted to the bathroom.

After a few minutes, Hannah tapped on the door and came in with a small packet of frozen prawns and a handful of kitchen roll. I said, 'I feel like one of those barmy people who line their rooms with tin foil to stop the government or aliens reading their thoughts or planting ideas in their brains.' I held the frozen packet to my nose and went on. 'It's irrational – I know, I know, *I know*. But I feel I'm being punished for even listening to you. And Hannah- *"We killed the wrong old woman"*. What does it mean?'

I was sitting on the toilet lid tipping my head back to stop my blood from dripping on the floor. The taste was intoxicating.

Hannah sat on the rim of her old-fashioned claw-footed tub. 'Guilt,' she began.

'Stop!' I cried. 'You're not listening. You're trying to explain away the irrational again.'

'Yes,' she agreed. 'Because if it isn't something in your mind, a critical imbalance of your brain chemistry caused by drugs...'

'Yes?' I interrupted. 'If I'm not crazy? What then?'

'What if there is no rational explanation? But Seema,' she said, touching my shoulder comfortingly, 'I know you're frightened, but there *will* be a rational, reasonable answer.'

'Even if it isn't vampirism?' I whispered. 'Even if it's... vampires?'

She glared at me. 'How can you disbelieve in god yet believe in vampires? Neither you nor I believe in the supernatural.'

'What if they aren't *super*natural?' I asked. 'What if, say, they're descendants of people who drank the blood of living creatures to survive?'

'Hmm.' Hanna tried to look as though she was taking me seriously. 'Well, I suppose vampires were also the stuff of folklore long before the Gothic horror novel was even thought of. Jung, of course, was a great respecter of the persistence of avatars in myths and legends. Anthropology. I suppose the vampire might be acceptable under such a category.'

She ran the cold tap over a flannel which she wrung out and

handed to me. I wiped the blood off my face and followed her back to her sitting room.

'Well,' she went on, when we were sitting comfortably, 'if you really want an irrational conversation about the paranormal let's discuss what we know about vampires – although that won't be of much use as what we know comes from fiction – not the most reliable source of indisputable facts. So? The un-dead: those who should be dead but, unlike ghosts, take corporeal form. They exist by draining humans of their life force, usually in the form of blood. As un-kosher a concept as you're likely to find, I might add.'

'They're supposed to be immortal but they can be killed,' I said. 'Wooden stakes through the heart. There's also beheading and sunlight. They're repelled by garlic and crucifixes as well.'

'Vampires figure in folklore from all over the world, including Africa and Asia where I don't suppose crucifixes would cut much ice. If they exist at all I imagine they're much older than Christianity.' She looked at me shrewdly, waiting for more information.

I felt I'd said too much already. I was betraying Lazaro. So I said, with a pretence of helpfulness, 'Then I think we can leave out the modern European and American incarnations from Dracula to all the film and TV fictions. Don't they all use Christian iconography?'

'I don't know,' Hannah admitted. 'I don't watch teenage programmes. Let's just look at what you've noticed.'

'Such as?' I said cautiously.

'Shadows and reflections?'

'Everyone I met at the Palatine Estate cast a shadow. It would've looked very odd if they hadn't, and it didn't look odd.' That was alright, wasn't it? Lazaro couldn't object to me talking about shadows. 'I don't think there were any mirrors in the living or dining rooms but, yes... ' I remembered looking at the wonderful Paula Rego Mr Rochester etching hanging between two windows, and I remembered seeing Lazaro's reflection in the glass. He had been standing behind me watching, enjoying my stunned appreciation of his collection. 'Yes, there were reflections,' I said.

'What else?'

'Well,' I said reluctantly. 'They ate a lot of rare meat. And they do seem to keep vampire hours. I haven't seen anyone in daylight.'

'That could apply just as much to people imitating a vampire lifestyle,' Hannah said.

'It snows,' I said, hesitantly.

'Go on?'

'Well, I know the weather's been weird this year what with climate change and all. And it's been exceptionally cold, but every time Pasqual turns up it snows.'

'Are you saying Pasqual controls the weather?'

'I'm just asking if that's a vampire characteristic. The first time I met Lazaro it snowed as we were getting into his limousine. But you said there hadn't been any snow in North London that night.'

'The Meteorological Office said that, not me,' Hannah corrected, writing busily.

I watched for a moment and then asked, 'Why me, Hannah? When Lazaro sat down beside me after Amy left the Italian Bar, I thought, well, I thought he was way too classy to be chatting up a gardener in Golders Green. And, actually, he *is*. I'm not putting myself down, honestly. You should see him and his house. I just don't belong in those circles.'

I could see she was going to begin her usual lecture about selling myself short so I shook a finger at her, and after a pause she said, 'I don't want to make a bad time worse for you, dear, but has it occurred to you that Amy might have set you up? Might she not have pointed you out to someone, hoping to lure you into an indiscretion she could use against you with Jacob? Bringing the situation between the three of you to a head? While you didn't know about her affair with Jacob, and he didn't want to tell you, she was the "other woman", the "bit on the side". Hardly a satisfactory position for her, as I'm sure you'll agree.'

'Amy wouldn't…' I began, and then stopped. Defending each other against all comers was a deeply planted habit that I'd have to pull out by the roots from now on.

'I'm sorry, but Amy would – and did.' Hannah handed me a tissue to dab my eyes with. It was only a little bloody. 'And so did Jacob.'

'I'm not crying for Jake,' I said. 'I'm crying for Amy.'

'I know.' Hannah pushed the whole box of tissues towards me. 'Actually you have a lot to cry about.'

When I was feeling better I said, 'Okay, I can see why Amy might want to set me up, but what about Lazaro? Was he on the prowl for just about anyone? I mean, I'm very ordinary and he's out of my league. And how did he know that apart from a little blow when I was at college, opium would be the only drug I'd ever be tempted by?'

'Maybe Amy told him. No, wait, Seema, apart from your own family, how many Mizrahi Jews do you know? A couple? And how many come from families born in Baghdad or Kolkata who traded in opium? And as I know the answer to those questions I'll ask one more – given your name, your background and your looks, how many times in your short life have you been called exotic?'

I sighed. Exotic is an insult. It means 'other', 'not one of us'. It's usually followed by, 'where are you from?' Or, worse, 'when are you going back?'

Hannah knows this very well. 'You may think you're ordinary, but you're not. In a very few sentences Amy could have piqued a stranger's interest in you.'

'And he just happened to have a stash of opium in the boot of his black limousine?'

'It wasn't opium, Seema,' Hannah said patiently.

'Okay,' I said, still, in spite of good evidence, not quite believing this. 'But it *was* an opium pipe.'

'If you say so, alright, perhaps the meeting wasn't a spontaneous piece of manipulation. Maybe Amy spoke to him on previous occasions. Suppose Lazaro came prepared?'

'Oh come on!' I said. 'Amy may be an opportunistic cow, but she isn't Machiavella.'

'Well then, we come back to the paranormal. A stranger picks you out of a crowd. He's already armed with what he needs to seduce a young woman with your unique background. He drugs you, wounds you and then takes you home. His driver knows where to find you the next night. How does he know?'

'He didn't seduce me,' I interrupted hotly.

'Enticed, then; lured you into dangerous behaviour; began to control you and your feelings about him. How do you feel about him now?'

I turned away, unwilling to meet her eyes, and unable to describe the longing, the emptiness caused by his absence. Where was he? Why didn't he send for me? Didn't he want me anymore? Had he forgotten me? Lovesick is a very good word for the way I felt.

Hannah watched me. Then she said quite sharply, 'I don't care if he's normal or paranormal, man or vampire, it's an effective but despicable tactic to encourage an appetite for something and then withdraw it. Drugs, love, sex – I don't care. He forces you to go to him because how else can you satisfy your longing? He stalks you, but without having to ask he makes *you* walk into his trap. He plays on your fear of abandonment. He makes you responsible for whatever fate *he's* chosen for you. It's passive but it works well. He's a passive predator. Whatever happens, whatever he does to you, it will be your fault. You will have brought it on yourself.'

'What fate?' I almost wailed.

'We'll never know unless you fall into the trap. He doesn't appear to want you at the moment but I see that you can hardly wait for sundown when...'

My phone rang. I answered it immediately because I didn't want to hear what Hannah would say next.

'Sergeant Ed Richardson,' said the brusque male voice. 'Where are you?'

'Here,' I said just as brusquely. 'Where are you?'

'Outside your front door. I thought you were going to wait in till I arrived.'

'You didn't make an appointment.'

'This is important police business.'

'And *this* is important family business.' I mouthed the word 'cop' to Hannah.

'Tell him to come here,' Hannah whispered. 'Tell him I'm unwell.' And it was nearly true. She still looked frail and exhausted.

After I'd given Ed her address, I made green tea with mango and found a packet of her favourite shortbread biscuits in the biscuit tin. We sat quietly, resting, watching the news: politicians wrangling, a mass of speculation and opinion but very few facts.

'Boring,' I said. 'The grownups don't know what they're doing. Again.'

Hannah gave a bark of laughter but didn't change the channel. In fact she must have found it soothing for, after a few minutes, her head drooped forward and she went to sleep.

I tried not to listen. Lately I've been news averse. There are more and more divisions in society, more and more paranoid rhetoric, more creeping xenophobia, racism and anti-Semitism. It isn't what I want to see so I don't look. I'm a coward. I live in a world of growing plants and making beauty. The news concentrates on the opposite. Often it depresses and frightens me. I don't like being depressed or frightened so I don't watch.

Instead I thought about Lazaro. His love for beauty was everywhere in his house. I was thinking of the bone-white Cycladic priestesses, arms folded under their breasts, straight and strong as columns, faces upturned to the moon. It had to be the moon I thought, although I didn't know anything about Bronze Age religion. Had the division between male and female, sun and moon, already begun four or five thousand years ago?

Although he was a man, I associated Lazaro with the moon. Was that because of the moonlight garden he'd described at our first meeting?

The doorbell rang and I went to answer it while Hannah shook herself awake and tottered off to wash her face.

Ed was as crumpled as before. He came in rubbing his face as if he were trying to erase all the lines on it, and failing. I sat him down while I made English Breakfast tea for him and more green tea for Hannah. When I returned with the tray she was already interrogating him on the results of his investigation. Looking somewhat banjaxed he was confessing that they hadn't got very far, that forensics hadn't turned up anything significant and that none of the neighbours had seen or heard anything.

'So,' Hannah said, 'the only anomaly is the visit of representatives from Sharpe-Harding Associates. What can you tell us about that?' She was so clearly in charge that I almost laughed. Sergeant Ed thought he was visiting a frail, unwell old lady? Well, silly him.

'They have an office in the City,' he said. 'They're mainly concerned with imports and exports, shipping and transport et cetera. It's not a big company, but it also provides security for and manages a couple of London properties. The gentleman I spoke to… ' he paused to look at a sheet of paper almost as crumpled as his jacket. '… Miles Thomas, a partner, said that you, Ms Dahami, were being considered for a garden design job and your credentials had to be checked before a formal offer could be made. It was, he said, the standard background check they run on all employees. As Ms Dahami is self-employed they included her mother.'

'I wonder why Ivy got so upset about it,' Hannah said innocently.

Sergeant Ed cleared his throat and looked at me as if he thought me fragile or dangerous but couldn't decide which.

I said, 'Go on, spit it out. I can take it.'

'Well, Mrs Dahami told quite a few people that the interview was hostile and that she was being dunned because you were badly in debt, having mismanaged your life and business affairs. And that you thought you were too good to waste time by celebrating the Sabbath with her.'

I sighed. I'd expected nothing else.

Noticing this, the sergeant said, 'I'm afraid your mother's friends don't have a very flattering opinion of you. One went so far as to suggest you might have organised a hit so that you could sell your mother's house to pay off your debts.'

That was too much. I opened my mouth to launch into wounded denials, but Hannah interrupted calmly, 'What did Mr Thomas say?'

'Mr Thomas said that as far as his limited investigation went, Ms Dahami has never been in debt, pays bills and taxes on time and has no police record. I can confirm that, by the way.'

'Thank you,' I said, exasperated. 'I don't understand my mother at all.'

'Mothers,' Ed began ruminatively.

'Without whom,' Hannah put in, 'I would not have had half so many disturbed clients.' She turned to Ed adding, 'About seventy-five percent of my income depends on mothers failing to live up to the huge expectations we heap upon them. And the even huger expectations we think they have of us.'

'Yeah, right, but back to the subject.' Ed didn't know Hannah at all if he thought he could interview me in her home without receiving a shed-load of input from her.

I smiled at him anxiously, 'Do you take the idea of me organising a hit seriously?'

'You aren't a suspect any more than anyone else at the moment, Ms Dahami,' he said blandly. 'It would help if you had someone who could swear to you being at home asleep.'

'But there isn't anyone.'

'No. And there's the rather odd fact that you were out of communication for hours after you were told of your mother's death and then turned up in a black limousine which we later discovered was owned by the Palatine Estate, which is co-owned and managed by Sharpe-Harding Associates.'

'Yes,' I said, 'I told you about that. Have you confirmed what I said?'

'No,' he said. 'You didn't tell me that. Nor did you tell me that the dogs you were so concerned about were also owned by the Palatine Estate.'

'Oh,' I said feebly. 'I thought I did. I thought you knew. The roof-top garden I might be commissioned to design is in the Palestine Estate. My patron is Mr Lazaro who lives there. Surely he can vouch for me.'

'Unfortunately, Mr Lazaro is away on business in Milan and won't be back till tomorrow night.'

'It isn't a secret,' Hannah put in. 'Seema told me all about it. But to be honest, I'm a little worried about the people at the estate.'

'Yeah,' the sergeant said. 'The very rich seem to have different priorities from the rest of us mortals. But fortunately for you the janitor, or as he calls himself "the security and maintenance manager", confirms that through a series of misunderstandings you kept his guard dogs overnight and he was forced to break your locks to get them back. He also agrees that you were taken to Belgravia instead of Golders Green and that Mr Lazaro personally rectified the mistake. He complained that they were "very international" at the mews and there were often language problems.'

'Have you done a background check on everyone at Sharpe-Harding and the Palatine Estate?' Hannah asked sweetly.

'Hannah, please!' I protested.

'Seema wants to be given this commission,' Hannah explained. 'She doesn't want to rattle Mr Lazaro's cage. But he's done a security check on her; it's only fair someone should return the favour.'

Sergeant Richardson shot her a dirty look and said, 'All aspects are being given due consideration.'

She returned the look and added a derisive snort, saying, 'They conduct all their meetings after midnight, Seema returns ill and exhausted with blank spots in her memory. I think they're somehow dosing her with illegal substances.'

'Hannah,' I said in my warning voice.

Sergeant Ed had the most sceptical eyebrows in the business. 'Are you being offered illegal substances, Ms Dahami?' His tone was borderline contemptuous.

I didn't know how to react. So I shrugged and said, 'Hannah's right, I have a shocking memory these days. And my sleep has gone to pieces. I don't know why my mother was killed. Was it a personal attack? Was it a hate crime? I feel threatened and targeted too. And I can't seem to eat properly.' I threw all this at him in no logical order as if it were connected to his question – and who knew, it might have been. It was certainly mostly true.

'Shouldn't she be having counselling?' Sergeant Ed asked Hannah. Then he actually blushed and added, 'On yeah, sorry, she's got you.'

'It's a good question though,' Hannah said. 'Why was Ivy Dahami killed?'

'I was hoping Seema here might be able to help,' Sergeant Ed said. 'You knew her best. At the moment it seems completely random. The neighbours, the members of her Synagogue, are getting more and more uneasy, linking the murder to the desecration of some graves in the Jewish Cemetery in Hoop Lane. There was quite a big hoo-hah about that as I recall.'

'Amazing,' Hannah said, 'how a few swastikas can cause such paranoia.'

'Yes,' the sergeant said, totally missing the sarcasm. 'So we were hoping you might know of a personal grudge or an enemy.'

'I don't,' I said. 'She was a bit abrasive sometimes – she could put people's backs up, but no one wanted to kill her.'

'She could be quite critical and quarrelsome,' Hannah said. 'As we all can. But Ivy more than most. In spite of that, she was a loyal friend even to those who annoyed her. Me, for example. We didn't see eye to eye on any subject at all, especially the one that interested her most – religious observance – but she remained in touch, worried about my health and even brought me soup when I had a cold last November.'

Ed turned to me.

'No,' I said. 'In terms of observance she was an example of a good woman. And most of her friends and acquaintances were part of the same community – Sephardic, strict.'

'What about other communities?' He shifted uncomfortably. I'd noticed that he didn't want to use the word Jew or Jewish.

Hannah just laughed. 'There are more ways of interpreting the Talmud than stars in the sky, Sergeant. If you're looking for consensus of religious opinion among Jews in North London you're doomed to failure. But if you think those differences are reasons for someone murdering Ivy, think again. Her throat was cut and she bled to death. The unease and paranoia you mention comes from that fact and its resonance with the way animals are butchered for the kosher market. This was not the act of a Jew. I'm sorry if that's inconvenient – but you *have* to look outside Ivy's community and her family. Even the suggestion is a deadly insult.'

He stared at his cracked shoe for a few moments before saying, 'Yeah, sorry. People are so sensitive round here.'

Again, the unsaid word, Jews, hung over his head like a thought bubble. Hannah and I waited silently. Then he said, 'I simply got to find the time to buy a new pair of shoes.'

When we didn't respond to that either he got up to leave.

At the last minute I said, 'When can I have my phone back?'

'Still with the techies,' he muttered, not looking at me.

Hannah showed him to the door saying, 'Please take a closer look at the Palestine Estate, Sergeant. Something there doesn't ring true.'

THIRTEEN

Hannah wanted me to stay, but I went home soon after the sergeant left. The sun was going down and I was restless. Her understanding of me was too complete but so cerebral that I felt she didn't understand me at all. Also she had too much inherited furniture – everything she owned seemed connected to the dead.

I heard trance music as I let myself into the flat. Amy and Jake were in the kitchen. They were making beef stroganoff which was an unfriendly dish to cook in my kitchen. It was a clear statement that they had no intention of sharing food with me again.

I went to my bedroom and wrote Amy an unambiguous note giving her a month's notice to leave my flat. I printed it, signed it and put it in an envelope. Maybe I could have a dog. A dog would be so much kinder than Amy.

In the kitchen I gave her the envelope and heated up a can of tomato soup. Jake threw me a sympathetic glance while Amy's attention was on the letter. I flipped him the bird. Was he *really* trying to pretend he was the good guy in all this?

Amy looked up from my note and said, 'Now you'll have two houses and I'll be homeless.'

Several mean answers popped into my mind beginning with, 'You should've thought of that before bonking my boyfriend', but I kept silence and dignity and went back to my bedroom to swallow my lonely bowl of soup.

I should get *two* dogs, I thought. One human being isn't quite enough for a dog. Dogs are pack animals – they need their own kind for company – someone with their own speed to run with. Chasing a ball must be second best. That thought brought me to the memory of the Beaus racing together on Hampstead Heath. I wasn't there to exercise them or entertain them. I was there simply to watch and admire.

But wasn't I a pack animal too? My own little pack used to be Hannah, Amy and Jake. It had been a comfort and a pleasure to come home, open the door and hear Amy's crappy music. Knowing she was there – my own kind, I'd always thought. Now she was the grit in my eye and the stone in my shoe. I wanted her gone. But when she'd gone, I would be alone. Till then, there she was, in my kitchen, using my pan to seethe beef in cream. She couldn't have chosen food more insulting to me and my mother's memory than beef stroganoff.

The tomato soup looked like blood but tasted of nothing. I sat at my desk gazing at the folder of drawings I hadn't managed to show to anyone, thinking about the two dogs whose future with Grigori at the Palatine Estate might be very uncertain. I thought about my mother's house, which Amy called my inheritance, and realised I could offer to buy the two wolfhounds. I could save them from being, at best, retrained; at worst put down as unfit for purpose.

I shouldn't leave the Beaus in danger I thought. Not for a moment longer. I should go and bargain for their lives right now. But I paused to put on smarter clothes and a little make-up.

While I was applying a second coat of mascara the phone rang and Mark Kirkby said, 'What're you doing? Am I interrupting something?'

'Not really,' I said, although it's bad policy to confess that you're not insanely busy and in demand.

He said, 'Mr Harding has invited me to some sort of reception tonight. I was wondering if you'd be my plus-one. I know it's really short notice, but my girlfriend came down with laryngitis at the last moment. I thought of you because you've already been to the house and I wouldn't have to explain the deal to someone who didn't already know.'

A reception. 'Wow,' I said. 'How formal?' Now that fate had played into my hands I began to lose my nerve. I am not a reception kind of woman.

'Well, I'm wearing a suit and tie, not evening dress, thank fuck. So I guess it'll be smart cocktaily clobber for the women.'

'Aargh!' I said sincerely. Then I remembered the white lounging pyjamas. 'Okay,' I said, and we arranged for him to pick me up.

After he rang off I realised that I was in mourning and white would be inappropriate. Normally, at this point I would've run to Amy to borrow something black and smart, but that source of help and advice was closed to me forever. Then I remembered that my family came from the East where white can be the colour of mourning and respect. I also remembered I had a vintage black velvet wrap with jet beaded borders and tassels.

But I was nervous. I washed my hair in conditioner because it behaves a lot better if I don't use shampoo. I moisturised thoroughly for a change, paying extra attention to my gardener's hands. Amy, in other circumstances, would've chosen one of her own nail polishes and applied it skilfully. I didn't bother – badly applied polish, I figured, was worse than none. At the last moment I found a crystal crescent moon I'd bought at a festival and sewn to a black velvet ribbon. I was tying it round my neck when I heard the doorbell. Mark was punctual.

By the time I sailed through the living room in my finery Amy had buzzed Mark in. He looked wonderful in a suit and green silk shirt with a pure wool overcoat slung across his shoulders. Not a tattoo was in sight but Jake, the sports fan, recognised him and was struck dumb by hero worship. Amy, well into her eyelash-flapping reaction to good looking strangers, was offering him a drink. So I swept past her and said, 'Another time, Amy, if you don't mind. We don't want to be late.'

Mark, bless his kind heart, said, 'Wow, Seema, don't you look gorgeous!'

I did not trip over my wrap, nor did I make a mess of climbing into Mark's Jeep which was treacherously tall – just as well because I caught a glimpse of Jake and Amy watching from the window. It couldn't have gone better if I'd planned it, written a script and rehearsed it fifty times. I almost purred, but instead I said, 'Thank you.'

'What for?'

'For making me look good back there.'

'Well, you do look good.' He was keeping his eyes on the road.

I laughed and said, 'You scrub up pretty good yourself.'

We both laughed and I felt so comfortable I told him about Jake, Amy and my mother, and why his brief appearance at my flat had done such wonders for my self-respect.

At the next red light he turned to look at me saying, 'Bloody hell, Seema, if ever a girl needed a night out it's you.'

I agreed, but I wasn't feeling sorry for myself any more, and I wasn't looking for sympathy – which surprised me a little. Instead I was feeling pumped. My folder of drawings was on my lap and my chequebook was in my purse. I could prove my value to Lazaro and rescue the Beaus in one visit. The Beaus would force Amy out of my flat and then I could concentrate on garden design and my duty to my dead mother. There would be a funeral my mother would've approved of and then I could put the misery behind me and give all my attention to Lazaro.

Best of all, I was not responsible for this visit. Mark invited me. I accepted. I hadn't done anything. This time I was passive and therefore innocent of making a first move. But I did take a couple of moments to wonder why I found it so difficult to ask for what I wanted, even longed for. But only a couple of moments – I was getting what I longed for without having to ask.

'Do they know your girlfriend's sick?' I asked. 'Do they know I'm coming?'

'I emailed. I wouldn't normally bother, but they're so formal there. I got a one word reply: "Acceptable".' He laughed. Good spirits fizzed in him.

'You have their email?' I was instantly envious. I hid it by adding, 'Does your girlfriend mind you taking someone else?'

'She's pissed off,' Mark said, 'but not about that. She's a health freak. She never gets sick. That's how we met – at Harvest Home in the vitamin supplement aisle. She was so beautiful she kind of shone. Know what I mean? I thought, wow, if she shops here, I'll never go anywhere else. Cat-Lynne's s a cosmetic model, but she hardly ever uses make-up when she isn't working. She doesn't have to.'

He wasn't making it easy for me to hide envy. I said, 'Lucky her. You must be a beautiful couple.'

'Yes,' he said simply. He was pleased. Clearly being half of a beautiful couple was important to him.

I sighed. I thought of Jake. He was a step up from what Amy and I used meanly to call 'standard-issue for Golders Green'. But it was a short step. No one would've called us a beautiful couple. Now we weren't even a couple. I sighed again. But as I was travelling away from him and towards Lazaro it wasn't with much conviction. I felt my sore heart ease with every mile.

Even though it was after midnight we hit a snarl of traffic on the Edgware Road. Police were directing a single lane of traffic around two crumpled cars. There was blood on the tarmac. We both craned our necks, but there were no grisly remains to see.

Mark drummed his fingers on the steering wheel. Neither of us wanted to be late. To distract himself he asked, 'What's in that folder you keep fidgeting with?'

'Just some drawings I did for the proposed roof garden,' I said modestly. 'I thought I might as well leave them for Lazaro to look at later.'

'Can I see?' He turned on the interior light and I gave him the folder muttering, 'They're nothing special.'

He turned the pages, at first idly and then with increasing interest. At last he said, 'Wow, Seema, you should be an artist, not a gardener.'

Of course he knew nothing about drawing or gardening, but I was delighted with his admiration. It seemed genuine.

I gathered the sheets of paper and put them back in the folder. 'I hope Lazaro agrees with you,' I said. 'It'd be a once in a lifetime commission – a whole career shift.'

'Well, good luck,' he said. And just then the traffic cop who'd been holding us up relented. We shot past the gruesome wreck and onto a clear road. We were almost there.

The gate was opened by a guy the size of a wardrobe. He was wearing a full-length black leather coat and a black leather drover's hat. He peered into the jeep, said, 'Good to see you, sir, ma'am,' and waved us through – although he looked as though he could've carried us, Jeep and all.

I whispered, 'Does everyone who works here look as if they stepped straight out of a movie?'

'Yeah,' he said laughing.

'And what's with the micro-climate?' I still felt I had to whisper. 'This has to be the coldest spot in London.'

Mark stopped outside the entrance. Another guy with shoulders like a double bed opened his door for him and then took his keys. I was surprised to see Pasqual on my side. He took in the drop from seat to ground, caught me by the waist as I was about to jump and lifted me down as easily as if I were a feather – which I manifestly am not. I was so surprised I almost forgot to thank him. The double bed drove the Jeep away and Pasqual led us into the hall.

There, someone took Mark's coat. I kept my wrap, but I handed her my folder of drawings and asked that it be left somewhere for

Mr Lazaro to look at later. She promised she'd see to it, but I watched anxiously as she walked away.

The next woman was dressed like an old-fashioned bellhop. She was in charge of a pair of recessed double doors which she opened, ushering us into a stainless steel lift. I was astonished. Who on earth would need a lift in a mews house? The next young woman pressed a button and instead of rising the lift fell so swiftly and smoothly that I felt a surge of nausea.

Mark and I exchanged a glance of complete disbelief as we stepped into a totally unexpected scene.

The space was enormous. Although the architecture seemed thoroughly modern, using the silver of brushed steel to contrast with polished black granite, the effect managed to echo the vaults, curves, pillars and caves of an old French wine cellar or, yes, a crypt. All along one wall were recesses. Some had been fashioned to look like miniature waterfalls and rock pools. Others were lush with black or white fur decorating private seating areas.

We were greeted by a server in a white shirt and black waistcoat bearing a silver tray of fizzing champagne flutes. I nearly accepted one, but remembered in time that Mark didn't drink alcohol. As his ersatz date, I felt I should go teetotal out of good manners. We both asked for a soft drink. All the servers were women dressed like men, their hair severely slicked back or cut boyishly short. They were all attractive.

'Central casting,' I whispered to Mark, hoping to hide my feeling of inferiority behind cynicism. I was intimidated by the architecture and the fact that we were so deep underground with, as far as I could see, only the one lift as a means of escape. I was daunted by the fact that the huge basement was filled with hundreds of strangers, drinking and talking animatedly in groups, their eyes shifting slyly towards Mark and me.

The only person I knew was Mark and I hardly knew him at all. I felt for his hand. It was large, strong and warm. He squeezed mine gently, but just then someone I recognised as one of Garth

Harding's acolytes came over, saying, 'How nice to see you again, Mark. Come and join Mr Harding.' He held out his hand and Mark had to release mine to shake it. The acolyte drew Mark away, making it clear that the invitation did not include me. As he left Mark looked back over his shoulder mouthing the word, 'sorry.' He wasn't half as sorry as I was.

I couldn't see Lazaro anywhere. I felt so exposed and lonely that I would have settled for Gemma or Pasqual's company but there was no sign of them either.

Against the far wall was a buffet table that seemed about half a mile long. I thought about filling a plate and eating just to give myself something to do with my hands which felt big and unkempt compared with the elegance of everyone else's.

But to my horror I saw that the centrepiece, decorated with garlands of black silk leaves and crystal baubles, was a boar's head complete with bared teeth and curling tusks.

Nothing could have made me feel more alienated. I backed away, turned and made for the lift. I couldn't tell Mark I was leaving because I didn't know where he had been taken. All I wanted to do was get out as fast as I possibly could. Claustrophobia and social stress were uniting to make me short of breath, and I was frantic to be above ground before I started to sweat or my nose, my constant enemy these days, began to drip blood.

I was intercepted in my rush to the lift by one of the boyish women who was carrying a tray of champagne. She had high cheek bones, a wide mouth and sly, humorous eyes. 'Take one,' she said, pushing the tray towards me. 'You'll feel a lot better.'

Loyalty to absent Mark made me hesitate, but in the end I accepted an elegant crystal flute and tried not to gulp the contents.

As calmly as I could, I said, 'I really need some fresh air.'

'That's how I felt the first time I worked here.' She grinned at me. 'I'll call the lift for you, shall I?'

'Yes please.' The rush of alcohol to my head made me afraid that I'd faint and make even more of a show of myself.

My new friend escorted me to the lift where she put her tray down on a small table and punched a button next to the concealed doors. A squawk answered her, and speaking into a microphone disguised as a design feature, she said, 'Come down, Lee, please. We've got a customer for the great outdoors.' She winked at me as she listened to the incomprehensible reply.

The champagne was hitting me hard. I said, 'I came with a guy who looks like a Norse god. He's about six foot three and has reddish golden hair, broad shoulders and a toothpaste smile. Would you tell him where I've gone?'

'That's your date?' she said laughing. 'I wouldn't leave him alone in this crowd if he was mine. You *must* be feeling crap.'

I didn't have to reply because the doors glided open and I stumbled into the silver pod.

I must have passed out then.

◆————◆————◆

I woke up in a red room on a scarlet silk bed. Gemma, wearing something black, clinging and bejewelled, was sitting in a plush armchair on the other side of the room. She was smoothing cream into her already perfect hands

I knew I'd been in this room before but I couldn't remember when. My brain seemed to whirl widdershins at high speed making the bed spin around me. It came to a halt just as I revisited my erotic dream.

My tongue was stiff with drink but I managed to say, 'It wasn't a dream. It was you. How *could* you?'

'Are you dreaming now?' she asked innocently.

I was almost buried under a slimy heap of mortification.

'Oh lighten up,' she said. 'It's only a dream. Don't be so damn bourgeois.'

'Consent matters.' I was trying to yell at her but it came out as a pitiful kitten's meow. And I didn't really know what I was accusing her of.

She looked at me blandly. 'Isn't it about time you took a long hard look at yourself and owned your own desires? Stop justifying yourself and take some responsibility. You're not a little girl anymore.'

'What have you done to me?' I whispered.

'Nothing you didn't want.' She yawned without bothering to hide her perfect dentition. 'Sir is studying your drawings now. But, admit it, this isn't about gardening. You want him to notice you, admire you and understand you, don't you?'

'Yes, but... ' I was barely audible even to myself.

She interrupted, 'You're a grown up. What've you got to give in return? And don't say "love" or I'll vomit. No one knows what that is anyway.'

My brain was pulsing like a heart. '*I* do.'

'No you don't. What you've got is a daddy complex: poor baby, lost her daddy and spends many useless years searching for the unconditional love she fantasises he had for her. Or should've had for her. Meanwhile you ignored your mother who was way more honest – she only gave her approval when you deserved it.'

Which was never. Was Gemma right? She was wearing a simple diamond choker that made my crystal crescent moon look cheap and tawdry. I watched the light play on her beautiful throat. Her skin looked as if it had been created for diamonds. Did that make her right? It certainly made me feel wrong. And very dizzy.

And then Lazaro walked into the room and I thought, what could a woman like me possibly give a man who had everything? He seemed to fill my entire field of sight. There was nothing and no one in the room except him. Gemma's diamonds might have been clinkers. What did she know about love?

She got up and gave her chair to Lazaro. He sat and placed my folder on the bed next to me. I struggled upright, still feeling woozy. Lazaro looked at me, then turned to Gemma saying, 'Would you fetch some iced water for Seema.'

He leaned forward and tapped the folder with the finger that wore his moon signet ring. Like the moon in the sky, the moon on his finger had fattened up a little.

'These are good drawings,' he said, smiling. 'You seem to have absorbed nearly everything I had in my mind.'

I was so thrilled I couldn't speak. Tears pricked my eyes, but I was grinning like an ape. He patted my hand gently. His touch went through me like a needle to my heart. At last I found my voice, but instead of saying something sensible I asked, 'How many signet rings do you own?'

'Twenty-eight. One for every day of the lunar month.' He beamed at me. 'You notice details. I like that.'

'Why did you send for me?' I asked.

'I didn't.' He was still smiling but his ebony eyes were serious. 'You found your own way here.'

'Mark invited me.'

'If you say so.' He sat back in his chair.

It was a withdrawal I could feel in the chill of my skin. I rushed on. 'I wanted to see you. I want to design a garden for you. I want to buy your dogs.'

He had been about to rise – to leave, I was sure. My offer to buy the Beaus stopped him and he sat back again.

I went on, 'Grigori mistreats them. He doesn't trust them anymore. He's angry. An angry man shouldn't be in charge of dogs.'

'This is your opinion?' Lazaro sounded haughty now.

I couldn't stop myself. 'No one here loves them.'

'You would throw away your love on dogs?' He was frowning now. 'I thought you wanted to see *me*.'

'No… *yes*.' Terror gripped my throat with an icy hand. 'I'd do anything for you,' I whispered, hoping he'd hear me, praying he wouldn't.

'Unfortunately,' he said, looking sad, 'I will not, probably, be able to employ you. It is a pity because I think you have a real talent, and it is a goal of mine to encourage the young and foster burgeoning talents.'

'Why?' I cried.

He withdrew further into formality. 'While, of course, we all sympathise with your loss, the committee thinks that your mother's death and the subsequent police investigation compromises our privacy. As did your removal of our guard dogs, without permission.'

'You weren't there to ask.' My heart was breaking, but I felt on firmer ground defending the Beaus than defending myself. 'Lazaro, please, I thought they were dead. I couldn't just leave them lying out there in the cold. I think those collars are illegal, and if they aren't they should be. Grigori hasn't trained your dogs properly. He can't control them without resorting to brutality. Please, if nothing else, let me buy the Beaus.'

Gemma, returning with a glass of water, heard the last part. She handed the glass to me saying, 'You really know how to ingratiate yourself, Seema.'

Pasqual, following her, added, 'I think you should give her the damned dogs, boss. Everyone's uncomfortable with them. And now that she's made them unreliable… ' He spread his hands and shrugged.

'As a reward for what?' Gemma snapped. 'For involving us in her chaotic life?'

I sat up and took a gulp of the ice cold water. 'I didn't involve anyone in anything,' I pleaded. 'Whoever killed my mother started that ball rolling. Whoever decided to check my credentials with my mother – *my mother* – and upset her so badly, involved Sharpe-Harding Associates. Not me.'

'You have talked about us,' Pasqual said.

'You *showed* yourself,' I protested. 'You stood outside my

window and everyone saw you. Of course I talked about you – you're beautiful.'

'No more beautiful than I am,' Gemma muttered.

'Children!' Lazaro held up his hand. 'This is unbecoming. Seema, the unreliable, opinionated people who surround you with their petty dramas, render you unsuitable. You should not have spoken.'

'Why?' To my horror I was starting to cry. 'Why not? You're the most incredible thing that's ever happened to me. You never told me not to speak about it.'

'Did I not?' He stared intently at me. Then he held out his hand to Gemma. She placed a lace handkerchief between his fingers. He leaned forward and dried my eyes with it.

'Maybe this has gone too far,' he said, holding the handkerchief up so that Pasqual and Gemma could see the blood stain.

Silence followed. I couldn't read their faces. Were they disgusted? I snatched the handkerchief out of Lazaro's hand and crumpled it into my fist to hide the stain.

'I can't help it,' I stammered. 'I don't know what's happening to me.'

Three pairs of eyes regarded me coolly. They were beautiful eyes, but in my anxiety I could see no emotion in them at all.

'Please, please,' I whispered to Lazaro. 'Please don't turn me away. I'll do anything, but don't leave me.'

He was standing now. What was he waiting for? I could think of nothing else to say until I suddenly recalled those readings at school from the Book of Ruth: 'Entreat me not to leave thee or to return from following after thee.' I felt my lips begin to move as I mumbled Ruth's words. At school they were taught as examples of steadfast kindness: in my mouth they sounded utterly abject. I bit my lip hard to stop myself from speaking and tasted my own blood.

Suddenly Lazaro leaned forward and kissed me. I heard Gemma's harsh in-breath and a tsk sound from Pasqual. And then my mind become void, completely absent, while my whole being concentrated on the touch of his lips on mine.

A moment later his lips, still quite close to mine, said, 'My pipe, Pasqual, if you please.'

I waited, eyes closed, hardly daring to breathe. Far away, in a distant corner of my mind, Hannah's voice said, 'Opioids, Seema; not opium.' And I knew I should ask questions. But how could I ruin this perfect moment? My mistake about the Beaus had almost caused catastrophe. Lazaro was not to be questioned or disputed with. His kiss depended entirely on my silence and acquiescence. I knew that now. His kiss was more important than anything else in the world.

FOURTEEN

Lazaro and I walked hand in hand through a field of golden wheat. The grain was ripe and heavy. The leaves, stirring in a soft breeze, sounded as dry and husky as an old man's breath. They whispered secrets to us as we passed. The sun beat down as bright as spotlights and warmed our backs.

I opened my eyes and stared into light so bright it hurt. I was inside a bubble of light. I thought, 'Have I died?' I closed my eyes but I could still see the light glowing crimson through my eyelids. My body felt languorous and at peace. I wanted to turn over and go back to sleep but a voice said, 'Seema, wake up now and pay attention.'

I thought it was Lazaro's voice so I opened my eyes and squinted into the light. I couldn't see him.

What I saw was Mark Kirkby sitting on a steel and leather Bauhaus chair. He was shirtless and his tattoos shone out like pictures in an exhibition. 'The Kuniyoshi exhibition,' I said, smiling at him sleepily. 'At the Royal Academy. Bauhaus furniture and Japanese print making – not a happy couple.'

Someone laughed. I turned my head but couldn't see anyone else. The laughing voice said, 'Well, we can all tell which one's yours, old boy.' There was more laughter.

Cautiously I checked my own clothing. I was still wearing the white lounging pyjamas and fittingly, I was lounging comfortably in a sofa on a sable rug.

Mark turned his head towards me and said, 'It's just skin art, Seema. Don't worry about it.'

But I did. I imagined him at the age of eighty-four with his skin hanging off him like a badly fitting cardigan, his glorious tattoos dangling from his bones as limp as wet laundry.

While I was thinking this Mark morphed into just such an old man. I wanted to cry.

Somewhere, outside the bubble of light that held Mark and me, words and whispers danced together, rising and falling. Then someone called, 'Silence', and all noise died.

A woman strode into our bubble without being invited and stood with her back to us. She was wearing a black satin robe. She raised her arms and said, 'We all know why we're here.'

I was offended. I said, 'I don't know. Do you, Mark?' I thought it was a fine time for an explanation.

'*Quiet!*' the woman barked. 'On my left is Mark Kirkby, a professional sportsman, supremely fit and at the pinnacle of a career as a popular, successful rugby football player. Degree of difficulty has been set at 5.4, ten posing the greatest difficulty and zero denoting no difficulty at all. Take a bow, Mark.'

Mark got up looking mildly puzzled. He bowed to left and right. Enthusiastic applause greeted him. I clapped my hands too, not wanting to be left out. I was glad to see he'd resumed his former god-like shape. As he sat back down he said, 'I don't really understand this, Seema, but I think it's some sort of game.'

'You win,' I said, 'I don't know any games.'

'On my right,' the woman said, as if I hadn't even spoken, which I thought was rude of her. I suddenly realised that she was Lesley Sharpe.

'Hello,' I said. 'We've met, haven't we?'

'On my right,' Lesley Sharpe repeated not very patiently, 'Is Seema Dahami, a gardener. Although she is a Mizrahi Jew by birth she is an atheist and a vegetarian. Degree of difficulty 8.7.

Stand up, Seema, and see if you can bow without falling flat on your face.'

I stood up. It was true that my legs wobbled and I felt light-headed so I just bobbed my head to left and right and then flopped down again. The applause was not enthusiastic.

'If it's a popularity contest you're ahead already,' I told Mark cheerfully. 'I lack charisma.'

'Don't put yourself down,' Mark whispered. This was kind of him because I could tell he agreed with me.

Lesley Sharpe said, 'I know most of you have been avidly following events on your devices, but let's just remind ourselves of the highlights.'

Suddenly the protective wall of light dimmed and vanished. To my horror I saw that it had been hiding a sea of pale faces staring at me. Hundreds of people, comfortably seated in an auditorium, were all looking expectantly in my direction. I've had nightmares like this, I thought, woozily. I pinched the back of my left hand. It hurt. I turned in panic to ask Mark what to do but saw that he was craning his neck to see a giant wall-mounted screen behind us.

A title, 'Death or Glory' came on the screen. There was music – phase music for two pianos. I felt a lurch of disorientation in my stomach, a little like sea-sickness. Phase music has this effect on me, I don't know why.

Maybe death and glory were out of sync too. I didn't like that idea much. I twisted round in my seat so that my back was to the audience and I could watch the screen more comfortably. Although I was pretty sure I wasn't still dreaming none of it felt quite real.

The first scene was a slow-mo shot of Mark leaping at full stretch, catching a lozenge-shaped ball one-handed, bringing it down to his other hand, side-stepping an enormous enemy and dropping the ball onto his right toe. The kick was sublime, the follow-through was perfect. The arc of the ball was high and beautifully curved. Even though he had taken the catch close to the sideline and a long way from the goal the ball flew end over end between the two white posts. A loud roar erupted from the crowd in the stadium. Mark, in the scarlet and gold colours of the Scorpions, ran towards his team-mates and modestly accepted their congratulations.

'Yes,' I said. 'That's what glory looks like.'

The scene ended with a close-up of his face, mud-spattered but with a smile of triumph which a gum shield left unspoiled. His blue eyes were the eyes of a warrior, blazing with excitement. Even ballet couldn't equal his catch and kick for muscular, masculine grace. The crowd's roar and Mark's face faded. The two pianos began their queasy oppositional patterns.

The next scene began with a woman wrestling a bag of compost up a ladder to a small ornamental balcony about four metres above the pavement. She was wearing jeans and a large red t-shirt. I thought sympathetically, 'With an arse like that, she wouldn't want to be videoed from behind.' The sound track featured the woman's heavy breath. 'Well, so what?' I thought. 'Lugging a full-sized bag of compost up to a first story window isn't exactly a walk in the park.'

Another, older woman strolled into the frame. She had a bulging supermarket bag in one hand and a dog's lead in the other. The lead was attached to a roly-poly pug who was pulling the woman's arm out of its socket. The woman walked one side of the ladder; the pug walked on the other.

'Luna!' called the woman. The pug took no notice. The woman jerked the lead. The lead caught in the ladder. The ladder began to topple. The woman on the ladder tried to steady it. She let go of the compost. The compost started to topple.

'Oh crap!' I cried shutting my eyes tight. Because I knew exactly what happened to the compost, I knew what happened to the pug and I knew how badly the woman in the red t-shirt hurt herself when she hit the ground. I knew all this before I fully understood that the woman with the large-ish backside and red t-shirt was me.

At least it wasn't manure, I muttered to myself. Then I vaulted over the back of the sofa and sat on the floor out of sight of an audience that seemed to have collapsed with laughter. I had a moment to notice that the sophisticated Palatine Estate audience had very crude taste in comedy before two of the servers hustled on stage and wrecked my hiding place by the simple expedient of removing the sofa.

I looked up at the screen again just in time to see the word: 'However… ' before it disappeared. Then there was a montage of still photographs of the pretty little balcony. We watched the plants grow until the sequence ended with a sustained shot of white clematis and dog roses interspersed with ferns and dark green ivy trailing over and woven through the ironwork in a lush curtain which stirred in a light wind making an ever changing tapestry. The laughter died away and a smattering of applause broke out.

I was not mollified. Yes, it had been a very successful piece of work but I'd begun it nearly a year ago. These were not clips taken from TV sports coverage. This was invasion of privacy. Someone had been filming me secretly for months.

I looked around. Where was Lazaro? How could he let this happen to me?

I couldn't see him anywhere. So I looked to Mark for support but he was now absorbed in images of himself and Cat-Lynne in a health food shop, browsing the aisles, filling their basket, paying at the check out. The commentary track told us that here was a couple obsessed by physical fitness and willing to pay handsomely for the supplements they felt necessary for their continued superiority. But as the sequence ended, Mark's credit card statement appeared on screen with everything he'd spent in the shop that month highlighted. The total was staggering.

That *did* get a reaction from Mark. He stood up suddenly and said, '*Hey!* That's private banking information. You've no right to it. It's *illegal!*'

This was greeted by an outbreak of sniggering. Mark peered into the crowd, astonished. On this occasion the audience was against him and he didn't seem to know what to do about it. For a moment I felt sorry for him: it's hard for popular, beautiful people to accept that they too might be subject to ridicule. It's so much easier to bear when you're more used to it.

Which was just as well because it seemed as if all the information on my phone had been captured, including the music, and there followed a series of short clips of me wearing my earphones when I couldn't seem to prevent myself from dancing. There I was, jigging around in an embarrassing way to David Bowie, Nina Simone, Adele or Beyoncé. It was always in inappropriate places like check-out queues, the garden centre or the post office. There was one shameful occasion when I bopped in place to Leonard Cohen singing 'Closing Time' when I got bored at a distant cousin's funeral in a Gants Hill synagogue. I love to dance but on this evidence I wasn't very good at it.

By contrast the shots of Mark and Cat-Lynne at night clubs were very cool and elegant. They never made a show of themselves. Always beautifully dressed, always the object of envious scrutiny and photographers, they moved like trained dancers. It was noticeable that neither one of them drank alcohol – which might've been responsible for their invincible dignity in public.

Amy and I at a hen night in North Finchley, on the other hand, presented quite the opposite impression.

As the assortment of candid shots of our lives progressed, Mark's and my circles were introduced too. Cat-Lynne was Mark's fiancée. His 'close' friends were about ten of his team-mates and two old girlfriends. His family was his mother who lived with a brother in a small manor house near Cirencester and his father who lived in Northampton with a second wife.

My so-called 'circle' was much smaller. There were my 'best

friend' Amy and my 'boyfriend' Jacob. Mr Lewin and Mr Sorkin were 'friends and important clients'.

Then there was Hannah. The video was of us coming out of a small art-house cinema having watched an afternoon showing of a Japanese movie. We went to a café and sat outside in the sun discussing what we'd seen. The conversation concentrated on the father-figure in the film. Then, to my dismay, the commentary voice informed the audience that Hannah was my 'much loved and respected mother'. He was ignoring the disparity in our ages. Hannah was wonderful, but she looked a lot more like my grandmother than my mother.

It hit me with awful clarity that if someone had meant to kill Hannah the film maker's research had contained a fatal flaw – fatal to my real mother, that is.

I leaped to my feet. *'Wrong, way wrong!'* I shouted. 'Whoever said "the wrong old woman died", stand up right now. How did anyone know that unless someone here had something to do with her death?'

The film paused, and suddenly the spotlights came on pinning me and my wildly gesticulating shadow like a dying cockroach to the blank screen. Lesley Sharpe approached me from the side of the stage. She put her hands on my shoulders and with surprising strength pushed me down so that I was sitting cross legged on the floor. 'Shut up, you stupid bitch,' she hissed.

She turned to the audience and said, 'Perhaps this is the right time for a change to the planned programme. Because of course, as some of you already know, a mistake was made by surveillance operatives which altered considerably the course of events which followed. We…'

I scrambled to my feet. 'This is outrageous,' I said. 'What the hell's going on?'

She shoved me out of the way with such force that I staggered backwards almost knocking Mark over. 'Mark!' I shouted. 'I think someone here murdered my mother. We've got to get out *now!'*

When he didn't move, I said, 'What's the matter? At very least they've been stalking you and your woman too.'

'Well no, they weren't,' he said. 'I knew all about it. They're making a TV documentary about me. You know – the build-up to me finishing the Tuareg Trek Trial. Mr Harding's company is sponsoring me.'

'And your credit card statement? Did you give them permission to show everyone that?'

'Well no…'

'So how did they get hold of it?' I shook his shoulder, but still he didn't get up. 'Let's *go!*' I was pleading. 'This stinks. I know you think it's okay, but it isn't.'

'Restraint!' called Lesley Sharpe. 'Would the sponsors please exercise some control over their contestants.'

There seemed to be some sort of commotion in the crowd which I couldn't see because of the spotlights in my eyes. I grabbed Mark's hand, intending to drag him to his feet and jump off the stage with him, but just then a thick black curtain dropped, cutting us off from the auditorium and the safety of a milling crowd. To either side of us I could see servers gathering in the wings. Garth Harding was pushing his way through.

'Come on!' I shouted to Mark. 'Maybe we can shove through the curtain.' I was gripping his hand as if it were the edge of a life boat.

He leaned towards me and whispered hurriedly, 'Don't tell them I had anything to do with stealing the dogs.'

'You're frightened too,' I yelled at him. 'I *know* you are. *Come on!*'

Garth Harding reached us and said, 'So much fuss! Come, Mark, this has nothing to do with you.'

Why hadn't Lazaro come to find me? Where was he?

Mark patted my hand and detached it from his own. 'It's alright, Seema,' he said. 'You'll see. Everything's okay.' He turned and followed Garth Harding into the wings.

'Where's Lazaro?' I shouted after him. But now I was surrounded by several of the servers who, politely but inexorably, ushered me offstage. One against half a dozen – I didn't resist. There was no point.

I was taken, by what looked like a service lift, up to the suite of scarlet rooms where I'd last seen Lazaro. Why hadn't he come to fetch me the way Mr Harding came for Mark?

I was so disoriented I didn't even know how many levels below the red suite the reception rooms were, and how many levels below that the auditorium was. And where was ground level?

'Is this an underground mansion?' I asked stupidly. No one answered. The only one I recognised was the woman with sly eyes who'd given me champagne – how long ago?

'What's the time,' I asked her. She just smiled a knowing smile and said nothing.

'You drugged me,' I told her. I didn't need an answer; I was stating it as a fact. 'If you don't let me go this will be kidnap.'

'Don't blame them,' Gemma said, appearing in the doorway.

I rounded on her, 'Where's Lazaro?'

'He's trying to repair the damage you've done to him and his standing in the community,' she said icily. 'You told him you'd do anything for him, but all you've done is humiliate him.'

'What the fuck are you talking about?' I was gobsmacked. 'Who's been humiliated? Where were you five minutes ago? Didn't you see what they did to me? You set me up. You spied on me...'

'I thought you trusted me,' Lazaro said, coming in quietly behind Gemma. 'I hoped a bond was growing between us.' He stood like a prince, taller than everyone else in the room. His presence, his authority, was overwhelming. I felt my viscera stirring and I suddenly understood the literal meaning of the phrase 'my heart melted'. I covered my face with my hands.

'Leave the room,' he said. And to my amazement I realised he didn't mean me. All the servers, even Gemma, disappeared.

He gestured to me to sit and when I did he pulled a straight chair close to mine.

His hair was as snowy as his shirt. I wanted to touch it but I didn't dare. His tanned skin was as smooth as silk. The fine lines on his forehead and around his eyes and mouth emphasised his beauty rather than detracted from it. I wanted to stroke his face but I didn't dare. His fingers were long, his hands strong. I wanted to hold them but I didn't dare. I was trembling and I was afraid he could smell my sweat. He smelled of nothing at all.

He leaned forward and with one finger touched the corner of my eyebrow and ran the finger down my face to my chin. He said, 'My dear, there are so many things I cannot tell you. But you must realise that there is a power struggle. You have become enmeshed in it because…'

He paused for so long that I said, 'Because?'

He sighed. 'Because,' he continued reluctantly, 'my enemies have become aware that you are precious to me.'

I thought I was going to faint. If I hadn't already been sitting I would have fallen. Falteringly I asked, 'Are you in danger?'

He hesitated and then nodded.

'What can I do to help?'

He smiled sadly then, and took my hand. 'I wish *I* could help *you*,' he said. 'I wish I could encourage you to display your full talent and potential. But…' He paused again. 'But all I can do until the situation is resolved is to ask you to trust me.'

'I *do* trust you,' I whispered. 'But I don't trust *them*.' I gestured to the hostile world outside the red room, the safe warm cocoon that contained only Lazaro and me.

'Rightly so,' he began, but I rushed on, 'They've been spying on me for nearly a year. A *year*, Lazaro. And that awful woman virtually admitted that someone here killed my mother, mistaking her for Hannah. And I think someone's tampered with your opium – the blood test at the hospital showed opioids.'

He took my hand in both his and his touch at once soothed

and excited me. 'If you care at all for your safety,' he said softly but urgently, 'these are subjects upon which you *must* remain silent – for tonight. Your life is in the balance.'

'I don't care about *my* life,' I exclaimed impatiently.

'What a glorious capacity for love you possess.' He stroked my hand. 'But I cannot ask you to die for me.'

'But I would,' I told him, astonished at myself and the revelation that I had at last found the true purpose of my life.

'You would?' He stared so deeply into my eyes I was sure he could see straight into my heart. We remained still and silent like that for several minutes. I felt completely happy. I was without any doubts whatsoever. Then he took the crescent moon ring off his own hand and put it on the fourth finger of my left hand. It was too big so he replaced it on my middle finger.

I stared at it, overwhelmed. 'It's too much,' I stammered.

'You would die for me,' he said simply. 'It's too little.'

'I'd much rather you gave me the Beaus,' I said before I could stop myself. 'I'm a gardener,' I explained hurriedly. 'My hands get scratched and dirty; my nails always look ragged and grimy. The ring belongs with you, it's part of a set.'

'Wear it tonight as my token,' he said, closing my hand around it. 'Are you serious about those damned dogs?'

'Yes,' I said. I couldn't explain.

But he said, 'Explain.'

I was stumped. I had angered him before, but he wasn't angry now. There was only one thing I could risk saying. 'Because they are beautiful,' I whispered.

He stared at me for a long moment before saying, 'Seema, you always manage to surprise me. Perhaps that is why I believe in you as an artist.' He got up and went to the door leaving me in a state of bliss.

'He believes in me as an artist,' I repeated to myself over and over again. It felt like the most powerful thing anyone had ever said to me.

Five minutes later Grigori came in without knocking. The Beaus pushed past him and ran to me, tipping me back into my chair. They stood on either side of me licking my face and neck. I put my arms around them and hugged them, kissing their ears, stroking their heads and muscular shoulders. All the while I was wondering why I could not love men with the same trust.

'You're a fool,' Grigori said. 'These damn dogs won't save you.'

'Who cares?' I replied, 'so long as I save them.'

His laughter was hoarse and cynical. 'Better stick them in the other room,' he said, 'if you want Mister High-and-mighty's company. Still, you're doing me a favour – I can't stand the fucking animals either.'

'Give me their leads, collars, especially those electronic ones, and their water bowls.'

'Say please,' he ordered, standing squarely in front of us. 'I ain't your servant. I ain't no-fucking-one's servant. You think I am and it's just another thing you're fucking wrong about.'

'Please,' I said without looking at him. He turned his back on our joyous reunion and stamped out of the room.

When he came back it was only to dump a cardboard box on the sofa before saying, 'More fool you.' I suppose it was the wittiest exit line he could think of. But I said 'Thank you.' Manners matter, my mother would have insisted.

Grigori had given me choke chains, the torture collars plus the gismos that activated them, a vicious riding crop, two muzzles, two water bowls and a hairbrush. I took them into the bedroom. I filled the water bowls in the bathroom and left them on the floor. I would take the leashes, collars and riding crop with me when I left – not because I wanted them but because I didn't want Grigori to have them.

While the dogs lapped their water I made a tour of the bedroom. I was happy to find my bag and folder of drawings on the dressing table. My phone was in the bag but I couldn't find a signal. Probably the Red Suite was too deep underground.

163

'What will I do with you?' I asked the Beaus when they too had finished sniffing around their new quarters. I was remembering a time when I was eleven or twelve when I had taken every hurt animal I saw back home or to the school boarding house. Birds with broken legs or wings, cats too starved to walk, a half mangled hedgehog, a stray dog dragging a paralysed leg. I even fed sugar water to a bumblebee that had been trapped for days between two sheets of glass. It drove my mother and the school matron crazy. But my dad approved.

No, wait – he wasn't there. He died before that phase in my life began. It was Hannah who encouraged me. What did she say? Something like, 'We have stolen the Earth from all living creatures except ourselves. That makes us responsible for the well-being of the ones that are left and the ones that we only allow to live because they serve our selfish purposes. Surely it is an obligation.'

The Beaus suddenly became alert and the hair on their backs rose.

Lazaro said, 'Leave the dogs where they are and come with me.' He stood in the doorway of the suite. I took off my black velvet shawl and laid it on the bed so that they could sleep comfortably on fabric that smelled of me.

He said, 'You look like Artemis and her hunting dogs.' I smiled at him, thrilled by the compliment although I was sure it was bullshit. I never knew what he was thinking but I'd stake my entire bank balance against the notion that he really likened me to an Olympian goddess.

I left my bag and phone on the bed too. 'I'll be back,' I promised, but they came with me to the door as I followed Lazaro out of the suite.

'Stay,' I said, laying my hands on each dog's head. They sat, smiling at me the way no human ever can. They were magical dogs. I wondered vaguely why I was following a man.

But when we were out of sight of the dogs he paused and took my hand. We turned into a small anteroom where Gemma and

Pasqual were waiting for us. We sat in a circle, our knees almost touching.

Lazaro said, 'There isn't much time to prepare you for what's about to happen. I'm so sorry but events have overtaken us. The film has begun again as you will see. I know you will find it painful, and I grieve for you. Please remember that this was done without my participation. But if you and I are to survive this night you must endure whatever happens in silence and with dignity. Do you think you can do that?'

'What's going to happen?' I asked, my stomach clenching with fear.

'If we knew that,' Pasqual said urgently, 'of course we would have prepared you.'

Gemma said, 'She isn't strong enough. Surely there's still time for all of us to escape. How can we put your safety, your very life, sir, on the line with only a woman as ignorant and unreliable as Seema to defend you?'

For an answer he held my left hand up so that she and Pasqual could see the ring. 'We are pledged,' he said. 'She believes in love. There is no other way.'

The three of them exchanged significant glances. But I did not feel excluded. Lazaro was holding my hand. His ring was on my finger. I felt almost complete.

I also felt about twelve years old; not like a woman in her mid twenties who had been disappointed by love at least three times already, and who had just lost a not very satisfactory boyfriend to her best friend. A classic Everly Brothers' line flitted through my head: 'I've been cheated, been mistreated, when will I be loved?'

I said, almost to myself, 'I just wanted to make a garden, why has this become a life and death struggle?'

'You're lying to yourself,' Pasqual said. 'You were looking for love and an end to boredom – a far more dangerous occupation.'

'Stop.' Lazaro held his hand up. 'She has found love. It is enough.'

'This isn't normal,' I said. 'This is an Alice in Wonderland world.'

'You *wish*.' Gemma muttered. 'Give her another pipe, sir.'

'She has reached her limit.' His hand on mine was warm and steady. He said, 'She knows we are unusual. She is sensitive – she will open her mind to me even if I am not beside her. We've already tested this. We will succeed.'

'What do you mean, you won't be beside me?' I asked, suddenly terrified. 'What's going to happen? What will I have to do?'

Lazaro gathered me into his arms and onto his lap as if I were a small child. He surrounded me. I was warm, I was safe, I was loved. He said, 'You will watch and listen to painful material – some of it true, some of it lies. You will watch and endure in silence. You must not fight or protest. Simply accept, knowing that my future depends upon your silent acceptance. You will be tested. When that happens open your mind to me, listen to my feelings. My ring, *our* ring, will give you strength. Deep inside, Seema, you will know what is right, and you will do what is best. I trust you, my dearest.' His kiss on my forehead was a blessing.

The inner door opened and Lesley Sharpe appeared, tall and straight in a black suit. A black robe was draped across her shoulders. The robe looked as if it had once belonged to a high court judge. Lazaro squeezed my hand and I stifled a sound that wanted to become a nervous giggle.

'As you have wasted so much time,' Ms Sharpe began without preamble, fixing her steely eyes on Lazaro, 'we have proceeded without you. And I have to warn you that you have lost a lot of credit. This one… ' she jerked an insulting thumb in my direction, 'is only still in the running because of mistakes deemed to be not of your making and, obviously, her 8.7 DD rating. Of course we all appreciate your famous sense of humour, but please do not turn this affair into a farce.'

'How sodding pompous,' I thought. But a last, light pressure from Lazaro's fingers informed me, as loud as spoken words, 'This woman is dangerous.' And indeed her eyes, as they rested on me, were as old, cold and ferocious as a Siberian tiger's.

I turned to look at Lazaro, but at that moment he released my hand and stepped back into the anteroom. I was alone with Lesley Sharpe.

FIFTEEN

It was a television studio set up for a live studio audience – not anywhere near as big as the previous auditorium.

The stage was in front of a curved screen on which, at the moment, was a rolling, roiling seascape. In front of the stage were what seemed to be half a dozen remote robot cameras. Flying above everything were what at first I took to be black dragonflies but which, as I swatted one away from my face, turned out to be drones.

The audience was ranged in a semicircle above the stage, and behind the seating was a control booth.

Set in the centre of the stage was a single strange looking chair. Lesley Sharpe said, 'Sit down, shut up and behave yourself.'

I looked at the single weird chair and said, 'Where's Mark?'

She said, 'Is "shut up" too difficult for you? Be quiet.'

A few giggles spread around the small audience. I guessed that there weren't many more than fifty– far fewer than in the big auditorium.

'From now on,' Ms Sharpe intoned, 'credits will be deducted for disobedience, non-cooperation or any sign of recalcitrance.'

It was on the tip of my tongue to say, 'What credits? No one told me about credits.' But just in time I remembered that Lazaro's safety depended on my silence and endurance. I walked to the chair trying to ignore the audience.

The thing I was supposed to sit on was a hybrid between an

airline seat and a dentist's chair. It could be tipped and swivelled but, apparently, not by me. On the left was a monitor screen. On the right arm was an array of coloured buttons, a joystick, a slide control and some other gizmos that I associated with the more sophisticated game consoles Jake was obsessive about.

I climbed into the chair which turned out to be surprisingly comfortable.

But as soon as I sat down the leg rest shot up and the backrest subsided. The whole seat tipped so that I was lying straight at an angle of forty-five degrees to the ground. I forced myself to lie still. A few murmurs of disappointment came from the audience. Perhaps some of them enjoyed 'recalcitrance'.

The monitor screen went blank. When it flicked into life again there was a split screen. One half showed Mark sitting alert in a comfortable chair; the other showed me lying stiffly as if waiting with great apprehension for root canal work. Momentarily a set of figures was superimposed over the two pictures. I didn't have time to take in more than that Mark had an AR of 76 and I had AR 23. AR, I guessed, meant Approval Rating. Whatever: Mark had lots more than I did. I was not astonished.

Then, out of nowhere a cultured male voice asked, 'In the past hour, other than champagne, have you ingested by mouth or by needle any drug or intoxicant? Press the green button for no; press the red button for yes.'

I could not remember exact times. I didn't know how long I'd been underground or how long it'd been since I'd passed out in the lift. There wasn't a button for 'don't know'. But as it's usually safer *not* to admit to being stoned I pressed the green button.

The voice continued: 'Place the middle finger of your right hand on the white button and keep it depressed until told to release it.'

I pressed the white button remembering Lazaro's voice when he said, 'Endure.' Simultaneously there was a sharp pain in my finger. It felt as if a needle had been inserted for a few seconds and then withdrawn. At the same time I heard the whirr of the robots approaching and one of the dragonfly drones hovered close to my face.

I suppressed my squeak of shock and pain and kept my expression as neutral as I possibly could.

On his side of the split screen Mark was watching his monitor intently. Was he watching me, I wondered; was Lazaro? How did Mark feel about bringing me to this reception and finding himself the object of such alarming attention? Had he sussed by now that we were pitted against each other in an unexplained competition?

He told me that his super-fit fiancée was sick and he'd chosen me as his plus one because... Why had he chosen me to be his plus one? However unlikely his reason had been, I hadn't questioned it. It was my chance to see Lazaro again and I'd grabbed it with both hands.

I looked at his handsome face on the monitor and it seemed as if he was staring back at me. I ventured a small smile. He hesitated and then smiled back. The smile warmed me, but the hesitation made me think, 'This was a set-up. I wasn't supposed to come. Lazaro didn't invite me – he was protecting me. Garth Handing told Mark to bring me. He's playing dirty. He's used me to hijack Lazaro, and I fell into the trap.'

This was my fault. I was a fool. I'd put him in danger. What should I do now?

The silent answer came: 'Do nothing. Be quiet. Accept.'

But was it my thought or was it Lazaro's? Women are always being asked for silence and acceptance, I argued, and any feminist worth her salt would resist. So it couldn't be my thought. And Lazaro was better than that. So it must have been someone else. Suppose the needle in my finger had delivered a drug to dampen my will?

Any urge to protest was interrupted by the male voice saying, 'Analysis complete.' An attractive bespectacled face appeared on the monitor. He was wearing a white coat and was reading from a hand-held device. 'The subject tested borderline adequate for opiates and stimulants. Blood iron and stored iron are at low but tolerable levels. Interestingly she has a rather rare blood protein that protects against both thalassaemia and sickle cell.'

A murmur of surprise went round the crowd.

Lesley Sharpe's face replaced the scientist's on the screen. She said, 'Which means, just let me check, yes, five credits have been restored to this account.' The result did not make her look any less threatening, but a ripple of applause went round the audience. I felt quite proud.

Mark gave a thumbs-up sign. Who to? Me? Or was he trying to prove to the audience what a gallant sportsman he was? I couldn't help noticing that a flash card on the screen showed that his AR had risen to 79.

What the hell did it mean? What on earth was going on? My vow of silence meant that I couldn't ask. I had to take whatever happened on trust. Lazaro's safety depended on it. I had to take that fact on trust too.

The picture on the screen changed to show a greenish image taken with an infrared camera. It was a fuzzy me hoeing the guerrilla traffic circle garden – one of my night time excursions with Jake. And there he was, leaning on a spade, talking. It hadn't occurred to me until now how much he talked and how little he worked.

The next shot was of the circular garden at its riotous best. It was, that year, a cunning mixture of flowers and vegetables. The border for instance had been alternating dwarf French beans, marigolds and strawberries. Local people had risked injury when crossing the main road to share the harvest. The commentary track explained this. My AR rose to 31.

In the end the locals wrecked the garden. They dug up the potatoes and there was evidence that there had been at least one fight about it. They left garden waste to litter the roadside; they tore through sweet peas and trampled whatever couldn't be taken home. I was quite pleased about this – I'd always wanted to involve local people, especially children. But I hadn't meant to cause conflict. This year I was planning something purely decorative – a traffic island so lovely no one would want to disturb a single living blossom.

I was thinking about white poppies so I almost missed the commentary: '... subversive as a gardener, she's happy to keep a secret, to enjoy the joke of being in the know and getting away with it. But in other areas of her life – her relationships for instance? No, that's quite a different story. She's wilfully gullible and laughably easy to fool. She seems to expect honesty and loyalty as her due, even from a man she does not love. Let me explain the "He'll Do For" game Seema and Amy have played together from the time they started dating.'

'Oh no, no, no...' I began before covering my mouth with my hand. Because there on the screen was the form Amy and I had devised over ten years ago. It was the version we both kept on our mobile phones. Clearly some vicious hacking had taken place.

The heading read, 'He'll Do For – A Monthly Update and Reminder.' Underneath in a smaller font was a list that went: 'A: He'll do for an hour if he buys the drinks and brings his own condom, B: all night if it's not at his parents' house and he brings his own condoms, C: a holiday. He pays and brings his own condoms, D: he'll do for now cos I'm too busy to go on the pull, E: he's replaced the previous one who'll do for now, F: forever.

Jake was ticked off under D and had not been upgraded for all the time I'd been with him. My AR plummeted to 22. I was mortified. How could Amy and I have continued with such a cold-hearted teenage game? A habit of friendship? No, there wasn't a valid excuse.

But it was something only Amy and I were supposed to know about. It had been a 'Cross your heart, cross your legs, never tell unless he begs,' oath.

I would've bet my future on the fact that Amy had told Jake all about it.

But was the commentator right? Had I expected more from Jake than I was prepared to give? Well, no, actually. However adolescent and hard-hearted the He'll Do For list looked, I hadn't bonked his best friend. Since starting with Jake there had been only Jake – except very recently and only in my dreams of course. Is treachery something you can be guilty of in your dreams even if your actions are blameless? I know what my mother's rabbi would say.

Meanwhile, on the screen, as a contrast to my juvenile cruelty, Mark and Cat-Lynne were walking hand in hand on a beach. Coming towards them was a joyous quartet of young women who looked the way only Brazilian beauties on a beach can look. Mark's eyes never even flickered away from Cat-Lynne's face.

His AR shot up to 82. There must've been a lot of women in the audience.

Then the screen bleached out, the lights changed and Lesley Sharpe and her two acolytes marched onto the stage under a brilliant spot. She held up her arms and said, 'This completes the introductory phase of the proceedings. You now understand the disparity which, at first glance, may seem insurmountable. This, of course has, to some extent, answered your many questions about the difference in Degree of Difficulty and what I'm sure must have appeared to some of you as sheer hubris.

'Still, as I'm sure you'll agree, this is what makes these bids for dominance such riveting entertainment for us all and well worth the time and expense.

'Now we come to the second phase of the experiment – the Demonstration of Impact by each aspirant on the developmental behaviour of his candidate. In order to minimise undue influence over later actions, the contestants will not witness the success or failure of his or her opponent.

'So, for the moment, goodbye Mark and Seema.'

The bleached screen vanished and the stormy sea took its place. I was just about to turn to see what the audience was being shown when, with a soft whirr and a pop, something emerged from the headrest of my hybrid chair. It clamped around my forehead so that I couldn't move my head. I let out a yelp of protest. Almost simultaneously restraints captured my wrists. I kicked out and managed to save one ankle. The other was fastened to the footrest. The chair flattened out. I was as stuck and helpless as sticky-tape to a parcel, except for one flailing leg.

'Is this what I'm supposed to endure?' I shrieked to unseen Lazaro. 'What sort of game is this?'

In reply, three thoughts converged on my panicking brain: my mother said, 'Just for once in your life, Seema do *what* you're told *when* you're told.'

Hannah said, 'A game of dominance and submission.'

Lazaro said, 'This has always been your decision... I am not forcing you one way or the other.'

The hopeless confusion I felt was resolved by the sly-eyed server who had given me the champagne. She emerged from the wings to push my chair – now virtually a hospital gurney – out of sight of the audience.

I didn't think it would do any good, but I kicked her, just because I could.

'Naughty, naughty,' she said, grinning and coming to the head end of the chair. She swung me round and pushed me, feet first, through thick black curtains and then towards a pair of swing doors. It took her three tries before she got me through them, partly because I used my free leg to impede progress where I could, and partly because she was having trouble keeping the gurney on course. We skittered from side to side, knocking into one wall, then another, of what looked like a service corridor.

'You're drunk,' I guessed.

'Am not,' she said, giggling. She took a sharp right. Almost immediately we came to a dead end. Rather than simply reversing she started to execute a three-point turn, which became a five-point turn until the gurney stuck fast, catty-cornered.

'You're either slaughtered or stoned,' I accused her.

'Well, only a bit,' she admitted. 'Why should the elders have all the fun?'

'What elders?' I struggled against the restraints. 'Can you sit me up a bit? I can't talk to you if I can't see you.'

'What's in it for me?' she asked, with only the smallest trace of a slur. I can't tell you how cheering it was to find even this tiny crack in the perfect façade of the Palatine Estate.

I said, 'Well, a chair is shorter than a bed. If this contraption was chair-shaped you could turn it round and we wouldn't be stuck.'

'Good point,' she said, and bobbed down out of sight.

I hoped she was examining the controls. I said, 'Who are you? Who are the elders?'

'I'm Kim,' she said from somewhere out of sight on the floor, 'As to the elders and all the other mysteries you're dying to ask me about – that's for me to know and you to find out.'

Then with a jolt the gurney folded into a right angle and I was left on my back with my legs stuck up in the air.

'Ow!' I yelled.

'Sorry,' she said, almost crying with laughter. 'I think I know what I did wrong.'

'Well, undo it,' I pleaded. 'This hurts.'

'Such is life, if that's what you want to call it,' she said. 'Suck it up.'

With another violent jolt I was suddenly sitting bolt upright, head clamped rigidly erect like a convicted murderer in the electric chair.

Kim scooted backwards and stood up, surveying me.

'Now,' she said, 'if you promise not to kick me I'll move behind you and push you out of here.'

'Where to?'

'I'm not supposed to tell you.'

'Then I can't promise not to kick you.'

She leaned against the wall glaring at me. Her boyishly slicked-back hair was coming unglued: a few ginger strands were sticking out. Her white shirt was now less than pristine, the knees of her trousers were dusty and the toes of her shoes were scuffed.

I smiled at her warmly. 'You look almost human,' I said.

'No need for insults,' she said looking disgusted. 'I hardly made the cut even as a lowly server and that was probably because it was such a huge Gather-in. You know, they've got nearly all of the Western Europe and East Coast North American honchos moshing around down here. All the Lords and Ladies and their favourites.'

'Who the hell are they?' I asked, desperate to know. 'Is it a TV or film company, or a secret society like, I dunno, the Rosicrucians?'

'And so *ad infinitum*,' she interrupted. She was laughing at me.

'Everyone in this sodding labyrinth thinks I'm a sodding joke,' I exploded. 'Even you.'

'Well you *are* a bit slow,' Kim said. 'I've just given you the biggest clue you'll ever get and you walked all over it.'

'Walked all over *what*?' I shouted.

Then I stopped shouting. I felt the beginning of the blinding head pain I'd come to fear so acutely, and the first drip from my nose. 'Oh shit,' I whispered resignedly – remembering too late Lazaro's request for silence and endurance. But surely he couldn't have foreseen the kind of duress I was under now? Besides it wasn't my fault that Kim was rat-arsed and disorderly.

'Oh, oh, oh,' Kim said urgently. 'I've got to get you where you've supposed to be.' She ignored my free leg and came to the back of the chair. She turned it easily and started off fast. In fact she almost ran for the first ten or so paces. Then she stopped just as suddenly. She came around to face me. I was horrified – her rather broad Slavic face had sharpened and paled to the colour of old bone.

'I can't help it,' she mumbled.

She leant in so close I could smell the booze on her breath. And she began to lick the blood from my nose and upper lip.

'They'll kill me,' she added, holding my cheeks like a lover.

I was revolted. But she kept licking and I couldn't stop her. She was standing beside me, leaning across, where my free foot couldn't reach to kick. All I could do was bend my leg up sharply to knee her in the ribs. She grunted and then with humiliating ease held my knee away from her body.

The world contracted. What remained was her tongue which was as rough as a cat's. I thought she was using it to scrape my skin away to expose all the blood vessels around my nose and mouth.

I couldn't move my head even an inch so I screamed straight into her mouth – as if my cries and my breath were filling her lungs like a perverted form of CPR. I arched my back and bucked, trying to jar her body away from mine.

At last she staggered back, swaying into the wall for support. She seemed exhausted, intoxicated and so terrified that she began to weep huge painful sobs. She whimpered, over and over, 'They'll break me.'

Her distress was so palpable that although I was furious with her and frightened of her, I was almost sorry for her. *And* I was beginning to sense the glimmer of an opportunity.

I said, 'I don't understand a thing, but don't you think we should move before they find us?'

'There's nowhere to go,' she sobbed.

'Yes there is,' I assured her. 'Get me out of this fricking chair and we'll go together.'

'You can't help me – you're too weak.'

'Don't you believe it,' I said in a powerful tone I had absolutely no belief in. 'Why do you think they had to restrain me like this?'

'You're a loose cannon. I heard them say so. "Ill-prepared,

ill-disciplined, culturally unpromising", at least that's what we heard.'

'Culturally what?'

'Maybe they said "unprepossessing". Don't ask me. They think your culture's ugly? Someone said, "This hasn't been tried since the Edict of Expulsion in 1492". Something like that. I don't understand.'

I said, 'Nor do I.' But of course I knew that the Edict of Expulsion was about Jews being kicked out of Spain. 'What hasn't been tried?' I persisted. 'What's happening here? It's a competition, isn't it? It feels like a reality show. And I'm the one set up for failure and humiliation. That's it, isn't it?'

Kim gave me the kind of look you give someone who doesn't know she has a fatal disease. She said, 'You really are an expert at missing the point, aren't you? I've committed the Forbidden Act. And I don't honestly know how that affects your status but I'm pretty sure it has destroyed mine.'

'Then get me out of this chair.'

She shook her head violently.

I said, '*You* may be dead woman walking, but I'm not, so for fuck's sake, *walk!*'

'There's nowhere to go.'

'Yes, there is. Get me out of this fucking chair and take me back to the Red Suite.'

'What's the point?' She was looking at me with hopeless eyes and something else I couldn't identify.

'Oh well, give up and die,' I said furiously. 'But don't take me down with you. I never volunteered to be your lollypop. And it's not my fault you have unspeakable habits. In fact it's hardly my fault I'm here at all. I keep telling all of you that I don't understand but no one listens.'

At last she crouched on the floor, out of sight behind me, and after an achingly long thirty seconds, the restraints silently retracted. I was free. I stood up and stretched my cramped neck.

'The Red Suite,' I urged her.

'Why there?'

'I have weapons.'

'You're *so* lying,' she said, with a trace of her old superior sneer. 'No outsider is ever admitted without a total electronic x-ray search.'

But she took my hand and led me back towards the thick black curtains and the place where she'd first taken the wrong direction. As we arrived a great clatter of applause rang out and Lesley Sharpe's voice intruded: 'An excellent result, I'm sure you'll all agree – centuries of prohibition defeated by a mere bacon cheeseburger.'

My heart plummeted. They knew about the cheeseburger. How was that possible? Someone or something had been following me for months, cataloguing all my failures. Who was doing this and why was Lazaro allowing it?

Kim tugged urgently on my hand. But as I turned to follow her Lesley Sharpe spoke up again: 'However, impetus was lost when we were brought to the attention of the Metropolitan Police – an unprecedented occurrence and a truly deplorable one. Retribution, of course, was swift and efficient.'

Kim chose this moment to drag me away with such force that I almost fell. 'What are they talking about?' I panted as I sprinted after her.

'You, dufus,' she hissed. 'Fucking hustle, can't you? I'm sure they'll have noticed by now that you aren't where you're supposed to be.'

'Who's they?'

'Security.'

So we ran, keeping to service corridors, always skirting public areas. It was like running around the edge of an underground shopping mall, a public place supported by a hidden structure of stairways and passages for goods and services. Or maybe it was an underground castle – all the stunning architecture and decor

179

reserved for the gentry while the dirty work was carried out, unseen, by an army of servants.

It was an army to be avoided. Kim was terrified of being seen. At the sound of a voice or a footstep we changed direction or hid behind a storeroom door, holding our breath and clutching the other's hand until the threat faded away. She knew, because she was one of them, that all the workers spied on each other – always looking for an advantage or a leg up on the promotion ladder. No one could be trusted.

At last, quite by accident, Kim found a door that concealed a flight of stone stairs. It was dark and dirty.

'Do we have to?' I shuddered.

'The Red Suite is three floors up,' she said, not looking any more eager than I felt. 'All the lifts are guarded. So, yes, we have to.'

Dirty was good, I decided. There were no footprints on the dusty floor so no one had used these stairs for a long time. Before I let Kim shut the door on us I found an ancient black Bakelite switch which actually sparked when I flicked it on. I jumped back, but to my astonishment a dim light bulb lit the empty landing above us.

Below us was dense darkness. 'What's down there?' I pointed.

'I don't know.' She sounded uneasy.

We pulled the door shut behind us and started cautiously up. There seemed to be a weird indoor-swimming pool echo. But what made the hair on my neck prickle was the smell. It was of chlorine, burned plastic and the sort of armpit odour you get if you iron a shirt without washing it first. It had a material quality that seemed to coat the inside of my nose and lungs. I searched the floor for rodent droppings but there were none. I would've preferred the signs of rats to the echoing silence and the smell of no living thing.

We were the rats; we scurried up to the first landing – twenty steps. Then another twenty to a door like the one we'd entered. This one – I could just see from the dim light below – had a key in the lock. I turned it, locking us in and the hunters out.

Then I pulled the key out of the lock and ran down to see if I could lock the first door too. I could and I did. But halfway up to the next floor I began to wonder if the first door had been left unlocked for a reason. The organisers of the Palatine Estate seemed to be plotters and planners. They weren't prone to human error. Except... My mother's murder. Lesley Sharpe announced publicly that it had been a mistake. What did she mean by 'a usually reliable operative?' A hit man? Or woman?

I came to an abrupt halt and Kim barged into me.

'That can't be true,' I said out loud. 'She can't have meant that.'

'What?' Kim stepped around me wanting to take the lead.

I'd already had thoughts about my own dreamlike voice chanting from the basement of my mind, 'The wrong old woman died.' But wasn't that shame speaking – the guilt I felt for sometimes wishing I'd never have to see or hear my mother burning a hole in my brain again. Or was it my fears for Hannah's safety? Real? Paranoid?

But my fears for my own safety were galloping like riderless horses in all directions. What if the open door was a trap?

'Did you know about this stairway?' I put my hand on Kim's arm to restrain her. Was she friend or enemy?

'No,' she said. 'But this site has been here for ages. I've been told it was excavated during one of the wars as an underground bomb shelter. I've even heard there is a secret tunnel to the garden at Buckingham Palace.'

We came to another locked door. And to my relief, another Bakelite switch. The darkness and the rusty chemical smell were pressing against my face like a stocking mask.

I said, 'You seem to have worked here quite often.'

She laughed. It was a bitter, echoey laugh. 'You've no bloody idea at all, have you?'

'What?' I said. 'What don't I know? Who are you?'

'I haven't got time to explain,' she said, her voice strained thin with fear. 'I am one of the larvae, a worm who's turned against the Lords and Ladies. At least that's how they'll see it.'

She started up the next flight of twenty concrete steps to the next landing that flickered in and out of existence, a victim of damp or ancient wiring. I followed, saying, 'I don't understand you. I'm trusting you with my life...'

'And I'm trusting you with mine,' she interrupted. 'You'd better not have lied to me. You'd better have weapons. If you let me down, remember, I'm way stronger than you.' She was taking the stairs two at a time without puffing or sweating.

I couldn't keep up. 'Wait,' I gasped. But she was so far ahead she didn't hear me. I trudged on, thighs and calves burning. I tried to do the maths – forty steps between each of the doors for three floors – one hundred and twenty steps up, steep steps in a toxic atmosphere. I was almost fainting by the time I found her waiting impatiently, leaning against the last locked door.

'Shut up with the heavy breathing,' she snapped. 'I'm listening.' She pressed her ear against the door.

I sat on the top step and sagged against the wall seeing red wriggling things behind my closed eyelids. I tried to control my breath. I was listening too. There was the ominous echo, as if we were trapped in a concrete drum, but I couldn't hear any sound of pursuit from below. Did that mean they, whoever 'they' were, would be waiting for us when I opened the door?

At last Kim said, 'I can't hear anything.'

I said, 'How far down is the Red Suite from the ground floor?'

'You think they let us in by the front door like guests? I've never even been up to the Red Suite before today. I'm a kitchen worm usually.'

'Stop calling yourself a worm,' I said. 'Have some self-respect.'

'Shut up.' She'd stiffened. Far below us I heard a muffled clang of metal on metal.

'That's not good,' I said. I crossed my fingers, slotted the big key in the lock and tried to turn it. It stuck.

Kim elbowed me aside with such force that I nearly fell backward, down the stairs. She snatched the key out of the lock, re-inserted it, applied much more force them I had, and then with a groan like a dying monster it turned. The sound reverberated round the empty stairwell, terrifyingly loud. Kim and I froze.

During the next heart-stopping seconds I heard Lazaro's voice in my head. He called my name and said 'Where are you?' And I remembered with horror his requests of me, my promise to him, and now my absolute failure to comply.

SIXTEEN

There was nothing I could do except say out loud, 'I'm coming.'

Kim clamped her hand over my mouth. She was listening intently. I hoped her hearing was better than mine – all I could hear was the rasp of my breath, the beating of my own heart, and a sort of tinnitus-like sound of streaming blood which resolved into a hissing anger directed at me.

I raised one arm to press my lovely white sleeve to my nose trying to staunch the newly dripping blood.

Not noticing, Kim opened the door a crack. The corridor was empty. She caught my arm and dragged me out into a plain cream service corridor and blissful air that smelled of nothing. My mind began to clear and I paused to remove the key from inside the door and lock it from the outside.

'Now where?' I whispered.

'I don't fucking know,' she mouthed back at me. And then stopped dead.

'Don't you sodding touch me,' I warned, because now that we were out of the dark and toxic atmosphere of the stairwell and she could see my blood, her face was taking on a carnivorous, hungry look.

'Back off!' I said, stepping away. 'You look like a hyena.'

'I can't help it,' she said.

'Yes you can.' I turned and marched off. I couldn't explain it but I was sure I hadn't picked the direction I'd taken randomly.

'Are we allies or are we not? Because I swear, if you start licking my face again you're on your own. I liked you better as a worm,' I added meanly.

'Why are you going this way?' She sounded uncharacteristically humble.

'I'm not sure, but I think Lazaro's calling me.'

With incredible speed she overtook me and blocked my way, arms outstretched. 'Are you suicidal?' she screeched.

'Lazaro is in danger,' I said. 'I have to rescue him so that he can save me.'

'You are *subnormal*.'

She sounded so like my mother I could've knee-capped her. Instead, gathering certainty around me like a costume, I said, 'Lazaro is my only friend in this shit-hole.'

'Is it *brain damage*? Where are your eyes and ears? Where have you been? Lazaro isn't in danger. Lazaro is your nightmare.'

I glared at her. 'You couldn't be more wrong,' I said. 'Garth Harding set me up. I don't know why but… ' I didn't have time to finish. Kim flung a hand over my mouth. She pushed me down and rolled me over till I was flat on the floor against the corner of the wall. Then she was gone.

I lay there stunned for a few seconds and then I too heard the footsteps. There was nothing for it but to stay still and keep my head down. If Kim was going to turn me in, now was the time – androgynous, carnivorous, contemptuous Kim who was wrong about everything that really mattered to me. Like Hannah, I thought. Like Hannah.

I heard voices. I heard Kim say, 'I'm sorry to bother you, mistress, but I've never been sent to this floor before and I got myself lost.'

'Where's your badge?' The strange voice was authoritative and peremptory.

There was a pause. Then Kim said, 'There was a small disturbance in the auditorium. It must've fallen off.'

I began to exhale slowly.

'Larvae wear badges at all times. What's your name?'

'Billy. I'm so sorry, mistress, I'll replace it immediately.' Her tone was so servile I could quite see why she called herself a worm.

'Carry out your orders first. Where had you been called to?'

'The Red Suite, mistress.'

'You should've turned left after exiting the service lift. Go back. No. Not that way. You've as much sense of direction as a damaged drone.'

Then there was silence. I stayed as still as I could, wishing I was a candle flame that could simply be blown out of existence. My breathing was so shallow it felt like I was drowning. I wanted desperately to cough the last of the toxic air out of my lungs.

At last I heard retreating footsteps. I counted to fifty-three until, unable to wait a second longer, I buried my head in what had once been a beautiful white tunic top and coughed so hard I almost retched. Then I scuttled back to the stairwell door, unlocked it, slid inside, and waited. I left a crack through which I could breathe and listen. I couldn't think of anything to do but wait for Kim.

Did I trust her? I thought I could only trust her if she was in as much trouble as I was. If she had really betrayed her bosses as thoroughly as she thought she had then she probably *was* looking to me for some sort of protection. That was the offer I'd held out to her. But I'd made the offer because I thought I was under Lazaro's protection – a thought Kim had dissed outright. And yet Lazaro himself had told me that his own safety was contingent on my behaviour, on my silence and obedience. And I'd failed him.

But he hadn't prepared me at all for what had happened or what was going to happen. I couldn't arm myself against restraint and coercion. How could I have anticipated being held captive and *forced* to submit to a stranger licking my nosebleed. Whatever Kim thought, Lazaro couldn't possibly have known what would happen to me.

Why had Mark and I been pitted against each other in such

a strange and unfair way? Mark knew all about the filming so he could present himself and his girlfriend in a flattering light. I'd been given no such advantage. I was hijacked.

Lazaro had been pitted against Garth Harding in a similarly mysterious way, and I presumed he'd been caught on the hop as badly as I had.

We'd spoken of love, he and I. We'd kissed – kissed with such tenderness and understanding. Maybe it was the kiss of friendship: maybe it was more. So why would Kim call him my nightmare? Why was Hannah so prejudiced against him?

And yet... I tried to shove Hannah's voice out of my mind but there it was: 'You are ignoring all contrary evidence. This means you are not thinking clearly. You have a good mind, dear, please use it. Your love does not make Lazaro a good man. You know you have a tendency to invent your men according to what you need, not what they deserve.'

'You don't know him,' I protested.

'Nor do you,' said unwelcome, imaginary Hannah.

'Come on!' hissed Kim, wrenching the door open and grabbing my wrist, not giving me time to relock the door before dragging me away. 'I know where the Red Suite is but we've got to hurry.'

So we ran, first to where this corridor ended in a t-junction, right turn, past the service lift 'mistress' had mentioned, on to a narrower passageway that had several doors leading off it. At the end there was a larger door opening onto a beautifully painted, generous hallway. Pictures hung on the walls, sculpture filled some of the alcoves and fresh flowers decorated others. It was a hallway fit for Lords and Ladies. We turned left.

This was not the direction I would have chosen. In fact I was feeling a faint tug in the opposite direction. The feeling had been strongest when we passed the service lift. I would've stopped there, undecided, if Kim hadn't been dragging me by the wrist.

But now we were in the palatial hallway and approaching what must be the door to the Red Suite. I recognised it because in the alcove beside it was a marble figure of the two-faced god, Janus, guardian of doorways.

'Janus,' I said. 'This is no accident. I'm neither in nor out. This isn't the beginning or the end. He didn't pick the Red Suite randomly.'

'If you're babbling about Lord Lazaro,' Kim sneered, 'which you usually are, nothing he does is random. Now *move!*'

I moved. A couple of paces from the door the dogs started barking – deep, warning voices the way only huge dogs sound.

Kim shrieked and let go of me. She jumped back to the opposite wall.

'Beaus,' I said quietly. You never have to shout at dogs to be heard. 'Hello there.' I was so relieved to hear them I almost wept. 'Now, sit down.' I said this quietly but firmly, and when I opened the door both the Beaus were sitting obediently, grinning, red tongues lolling.

Their compliance only lasted till I was kneeling in front of them, arms around them, hugging them. Then they knocked me down and stood over me licking every inch of bare skin they could find. This was their welcome, not blood-lust. And I buried my face in their rough fur smelling the friendship in their warm, thick scent.

The Beaus were my scouts – I could follow them back to my own identity. With them I was no longer bewildered, confused and torn. Nothing could be simpler than an ecstatic welcome from two beautiful dogs. It was love I could accept and give without fear.

But I was forgetting Kim. She was standing in the hall outside peering in with an expression of such fear and horror on her face I almost laughed.

I disentangled myself, stroked the Beaus and gave each of them a kiss on the top of their heads. 'Sit,' I said, 'and be quiet. She's scared of you so don't frighten her even more.'

I beckoned her inside. It took her quite a while, but eventually she came in and shut the door. 'What are they?' she asked.

'True friends,' I said. 'Weapons.' Then I remembered something. I looked for my purse and found it on the little desk by the window along with the folder of drawings. My black shawl was still on the bed, now rumpled and covered with dog hair. Of course no one had come in since I left. The Beaus were here guarding their territory. That was why no one was waiting here for me, and why no one had opened the door to take the key from the inside to lock me out.

'You're the best,' I told them. First I took them to the bathroom to refill their empty water bowls. Then I took the chequebook out of my purse. This was the reason I'd given both myself and Lazaro for coming. He hadn't believed me, nor had Gemma, and, if I was honest, nor did I. But now I was going to make good. I wrote a cheque for two hundred pounds, signed and dated it. I looked for paper in the desk, couldn't find any. I thought about tearing a corner off one of my drawings but couldn't bear to. In the end I wrote on the back of the cheque in my finest, smallest handwriting. 'Dear Lazaro, I am sure your dogs are worth more than a hundred pounds each, but this is all I can afford until my mother's will is probated. After that I'll pay whatever you ask.' I bit the end of my pen before starting a new paragraph: 'I really, truly hope you're alright. I know I've let you down. I'm so sorry. I just didn't understand what you needed.' I wanted to say so much more. I wanted to end the note, 'With all my love,' but somehow I couldn't; not with the Beaus sitting so close to me, water dripping from their beardy muzzles. I simply managed to cram 'Love, S' into the bottom right hand corner.

I left the cheque in the middle of the desk and turned to Kim. Her teeth were chattering audibly. I said, 'Come over here and make friends.'

'No,' she said. She'd been frightened before, but now she was both terrified and disgusted. 'They're dreadful animals. Their teeth are covered with germs. I can smell it on their breath even from here. Their bite is poisonous.'

'They won't bite you. You're with me. I'll protect you. I don't know why everyone here's so scared of them, but don't you see, that's to our advantage.'

She thought about it for a moment, then said, 'Okay, but keep them away from me. Don't let them touch me. To be eaten by a dog is the worst of all fates.'

'What a ridiculous thing to say,' I said. But at the same time I thought about Jezebel and Ahab. Queen Jezebel was supposedly eaten by dogs, while King Ahab's body was licked by dogs and pigs. And I wondered again about how much the people here knew about dietary laws and what Kim had meant when she talked of my 'unprepossessing' or 'unpromising' culture.

I stared at Kim; at her androgynous clothes and body, her high cheekbones and sly eyes. She looked like a modern young woman who never in a million years would have read either of the two Books of Kings. And yet there was something off-kilter about everything she said and did. I wanted to think more closely about this, and about everything Lesley Sharpe had told her audience. But as usual there was no time for reflection. Kim was almost squirming with anxiety, and I knew exactly how she felt.

I went back to the bathroom and collected the box Grigori had thrust at me when he brought the Beaus. Quickly I discarded the abominable choke chains and whip, but I kept the electronic shock collars and the gizmos that activated them.

First I tried to phone the emergency services but couldn't get a signal. Then I tied my shawl round my shoulders, grabbed my purse, and called the dogs to heel. My drawings had been paid for. They belonged to Lazaro. So, with a pang, I left them on the desk with my cheque for two hundred pounds.

We hurried through the eerily empty corridors straight to the service lift where Kim punched the button for the ground floor.

'Maybe they'll be as glad to get rid of us as we are to go,' I said hopefully.

Kim, who was standing as far away from us as she could, said nothing. Her face was marble-white.

The lift door glided open and we stepped out into a service corridor identical to the one we'd left below. The only difference was two security guards armed with batons. One was close by to our left; the other was about fifteen yards away to our right, next to an open door.

Before I could jump back inside, the lift door closed. And no matter how hard I punched the button it refused to open again.

The dogs' heads were down and all the hair on their backs from neck to tail was bristling, making them look huge, and bear-like. The guard on our left edged forward. No one said anything and no one gave an order to attack but I could see quite clearly we were being directed towards the open door.

There was, in any case, nowhere else to go so I marched firmly towards the open door as if it was my own idea. My heart was a doorknocker – I was sure everyone could hear it.

I found myself in the grand entrance hall. As soon as Kim and the Beaus came through behind me, I whirled around and slammed the door on the following guards. Again, bless Palatine efficiency, there was a key in the lock and I turned it.

It was no more than a gesture of independence and defiance because facing me were Garth Harding and his two assistants, Lesley Sharpe and hers, Pasqual, Gemma, Grigori and another handful of guards in riot gear. There was also a beautiful blond person of no identifiable gender who was operating a steadicam.

'Where's Lazaro?' I said.

Kim said, 'Ladies and gentlemen, forgive me. This woman was my captive until she overpowered me...'

I almost laughed.

'*Kneel!*' thundered Garth Harding.

Instantly, Kim fell to her knees and bowed so low her head touched the floor. Any urge to laugh I might have had died.

The Beaus snarled, 'Rmaaarrr,' and stepped forward gathering themselves.

'Stay,' I said urgently.

'Very wise,' said Lesley Sharpe. But I noticed that not even the guards took so much as a step towards me.

'Get up,' I said to Kim. 'You look ridiculous.' She didn't more a muscle; she didn't even raise her head. My judgement when picking allies is flawless.

'I want to see Lazaro,' I repeated. 'Where is he? What're you doing to him?' This was greeted by silence, but Lesley Sharpe smirked.

'I really don't like you,' I thought. Out loud I said, 'I choose you.' And, flanked by the Beaus, I walked straight up to her.

To her credit, she was the only one who didn't retreat. She even kept the smirk on her face. I was glad of that because I didn't know how badly I was going to hurt her.

I pressed the business side of one of the shock dog collars to the middle of her chest and flipped the switch on the remote control.

Lesley Sharpe fell like a ripe apple and her head hit the marble floor with a dull thud. I caught her arm, dragged her back to my side of the hall and laid her out beside kneeling Kim.

'On guard,' I said to one of the Beaus, and he stood over her with bared teeth, growling deep in his throat. Her horrified eyes were open. She was, it seemed, conscious but disabled.

This took place before anyone could react. Then a hubbub broke out.

It was only at this point that I checked the remote control and saw it was turned up to maximum.

'How about you?' I asked Grigori who was staring in astonishment at Sharpe's inert body. 'Want some? Or are you one of those guys who can dish it out but can't take it?'

'You fucking brainless cretin,' he yelled at me. 'You got no sodding idea what you're dealing with.'

'Then please would someone effing tell me.' But my voice was lost in the cacophony of everyone else talking at once. So I yelled at the top of my voice, 'Get Lazaro! *Now!*'

This caused more conversations. I used the time to buckle the shock collar round Lesley's neck. I checked that it was still set to maximum. While I was at it I made sure that the setting on the second collar would be similarly effective. I was stunned by the success of the manoeuvre and I was doing my best not to look as clumsy, dithery and incompetent as I had been portrayed by the outrageous stolen footage they had all watched and sniggered at; were probably still sniggering at if the steadicam operator was anything to go by. I'm more than that, I kept telling myself, as if repetition would cover me like a layer of paint. I wanted to be an artist's impression of myself, not a bad photographer's.

I was so dirty, untidy and frightened that even the appearance of confidence was hard to come by. But I stood up straight and tapped my toe to show impatience.

'Lazaro?' I prompted.

To my amazement Pasqual ran up the grand staircase to the reception room – the room I'd first visited when Lazaro showed me the Cycladic figures, Rodin maquettes and Paula Rego prints. At least, I thought, he wasn't being kept constrained in some basement service area as I had been.

Unwillingly, I caught Gemma's angry gaze. I wasn't going to look away although I wanted to. What did she have to be angry about? Wasn't I trying to save her boss? Of course she'd never liked me and she probably thought he was in trouble now because I'd behaved badly and hadn't obeyed orders. Well, she was right. But wasn't I risking my life in an attempt to put things straight?

Risking my life? How had this happened?

'How has this happened,' I asked Gemma. 'All I did was accept a vodka and tonic from a sweet old gentleman in a bar in Golders Green. And now we're involved in murder and blood and secret surveillance. What's the effing story? No one tells me anything.'

'You *know* what the "effing story" is,' Gemma said contemptuously. 'This so-called ignorance is wilful blindness on your part. Nobody can be as stupid as you want us to believe.'

'What about Mark?' I asked Garth Harding. 'Does he know what you've been doing to him? How stupid or wilfully blind is he?'

'He's a competitive sportsman,' Garth said. 'He knows about the sacrifices he has to make to stay on top. He accepted the terms and conditions long ago.'

'What terms and conditions?' I asked.

'Here we go again,' croaked Lesley Sharpe from somewhere near my feet. 'Ignorance is not the same as innocence no matter how much you want to tell yourself otherwise.'

'And you can just shut up,' I said, waving the remote control in front of her. 'I've heard enough of your snide remarks. As a presenter of reality TV, or whatever you think you're doing, you suck. Big time.'

For some reason everyone, including a few of the guards and the camera operator, burst out laughing.

'Have a little patience and understanding,' Lazaro said. I didn't know if he was addressing me, Lesley or the whole crowd.

I looked up and saw him on the last step of the grand staircase with Pasqual a couple of paces behind him. He didn't look like a prisoner. His suit, shirt and shoes were as immaculate as when I'd last seen him. I felt enormously relieved, but simultaneously resentful. I was, by comparison to everyone, except maybe Kim, a bag of unwashed laundry.

'Are you okay?' I asked tremulously.

He looked just a little startled, and then said, 'As you can see.'

Pasqual smiled but Lazaro looked almost regretful. He walked across the hall to stand beside Garth Harding. His eyes, clear, dark and beautiful, took in the stand-off that my unexpected capture of Lesley Sharpe had caused.

He said, 'I don't know how you've accomplished it, my dear, but again you have surprised me.'

'Maybe you've always underestimated her,' Gemma said.

'Maybe, old chap, you've always overestimated yourself,' Garth Harding responded.

'I'm sure both suggestions have merit,' Lazaro replied coolly. 'But now, perhaps I can ask you all for a little privacy. Seema and I need to resolve this dilemma. We shouldn't allow Lesley's discomfort and embarrassment to continue. Nothing will be gained by all of us standing around arguing. Nor will we profit from the threat posed by our security forces. They should stand down. Force is not a solution.'

'Are you mad?' Garth Harding asked.

'Sir!' Pasqual protested.

'You can't possibly let this insult go unpunished,' Lesley Sharpe wheezed from the floor. Maybe I'd pulled the collar too tight. What a pity!

'Just give me the order,' Gemma said. 'I can take her down easily.'

'Like Ms Sharpe did?' I asked her sweetly, waving the second collar. The Beaus turned their massive heads towards her and glared as if to back me up.

Lazaro took three steps towards me. Three steps away from his people. He ignored the bristling wolfhounds, and turned to face the group. Now, I couldn't see his face but I could hear how his voice rose above the clamour the way a singer's voice can pierce the sound of a full orchestra. He said, 'Let's not waste any more time. Please leave quietly. This conundrum is of my making and is mine to solve. As Lesley is *hors de combat* we can have no unbiased adjudicator. Therefore, Garth, I am asking for a temporary suspension of our normal procedure.'

'Normal procedure?' I said. 'What the hell is normal here?' I was unheard or ignored.

Garth said, 'This will cost you. And you're wrong about force: it has always been the solution in the end.'

Lazaro simply nodded.

Pasqual said, 'Sir, of course we support whatever decision you take...'

'We always have,' Gemma interrupted. 'But please sir, think again. Is this –' she jerked her thumb towards me '– worth the risk?'

'But she –' Garth too jerked his meaty thumb at me, '– must relinquish her hold on Lesley.'

'I believe that will be unacceptable,' Lazaro said.

'You really do think I'm stupid,' I said to Garth, absurdly hopeful. Lazaro was taking my side.

'Why are we dicking around?' asked one of Garth's assistants. I'd never heard him speak before. 'Jump her,' he continued, 'off her; game over.'

'And that,' Lazaro said coldly, 'would be unacceptable to me.'

My answer to that suggestion was to dial Lesley's remote down to halfway and flip the switch for a micro second. Her body writhed and she squealed with pain. I made a big deal of dialling back up to maximum, forcing all of them to notice my influence over their choices. I wasn't proud of myself and I wished I wasn't enjoying Lesley's plight so much.

'Very well,' Garth said at last. 'I'll give you ten minutes.'

'You'll give me as long as it takes,' Lazaro replied.

The steadicam operator was swinging the camera between Garth and Lazaro as if it was a tennis match that was being recorded.

I said, 'Lesley stays where she is. All the rest of you can take a hike.'

'What about Kim?' Grigori asked.

I looked at Kim. She was still kneeling with her forehead on the floor. I said, 'She stays here.'

Lazaro said, 'I take full responsibility. I will see to it that Lesley comes to no harm.'

'I'm already harmed,' Lesley said. 'I can't feel my legs.'

'No *further* harm.' Lazaro was beginning to sound tetchy.

I said, 'The effects will wear off. These dogs were given a full blast. I thought they were dead but they recovered fully. Unfortunately I can't answer for what might happen if any of you forces me to blast her again so soon.' I felt like a character in a bad thriller, saying 'this gun has a hair trigger.' Guns were killing machines. All I had were two shock dog collars.

'Seema doesn't want to hurt anyone,' Lazaro said. 'She isn't the type. You've all seen the footage. Now please leave us to talk.'

Grumbling, disapproving, worried, they made for the stairs. The last to go was the steadicam operator, walking backwards until the last moment.

Lazaro waited, listening till the last vestige of voices and footsteps faded. Then he turned towards me.

But I had one more thing to do. I went to Kim and pulled on her arm to make her stand. She had cramp in both her legs and her feet so I helped her sit against the wall. I said, 'If you act like a worm, they'll treat you like one.' I stooped to massage her feet but she pushed me away.

'Is that what she called herself?' Lazaro asked. 'A worm?'

'You lot don't treat your employees very well,' I said.

'She isn't an employee,' he said after a short pause. 'She or he is a child of the house.'

'Excuse me?' I stared at Kim then back at him. 'You've got a lot of explaining to do.'

'Think of the honey bee,' he said. 'Its development – each one, for a time, had the potential to become a queen. You might say that Kim is in a state of gender suspension.'

I must have looked like a slack-jawed chimp because he laughed and said, 'You are at the very edge of a decision that, if you step one way will blow your mind, but if you step back will leave you with nothing more than what you already know. Is that enough for you, my dear?'

'Be silent,' hissed Lesley Sharpe. 'This is classified.'

'Am I really your dear?' I asked. There was an embarrassing shake in my voice, but no one can say I don't tackle the really important issues first.

'Shall we sit over there?' he said, indicating two carved throne-like chairs on the other side of the hall. 'We'll be less likely to be overheard.'

I made sure that Lesley knew that her shock collar had a range of at least five hundred yards. She looked at me with such loathing and contempt that if I'd been a flower I would have withered and blown away. But I wasn't a flower. I was a woman following a man who wanted to talk to me without being overheard. I stepped lightly with hope in my heart.

The carved chairs were there to impress but not to be sat on. They were very uncomfortable.

He sat first, and I had to move my chair around so that I could keep an eye on Kim and Lesley. As if they'd made a deal, one of the Beaus stayed threateningly close to Lesley while the other came to sit by me. Lazaro showed no sign of nerves but he wasn't happy. His eyes, whenever a Beau moved, were the eyes of someone watching a poisonous spider.

Nevertheless, he leaned forward to take my hand, holding it as if he hadn't heard my Beau's threatening snarl. I sighed with complete happiness until I glanced down and saw what our clasped hands looked like. His skin was tanned where mine was weather beaten. His was soft, pumiced and moisturised; mine was roughened by gardening and scarred by kitchen accidents. His nails were buffed, shaped and above all clean; mine had picked up all the grime of the stairwell and the nail beds were disfigured by hangnails.

I thought, 'How can such a beautiful hand bear to hold mine?' Then I wanted to hide the grubby thing in my sleeve. I remembered my mother once pulling away from me in the supermarket and asking me why my hands were always so 'clammy'.

'How can I be your "dear"?' I asked, close to tears.

'I chose you,' he said. 'We talked and there was a connection. I thought, This young woman loves what I love. Do you know how rare that is?'

'Yes,' I whispered.

'I have lived a long time,' Lazaro said: 'And I have been lonely for a long time.'

My heart pumped and tingled. What could be wrong with any of this? But he had answered my question without answering my question. Instead he'd said something to delight me and that was a different matter entirely.

'What did you choose me for?' I asked.

'I could ask you the same question.' He smiled.

'I didn't choose you,' I said. 'You happened to me. It's not the same thing. You have a purpose. You're involved in that appalling thing that happened downstairs. You said you were in danger, but everyone's treating Mark and me like we're a game.'

'Cannot both things be true at the same time?'

'Well, if they are, shouldn't you explain it to me?'

'I felt, with a connection like ours, no explanation would be necessary.'

How I longed for this to be so. Then I could smile, nod and shut up. Just give me one more minute to hold your hand and think of love; one more minute when I don't have to disappoint you and see you walk away in disgust.

After a long pause, I said, 'You see, I don't know who you are. You have a name and an address, and you're obviously a man of great wealth and taste. But men of wealth and taste don't pick up women in North London bars and offer them opium. You could afford the best architects and landscape gardeners to do your job for you. You don't need a scruffy one-woman operation. But you've involved me in something I don't understand. Soil structure, when to plant the crocus bulbs – *that* I understand. But I don't understand this.' I waved my free hand in the air. 'Gender suspension, Lords and Ladies, nosebleeds, neck wounds. What are you? What do you want with me?'

'Questions you should have asked when we first met,' he said. 'Why did you not?'

'Actually,' I said, trying to hold on to his hand and my rational mind at the same time. 'Actually these questions should address the time about a year *before* we met. You, or people you do business with, have been following me at least since I planted Mrs Redland's balcony.'

'Yes,' he admitted, smiling. 'And didn't that turn out beautifully? It has been a privilege to watch how your imagination grows from hard physical labour and, yes, dirty hands, falling off ladders, and everything else that is required to create a beauty that will only be apparent months or years later. It's the way art used to be made. Whether it be bronze doors, sculpture in Carrara marble, murals or tapestries – there were no quick ways as there are now. An artist had to hold a vision in his head and heart for a long, long time before he could see the result. And so do you.'

'Oh yes,' I sighed, stunned that he saw me and my dirty hands as part of a Renaissance tradition that included Michelangelo's filthy feet. He was offering me a vision of myself that contradicted everything I'd seen on the screen downstairs.

I said, 'You're dazzling me.'

'You're dazzling yourself,' Kim shouted from across the hall. I jumped. I'd forgotten all about her. She must have ears like a hare's.

Lazaro merely smiled, but Lesley muttered something that made Kim bow her head and cover her mouth with her hand. I thought I caught the words, '… watch an expert at work.' But I must've been mistaken.

Or was I? Had Lazaro answered any of my questions?

'Who are you really?' I asked in the end.

'Who do you think I am?'

A tiny movement made me think he was going to take his hand away. Quickly I said, 'Hannah thinks you're trying to engage me in a game of dominance and subservience. She thinks, because of the puncture marks on my neck, that you're involved with a blood fetish.'

Now he really did remove his hand.

He leaned against the arm of his hideously uncomfortable chair and regarded me speculatively.

After a moment, he said, 'Hannah David is an astute woman, but she has no imagination and sometimes falls a long way short of the mark.'

'What are you saying?'

'Nothing. What are you thinking?'

I gulped. Now that he had withdrawn his hand it seemed as if a chasm many miles wide separated us. I whispered in the tiniest voice I could possibly produce, 'Are you a vampire?'

SEVENTEEN

He laughed. It was an amused chuckle which said, louder them words, 'Are you joking?'

I can't describe how much I longed to say, 'Yes', and have him lean towards me and accept my dirty hand in his.

What I should've said was: 'There are just too many things that need explanation and straight answers. You, who I love beyond all reason, *must* be a tricky bastard. If you weren't I wouldn't be in this bewildering mess and my mother might still be alive. Lesley and Gemma are right: I've overlooked too much for far too long.' But my terror of abandonment was so strong that I just stared at him wordlessly.

The silence seemed to go on forever until he said, 'I see you are serious. You will have many questions. Ask them. I promise I won't lie to you.' He leaned towards me and again offered his hand.

Suddenly all my questions seemed absolutely trivial compared to the warmth of his palm and the acceptance in his gaze.

At last he said, 'I believe you once told me that although you are a Jew you are also an atheist.'

I nodded.

'Then presumably you do not believe in the supernatural?'

I nodded again.

'So?' he said as if the one word would be enough.

Again there was a long silence while I searched desperately for something that wouldn't insult him or make me look like an idiot. I was becoming more and more aware that my need for his acceptance was interfering with my need to understand.

At last I said, 'Why do vampires have to be supernatural?'

He laughed suddenly. 'Interesting,' he said. 'If you analyse the folk tales and the fantasies in popular culture, you have the immortal living dead who can be killed; the victorious who can be defeated; the heartless who can be slain with a wooden stick through the heart; the corporeal who leaves no shadow or reflection; the embodied ghost who needs food; the creature with no circulation who lives on blood. Shall I go on?'

'None of it makes any sense at all,' I admitted, but I did not add: 'Forget I ever mentioned it', or offer my humble apologies. I just let my original question hang.

'What are you thinking now?' he asked.

'About the Maasai,' I said reluctantly. My jaw was aching with the attempt to stop my teeth from chattering.

'Another interesting thought in the current context,' he said. Again I felt he was complimenting me and I felt the glow of his approval.

He went on, 'You do realise, don't you, that Maasai dependence on both blood and milk makes nonsense of your compartmentalised dietary concerns about theft and gift. These people sustain themselves on blood, which you would call "theft", but without killing the source. But they also drink milk, which you characterise as the "gift". Both blood and milk, therefore, can exist side by side as gifts.'

I had not expected this. My pinball thoughts had been travelling in a different direction. I tried to clear my head.

He ran his thumb across the inside of my wrist and my critical faculties vanished. I said, 'I'll think about that later. In fact I was wondering about genetic characteristics inherited from one extremely ancient civilisation by a few surviving descendants in the present.'

'We *all* inherit characteristics from ancient civilisations,'

Lazaro said. 'We also inherit characteristics from animals that have no recognisable civilisation. We even inherit genetic material from fish. Consider the development of the foetus.'

'Yes,' I said. I *was* interested in the development of the foetus, but at the moment it was a distraction. I ploughed on, 'But why is this social group...' I waved my hand vaguely to include the house, Lesley, Kim and himself. 'Why are you all so interested in blood? Are there other groups of humans, as opposed to insects, who have "gender suspension" as an evolutionary survival mechanism?'

'You might be surprised at how many babies are born without an identifiable gender, at how many ambiguities there are on the spectrum between clear male and female. You might also be surprised to hear that some of these ambiguities run in families.'

I really *was* surprised. 'Are you saying that everyone here is related in some way?'

'Only in the sense that, for instance Jews, whether they are Ashkenazi, Sephardic, or, like yourself, Mizrahi, are related.' His expression was unreadable, I looked at the Beau who was sitting beside me. I could not look at Lazaro and think clearly at the same time. Beau stirred when he felt my attention was on him and I put my hand on his head to steady myself. I was thinking that I should only ask one question at a time. I shouldn't give Lazaro any choice about what question to answer. He was derailing me with fascinating but irrelevant information.

'Are you part of a religious sect?' I asked bluntly.

'Like you,' he said, 'I do not believe in a god.'

'What is going on downstairs?'

'You'll have to be more specific.' He gave me another of his beautiful smiles. And again my brain went walkies.

I concentrated on the modelling of Beau's skull under my hand and the harsh feel of his rough coat on my fingertips.

In the end I said, 'There's a cinema down there, and an auditorium for hundreds of people. There's a TV studio. There's a crowd of people who are acting like a live studio audience. It felt to me like a reality gameshow that you and Garth have been organising for over a year. It seems to be a game for which Mark was way more prepared than I was. He was set up to be a hero against me, the fool. But that's beside the point. There appears to be a much more serious agenda.' I looked up and saw Lazaro watching me with the sort of intense affection and attention I have always craved. 'Please explain,' I said quickly, before my brain tiptoed into the tulips again.

'I should apologise,' he said, gently. 'None of that should have happened. It was not my intention.'

'Then whose was it?'

'I don't want to point a finger at any of my colleagues. That would be disloyal, and the knowledge would neither profit nor console you.'

'I'm already unprofited and unconsoled,' I said. 'But I have been stalked for a year. Why? Our meeting at the Italian Bar was not a co-incidence, was it?'

'I have never stalked you.' He said this with such conviction that I couldn't help believing him. 'Further,' he went on, 'I did not invite you here tonight.' Of course this was true. I felt myself blush when I remembered how eagerly I'd accepted Mark's invitation.

'Mark did,' I said. 'Did Mark know he was setting me up?'

'As I have never even seen Mark before tonight I simply can't tell you.' He had been sitting very still. Now he stirred and said, 'I have answered a lot of your questions but this chair is unkind to old bones. Why don't we go somewhere more comfortable and alone, just you and I? The dogs will guard your prisoners.'

He got up and held out his other hand to help me up. I got slowly to my feet. This was all wrong. I knew for certain he was lying to me because Mark told me he'd thought Lazaro was the interior decorator. If Mark had seen Lazaro, then Lazaro had seen Mark.

But, yes, I took his hand because, heaven help me, I wanted to touch him. Or rather, I wanted him to touch me. And I longed more than anything to be alone with him. I wanted, more than life itself, to believe him – *in* him. I was forgetting. I could actually feel my mind drifting as if it didn't belong to me. Instead, like an unanchored boat, it was being carried out to sea on the tide. So I allowed him to draw me away from the chair that hurt him, away from Kim and Lesley, away from the Beaus, towards the stairs at the other end of the hall.

I wasn't thinking at all; I was simply feeling, mindlessly, that my life was with him. My hand wasn't just holding his: it *was* his.

And then Lesley spoiled it. She made a choking sound. I turned to look at her and saw that she was biting her own arm in an attempt to cover her mouth and smother her laughter. She was still lying flat on her back exactly where I'd put her but her whole body was shaking with suppressed mirth.

Half a second later I noticed that both the Beaus were growling and looking ready for action. In fact the one closer to me had come around in front of me and was trying to bar my way.

Astonished out of my fugue I turned to Lazaro and saw that he was staring at Lesley with an expression of such frustration and loathing that I barely recognised him. I dropped his hand and he rounded on me trying to snatch the gismo that controlled the shock collar around Lesley's neck. I thought, 'He wants to kill her.'

Instead, Grigori appeared at the bottom of the stairs as if shot from a harpoon gun. He shouted, 'Boss, there's a bunch of frigging coppers at the gate. What do you want us to do?'

There was no time for a reply. Both Beaus, bristling with murderous rage, turned on Grigori, teeth bared. My split second assessment was of a co-ordinated attack – one taking the high road, the other the low – throat and groin.

Why not? They owed him pain. And hadn't *he* trained them to… to do what? Kill? More blood. More blame.

'No!' I shouted. 'Down! Come here!'

These people hated dogs. If the Beaus killed Grigori, *they* would be killed. I wouldn't be able to save them. I was vastly outnumbered. Their only hope of survival was no blood and no blame.

The muscles in their haunches were bunched for the leap. Grigori screamed in fear and cowered back against the wall.

But the Beaus heard me. They stopped. Love does, very occasionally, conquer all.

Keeping my voice calm and level, I said, 'Come on over here, my beautiful boys.' They came, red tongues lolling, almost grinning as if it had all been a joke. I crouched and hugged them both. 'Well done,' I said. 'Good, good boys.' I wanted to cry – I'd so nearly lost them. But they hadn't lost me.

To my astonishment I saw that Lazaro had retreated behind one of the unkind chairs and was holding it up as if he were a lion tamer. It was an oak throne-like thing and it must've taken considerable strength. He saw me staring and put it down. Straightening his jacket and tie he turned smoothly to Grigori and said, 'The police? What do they want?'

Grigori was walking backwards very slowly towards the stairs, never taking his eyes off the dogs. If he could've made himself invisible he would have.

'Grigori!' Lazaro snapped. 'What do the police want?'

'Her.' Grigori jerked his thumb in my direction. 'Boss, I told you she weren't our sort.'

'In case you've forgotten,' Lesley put in, 'so did I. But that, apparently, was the challenge.' She was starting to get to her feet so I gave her a mini jolt from her collar and she fell back down.

'Seema,' Lazaro began, 'my dear, who did you tell… ?'

But I was already on my way over to Lesley. To my delight she looked scared of me. I said, 'What did you mean downstairs when you reminded the audience that an error had been made and that a surveillance operative had mistaken Hannah for my mother? Did you kill my mother? Did you mean to kill Hannah?'

She could see that my finger was poised over the zapper and that I was flanked by both Beaus. She looked behind me at Lazaro.

I said, '*You* were the MC downstairs. I'm asking *you.*'

Grigori, flustered, said, 'What we going to do, sir?'

Lesley said, 'I haven't killed anyone.'

'Tell Mr Harding to delay,' Lazaro said, for the first time in my experience sounding urgent. 'And tell him we are in evac mode.'

'No shit,' Grigori said, leaving fast.

I persisted, 'Did you *have* my mother killed?'

'You're asking the wrong person,' Lesley cried as one of the dogs lowered his huge head over her and let her see his teeth and smell his breath. She turned her face away. She was very pale under her cleverly applied make-up. But there was a nasty red weal showing from beneath the dog collar. I wish I could say I felt guilt about this, but I didn't.

'We don't have time for this,' Lazaro said impatiently.

'I'll take that as a yes, shall I?' I said, still addressing Lesley.

'You're catching on,' Kim said. She'd been quiet for so long I'd almost forgotten she could talk.

'Silence!' Lesley barked.

Kim looked at her and her predicament. 'Ask her about Leigh-Sampson Security,' she suggested, with a ghost of her old sly smile.

'Is Leigh-Sampson the operative you were talking about downstairs?' I asked, nudging Lesley with my foot to get her attention.

'You'll pay for this,' Lesley told Kim.

'Disloyalty is punishable by death,' Kim intoned as if it was something she'd learned by rote when she was five years old. 'According to you I'm already dead.'

Suddenly I was completely fed up with having perfectly straightforward questions ignored. I rounded on Lazaro. 'Do you people employ a company called Leigh-Sampson Security?'

'My dear, we employ so many companies, I can't keep track of them all.'

'You know what I'm asking,' I said. 'Your evasion and obfuscations are so blatant I'm coming to the conclusion that you have no respect for me at all, and the words "my dear" are effing lies. You've been manipulating me for your own purposes. You've injured me. You've put me in hospital. You've made a fool of me and humiliated me in public. You and these weirdoes you live with are probably responsible for my mother's death. I don't know what your effing game is, but I want nothing except to be out of here.' I refused to meet his eyes when I said all this.

'I'm sorry you should think so,' Lazaro said. 'But how can I let you go? Think of the bond, the love that has grown between us. *Us* – you and me. Don't be afraid, my dearest, look at me.'

'Don't look at him,' Kim warned.

Staring determinedly at his silver grey tie, but with unbearable sadness in my heart I said, 'I love you, Lazaro. I can't imagine a time when I won't. Ever. But I don't know what you want with me. I'm pretty sure it isn't a roof top garden. I'm pretty sure a guy with Paula Rego etchings on his walls can't admire my poor drawings. I've stopped believing, Lazaro. What happened downstairs… well, I can't think about it properly yet. But I will. I have to. If I don't I'll always be the weak, needy fool you took me to be. I'll be your victim, and I'm stone fed up with being a victim.'

By the time I finished talking I was weeping openly.

The tension in the hall ratcheted up several notches. I saw Lesley and Kim start up, their faces sharp as knives.

'Be still!' Lazaro ordered. 'She's mine.'

I wiped my eyes on what used to be a lovely white sleeve and saw to my acute embarrassment that it was again stained with a fresh bloody smear.

Holding my arm up, I said to Lazaro, 'What have you done? What does this mean?'

'It means, child, that you and I are of one blood. What's yours is mine and mine alone. It is a connection far more powerful than the love you yearn for. We are bound by forces you cannot yet imagine. But you will learn, and then you will never be alone, isolated or lonely again.'

Something inside me relaxed. Why did I need my questions answered? Wasn't feeling way, way more important than meaning?

Lazaro held his arms out to me. He was so tall, so straight, so handsome. He turned other men, like Jake, into spotty boys. This strength would shield me, protect and support me against everyone and everything.

And yet he hated dogs. At the last moment I noticed the Beaus' anxiety and protective stances. They were ready to go to war for me..

'Tell them to lie down,' Lazaro said gently, lovingly. 'We'll take care of them later.'

'We,' he'd said. The two of us. Together. 'What's yours is mine,' he'd said. Another question: was he talking about my blood? And if mine was his, was his mine? Would he want me to lick *his* bloody tears? The lining of my stomach seemed to cringe. The thought of drinking blood – even Lazaro's – made me want to throw up.

He seemed not to notice. 'Well?' he asked. There was no hint now of impatience in his voice. We might have had eternity to talk through my doubt.

'Is it my *blood* that's yours?' I asked, my voice sounding weak and kittenish. 'Does that mean that your blood's mine?'

'Would that be so bad?' His smile was almost playful. 'You said you would die for me.'

'I know,' I said, swallowing the urge to vomit. 'But I never said I'd kill for you.'

'Not necessary.' He laughed. 'We agreed, didn't we, that your archaic notions of theft and gift were immaterial.'

'Did we?' My mind felt as if it were being torn in two. I looked at the dogs. They ate meat. Given half a chance they would lap up blood. But.... But what?

But they were dogs; they had no choice. That was the difference.

I said, 'You have already taken my blood, haven't you?'

He said nothing, but his irresistible dark eyes loved me.

I couldn't think of anything intelligent to say so I quoted Hannah: 'What's taken by force or subterfuge can never be yours.'

'Don't you believe it,' he said with such careless certainty that I suddenly saw a shadow of cruelty in his loving eyes.

Just then, a tremor, like a minor earthquake, made the floor shake. Garth Harding almost flew into the hall shouting, 'They are ramming the gate with what looks like an armoured truck. Lazaro, we must abandon the house and close off the tunnels.'

'Stall them,' Lazaro ordered.

I said, 'Did you have my mother killed?'

'No,' he said, looking me straight in the eye.

And, god forgive me, I believed him even though I knew he was lying. Then another quotation infiltrated my brain and I said, '"The dead shall not rise. Those requiring a cure will not rise."'

He raised his eyebrows.

'What's done is done,' I said with a heavy heart. 'Only Isaiah said it better. I'm going now, and I'm taking the dogs. And Kim if she wants to come.'

'I can't let you go,' he said simply.

'It's not up to you anymore,' Garth Harding said. 'Face it old boy, you lost. I'm giving the orders now.' He turned to me. 'Go,' he said. 'Take the fucking dogs and go. But unless you want more death on your hands you'll play for time at the gate.'

'What about Mark?' I asked, already on my way to the front door. 'I came with him and I want to leave with him.'

'You're too late,' Garth said. 'He's made his choice. And so, it appears, have you.'

Later I would hear the important part of Garth's speech, but at the time I was deaf as a stump.

EIGHTEEN

I slept until the afternoon when Amy woke me, roughly shaking my shoulder.

She said, 'Those bastard dogs won't let me in the kitchen and it stinks of dog poop. Do something!'

I'd thrown myself on the bed when I got home at mid-day. I hadn't showered or changed. I felt like the bottom of a rubbish bin.

'You look like shit,' Amy confirmed kindly. 'And who's that person sleeping on the couch? It looks like a refugee from a leper colony.'

'Fuck off, Amy,' I said. I wanted to go back to sleep and never wake up. But I staggered to the bathroom and stood under the shower, trying to scrub myself clean of sorrow, guilt and memory. I had two dogs to feed and exercise and, according to Amy, to pick up after. I concentrated on this thought. As it happened, the dogs posed the only problem I could solve that day.

I drove them in the van to Hampstead Heath and then let them run and roam free. They caused some concern amongst owners of smaller politer dogs who were kept on leads. But the pair simply weren't interested in causing trouble. The only time they showed the slightest aggression was when a professional dog walker scolded me for not using either leads or collars. Then they ran up to investigate and their sheer size intimidated her and her handful of pugs and poodles.

They'd earned their freedom, I thought. I did not want to

control them at all. I was repelled by the very idea of control. They came back to me when they were ready and we went home via Pets R Yours where I bought large quantities of food for carnivorous animals. There were no dog baskets big enough for them so I thought I'd better buy them a sofa of their own. That could wait for another day. Meanwhile I would have to figure out what to do about Kim.

I'd left her fast asleep on the couch, and I didn't want to think about her at all. She'd been silent and useless at the police interviews, not backing me up or confirming my story of an underground labyrinth. She'd left me dangling: clearly, in police eyes, a delusional lunatic. All she'd done was complain of fatigue and stomach cramps. So when we finally got back to my flat all she wanted to do was to close the curtains, cover her head with my spare duvet and sink into a sleep so deep that I didn't even have time to show her the bathroom or the kitchen. I was disgusted and disappointed with her and I figured the flat was small enough for her to find whatever she needed without my help.

Jake arrived after work and he and Amy stalked off to the movies, unwilling to share with an unexpected house guest. I went to my room.

I had nothing to do. Yesterday I was eagerly getting ready to go to a reception. I felt as if years, not hours, had passed. I was as different from who I was twenty-four hours ago as I was from who I'd been ten years ago – a huge shift in a very short time. I wondered if what I was experiencing was jetlag.

The Beaus clambered onto my bed and went to sleep. I gazed at them in wonder. I was now responsible for two dogs large enough to fill a double bed. Forget the sofa idea; I needed to think bigger. And I would have to learn to distinguish one from the other. But they were twins. Tentatively I said, 'This one is Beau; that one's Bro.' This was going to take patience.

I sat at my desk and watched daylight fade, to be replaced by street lamps and windows lit by electricity. My pens, pencils and brushes filled a carved wooden pot. Drawing books of varying sizes were stacked ready to receive visual ideas. But I had none. The paper, like my mind, was blank. My last, my best, work was gone. Maybe Lazaro took it before he, like the other occupants of the Palatine Estate, vanished. Maybe it was forgotten in the Red Suite.

There was no one to talk to. No one who would believe me. The police when they finally broke down the gate and unearthed the appropriate paperwork to allow them to search the house found a lower ground floor with half a dozen guest bedrooms. Beneath that that was a basement containing nothing more suspicious than kitchen, boiler room, utility rooms and three chest freezers packed with meat. The officer I talked to said there had not been a single green vegetable or piece of fruit in the house. He found that slightly odd but it was hardly evidence of anything but my 'vivid imagination'. The hours that had changed my life, my confidence, and my understanding of the world had been wiped away like a spot of grease on a kitchen counter.

I had Kim and two giant hounds for proof. But one of them wouldn't talk and the other two couldn't. Hannah, who had, by magic all her own, galvanised the police into action and was sure she'd saved my life, suddenly and inexplicably had nothing more to say.

I was furious with her. Maybe she *had* saved my life; maybe she'd ruined it. I simply didn't know. But as far as police interviews went she, like Kim, had left me dangling – a fantasist who was probably spinning a yarn to cover up something shameful and interestingly sexual. Maybe, the officer insinuated, my mother's violent death had destabilised me to the point of schizoid visions. I was lucky to be allowed home – under Hannah's expert supervision, of course. Otherwise, he said, he would have had me committed for assessment at the nearest barmy house. No: I wasn't speaking to Hannah.

Then I heard Kim stir and begin to moan. I went straight

through to the living room. She had tried, I suppose, to kick off the duvet but had fallen off the sofa and was lying in a tangled heap on the floor. When I turned on the light, she attempted to cover her eyes with her forearm, but I could see what Amy meant when she mentioned a leper colony. Kim's face was covered with a rash which was beginning to blister. The blisters were filling with yellow pus. It looked at first sight like chicken pox.

'Bloody hell, Kim,' I said, shocked. 'Does it hurt?' I asked this because the other thing the rash reminded me of was when Amy had shingles in her late teens. It hadn't been on her face, but it was just as ugly, and very painful.

Kim groaned and tried to talk through teeth clenched against pain. That was answer enough, but I thought she said, 'I've been cursed,' or 'I've got the curse.' So I lifted her off the floor, half carried her to the bathroom and showed her where to find sanitary products and how to use the shower.

I fetched my phone and retreated to the living room where I Googled shingles. After that I Googled herpes because Amy, at the time, had been absolutely paranoid about sexually transmitted diseases but of course couldn't possibly share her fears with her mother. I remembered too that her mother mistook Amy's symptoms for a second case of chicken pox and only found out later that she could have helped Amy by taking her for an antiviral shot early on.

My mother had been very smug because she'd told Amy's mother that you couldn't get chicken pox twice and that you could only get shingles if you'd already had chicken pox. I did not discuss the possibility of herpes with my mother. Are you insane? Two Jewish mothers discussing symptoms is already a terrifying phenomenon; the addition of a possible sexually transmitted infection was too much for a teenager even to contemplate.

With all this in mind I rang my GP's surgery only to hear a recorded message saying the surgery was closed for the night. The recording gave the number of a locum service, but when I rang I was told by another recorded message that I was thirty-seventh in the queue. I was about to request a call-back when I heard a crash. I flew to the bathroom and found Kim on the floor. She had a red swelling on her blistered forehead. She must have hit her head on the edge of the bath or basin when she fell. The lavatory pan was dark red with blood.

'Kim!' I cried, shocked. 'What's happened?' I was so perplexed by the sight of her blood, and hopelessly confused by the possibility that what Lazaro had called 'gender suspension' might have been reversed so suddenly that she'd been caught unprepared. I was paralysed by indecision. All Kim could do was clutch her stomach and moan. I fixed her up as best I could and half carried her back to the sofa. She couldn't walk properly and cried at every step.

'Okay,' I said, wrapping her in the duvet because she was shivering uncontrollably. 'This is an emergency. I've got to do something. Immediately. What do you want me to do?'

She said something. I could only catch the words 'punishment' and 'curse'. At least that's what I thought she said.

I simply couldn't face the idea of putting her in my van, driving us to hospital and looking for parking so I punched in the number and ordered a cab to take us to the nearest A&E department. It came within ten minutes and while I was waiting I did my best to hide my anxiety and talk to her in a calm, reassuring tone of voice. It didn't work. Kim's reddish hair was black with sweat and the rash seemed to be spreading to her wrists and hands.

While trying to reassure her I was frantically wondering what to say when we got to the hospital. Was there some sort of medication she was supposed to take regularly but because she'd left the Palatine Estate without it she was suffering from a dramatic withdrawal reaction? How on earth would I explain that to the triage nurse at A&E?

By the time we arrived at Pond Street Kim could not walk at all. Someone brought a wheelchair and decided, on the spot, that she should be seen immediately. As they were about to wheel her away I caught a look at Kim's face under the bright hospital lights. She looked ten years older. Pain and desperation were scratched and scrawled on her poor skin alongside the blistering. And to my horror I saw that on top of everything else she seemed to be growing a moustache.

I was pushed to the head of the queue at the registration desk where I gave her name as Kim Harding and her address as the Palatine Estate. I was asked a lot of questions I couldn't answer, which I explained away by saying that I'd put her up for the night after a party. She was not a relation and I didn't really know her at all.

I asked if I should stay, and was told to leave my telephone number. I would be called if I was needed to take her home. Whose home, I wondered, as with enormous relief I left Kim behind in what I fervently hoped were professional hands.

After being enthusiastically welcomed home by the Beaus, I managed to tidy the living room and clean the bathroom without thinking about Kim at all. Then memory of her blistered, hairy, tormented face intruded. I'm ashamed to say that my first action was motivated by fear for my own health. I sealed the duvet and pillow she'd used into sturdy black bags. I would have them steam cleaned or dumped.

Shame punched me in the gut. Hadn't Kim helped me? She'd released me from the chair manacles and shown me the way through the maze of service corridors and up the disused concrete stairs. Why? I hadn't been at all persuasive, so what made her change her mind? I thought back through all the fear and incomprehension – until I realised that Kim only decided to release me after licking my nosebleed. I cringed at the memory. Up until that point she'd been smug. She'd been associated with the powerful; she dismissed me as a bit of a joke victim. After licking my blood she'd become, it seemed, as scared of my captors as I was. Perhaps my fear was carried in my blood and she had caught the contagion.

I tried to think about blood but my mind seemed to be rejecting thought. I needed to talk to Hannah. What was left of rationality went to war with anger and pride. Rationality, to my astonishment, won. I fumbled in my pocket for my phone but before I could use it Jake and Amy came in. Instantly, Beau and Bro came to my side, alert but not yet aggressive.

Jake and Amy stopped in the doorway. She took his hand in a gesture so blatant she might as well have tattooed 'Amy's Property' on his forehead or burned her brand onto his butt. He merely looked uncomfortable. Poor little Jakey.

I don't know what I felt. Maybe it was jealousy, maybe humiliation. Mostly, I think it was rage. They'd hurt me and betrayed me and yet they were still insisting on their right to live in my flat – whereas I didn't even want them to live on my planet.

The two dogs began to crowd forward belligerently. I stuck my chin out and said, 'Yes, I'm now the proud owner of these hounds. If you don't like it, you know what you can do.'

'You're using slumlord tactics to evict me,' Amy accused. 'What about that leprous vagrant you brought home to sleep on the sofa?'

'Don't be such a drama queen,' I replied – I might even have sneered – adding meanly, 'Kim doesn't have leprosy. It's probably only a virulent case of herpes. You might want to wash all the towels before your next shower.'

Amy shuddered, I was happy to note, and Jake looked even more uncomfortable.

I went on, 'As for Beau and Bro, they're rescue dogs – I couldn't leave them to be mistreated so I bought them. I will of course have to live somewhere with more space, but that will take time. If you want to continue living here you'll have to put up with them till the end of the month. Or you can buy me out. But I'm warning you now: don't expect any favours in the matter of property prices. If you, either of you, wanted any consideration from me, you should have treated me better. And if you must know, I never want to see either of you ever again.'

'I never knew you were such a vengeful bitch,' Amy said, beginning to tear up.

'And I never knew you were such a treacherous, spiteful woman,' I shot back. I couldn't call Amy a bitch – it would be an insult to female dogs. But I really was that angry; furious, in fact. Amy glared back at me. She was furious too.

Jake, with his wonderful deaf, dumb and blindness to emotions, said, 'I say, Seema, was that really Mark Kirkby of the London Scorpions you went out with yesterday evening? Are you seeing him again? Any chance of a couple of complementary tickets to their next home game?'

Both Amy and I gaped at him.

'What?' he said puzzled.

I was almost struck speechless but managed to say, 'In your dreams, moron.' Then turning to Amy, I added sweetly, 'You wanted him; you got him. Were you so sodding busy campaigning against me and beating me out that you failed to see what an emotional illiterate your prize was?'

'It's all about you, isn't it?' Amy said. 'Couldn't Jake and I just have grown together naturally because *you* are such a self-centred mare?'

'And our friendship lasted as long as it did because I was so self-centred?'

'Well you're accusing him of emotional illiteracy, but you never loved him. "He'll do for now", that's what you said.'

I was right: she had dobbed me in to Jake. I was mortified, but there was nothing to do but take it on the chin. I said, 'That was juvenile and unkind.' I turned to Jake. 'It's true: what Amy showed you was part of a stupid game we should've given up years ago. I apologise. But, Jake, it's also true that even though you were not the love of my life, I was fond of you. You were never a grand passion and I don't think I was that for you either. I can't speak for you; I can only tell you what I observed. If I'm wrong I apologise again.'

'You're not wrong,' Jacob Silver said. 'So why are you taking it this hard?'

'Because we'd been together for three years and I thought there was enough affection and respect between us that you'd be straight and decent with me. Instead, half the time we were supposed to be a couple was a sham. You were leading a double life and bonking my so-called best friend. I'm angry with you, but I don't want you back. The one I'm really fighting with is Amy who seems to have despised me, envied me and taken advantage of me for many, many years.' I cut my eyes hard towards Amy. 'I don't want you back either. I'm way better off without friends like you.' While I was saying all this I was wondering if I'd had the moxy to speak my mind because the dogs gave me the courage. With two gorgeous wolfhounds for company I wouldn't be lonely when my ex-best friend left with my ex-boyfriend.

It wasn't that I was feeling brave. It was as if my relationship with Lazaro – even if he was the cruellest, most malicious, evil man in the world – was still the most vivid and important one I'd ever had. He had taught me something about love that obliterated Jake completely. If I'd felt even a hundredth of that intensity for Jake I would have considered myself in love with him. But, I supposed, not even that much feeling for Jake would have saved me from Lazaro.

'Tell me something,' I asked Amy. 'Did you set me up with Lazaro?'

'Where would I meet a guy like him?' Any answered. Or rather, she didn't answer.

I continued to stare at her. But to my surprise it was Jake who took up the question.

'Come on, Amy,' he said. 'I want to know that too.'

'I don't want you to be angry with me,' she said snuggling up to him and raising her head so that she could kiss his neck the way I knew he liked. I watched his arm tighten around her. And, in spite of everything I'd only just felt, rejection hit me like a wave on a beach. It seemed to blow my guts out of my body, leaving me as hollow as an empty bottle. I'd lost him. I'd lost Amy. I'd lost, or never had, Lazaro.

Amy said, 'Well, remember that time when you and Seema went out to that stupid roundabout you were so proud of? That afternoon, we'd been together while she was working, and she came home late so we had to pretend we'd just been watching Living Dead on TV? And I was pissed off cos you were keeping me a secret? Remember?'

'Not really,' Jake said. 'There were lots of times like that.'

'Well,' Amy went on, looking annoyed, 'that night, I couldn't bear to be alone so I came out with you. She was driving the van so we were squashed up on the front seat. In fact I was almost sitting on your lap. We were so close I could feel, you know, that you wanted me again, and it was so exciting – our secret. But even so I was thinking we could be like this all the time if you'd just man-up and tell her the truth. But you always droned about her not having done anything to deserve being treated so badly, poor baby, and you didn't want to admit to being such a bastard. But I thought if she found someone else she'd be the guilty one. I *knew* she'd tell you cos she can't keep a secret to save her life. And then you'd go away and after a month or so we could inform her we'd just met by accident and pretend it was a new beginning – a new chapter. By that time she'd be with the new guy, and even if she still felt possessive about you, she wouldn't have a leg to stand on.'

Amy got up abruptly and went to the kitchen leaving Jake and me to stare after her. I did not want to look at him. It was exactly the sort of plan he'd sign up to because it allowed him to be the injured party. In fact, thinking back, I was sure he *had* signed up – if the speed with which he'd accused me of double dealing when I first met Lazaro was a clue.

Amy came back with a bottle of Prosecco and two glasses. Jake gave her a quizzical look and went to the kitchen for a third which he filled himself.

I thought Prozac would be more use to me than Prosecco but I accepted the glass. Jake went quickly back to his seat next to Amy. Perhaps he was afraid he'd given me something I could chuck in his face. But I was thinking, 'If he knows this already, why is Amy pretending to tell him about it for the first time, and why is he pretending to hear it for the first time? What the fuck are they up to now? Am I going to be paranoid about everything forever?'

Then I didn't know what to think so I just said, 'Go on.'

She decided to speak to me directly this time. 'You were planting stuff or weeding or whatever gardeners do. And I was just sitting in the van thinking that Jake should be in bed with me right now, but instead you'd dragged us out in the cold. You think he's with you, but he's not: he's with me. *We're* the couple; *you're* the spare wheel, and it's about time someone put you straight.'

Jake nudged her gently and said, 'Dial it down, sweetie.'

Amy had been my friend for over twenty years. I took a huge gulp of wine and nearly choked. Beau and Bro edged closer to me, laying their heads on my lap and their paws on my feet.

Amy took a deep breath and went on, 'Then a weird thing happened. An old guy tapped on the window and said, "Are you part of this gardening team?"

'I said I was just waiting for my boyfriend. So he said, "Is he the gardener?" And I said no. Then he asked about you, Seema. He said he'd watched the garden grow and was very interested in meeting the person responsible.

'He was old, but he had something, you know – charisma – and I couldn't take my eyes off him. So I thought maybe he would be a start. He might pry your sticky fingers off my Jakey. But the old guy said he was too tired to talk to you now. But he gave me his card and said, "Can you keep a secret?"'

My phone rang, interrupting Amy's story. I didn't recognise

the number but Amy's words were so hurtful that I took the call anyway. It was the charge nurse in the Observation Unit at the Royal Free. He told me Kim would be staying over night. There were tests. I could ring after the specialist's rounds in the morning at eleven.

'What tests?' I asked.

'It's too early to say,' he told me. 'There'll probably be more in the morning.'

'Yes, but what do you suspect? What am I supposed to tell her family?' Not that she had a recognisable family as far as I knew.

'Well,' he began reluctantly, 'all I can say at present is that the first tests are for lupus.'

'What's lupus?'

'I'm sorry,' he said. 'You'll have to ask one of the doctors. These are just tests. Now I have other calls to make. Ring back tomorrow: we'll have more information by then.'

'Is lupus contagious?' I cried, but he'd already rung off. I stared at my screen, and then saw that Jake had his phone out and was Googling lupus.

'*What?*' Amy asked urgently. 'What's lupus? Hurry!'

'Don't get your knickers in a twist,' Jake said. 'It's an auto-immune thing. Hereditary. You can't catch it. There's a rash, sensitivity to light, joint pains etcetera. Did this person have that?'

'She had a rash like pepperoni pizza,' Amy said.

'Yes,' I said, 'and she kept covering her eyes and she was crying with pain. In the end she could hardly walk.'

'Poor thing,' Jake said soberly. He was still reading from his phone. 'I don't think it's life-threatening. In fact it's a life-long condition which may be asymptomatic for long periods and then flare up dramatically.'

'It certainly did that,' I said. I decided not to mention the moustache and the blood. Those were details Amy would take ghoulish delight in. I didn't want her to have fun at Kim's expense. I didn't want her to have any fun at all.

'But it's not an infection?' she said. 'And there are tests?'

'Yes.' Jake read on. 'They look for certain antibodies in the blood.'

Blood, I thought. It's always about the blood.

NINETEEN

I couldn't sleep till nearly dawn, and then I slept like the dead. I dreamed I was standing on a dangerously rocking iceberg which was at the centre of a compass. Four voices were calling to me. My mother's voice came from the North; my father's from the West; Hannah's from the South; Lazaro's from the East. My arms were outstretched because I was trying to keep my balance and not tumble into the freezing ocean, but I was whirling like a confused magnetic needle.

The dogs woke me at nine-thirty, licking my face. For a couple of awful seconds I thought it was Kim licking my nosebleed. But I tumbled out of bed, fed them, dressed in trackies and a puffer jacket and took them out, glad that Amy and Jake had already left for work. We went to Golders Hill Park and I promised them a longer run later. On the way back I bought coffee and Danish for breakfast.

I was almost as disoriented as I'd been in the dream. I needed to do something completely unconnected to my disorientation. In fact, I wanted to work. I hadn't worked for a week. With a shock I realised that it was again almost the eve of Shabbat – a week since I'd met Lazaro and had my comfortable humdrum life shattered.

I rang Mr Lewin and Mr Sorkin. Mr Lewin makes his retirement comfortable by composing crossword puzzles so I knew he'd be at home. Mr Sorkin uses driftwood out of which he whittles eccentric chess pieces that his grandson sells at weekend markets. He more or less lives in a wheelchair. They are both kindly old geezers. Both are creative but lonely. They live only a quarter of a mile apart and you'd think they'd get on well. But they don't. In fact I can't tell either of them that I also work for the other. I don't know how they met or why they fell out, but Hannah, who knows them both, thought it had something to do with a woman.

Of all my clients they were the least likely to ask intrusive questions about my mother's death. As it turned out they were both fond of dogs and interested in why I'd suddenly acquired two huge wolfhounds. So I took Beau and Bro with me.

On the way to Mr Lewin's I devised a short, nearly true story about buying them from a cruel owner. Both of the old guys liked stories but were impatient of too many complicated details. And neither of them was any good with feelings. That was why I could trust them not to ask about my mother.

I spent over an hour on Mr Lewin's patio, pruning and reshaping his myrtle, his blueberry bush, his fig and his supposedly dwarf cherry. I had warned him about the cherry and the fig, both of which wanted to take over the world and were prone to black fly. Neither was suitable for a patio but Mr Lewin hadn't listened because he loved figs and cherries. It was true that his cherries were delicious and his figs, though tiny, were sweet, but this year, as well as cutting back the branches, I had to prune the fig's roots which had burst out of their container. It was hard, sweaty work and I was delighted to be doing it.

Mr Lewin gave me a mug of tea and a plate of digestive biscuits. He gave the dogs a bowl of water and a biscuit each. They accepted gracefully. I was pleased to see that although they weren't over-friendly they were beginning to be sociable.

Mr Sorkin's problems were quite different: he had two window boxes at the front that were completely redesigned each year. And at the back he had a tiny south-facing yard which I'd transformed with raised beds and wheelchair access. Unlike Mr Lewin, Mr

Sorkin liked to get his hands dirty so he did whatever weeding he could reach himself. My work at this time of year was helping to plan what he wanted and preparing the soil to support his choices. He loved vegetables, and this year he'd chosen sweet corn, mange-tout and courgettes. The job was made easier because he adored asparagus and I'd managed to establish a permanent, vigorous asparagus bed at the back. Beau and Bro investigated every inch of his flat and yard while he and I drank tea and talked. I made notes while the dogs lay at my feet and snoozed. I felt easy and useful.

'Well,' Mr Sorkin said, as I was putting pencil and notebook back in my bag, 'how's that old friend of yours?'

For a moment I thought he was talking about Amy and my heart instantly responded to her loss by lurching downwards in my chest. But he was talking about Hannah. 'I wish I saw more of her,' he said. 'Interesting woman. Logical mind. Should have been an engineer. I don't know what attracts women to the soft sciences. All those bleeding hearts.'

Blood again. I narrowed my eyes at him. 'Women don't always want to work in a man's world, with men's rules, everything set up to suit men. A man's world bends women out of shape. Maybe Hannah wanted to keep her own hours, make up her own rules and see what she could do about people's bleeding, broken hearts.' Blood – it gets every where. 'She's no softy,' I added.

'True. I expect she's been quite a help to you in the past few days.' And that was the only reference Mr S made to the death of my mother, which, by all descriptions, truly *had* been bloody. And had, possibly, saved Hannah's life.

I sighed and took the dogs home. Then I set out to see Hannah. It was time to mend fences.

On the way I changed my mind. It was after eleven. I checked my phone. There was nothing from the hospital. Good, I thought at first. I was not responsible for Kim. I wanted my own life back: my own hours and my own rules. Like Hannah.

I'm a gardener, I said to myself. I'm not built for weirdness. I have a good eye and a strong back; I have a feel for growing things. But I'm not an aesthete. I'm not sophisticated or intelligent enough to deal with the tricks and games cooked up by sophisticated, intelligent people. Shit, if I couldn't even deal with Amy's tricks and games what chance did I have with Lazaro? Not even a pop tart's chance at a teenage breakfast.

So I drove to Hannah's via the Royal Free telling myself that if I found a parking space for the van nearby I would take it as a sign I should go in and find out how Kim was getting on. To my dismay, I found one.

Inside the hospital I was told that Kim had been transferred from Observation to a women's general medical ward. I went up in the lift and found myself trying to negotiate with a dragon behind a desk.

'Kim Harding?' He gave me a forbidding stare before consulting his computer. 'In isolation: pre-assessment. No visitors. Are you a relative?'

'No, but…'

'No exceptions.' The fire-breather turned his back on me to pick up a phone that sounded so exhausted it might have been ringing for twenty minutes.

'God bless the NHS,' I said, relieved of all responsibility. I went back to the lift where I was accosted by a skinny woman who was pushing her own drip stand. She was barely covered by a hospital gown and had hair like rusty wire wool. She said, 'Friend of yours?'

'Excuse me?'

'That new one. Came up from Observation an hour ago. Friend of yours?'

Caught between saying 'Maybe' or 'Not really,' I murmured, 'Mmm?'

'I told them.'

'Told who?' I punched the call button twice.

'I'm not stupid,' she replied. '"Wait till the full moon", I said, "you'll see I'm right".'

'Of course you are,' I said, because it's what I say to total strangers who seem to be deranged. It's safer than saying, 'Piss off.' This is London – sometimes known as Loondon – after all. I punched the call button again. The doors ground open much too slowly.

'You can tell me.' The woman leaned towards me, her sweet pharmaceutical breath tickling my cheek. 'I can keep a secret.'

'Of course you can,' I said, stepping into the lift, pretending not to hurry.

The woman hopped up and down excitedly. 'I knew it,' she screeched. *'She's a werewolf!'*

Three women with the word, 'Physiotherapy' on their badges rushed in after me. The doors closed and the lift jolted into action. Although they must have heard the exchange because they'd been waiting right next to us the physios gave no sign of it. They were talking about a charity Fun Run. They sounded so English and ordinary they made me feel like an alien. Who was going mad round here, I wondered. Was it the woman with the wire wool hair, the physios who apparently hadn't noticed someone shrieking about werewolves, or was it me who had recently asked the man I loved if he was a vampire? Had the woman actually said, 'She's a werewolf'? Or is that what I, alone, heard? If what I heard hadn't actually been said, what was wrong with me?

I bought French Onion soup at a deli in Belsize Park and a loaf of freshly baked bread, a tub of expensive out of season raspberries and some cream. Seeking forgiveness is easier done with food offerings. And it was time for an early lunch.

Hannah opened her door, saying, 'Seema, how nice. We were just talking about you.'

I held out my offerings and said, 'I'm so sorry, Hannah. You did rescue me from something horrible but I don't know what, and I'm afraid I'm going mad.'

'Onion soup?' Hannah said. 'My favourite. Thank you. And there's enough for three. How thoughtful. Come in and meet my friend, Titus.'

'I should've rung,' I faltered. 'I'm not fit for company.' I gestured to my work jeans but to my horror I knew I was going to cry. I tried to push the bag into Hannah's hands and back away at the same time.

'No, no,' she said. 'Come in. You look so tired. Oh dear, you're crying. Yes, I think this is the perfect time for you to meet Titus.' She took my arm and shepherded me into the house.

'Is there blood?' I asked, trying to blot my eyes on my sleeve. Where the hell do tissues hide when you need them most?

'Only a little,' she said. 'You've been much worse. No, don't go and wash your face – I want Titus to see you just as you are.' This was the opposite of what I wanted, but she was the injured party as far as my behaviour to her was concerned so I followed meekly.

As usual her sitting room looked like an overcrowded antique shop – absolutely the wrong setting for the enormous man who got up to greet me. Pale brownish hair sprouted in all directions like badly mown hay and bright blue eyes examined me critically through steel-rimmed academic spectacles.

'Titus is Dutch but he's a professor of deviant behaviour at Berlin,' Hannah told me unhelpfully. He looked more like a weightlifter than a professor to me.

He enveloped my rather grubby paws in dinner-plate hands which would've better suited a riveter.

'Deviant behaviour?' I stammered, wondering fearfully what Hannah might have told him.

'Ah, Hannah,' he said, looking at her fondly. 'She does love her little jokes, no?'

Hannah said, 'No,' and I said, 'Yes,' more or less simultaneously.

She said, 'Do you like onion soup, Titus? Seema's brought some and I think it will complement the quiche perfectly.'

'Quiche?' I asked, thinking I'd never seen anyone who looked less like a quiche man.

'Wonderful,' Titus said, still staring at me. He leaned forward and, without asking, ran a golf-ball sized thumb under my left eye. He sniffed his thumb and then, to my disgust, licked it.

'Oh gross!' I snapped. 'Are you one of the Palatine people? What've you done, Hannah?'

'Don't worry,' Hannah said, on her way to the kitchen. 'Titus is one of the good guys.'

'That's what I thought about Lazaro,' I said, trying to edge round Titus and escape to the kitchen too.

He was a hard man to edge around. He said, 'In fact, that is not true: you never even considered Lazaro's *goodness*. It would not have mattered whether he was good or evil. You felt the danger but you did not care. He was worth the risk. Your judgements, even simple thought processes, were held in abeyance. You were enchanted.'

I might've hit him, although it would've broken my hand, if I hadn't been convinced that he would hardly notice. Instead I gave him a chilly look and said nothing – the cowardly woman's solution to violent impulses when facing an enormous opponent. I should have brought the wolfhounds, I thought, and regretted my fears for the safety of Hannah's fragile furniture.

'Why are you angry?' he asked. Then, without waiting for an answer he turned his head and called to Hannah, 'Do you have some hot chocolate in your kitchen? This young woman looks to have low blood sugar and she is too tired and anxious to listen with rational attention.'

This hulk should have been insensitive but he wasn't. Don't appearances count for *anything?* I thought wearily.

Hannah came back almost immediately with a jug of hot chocolate, three mugs and a smug smile. She said, 'I anticipated the suggestion, my dear Titus.'

'Of course.' Titus gave her a small, respectful bow. He took the tray and placed it on a spindly-legged table close to Hannah's favourite chair.

'Sit,' Hannah said to me, 'on the sofa with your feet up.' She poured the hot chocolate into the three mugs, and after we'd all had a couple of sips, she went on, 'What's on your mind, Seema? Why did you come?'

'To apologise,' I admitted. 'You called the police and got me out of a very tricky situation, but you refused to stay and back me up. I didn't know what you'd told the cops, but they were obviously looking for evidence of drugs and abduction and I couldn't provide any. In fact they couldn't even find the underground labyrinth I described and I looked like a total pronk. Kim was getting sicker and sicker and was too terrified to say a word. I needed help but you wouldn't stay. So I was rude and ungrateful. I'm very sorry.'

'It was nearly dawn,' Hannah explained. 'I was tired; I needed to go to bed.'

'I know,' I said. 'I wasn't thinking about you; I was only thinking about myself.'

'Under the circumstances that's quite understandable. How is Kim?'

'I took her to the Royal Free last night. She looked awful and could hardly walk or talk. When I rang to ask how she was doing someone told me they were testing for lupus.'

'Lupus?' Titus said, exchanging a long look with Hannah. 'Of course you know people at this hospital?'

'She isn't allowed visitors,' I put in. 'I'm not a relative so I couldn't insist.'

Hannah said, 'Seema dear, just tell us why you thought she was sick enough to take to hospital.'

I described the blisters, Kim's pain and near paralysis. I even told them about the blood in the toilet bowl. I explained why this was worrying in light of what Lazaro had said about 'gender suspension'. Then I told them about Kim beginning to grow a moustache. After that I paused and finally, reluctantly, I repeated my exchange with the rusty-haired woman while I was waiting for the lift.

Silence followed. I finished my hot chocolate and Titus poured more for all of us. I was beginning to feel better. Hannah reached for the phone and pressed the key for her contact list. She looked at Titus and said, 'Irvin Malloy.' When he nodded she tapped another key, waited a few minutes and then said, 'I'd like to speak to Doctor Malloy urgently. It's Hannah David. He has my number.' She waited a few more minutes, then said, 'Irvin, how are you? ... I agree – we shouldn't leave it so long... I miss you too... Listen Irvin, I'm sorry to interrupt your busy day but I need urgently to know the status of a patient on one of the women's medical wards. Her name is Kim...' she looked at me.

'Harding,' I supplied.

'Harding,' Hannah said. 'She was brought in last night and is being investigated for lupus... Yes... Thank you so much Irvin, you're a mensch.' She rang off.

'Fifteen minutes,' she said. 'He was a student of mine many years ago.'

Titus laughed. 'I also was a student of Hannah's,' he told me. 'I too respond at great speed.'

She dismissed his words with an airy wave of her hand. I noticed that as well as the usual gold band she was wearing a diamond and sapphire eternity ring. She was carefully dressed in a long sapphire blue skirt and a soft black mohair cardigan. Her scarf was black, white and blue in a bold African design. I was beginning to see that she had dressed up for Titus, and that she looked spectacular.

I smiled at her, and as usual she read me perfectly. She said dryly, 'While we are waiting, Seema, perhaps you'd fill us in about what happened after you left your flat with Mark Kirkby to go to a party in Belgravia.'

'How do you know about that?'

'Jacob Silver rang me, perturbed. He seems to have retained

some feelings for you despite Amy's best efforts. He might have been motivated by jealousy but all he admitted to was concern for your safety. He told me that, in spite of all our warnings and misgivings about him, you were going to see Lazaro. He said he had "a very bad feeling about it". This was correct, wasn't it?'

'Yes,' I said. 'I'm grateful you took him seriously.' That, I thought, was enough gratitude, even for Hannah. I still had strangely mixed feelings about her intervention. But I began to tell her as accurately as I could about what happened: about the reception, the table with the boar's head on it, about my attempt to leave and accepting a drugged drink from Kim.

Titus, who had been writing in a spiral notebook looked up and said, 'But Lazaro had not, at this point, appeared, even to greet you?'

'Well,' I began defensively, 'he wasn't the one who invited me.'

'Hah!' Hannah snorted. 'This has been his passive-aggressive approach all along.'

'So you have informed me,' Titus said, not looking up from his notebook.

Hannah was about to reply when the phone rang. She picked it up. 'Irvin,' she said, 'how good of you to call back so quickly. What news?'

After a few minutes she thanked Irvin profusely and rang off. 'Extraordinary,' she said to Titus. 'Now Kim's doctors are investigating porphyria – in its acute *and* cutanea tarda presentations. If that is what it is, they say they have never seen such dramatic or speedy deterioration.'

They stared at each other while I waited for an explanation.

Eventually, Titus made another entry in his notebook, looked up and said, 'Well, Seema, if that is so, it might account for what you thought of as blood in Kim's urine. In fact it is the colour of the urine which changes. The name porphyria is derived from the Greek word for purple – which in turn describes the colour of the sufferer's urine.'

'Plus,' Hannah said, not to be outdone, 'porphyria cutanea tarda is light-sensitive and can cause blistering and facial hair.'

'Poor Kim,' I said, shocked.

'Indeed,' said Titus, looking more curious than sympathetic.

'Now we must wait for further information,' Hannah said. 'So continue with your narrative, Seema.'

'Is it dangerous?' I asked, 'this poor-fear whatsit?'

'Porphyria,' Hannah said. 'Not if it's treated quickly. Although there is no cure. There's only management.'

'It's hereditary,' Titus said. 'A genetic defect.'

'But let's not scurry down *that* rabbit hole yet,' Hannah interrupted. 'We don't have enough data. Tell us instead about this reception you went to with Mark.'

I paused, remembering what happened when I woke up in the Red Suite. I wasn't going to report my conversation with Gemma because that would involve me confessing the erotic dream that just possibly wasn't a dream. No way would I tell Hannah and Titus *that*. Of course it was one of many things I was ashamed of; one of the enormous number of things I didn't understand.

To give myself a bit of a boost I began with Lazaro approving of my drawings. Hannah took her phone out and showed Titus the pictures she'd sent to her friend at the Royal Horticultural Society. I'd forgotten about those, and I felt a sudden burst of relief – there was a record of them. They weren't lost completely.

'They aren't my normal style,' I said. 'Usually, when I'm pitching for a job I'm a lot less fanciful – more factual, academic if you like.'

'Please to send these to my email?' Titus asked Hannah. Then, turning to me, he added, 'But of course you were not merely "pitching for a job", were you?'

'That's what Gemma said!' I exclaimed unguardedly. Hurriedly I explained Gemma and Pasqual's relationship with Lazaro, and went on to talk about how I'd bought the dogs and how Lazaro's attitude to me changed. I could still feel the cold despair of his rejection when he told me he would not employ me; how he'd linked his refusal to police intrusion caused by my mother's death.

'In which our good friend, Hannah, believes he is involved,' he said.

'Yes, but...' Again, I was forced to defend Lazaro.

'But?' One of his eyebrows shot up making him look both quizzical and sceptical. Then he leaned forward. I drew back, afraid he would do something disgusting again – like licking my blood off his thumb. But he simply touched the palm of my left hand with his forefinger and said very sweetly, 'Time to come down to earth. There is no moonlit garden.'

I was suddenly almost suffocated by sorrow.

Seeing this he said, 'Someone has taken great advantage of your guileless need. Now you must come back home and be tough. You are still in danger, and so is your good friend, I think.' He gestured towards Hannah who was having a rather comical struggle with her mobile phone.

She saw me looking, and wordlessly handed me the phone. I ignored Titus's request that the photos be sent to his computer and sent them to his mobile instead. It was much simpler. But the pause and the sense that I had done something to help Hannah steadied me. When I'd finished I told them what Lesley Sharpe had said about a mistake made by a 'surveillance operative', and the voice in my head which said, 'the wrong old woman died.'

'Less of the "old", Hannah said, making Titus laugh too loudly and too long.

I studied him, noticing his strong, slightly crooked teeth. He was untidy and ungainly, but had I not been comparing him to Lazaro's grace and perfection, I suppose I would've thought him quirky and amiable. Without any evidence at all I decided he was a smoker.

'Do you like dogs?' I asked him suddenly.

'Yes,' he said, surprised, 'unless they are very small and easy to crush when I pat them.'

Hannah glanced at us over the rims of her spectacles and said, 'How much did you pay for the dogs?'

'A hundred pounds each. But I wrote him a note saying I'd pay whatever he thought they were worth.'

'Has your cheque been cashed? Look at your bank statement.'

I fiddled with my phone, looked at the latest transactions and saw that Lazaro's cheque for two grand was safely lodged in my account, but no one had removed two hundred pounds. Rejected again, I thought.

Titus said, 'You say everyone at this place was afraid of dogs?'

I nodded.

'Everyone? Most un-English. Now tell us more about this so strange evening.'

I tried to explain the weird competition between Mark and me; how it was evident that I had been followed and filmed for at least a year; how, apart from Mark's hacked credit card records, everything had shown him to great advantage while I'd been made to look like a clumsy fool.

'But,' Hannah put in, 'the competition was not between you and Mark.'

'Exactly.' Titus nodded vigorously. 'It was between your Lazaro and Garth Harding.'

'It sounds like a contest for leadership.'

'But who wishes to lead what?'

'Quite,' Hannah said, and they both looked at me.

'I don't *know*,' I wailed. 'But it was Garth Harding who won.' I repeated Garth saying, 'Face it, old boy, you lost.'

I continued, 'The woman, the kind of announcer and referee, called Lazaro and Garth Harding our "sponsors", and Mark and me their "protégés" and "contestants". We were being awarded points or credits. I was behind by a country mile.'

'She means she was a big loser,' Hannah explained cheerfully to Titus who was looking puzzled. 'Don't be distressed, Seema, we're collecting information about a cruel game which has absolutely nothing to do with your true worth. Now go on, dear, and tell us as much as you can remember.'

But I was still stung by being called a big loser, so I said, 'I was awarded an 8.7 degree of difficulty compared to Mark's 5.4.' And then I told them about Lesley Sharpe's comment that Lazaro's choice of me as his contestant was evidence of his 'hubris and sense of humour'.

There was so much I didn't want to tell them. I wasn't, for instance going to admit that I was wearing Lazaro's ring. It was on a fine gold chain around my neck, under my clothes. I'd never worn the chain before. My mother gave it to me when I passed enough A-level exams to leave home and go to university. My mother's selection of a suitable prize was a Star of David on a gold chain – something she expected me to wear always, as she did – a sign and symbol of who I was and where I'd come from – a small world of no choices. I saw the gift as a ball and chain. It was as if my name, Seema Dahami – which I had to explain and spell for every new person I met – was not enough to mark me out in British society as 'one of the others'. All I wanted to do was fit in. Fat chance.

Now I'd exchanged the Star of David for a ring that bore a waxing moon etched into a cornelian, given to me with a kiss by Lazaro. It was a secret, something I literally kept close to my heart, something I'd felt compelled to do. But I was forced to confess to myself that that I wasn't comfortable about the exchange.

I realised I'd been silent too long when Hannah asked, 'What are you thinking, dear?'

I lied: 'I was trying to remember what Lesley Sharpe called the next phase of the contest. I think it was Demonstration of Impact. But I don't know what it was about because she had our monitors switched off so that we wouldn't experience "undue influence". But that's when the damn chair became a restraint. And then I panicked and forgot to "endure in silence".'

Then I had to describe the chair to Titus: the button I'd pushed as a sort of lie detector, and the needle which gave me a blood test.

'All controlled remotely?' he asked. 'By who?'

'There were control rooms at the back of both the big auditorium and the TV studio. There were drones and remote cameras too. But I couldn't see who was doing what.'

'These places,' Hannah began, 'according to the police who searched the building, do not exist. There are only two floors below ground: one is for luxurious spare accommodation, the other for kitchen and utilities. They could find no secret stairs or lifts that descended below the utility basement.'

'I am *not* making this up,' I said with deliberate emphasis although actually I wanted to throw a gigantic tantrum about being treated as a fantasist by the cops.

'There may be at least two alternatives,' Titus said, tapping his front teeth with a slightly yellowed fingernail.

Yes, you *are* a smoker, I thought, glad to have discovered a small sign of something I'd been right about.

'It may be that the police are looking in the wrong place. Maybe this underground labyrinth, as you say it, is not directly underneath the house they searched. Maybe access is found through a door they did not find.'

'Yes, I thought that too,' Hannah said. 'When you look at the Palatine Estate on Google Earth you can see far more clearly how extensive it is.'

'My other thought,' Titus said, looking at me more cautiously, 'is that these people, are making something with mind control. This Demonstration of Impact is to show the success of what you call "brain washing". They wish to show that they can make you believe something that is not.'

'Quite so,' Hannah said eagerly. 'I think they have been testing and playing on your suggestibility for quite a while. I told you, Titus, didn't I, about the bacon cheeseburger?'

'Indeed – most significant.'

'How long have you been here?' I asked him suspiciously.

'I came here since yesterday morning.'

'I called him as soon as you'd been released from the Palatine Estate,' Hannah said. 'So many extraordinary events have taken place, and I thought Titus was exactly the right man to help us think about them. And now I think we should stop for lunch.'

So we ate quiche, onion soup and good bread while I tried to find out more about Titus.

'Just a teacher,' he said, waving his soup-spoon casually.

But when he went outside for his 'postprandial' smoke Hannah told me a little more. 'He's done extensive work on some of the odder manifestations of group dynamics,' she said. 'His book "Cult and Club Cultures" attracted a lot of attention in the profession, and now, of course, he is sometimes consulted by the police in many Western European countries. It isn't simply disturbing belief systems he's interested in; it's also the more radical political groups, of which there are too many these days. And then, also, there are clusters around deviant sexual behaviour – dangerous desires that are all too easily satisfied now. But it is the faux family groupings and associations that reinforce the deviant behaviours which interest him most.'

I cleared the table and began washing dishes while she talked. Then, as she went through to her living room, leaving me to make the coffee, she murmured, 'Titus is in great demand – the zeitgeist being so fractious and fractured. I am not a fan of the times we live in.'

'I know,' I said, remembering her work with holocaust survivors and knowing that she had spent her whole working life among the fractured and fractious.

We ate small bowls of raspberries and cream with our coffee and I imagined Titus making short work of huge plates full of red meat and fries while dragging on a cigarette. It made him seem less intimidating. Why? I didn't know. I wanted to go home to Beau and Bro – company I could be sure of.

Instead Hannah wanted me to talk about Kim. 'Who is she?' she asked after I'd tried to explain how she'd turned out to be a rescuer as well as a captor. 'Clearly she wasn't just a server. From what you describe, she has to be part of the social structure of that group. A lowly member or a member in waiting but certainly not someone hired for a night's work. And what's this about her licking the blood from your nosebleed?'

'That was so revolting,' I said, not looking at Titus. 'She kept saying she couldn't stop. And afterwards she was in a total funk, as if she'd committed a huge sin. That's when we *both* became the hunted ones. We had to rely on each other.'

'Interesting,' Titus said. 'So only specific people or classes of people in the hierarchy are allowed to taste blood.'

'Hierarchy?'

'Yes, always, Seema, there is a hierarchy.'

'But what has it got to do with blood?' I asked. 'And why –' I gestured to my nose and eyes, '– I never got nosebleeds before. And what's the meaning of red tears?'

Titus said, 'Nothing weird or mystical, Seema. You will not have heard of Haemo lacria, I suppose? No. It is a rare condition, sometimes caused by, for example, conjunctival injury or tumour. But in your case, I think, it must be related to the unaccustomed nosebleeds. A backflow, you might say, through the naso-lachrymal system.'

'Nose and eyes are connected,' Hannah put in helpfully. 'It's why your nose runs when you cry.'

'But this is a diversion,' Titus cut in again. 'You were telling us about the contest. Did you receive any clue about who these people were?'

'No. At first I thought it was a grotesque reality TV production company.' Then Titus's use of the word 'clue' reminded me of something: 'When I asked Kim if she was part of a weird religious sect like Rosicrucian she said, "And so *ad infinitum*." Then she laughed at me and said I'd stepped on the biggest clue I was ever likely to get.'

'*Ad infinitum?*' Hannah said, looking at Titus. 'Forever, always, without end, in perpetuity, eternally? Does anything ring a bell?'

'An organisation that calls itself Ad Infinitum? There's something, maybe – but I need my library.'

'Vampires are supposed to live forever,' I said quietly, hoping I wouldn't be heard; hoping I would be heard.

Hannah and Titus stared at me, each waiting for the other, I supposed, to tell me what an idiot I was. So to delay the inevitable, I said, 'Lazaro called Kim a "child of the house," and he said she was in gender suspension. He said, "Think of honeybees". I asked him directly if he was a vampire. Don't look at me like that, Hannah. Then I asked him if vampires actually had to be supernatural. He never answered a direct question directly, but he wanted me to think about inherited characteristics. He talked about the Maasai as maybe being survivors of an ancient civilisation that depended on both milk and blood. He was saying that both could be gifts. He was arguing against my compartmentalised thinking about diet.'

'Aha!' Titus exclaimed to Hannah. 'The bacon cheeseburger?'

'I suspect it was one of Lazaro's Demonstrations of Impact.' she said. 'If he could influence Seema to act against one of her most strongly held positions it would be clear proof of his dominance over her.'

'Her compliance would earn him credits in this bizarre contest of strength between himself and the Harding man?'

I said, 'But I didn't *comply* – it was not something I decided to do. I did it without knowing I'd done it. I never changed my mind about eating meat. Even when he suggested we could exchange blood my stomach almost turned inside out in revulsion.'

Hannah looked taken aback. 'He actually offered you his blood?'

'Well, yes and no.' I stopped. My throat was closing as if a giant hand was strangling me. The little wounds were throbbing. I was shaking, and I could feel sweat crawling down my sides.

'What is this?' Titus asked.

'For want of a better interpretation,' Hannah said grimly, 'I'm calling it one of her panic attacks. Heat up some milk, Titus. No caffeine but maybe a little honey.'

'One small diazepam?' he suggested.

Hannah brought me a damp towel to wipe my face and hands, arranged cushions on the sofa and covered me with a soft rug. Titus came from the kitchen with a cup of warm sweet milk in one hand and a small white pill in the other. I felt like a sick child. Cosseted but embarrassed I fell asleep for about an hour.

I woke with a start when the phone rang. Hannah picked up quickly, saying, 'Yes, this is she.' Then, 'Yes she's here... but, no, that's just not possible... why? – because she has been here all afternoon ... no, no knowledge at all. Who am I speaking to?' She transferred the phone from her right to her left hand and made a note on her phone pad. 'Yes,' she said. 'I will make enquiries and call you if I learn anything new.' She closed her phone, took a deep breath and said, 'Kim has disappeared from hospital.'

'What do you mean?' I was awake but fuzzy.

'One minute a nurse was inserting a cannula into her arm – they were afraid her liver and kidneys were failing – and the next minute, when someone else came in to assist with the drip he found the nurse on the floor unconscious and Kim's bed empty.'

'This nurse?' Titus asked.

'She said she felt dizzy and must have fainted. No one saw Kim leave. They say she was in no condition to walk without assistance. Someone is checking security tapes.'

'Was it snowing?' I asked.

Hannah and Titus looked at each other as if I'd sprouted floppy green ears. But I was staring at the gathering dusk outside the window. Cold seemed to be swarming up to the glass as if it wanted to creep in through the cracks. I threw off the blanket and got to my feet. 'The dogs,' I told Hannah. 'I've left them alone far too long.'

'Go with her.' Hannah almost snapped at Titus. 'Talk to her about Lazaro. I can't do it without losing my temper.'

'What will you do?' Titus said, and almost at the same moment I said, 'No, I don't want to leave you alone.'

'I'm going to the hospital,' Hannah told us. 'I'm meeting Irvin there. I won't be alone.'

'This is not a good plan,' Titus grumbled as he lumbered behind me to the van.'

'Then stay behind and argue with Hannah,' I answered, unlocking the passenger side door for him.

'That is not a good plan either: I have nearly never won an argument with her.'

'Me neither,' I said as I scrambled in and started the motor.

TWENTY

We took the dogs to Hampstead Heath and they disappeared into deep dusk as soon as their paws hit grass.

'These are the hounds that guarded the estate?' Titus asked. 'That Lazaro was afraid of?'

'That everyone was afraid of – even their handler,' I corrected him. 'And they were a lot more scary a couple of days ago.'

'Then I wonder why such animals were required. You say there were electronic security measures, very sophisticated technology. So maybe those who were high in the organisation were afraid of attacks from within?'

I considered this, then said, 'It's possible, but the only time I saw them loose outside the house was in the daylight. Listen, Titus, I know you're a stone rationalist like Hannah, but the people who lived there kept vampire hours.'

'Invisible, you say, from dawn to dusk? But Seema, it is only because *you* didn't see them. Think of this: if maybe as Lazaro suggested, there is a genetic connection between all of them, then, have you thought, they might all have inherited a light-sensitive disease?'

'Porphyria? Like Kim?'

'This, until proved by examination of blood, is only hypothesis. But Seema, now, while Hannah is not listening, please describe to me Lazaro.'

'It's difficult,' I began. But then Beau and Bro came galloping back and I fed them each a couple of Doggie Treats from my pocket before they raced joyfully away again.

'Your face,' Titus said, 'when you look at your dogs, is radiant. When you are thinking of Lazaro you look afraid and secretive.'

'Oh great!' I said, offended. 'Now I'm being attacked by a professor of deviant behaviour who can see in the dark.'

'Observing, not attacking.'

We had been walking along an up-hill path. It was so cold that we huddled down into our puffy coats and met hardly any other walkers. Now we stopped and sat on a bench close to a dim lamp. He reached in his pocket and brought out a packet of Drum rolling tobacco. Although he was probably at least fifty years old he rolled his cigarette carelessly, like an art student. When he lit up, burning flakes of loose tobacco floated down onto his thick chest and he brushed them away without looking. He was staring upwards, blowing smoke at the blackening sky, taking no notice of me.

I took a deep breath and began, 'I'd say Lazaro is a little less than six feet tall.' I went on to describe him in minute physical detail. Then I stopped and waited for Titus to ask me what he really wanted to know while he, presumably, waited for me to continue.

Then he said, 'This has been an extraordinary and terrible week for you – your mother's murder, the loss of your boyfriend, the betrayal by your best friend, and now this – when you are sucked into something you do not understand. I am in awe of your strength and resilience. You don't have to fight me, Seema. I'm here to help you.'

'You don't understand,' I said. 'I can't explain this to Hannah but I feel all my so-called strength comes from Lazaro. His... interest... in me is what has sustained me.'

'Yet his "interest" has possibly caused everything. Some co-incidence, I agree, but consider: his "interest" in you began, as you say, at least a year ago. For how long has your boyfriend been cheating on you with Amy? Could these items be linked? Hannah says that Amy "set you up" with Lazaro – gave information to him before you actually met. And then, your mother...'

'I know, I know. It's almost certain that the people who were following me, agents from a firm of, I dunno, investigators, called Leigh-Samson, caused her death, but...'

'You mean "killed her", "murdered her". Caused her death, Seema, no, no – this is too passive. You might be talking about a virus or a cycling accident. Again you are absolving Lazaro.'

I felt there was an invisible shield separating us. I heard his words, but they didn't penetrate my mind or my heart. I said, 'How do you know there was anything to absolve him for? His enemies, Garth Harding and Lesley Sharpe, could have done it to discredit him.'

'What has he done to you, my dear girl? For only one week he has made an addict of you – if not to opioids, then to himself. He can do this because for one *year* he has, with the help of outside agencies and your ex-friend, gathered all the information he needs to trap you, turn you emotionally inside out and dominate you. The night you met he already knew you far too well.'

'I expect that must be true because I saw the evidence. But my experience of meeting him seems to upstage the evidence. We met. He transformed my life. He made me feel I was transforming his.'

'Okay,' he said, relighting his cigarette. 'Then I must ask, why did he choose you?'

'That's what I keep asking: "Why me?" I remember thinking, before we began talking in depth, that given the way he dressed, his looks, his tan et cetera, that Golders Green was not his natural stalking ground. I thought of old Fellini films where an aristocratic guy like him would always be yearning for mysterious beauties.'

'But he was not looking for a mysterious beauty; he was looking for you. I want you to think about the words "degree of difficulty". In sports, such as diving or snow boarding, this is taken into consideration when judging a performance: the skill required to perform a particular manoeuvre. So, if Garth Harding, for instance, took a lot more time to groom a famous sportsman than Lazaro took to groom you for this grotesque competition, the degree of difficulty attached to you would be greater and would give him an edge.

'So. You come from a religion that has many prohibitions about diet, about blood in particular, and you are vegetarian.'

'Exactly,' I cried. 'But those things only matter if you want someone to drink blood. And who would be interested in that?'

'You want me to say "vampires". But I won't.' Titus gave up on his cigarette and absent-mindedly put it in his pocket. 'There is also this thing called vampirism which is a deviant fantasy of dominance and submission and that has in its heart a fascination or fetish with blood. This is far more reasonable, is it not? It is a vampire *game*, Seema. The competition you describe is a game within a game. This Palatine Estate hosts a club of men and women of the same quasi-sexual interests. It is time to vote, for instance, for the new president. So they make a sport of it. That's all, Seema.'

'That's not all.' I could feel my temper rising. 'You and Hannah are so totally in love with the rational. What about the snow? What about Kim and gender suspension?'

'There is, from what little I know about porphyria, a hormone component. Suppose a child has all the markers for the disease and, as it is inherited, her family knows the condition will become active at puberty. Will not the family and the child herself wish to delay the evil day? There are drugs, Seema, employed by transsexual children – invented in East Germany many years ago for use by little girl gymnasts when their trainers wanted to keep their optimum power-to-weight ratio static. These drugs interrupt development of secondary sexual characteristics like breasts. If you knew you had this sickness in your future would you not want to take the drugs?'

'You've got an answer to everything,' I said crossly.

'Yes I have. I am not playing a game with you. I only wish you to think with clarity about alternatives to the unreasonable. Look what happened when Kim left the Estate. She probably has no access to her medication. She goes out in daylight and the result is devastating.'

'There's no talking to you.' I got up and began to walk away. After a moment or two I heard him thumping along behind me. He was not light on his feet.

'Why are we quarrelling?' he asked when he caught up.

'Because you and Hannah are treating someone like Lazaro as if he's a collection of symptoms – of both disease and perversion. You haven't even met him. You're always twisting facts to suit your theories.'

'Aha!' he crowed, delighted. 'You are quoting the estimable Sherlock Holmes at me, I think?'

'It's a good all-purpose quote. You ignore everything you can't explain.'

'For example?'

'The snow, my dreams, the way I have felt that my mind is not my own. Did Hannah tell you about the ugly stuff I said to her?'

'Indeed,' he said thoughtfully. 'But, Seema, you live in a xenophobic world. You are of a race that is treated with dislike and suspicion. It is common in people of such a background as yours to sublimate the frightening opinions that surround you. *In extremis* your *internalised* anti-Semitism finds its voice. It is not Hannah you hate in such moments. It is yourself. Think, Seema: your mother's throat was cut. She bled to death in her kosher kitchen. How terrifying is that? Hannah tells me that you have not mourned.'

'I can't. It isn't real. The police haven't released her body and they won't let me go into her house. According to all her friends and congregation, the autopsy is a desecration and she should have been buried days ago.' While I was saying this I was wondering why I hadn't heard from DS Richardson. But it was one question too many to cram into my overloaded mind, so I dismissed it.

Titus was saying, 'As for Lazaro dominating your thoughts, this is exactly what is worrying Hannah. For myself I would say that this, for a young woman infatuated, is not an uncommon problem. And because he is the supplier of addictive drugs it is no surprise either.'

Furious, I said, 'Oh *right*. Love and drugs make you do the whacky?'

'Well, don't they?' he said in his most patient and reasonable tone. 'Listen, terrible things have happened. Some people might find their explanation in believing it is the will of God. But you and God are not compatible.'

'Listen yourself – I don't believe in the supernatural. I keep saying that. But what if the folk lore and legends about vampires have as their source a race of very secretive, self-protective people whose skin is light-sensitive; who maybe, at certain times in history, have had to subsist on blood?'

'Blood, you say?' Titus stopped and then lengthened his stride to catch up with me.

'Or maybe not,' I corrected myself hurriedly. 'When people are afraid, or want to terrify children, or set a population against outsiders, they often throw up the *scare* that strangers are monsters who will drink their blood.'

'You are thinking perhaps of the persistence of the Blood Libel? Yes, of course you are right. But Seema, you admit yourself that the people at the Estate are fixated on your blood. The nosebleed I have seen myself of course, and what you call the red tears. But now *you* are on the side of the rationalists. You are arguing both sides of the question.'

'I'm arguing against vampirism, against that syndrome that begins with an R...?'

'Renfield's.'

'I'm arguing for a rational explanation of vampires. This does *not* mean I believe in the supernatural. But at the same time too many things are too effing weird.'

'I think you do not wish to associate Lazaro with anything underhand or perverted. I think you are protecting your abuser.'

'And I think you're full of shit,' I shouted in a sudden burst of fury that startled me and caused an instant headache.

Far from taking offence, Titus looked gratified. 'From what you say, I believe, at the Palatine Estate, there is a triumvirate of Garth Harding, Lesley Sharpe and your Lazaro. Maybe, such a contest for leadership is normal for this group, or maybe they have become bored with the usual method of decision-making. Maybe they have turned democratic voting into a blood sport which is intended to entertain and titillate the mass of the group's members. Recall for me how the audience reacted to the videos of you?'

I was still close to boiling point but I was forced to remember the applause for Mark and the derisive laughter I'd provoked. 'Yes,' I muttered feeling my face burn with shame.

'Lazaro *himself* put you in that position. He chose you as his representative. He set you up as a comedy of ineptitude to entertain his audience. His intention was to present you as totally unfit for purpose and then show everyone how great was his skill when he forced you to do whatever would win him the contest.'

'Drink his blood?' I whispered.

'I very much doubt it would be *his* blood,' Titus said shaking his shaggy head. 'No, Lazaro's blood will be forbidden to a foreigner: his supremacy contrasted with your subservience. Possibly it would be Mark's, or maybe they had some other victim hidden away to sacrifice.'

'You're guessing.' But somewhere at the back of my mind was the memory of Lazaro saying, 'You would die for me? Yes. But would you kill?' Had he really said that? I tried to kick my brain into life.

Titus was looking at me with a kindly, speculative expression.

'Lazaro did say he chose me,' I told him, but not as if it was a matter of pride anymore. 'Later he said the situation was none of his making and he was in great danger. And I said I'd die for him.'

'Yes,' Titus said sadly. 'I expect you meant it.'

'Have I been the biggest idiot on the planet?' I asked. I was feeling as empty as a grapefruit skin after someone scooped out the contents with a sharp, cruel spoon.

'No,' he said. 'You are not an idiot. You met someone far stronger, far more experienced than yourself. You have been lied to and controlled by a man who was focussed solely on his own success. You have been put in an extraordinary position you had no hope of understanding. And you became entranced. It is not your fault. You must not judge yourself.'

'Why not?' I said. I felt numb and dull now. 'I've been fooled. It isn't just Lazaro. It's Jake and Amy too. Especially Amy. Men could come and go, but she and I would be solid till one of us died. How could I not have seen that was just my stupid fantasy? My need for my friend blinded me to what was happening under my own nose. Kim was right when she shouted, "You dazzled yourself." Every mistake I've made was caused by my own needs.'

I knew everything Titus had said was on the money. Lazaro, in that last conversation we'd had in the hall of his house, had more on less confirmed Hannah's worst interpretations and my deepest fears. But he'd talked too of love and our connection. He gave me his ring. I was bound to him.

I tried to explain some of this to Titus. He nodded almost impatiently, and then said, 'What is the future?'

The question silenced me. There had been so many endings; I couldn't imagine a future. There *was* no future. As this dreary thought hit me like a bullet in the middle of my forehead the dogs capered out of the dark and knocked me flat on my back in their eagerness to greet me. They also, for a few glorious minutes knocked the depression out of me while I tussled with them and hugged them and endured their long wet tongues. Titus stood well back and laughed out loud.

'You are a much loved young woman,' he said. 'You will remain a gardener, I hope.'

I stared at him, so he went on, 'I could see on your face the doubt. But Hannah has shown me pictures on her phone. Did you know she takes pictures of many of your works? They give her pleasure. She is proud. I ask my question because someone who has lost so much in such a short time will sometimes lose belief in herself. But you should know that in the end you had the strength to resist Lazaro.'

'No I didn't,' I said. 'The police came because Hannah sent them. I had been abject. I even quoted the Book of Ruth to him. You know, "Entreat me not to leave thee... "? Even at that last minute when he held out his hand to me, I might have gone with him if Grigori hadn't interrupted.'

I got up and we turned to go back to the van. Beau and Bro walked quietly beside me now and only made short forays into the bushes if they heard or smelled something interesting.

'You see, your dogs will protect you,' Titus said, 'just as Hannah protected you. And why is that? Is it not because you love and protect them?'

'That may be the deal with the dogs, but between Hannah and me it's always she who has been the protector and giver.'

'I don't think so. She is an old woman who has no children. You are her ersatz daughter. You give her your physical strength, your company and your vigilance when she is sick. You think you have nothing to give?'

'Nothing as important as what she gives me.'

'You should try to ignore your childhood memories sometimes, but do not tell Hannah I gave this unorthodox advice,' he said. 'What else is in your future?'

'I must talk to the cops and bury my mother,' I said gloomily. 'I must find out how to clean her house so that it will be kosher again. So I'll have to talk to the rabbis. Then I'll sell it because I need a house with a garden for the dogs. I'd like to move to the country but I can't leave Hannah and my clients.'

'You can't?'

'Okay, I don't *want* to.'

'That's better,' he said, 'so long as it's true.' Then he threw back his head and laughed a deep bray of laughter which resounded around the deserted heath and made the dogs look up at him in amazement. A single owl hooted in reply.

TWENTY-ONE

I intended to drive Titus back to Hannah, but when we checked our phones and found no message he told me she'd instructed him to stay with me until he heard from her. So reluctantly I took him to my flat where I found Amy about to leave for Pilates and Jake on the sofa cuing up a recorded football match he'd missed the evening before.

'You're full of surprises,' Amy said, taking in the bulk that was Titus as he filled the hallway and prevented her from leaving. 'I liked the last one better.'

'The last one was Mark when he took me to the reception,' I told Titus.

Titus looked Amy up and down without making eye contact, showing no interest at all. He certainly knew how to annoy women – a skill that warmed my heart when it wasn't me he was annoying. The dogs ignored both her and Jake as they bustled through the living room to the kitchen. I followed them and gave them food and fresh water.

In the living room I saw that Titus was sitting on the sofa beside Jake. Already enormous, Titus had placed himself too close to Jake and was adopting the dominant male posture – legs and arms akimbo, taking up more than his fair share of space. Jake was forced to make himself small and edge into the corner. I was sure this was intentional. Again, I admired his talent for provocation.

I sat in the armchair with my hands folded demurely in my

lap. For a couple of minutes we all watched the beginning of the match. Then, when the dogs ambled in from the kitchen and flopped down at my feet Titus said, without looking at him, 'Jacob, turn the TV off. It's time for you to go home to your mother.'

Jake's face flamed but he said, 'I want to watch the match.'

Titus yawned and stretched. Jake had to get up to avoid physical contact. I could see he was enraged: his face was scarlet.

'Just be a good boy and turn that off,' Titus said coldly, jerking his chin towards the screen. 'This is not your television set I think.'

'Amy said...' Jake began. But this time I interrupted him. 'You can visit Amy when she specifically invites you,' I said. 'But you can't just hang here, blobbing out on my sofa and commandeering the telly. And I want my keys back.'

I could see him struggling with himself. Eventually he controlled his temper and with reasonably good grace switched off the TV. He reached in his pocket for the keys I'd given him. How long ago? Way back when I trusted him and was happy to see him whenever he showed up. He put the keys on the arm of my chair and said, 'I'm sorry, Seema, I never wanted any of this to happen. I love you. I never wanted you out of my life – you must believe that.'

My throat constricted. I could scarcely breathe. But he was waiting for an answer so I swallowed and said, 'If that's how you treat someone you love...' I couldn't finish.

He began to speak again until we both noticed Titus half singing, half humming, 'Will you still need me, will you still feed me when I'm sixty-four?' He looked bored. Now he was pissing me off too, so I gave him a look that was supposed to convey the message that I wanted to feed him one of his own size 18 desert boots – slowly – with his severed foot still inside. He returned a smile of stunning sweetness that unbalanced me to such an extent that I almost didn't hear what Jake said next.

'I know I've hurt you,' he said, 'and you'll probably never forgive me, but I meant what I said: I do love you. It's going to be hard for you to deal with your mother's estate. I could help. And if you need money to tide you over till the will is probated, well, I don't have enough now, but I could buy the lease on this place from you in instalments. You won't have to deal with Amy. This will be just between you and me.'

I had a moment of blank astonishment. He really seemed to think he was offering to do me a favour. I looked at Titus. He was staring at Jake as if he'd just discovered a new species of insect.

When I could trust myself to speak I said, 'Have you discussed this plan with your girlfriend?' I spoke evenly. It was probably better than screaming, '*You arsehole,*' at the top of my voice. But possibly not.

'Not yet,' Jake said. He looked down at his right hand and noticed at the same time I did that he was automatically rubbing his fingernails with the ball of his thumb. A tell, I thought: he was lying to me. He quickly put both hands in his pockets saying, 'I never stopped thinking of *you* as my girlfriend, I swear.'

I gaped at him, big eyes, big mouth – a pantomime. I said, 'Okay, you lying piece of shit, I know you're cooking up something devious with Amy that will give you the right to stay here and evict *me.* Don't try to weasel out of it because I'll never believe another effing word you say to me. So why don't you do what Titus said? Put your coat on and go back to your mother. If you have any self-respect left at all, you'll never let me see your face again.'

Whatever his plan was, he'd lost, and he knew it. Five minutes later he was marching out, looking like a victim, with his bulging overnight bag.

'*Burn!*' Titus pronounced happily.

I grinned at him, wondering uneasily whether I would have been so direct if he hadn't been a witness. Was I now looking to Titus for an older man's approval? Some of the things Gemma had thrown at me were sticking like jam to a jersey. I was unsure and self-conscious.

He said, 'Jake matters less because Lazaro matters more? Or did you always care for Jake so little?'

'I don't know. I'm so sodding angry with him.'

'And are you angry with him because you cannot let yourself be angry with Lazaro?'

I was composing a sharp reply but stopped suddenly.

We both turned towards the window.

There was a slapping sound like bat's wings beating at the glass. We bumped into each other while hurrying to open the curtains. There we saw the great flakes of sleet whacking the window pane and sliding down as they melted.

'Pasqual!' I cried, and opened the window. Gusts of wind blew the sleet into my face as I leaned out. The wolfhounds started barking, loud and aggressive, as though we were being attacked.

'Hush,' I said, wiping sleet out of my eyes, peering into the dark. I thought I could see someone standing in the shadows on the other side of the road.

'What is it?' Titus elbowed me out of the way and squinted into the driving sleet. 'I cannot see anything.'

'Across the road,' I shouted, trying unsuccessfully to push him away.

Without pausing to put my coat on, I ran out of the flat and the building onto the silent, sleety street. The dogs brushed past me tripping me on the doorstep. They hesitated momentarily then set off galloping, first to the other side of the road, then veering to the right. They bayed, deep in their throats. The sound was so ominous I had to remind myself that they were my friends. Then suddenly the street lights failed and all the windows of nearby buildings went dark. The dogs raced away into the night.

I scrambled to my feet, calling out to them. But they moved so fast that within seconds they were out of sight. I could hear them, but they were making so much noise they couldn't hear me.

Titus exploded through the door, knocking me over again. He

skidded on the slippery pavement and ended up on his backside. We sat facing each other, helpless in the wet slush.

Far away, to my right, I thought I heard the roar of a motorbike starting up.

I got up and as I limped to the other side of the road the sleet stopped as suddenly as it had begun. I was shuddering with cold and scanning the pavement when Titus joined me.

'Give me your cigarette lighter,' I demanded.

He fumbled in his pocket and handed it to me. I flicked it on and by the light of the tiny flame could just see the fading signs of two footprints in the snow. They were facing my living room window.

'What?' Titus asked, bending low.

'Footprints,' I said. 'Can't you see them?'

'Maybe.' He bent lower. 'Who was it? Did you see?'

'No.' I was close to tears. 'It always used to be Pasqual. Did you hear the motorbike?'

'Who can say? Traffic is always so loud in London.'

As he said this I realised that I had not heard normal traffic noise. The strange silence had only been broken by the dogs. Now ordinary street sounds re-asserted themselves, the lights came on and Beau and Bro came trotting back down the middle of the road. One of them was carrying what looked like the cuff and part of the sleeve of a leather jacket which he refused to release until we were back in my flat. Both dogs were jittery and wouldn't settle until I'd dried them off. Then I fed them dog treats and massaged the tension out of their necks and shoulders.

Titus, wisely, didn't touch them. He found my boiler and turned the heat up. While I was calming the dogs he took a hot shower and put his sopping clothes into the dryer. He seemed to know, without asking a woman, how domestic appliances worked – a trick Jake had never mastered. I gave him points for that and concluded that he must be unmarried. I did not give him points for style while his clothes were drying. He wore a towel that barely stretched around his waist, and his puffer jacket, open, over his hairy chest – not a good look on a big man.

I showered quickly and put on clean jeans and the long soft sweater Amy gave me for my last birthday. It was the sweater of choice when I needed to warm up quickly. Now I wondered if it had been a guilt-gift and nearly tore it off again. But I heard the house phone ring and hurried into the living room only to watch Titus absent-mindedly pick up the receiver as if it was his house and his phone.

'Hannah,' he said. 'What news? Yes, she's here.'

I switched to speakerphone. 'I'm just leaving the hospital,' she said. Her tinny voice sounded tired.

'Come to me,' I said, 'I'm going to cobble together a pasta sauce. There'll be plenty.'

'And Titus, no doubt, will consume all of it. Thank you, dear, but Irvin is fetching his car and he will give me a lift home. I'm rather tired, but I wanted to tell you both what has happened here.'

Titus huddled close to me so that we could both hear the unclear speaker. The smell of his soap made me sneeze.

I said, 'Shall we come to yours?'

'I want to go straight to bed. But first I need to tell you that the news here is that there is very nearly no news. We waited for a long time for the security tapes only to discover that the cameras at all the entrances and exits and the ones in the public areas outside Kim's ward showed no strange activity at all. There is no sign of her leaving her ward, and there was, apparently, no visitor who could have helped her leave. Nothing at all. Then one of the security team noticed that the time counter was malfunctioning and we had to wade through a lot of extra footage. Even so, there is nothing on tape that explains Kim's absence.'

'Could someone have interfered with the CCTV system?' Titus asked. 'Blocked it for the time required to abduct Kim?'

'That is what everyone supposes. An expert from the

manufacturers will come tomorrow to, I believe the term is, "run a diagnostic".'

'Do they often lose patients at the Royal Free?' I asked.

'Their security, they say, is about as good as it can be given the size of the place and the chaos that occurs even in the best run hospital. They're taking this abduction very seriously.'

'They're calling it abduction?'

'The medical team say she was in no condition to leave of her own volition. She was on an IV drip, she couldn't walk and she was incoherent.'

'Speaking of diagnostics... ' Titus began.

Hannah cut him off. 'And that's another thing: all of Kim's blood and urine samples mysteriously failed to arrive at the lab. The doctors and the senior nursing staff in charge of her treatment told me that they couldn't seem to reverse the symptoms of catastrophic liver and kidney failure. They said that if her condition was indeed porphyria it was rampant to a degree none of them had witnessed before. But unless someone can track down the samples we'll never know.'

'What do you make of all this?' I asked cautiously.

'I think they do the best they can,' Hannah said vaguely. 'But you know how badly funded public medicine is: mistakes are made all the time.'

'Chaos in the NHS?' I asked, lifting an eyebrow at Titus. I was worried about Hannah's vagueness. 'Have you had anything to eat since lunch?' When she didn't answer I said, 'Hannah, there's some chocolate in your handbag.'

'Ah, so there is,' Hannah said to the sound of rustling. 'I forgot.'

Amy chose this moment to storm into the flat in a towering rage. 'You have no right to evict my boyfriend!' she yelled, waking the dogs who rose up to full height growling and bristling.

'I'm on the phone,' I said.

'That must be Amy,' Hannah said more cheerfully.

'Jakey's in tears,' Amy screeched more quietly. 'And we know you brought in those fucking dogs to intimidate us. You're an emotional fascist and a pathetic loser.'

'Grrrr-ro-row!' went Beau and Bro advancing stiff-legged.

'She's wearing pink yoga pants,' Titus told Hannah. 'Not a good colour I think. Like fuchsias.'

'Are you catching the gardening bug from Seema?' Hannah asked.

Amy at last noticed Titus in his towel and puffer jacket. She burst out laughing. 'Is this what you're reduced to now?' she hooted. 'A hairy old bloke with a paunch?'

'Is she talking about you, Titus?' Hannah asked.

'So I believe,' Titus said. 'I cannot see any other hairy old bloke with a paunch.'

'Have you eaten some chocolate?' I asked.

'I'm eating now. And Irvin has just arrived. He's waving to me.'

'Hannah,' I said urgently, 'don't go straight to bed. We'll come over as soon as Titus's clothes are dry enough to wear and we'll pick up some Chinese noodles on the way.'

'I need sleep,' she replied and rang off before I could argue.

I turned to Amy in a fury. 'Don't you *ever* call me a fascist again! And don't you come on to me like you're my victim. *You* are the lying, cheating troll. Obviously, since you're insisting on your rights as my tenant, you can invite whoever you like – when you are here to receive them. But if you think I'll put up with Jake hanging around when you're out, you've got another think coming.'

'I'm surprised she trusts Jacob to be alone with you,' Titus remarked to me. Yes, he really did know how to pour petrol onto flames.

'He calls her the *heifer,* for fuck's sake,' Amy exploded. 'He wouldn't touch her with a ten-foot pole.'

'So of course you know about the deal this so virtuous man proposed to the heifer that he still claims to love?'

'Shut up, both of you!' I shouted, close to furious tears at Jake's treachery, Amy's treachery and Titus, just for being a witness to my humiliation.

'Jacob tells me everything. I said it wouldn't work but he insisted it was worth a try.' She lifted her chin and looked smug.

I studied her expression, searching for even a flicker of self-doubt. I used to love and rely on her confidence. Now it frightened me, so I turned away, focussing on the dogs instead. I noticed that they were creeping closer to Amy, pinning her against the wall. They were reacting to the enmity in the room. 'Come here boys, and sit down,' I said, kneeling on the floor next to the phone table. I could bury my burning face in their fur and hide the hurt and shame behind their bulk. Jake described me as a heifer and Amy blabbed it in front of Titus. I wanted to vanish.

Free to move, Amy walked into the centre of the room. She didn't just sit down in the armchair – she occupied it as if she'd won it in a battle. She took her phone out of her gym bag and thumbed in a number. 'Hi, sweetie,' she cooed. 'You can come in now... what? Yes, he's still here but they're leaving soon... yes, they're still here too... oh, don't be such a wuss... no, she won't.... because she knows I'll sue the knickers off her if either one of us is hurt even the tiniest bit.' She stared at me coldly as she hung up, daring me to contradict anything she said.

I got up, turned my back on her and went to the kitchen. Titus followed me. We both looked at my dryer which was grinding away, whining every now and then in protest. We watched his trousers flopping around like a falling man. I said, 'If I cook a simple sauce now, you could take it to Hannah when you leave. She needs to eat little and often, but she forgets or thinks there's a better way to use her time.'

'We could take food to Hannah together,' Titus said. 'We could cook together. Then my clothes will be dry and we can leave the toxic twins to poison each other.'

Two gigantic hounds, Titus and I filled the kitchen to bursting. We heard Amy letting Jake in but by that time Titus was weeping over the onions and I was chopping pimentos, garlic and Portobello mushrooms which I fried up in olive oil before adding tomato puree, tinned chopped tomatoes, quorn mince and a fat handful of basil. Because of Titus I made twice as much as I would for myself, Jake and Amy. I would never cook for Jake and Amy again. Another door closed.

I would never see my mother again. That was one more closed door. To my own surprise I found myself talking to Titus about her while the dryer wheezed and the sauce simmered down. 'She wanted a son,' I told him. My dad died of meningitis when I was eight. We'd been to the swimming pool at Camden Sports Centre together and she blamed me for his death. Then, because of his death she blamed me because she'd never have the son she wanted. She said I'd taken away her last chance.'

'Was the pool tested for the meningococcal bacteria?'

'I don't think so. Hannah said he was far more likely to have picked it up in the school where he taught. Mother thought he had flu and a heat rash. She didn't think adults were susceptible to meningitis so it was diagnosed far too late.'

'Where were you when he died?' Titus took a spoon out of the cutlery drawer and 'tasted' the sauce. He took several large spoonfuls before expressing his his satisfaction.

'Hannah came and took me home with her. I stayed with her for about six weeks and then I was sent to boarding school. When I was allowed home for the winter holiday, Mother was already well on her way to becoming a religious nut with a massive kosher kitchen. There was no sign that Dad had ever lived in the house. That crappy kitchen had even gobbled up his study.'

'Mmmm,' Titus said around another mouthful of sauce.

'Leave some for Hannah,' I said anxiously.

'She says your mother was a very angry woman.'

'Yes,' I said, confiscating the spoon.

Titus changed the subject, 'You know that I am going to blame climate change for the snow, don't you?'

'Of course. So do I.'

'But?'

'But it's one of the weirdnesses. In dreams, Pasqual is a being who lives in permanent winter and takes it with him wherever he goes.'

'The Iceman Cometh?' Titus suggested dryly.

I laughed and relieved him of a second spoon.

'You dream just of him?'

'I dream of them all. There were the opium dreams. Hannah says it wasn't opium. So maybe they weren't dreams.' This was as close as I'd ever come to confessing a shaming belief that, although I didn't understand how, I'd been abused by Gemma. I hurried on, 'Someone was there tonight. The dogs went after him. They attacked him – must have: they brought back a chunk of his leathers. And what about Kim's abduction? Don't you think the hospital CCTV system was tampered with?'

'Probably,' Titus said. 'That is not weird. It is a staple of mystery stories. I don't know if it's so easy in real life. But why this conspiring? Why go to all the trouble?'

'To protect the identity of whoever took her away.'

'Again I ask why. This is a very sick girl who may, in any case, die. Why steal her medical records? What, here, is being concealed?'

'Kim herself?' I suggested.

'Yes – because she is part of a household that conducts itself in a most peculiar way and uses outsiders for entertainment.'

'She knows too much?' I said, trying to keep the edge of sarcasm out of my voice. I was annoyed with myself: again I was thinking of too many things at once. And true to form Titus had picked the most obvious one to examine – ignoring the bigger picture.

I said, 'If we take each incident separately it's like examining a painting inch by inch.'

'But,' Titus began, eyeing the simmering sauce wistfully, 'that

is how scientists think. We build our picture from small facts.'
He paused and looked at me. 'Aha, but you are saying we already
think we know what is happening and are twisting the facts. Well,
we are scientists of a sort, Hannah and I, and we must ignore
certain outcomes – such as the existence of vampires or trolls or
gods. Our conclusions must have provable, fact-based credibility.
It is not a fantasy-based picture we are making. Human behaviour
is usually all that is required to explain the weird.'

'That's what I'm saying too.' I said excitedly. 'I'm saying there's
a possibility that vampires are human and not fantasy. They aren't
"made" by exchange of blood like the stories say; they're born that
way – conceived and born the way all mammals are: a lost tribe,
sort of. Think how many types, shapes and sizes of cat there are.
Why should human beings be so one-size-fits-all?'

'They aren't.' He sounded exasperated. We stared at each other.
I blinked first, looking away, turning off the hob and collecting
vegan parmesan from the fridge and an unopened packet of fusilli
from the cupboard.

Amy opened the door. She'd changed into tight jeans and a
low-cut sweater. She smelled of shower gel. 'You're hogging the
kitchen,' she complained. I ignored her. Titus leaned back against
the counter looking comical and obscene in his inadequate towel
and open jacket. She wrinkled her nose in distaste and backed
away.

The dryer stopped grinding and the trousers, exhausted from
running on a treadmill, dropped to the bottom of the drum,
cushioned by the rest of Titus's clothes. While he went to my
bedroom to dress I stirred the pot of pasta sauce, turning it over
and over, hoping it would cool quickly so that I could decant it
into something Titus could take to Hannah. The dogs lay in the
corner close to their bowls, opening one eye every now and then
to check they hadn't missed anything.

I'm in my kitchen, I thought, with my sleepy dogs. The room
is fragrant with Mediterranean smells. A man is getting dressed in

the bedroom. What is wrong with this quiet domestic scene? Why can't I live in this moment without anxiety, without yearning for something, someone, a lot more dangerous and strange?

I picked up my knife and chopped another handful of basil. I would let it wilt in the heat of the cooked sauce. But instead of acting on the thought, I stabbed my thumb with the knife while it still had traces of basil on it. I squeezed and watched the scarlet blossom swell. Like a rose it was decorated by the lovely mid-green of basil leaves. Something was telling me to let the blood drip into the sauce. The voice in my head said, 'It is your own blood, given freely. It cannot be a theft.'

Then Titus said, 'You cut yourself. Let me see.' His clothes were wrinkled and tight from the dryer.

I put my thumb in my mouth and sucked swallowing the blood myself. 'It's nothing,' I said as I did the sensible thing – washing the little wound with soap and water, finding a plaster in the first aid box and covering my thumb.

There was a plastic container in another cupboard and I went through the motions of emptying the sauce into it and sprinkling chopped basil over the top. After that, resentful and bored, I washed the knives and pan and cleaned the kitchen counter. This time Titus watched me without offering to help. He looked puzzled. I was puzzled too. A fragile connection between us felt damaged. I didn't know why, but it had something to do with him interrupting me and seeing my blood. I'd wanted to turn on him and say, 'Not for *your* eyes, mister.' Now I wanted him gone.

Lazaro, I was convinced, had sent Pasqual to fetch me. He had forgiven me, or if he hadn't he would allow me to ask for forgiveness. I would kneel and touch my head to the floor the way I'd seen Kim do. He would tell me to abandon interfering Hannah and nosey Titus. He would tell me to get rid of the dogs. Then he might, if I was very, very good, open his arms to me again.

When I'd finished cleaning and packed the food in a bag I handed it to Titus saying, 'Take this to Hannah and make sure she eats some. Don't you scarf it all down before you see her. I'm not coming. I'm tired. I want to go to bed.'

He put the bag down on the clean counter and stared at me. 'Have you been scratching those bites on your throat?' he asked. 'There's blood on the neck of your sweater.' He reached out to touch me, and I stepped back quickly.

'What?' he said.

'What you did last time was totally yuk.'

'Last time?' He looked bewildered. 'What did I do?'

'At Hannah's.' And when light did not dawn I followed up with, 'When I was crying.'

'Oh?' he said. Then, 'Oh. That.'

'Yes, that. It made me wonder if you were one of them.'

He looked as if I'd whacked him on the head with a brick.

'One of the deviants you and Hannah think Lazaro is,' I said, to help him out. 'But as Hannah's vouching for you I'll give you the benefit of the doubt – which is more than you're giving Lazaro.'

He bent his head for a moment, gazing at his canoe-sized shoes. I picked up the food bag and thrust it into his hand again. From my point of view this was as good as saying, 'Now bugger off'.

'No,' he said, understanding me. 'I was instructed not to leave you. You must come too or Hannah will not eat.' He rubbed his chin and I could hear his fingernails rasping over the night-time bristles. For a moment the tiny noise was too loud and aggravating. It even hurt my skin.

'If you don't come,' he said, 'Hannah will be hungry. You say, yourself, she should eat often. What has she eaten since our lunch? A bar of chocolate? What good have you done by cooking if you do not also give the food?'

'You can give the food,' I said furiously.

'No.'

'You are just one more manipulative bastard,' I hissed. 'Just one more arsewipe who thinks he matters more than I do. Why do you blokes think testosterone gives you the right to trample over *my* thoughts and feelings?'

'Hannah is more important than a quarrel about men and women.'

'Even that doesn't give you the right to use force – not emotional, moral or physical.'

'Okay,' he said amiably. 'But *I'm* hungry. Let's eat.' He began to unpack the bag.

'You conniving prick.' I grabbed the food and headed out of the kitchen to the front door, only pausing to grab my coat and bag. The dogs followed quickly, unnerved by my anger.

'About time,' Amy said, as we marched past. Jake gave me a covert sympathetic smile. Talk about conniving, manipulative bastards.

I did not manage to drive off leaving Titus on the pavement the way I'd planned. Nor could I give him an uncomfortable ride without hurting the dogs too. At the first set of lights, one of them reared up, his huge paws trampling the wire netting, to snuffle into my hair trying to lick my ear. I could feel his anxiety. I turned in my seat to smooth his head. 'It's fine,' I mumbled. But it wasn't.

At last Titus said, 'If vampires are born, not made, why does Lazaro want to drink *your* blood? What possible reason would he have to subvert your beliefs and your culture unless it was to prove his power and dominance over you to an audience of his people? You call me manipulative. Your attack on me for using manipulation was instant and convincing. And yet, in spite of everything you had told to me, you are still accepting Lazaro's use of force against you. He has abused you in nearly every conceivable way and yet you defend him. Who, now, is twisting facts, Ms Dahami?'

I knew I shouldn't answer him. The lights changed and I drove on, keeping my mouth tight shut.

He continued, 'This Lazaro has drugged you, hurt you and humiliated you. He most surely has caused death to your mother.

He will let Kim die for lack of medical treatment rather than allow her to reveal him. He has shown in many ways he owes to you no loyalty. He uses you without mercy. And yet you, against your own logic, defend him. Are you a fool, an addict or a wimp?'

My lips were pressed together, trapping angry words behind them. Whatever I said, he would use it against me.

'You will, like any poor beaten woman, say you love him,' he said, angry too but speaking in measured tones that annoyed the shit out of me. 'Even while your neck bleeds and your wrists ache with bruises from the restraints he forced you to wear. What are you trying to prove about your capacity for love and loyalty? And to whom? What do you people call it? "Gluttony for punishment"? Do you enjoy pain? Are you as stupid as that?'

I was on Lyttleton Road, avoiding roadworks. I risked a hate-filled glance at the man who was yammering at my profile. His pale hair was grey under street lights and sticking out like a cartoon character's. He had the patient look of a man talking to a stupid child. I wanted to jolt him out of his paternalism with a blast from a shock collar.

Instead, four or five things happened one on top of another. Just as I was grinding my teeth in frustration and looking back at the road ahead, a motorbike roared out of a turning to my left cutting straight across me. I stamped on the brake and flung out my arm to stop Titus or either of the dogs from hitting the windscreen. I swerved left. The van lurched over the kerb and I saw a red pillar-box flashing towards me.

I don't remember the impact and I don't remember my head hitting the steering wheel. But that's what Titus told me happened.

I felt as if I'd just blinked, but obviously I'd lost more time than that because, when I opened my eyes, Titus and the dogs were on the pavement. Titus was having a furious argument with some men. The dogs were battle ready, squared up between the men and the van. The van door on my side was crumpled and jammed against the pillar-box. I couldn't move my right arm.

'No.' Titus shouted. 'We do this the proper way.'

'But we've got the motor right here,' someone shouted back at him. '*We'll* take her to the hospital. What're you waiting for?'

'Johnny Foreigner wouldn't know the "proper" way we do things if it bit him on the bum,' yelled someone else.

'I phone police.' Titus brandished his phone.

'How long will *that* take?' said another angry voice. 'Taking statements, filling in forms…'

'She needs a doctor *now!*' yelled the first man. He must've moved forward because the dogs went into full attack mode, snarling and barking like mad things. The man squealed.

I closed my eyes and kept still. Pain was whispering to me just out of earshot. I didn't want it to come any closer. No one could open the driver's side door. I couldn't get out unless I scooched across to the passenger side. But I didn't want to move and I *so* didn't want anyone to move me.

'She could be dying,' a man said accusingly. 'If she dies it'll be your fault.'

'Am I dying?' I asked. No one answered.

'I don't know why you want to take her,' Titus said loudly. 'She should not be moved except with help of experts.'

'Can't you control these 'orrible sodding dogs?'

'No,' Titus said simply. 'They'll calm down if you go.'

'Sirens,' the first man said. 'The fucking moron did call Old Bill.'

Then it was quiet enough for me to hear the sirens too.

TWENTY-TWO

It was well after midnight when Hannah at last ate the meal I'd prepared for her hours earlier. She was surprisingly chipper about it. But then Hannah prospers on emergencies.

Titus, who had dealt with the police, the emergency room, the van and the dogs, wolfed down three-quarters of everything while the real wolfhounds slept in Hannah's utility room.

I wasn't hungry. I'd been given painkillers which actually worked, and my cracked upper arm was immobilised, but the shock of the accident was still making me feel twitchy and remote.

It was Titus's statement to the cops that was the real stunner. He was recounting it to Hannah now, while mopping his plate and the serving bowl with the last of Hannah's bread.

'I told them,' he mumbled through another enormous mouthful, 'I said the accident was caused by a man on a motorbike, probably a Harley, who speeded out from a turning. Of course I couldn't see his face but his leather jacket was torn of the sleeve. I said also that I thought the accident was not so much accidental. I heard the cough of the bike before it roared, as if he was idling, waiting for us.

'Waiting for us also was three men. You wouldn't see this, Seema.' He turned to Hannah. 'Seema first was trying to avoid the bike, pumping her brakes, then trying not to hit the mailing box head on. She was throwing out her arm to protect me and the dogs from the face-forward crash, so she took the impact herself,

272

you see. She hit her head and broke her arm and did not notice how quickly three men walked out of three dark doorways. This fact, I told the police, was most suspicious. The men were spread out but acting together. It was an ambush.'

'But how did they know where to set an ambush?' Hannah asked.

'It's the route I always take to your house,' I said. 'There were roadworks where I had to slow down, so they had plenty of time to recognise my van and signal the biker.'

'But who knew you were coming here?'

'I knew,' Titus said, 'you knew and Seema knew.'

'And,' I added, 'if Amy was listening at the kitchen door – which I know she does – she knew. And if she told Jake, he knew too.'

'Or these people, whoever they are, could've put a bug on your van,' Hannah said.

'Or that,' Titus agreed. 'The police took the van to their pound, and I told them to look. They think I am mad.' He laughed. There was a smear of sauce on his chin and another on the front of his cable-knit sweater.

'But of course what they'll really be looking for is evidence that my van wasn't safe or maintained properly. At least they knew I wasn't pissed – they breathalysed me before letting me get into the ambulance.'

'Because as soon as they heard the sirens, the three men ran away from us.' Titus stared sorrowfully at his empty plate. 'So when the cops come there is no sign of a biker and three other men. Maybe we are two mad people or covering up for something.'

I could feel my head drooping over the table. I got up and took our plates one by one to the kitchen.

'Stop that,' Hannah ordered. 'You will sleep on the sofa tonight. Titus of course is in the spare room. If you want to do something before using the bathroom, bring in the old cake tin. I have a brick of fruit cake far too dense for me to eat which might suit Titus.'

When I came back from the kitchen balancing the cake tin, a

plate and a knife in one hand Titus was saying, 'I think you must be right: the men were not expecting me or the dogs. They appeared only to expect Seema. If their information came from Amy they would have known. But they didn't. So they were tracking the van only.' He got up and relieved my one useful hand of its burden. 'Before you go, Seema,' he said to me, slowly and seriously, 'you must know what I think, and Hannah too. This means the men were not ambushing me or the dogs. It was you they are waiting for. I think they would make you disappear like Kim.'

'But why?' I asked, nonplussed. 'You think this is Lazaro's doing, don't you? But you know, and Lazaro knows, if he wants me all he has to do is send for me.'

'Unfortunately we all know that,' Hannah said sadly. 'But we don't think he *wanted* you; we think he hired people to clean up loose ends for him.'

I stared from her to Titus, stricken. Titus nodded, 'They are rich, important people in this group – this secret society. They fear exposure by you, perhaps. It is possible that they always expected you to choose death for Lazaro's sake.'

What had I told him or Hannah? Had I really blurted out that I'd told Lazaro I'd die for him? Surely not. But I couldn't remember.

'This may be a cult with death as its object,' Titus went on. 'It is not unknown.'

'Or,' I began dully, 'it could all be Garth Harding's and Lesley Sharpe's doing.'

'Picture this,' Hannah said. 'I am sitting here, waiting and waiting until I'm faint for want of food. Eventually I ring the police who soon tell me your van had been found on Lyttleton Road. There'd clearly been an accident but the driver was missing. A bag containing food was found on the floor of the cab. Some blood was noticed on the steering wheel.

'Eventually you are put on the missing person's list. You are never found, Seema, and I never see you again – never. Kim will never be found either. *Listen* to me: no one goes to those lengths to cover up an abduction if their intentions are benign.'

'And where *are* you, Seema, tell us that,' Titus asked. Because of course he had to add to the bleak picture. He couldn't just shut up, could he?

I said, 'The story won't be complete until, come the revolution, my bones are dug up when the whole of privileged Belgravia and Buckingham Palace are flattened to make way for high-rise blocks of flats for the proletariat. Then they'll find a labyrinth of tunnels and underground castles and wonder what went on there in the good old days.'

In fact I was fantasising about sitting beside a pool, surrounded by white irises, in Lazaro's Italian Moonlight Garden. Someone close beside me is saying, 'It's better here, isn't it, my dear?' I don't look up from my drawing, but I can feel his warm breath on the back of my neck.

I don't need opium to dream, I thought. Then I saw two unsmiling faces staring at me.

'You are still in danger, Seema,' Hannah said angrily. 'What can we do or say to bring you back from cloud cuckoo land?'

I was going to say something light and superficial, but suddenly I felt time draining out of me. If I looked down, I thought, I would see a pile of sand, as if my whole body had become a broken hour glass.

I slept for nearly nine hours and woke in the same position I went to sleep in. Hannah was offering me a cup of coffee. She said, 'Titus has gone to The Corner Shop for dog food. Drink this.'

I drank. She looked better. She taped a bin bag round my arm so that I could have a shower and wash my hair. Then she told me that Detective Sergeant Richardson would be visiting me soon.

By the time I was clean Titus was back. He'd fed the dogs and taken them round the block for a quick bathroom break. All five of us seemed to have had a decent night's sleep.

But I looked down at my bruised and puffy hand. It was ugly; there was no other word for it. I flexed my fingers. They felt stiff and clumsy. I hadn't summoned enough moxie to look at my face in the bathroom mirror but I could feel the swelling on my cheekbone and forehead: the inheritance of a crash I couldn't remember.

I thought about the beautiful people at the Palatine Estate reception – especially Gemma and Pasqual, Lazaro's chosen assistants. They'd been picked for their perfection, I was sure. Even androgynous Kim was smooth and shiny, until she allied herself with me. After that she became as dirty and untidy as I was. And even grew a beard – the Seema Dahami effect?

I was never a beauty. Maybe I could be called interesting-looking. Some ignorant people describe me as exotic. But not pretty. So Lazaro did not pick me for my looks.

I pride myself on my strength. But he hadn't picked me for that either; or my affinity with dogs. There were thousands of better draughtswomen and more experienced gardeners too. He picked me, I thought with sudden clarity, because I was both culturally difficult and disposable. My so-called boyfriend wouldn't miss me, nor would my best friend. I wasn't part of a community or family. When he had my mother killed he must've thought he'd got rid of the one old woman who would care enough to create a fuss. Oh yes. I believed that now. Perhaps I always had.

I looked again at my hand. Would I be able to work one-handed? Or had he taken work away from me too? I tried to clench my fist and a bolt of electrical pain shot up my arm to my shoulder, making me gasp.

'What?' said Titus, looking up from his phone. Beau and Bro crowded into the small dining room to cuddle close to me.

'Will rage break the spell?' I asked. I experimented with the idea. All I could conjure was crushing disappointment.

'Eat your toast,' said Hannah. But I only managed half a slice before the doorbell rang.

When Titus showed Ed Richardson into the packed living room the first thing he said was, 'You got the hounds back, I see.'

'I bought them from their owner,' I told him. 'I found I couldn't live without them.'

The dogs positioned themselves between the stranger and me. I could see from their posture that they had their don't-give-us-any-shit faces on, making the Detective Sergeant's smile when he said, 'I hope you don't think you need that much protection from me.'

He and Titus had more buttock than chair seat, and they squirmed uncomfortably while Hannah sat serenely in her usual armchair. I stood until I realised with dismay that this would not be a private interview. Then I sat on the small sofa with the dogs on guard in front of me.

Ed Richardson began with, 'I'm happy to tell you that your mother's body will be released on Monday so you can go ahead with your arrangements. Your mother's rabbi, who I have to say, has kept in closer touch than was convenient, has been informed. I hope that's alright with you?'

'Thank you,' Hannah said. 'Then I assume we can clean the house now?'

'Forensics has finished with the crime scene,' he replied, shaking his head and frowning at Titus who was leaning forward looking interested. 'Nothing was found that was unconnected to Mrs Dahami, her family or her friends. And I'm afraid none of our enquiries have proved any more successful. The case will remain open, of course, but... ' He shrugged and spread his hands. He wasn't happy.

Because Hannah looked as if she was going to butt in again I said quickly, 'I know you've interviewed someone at the Sharpe-Harding offices. Did you ever speak to whoever it was who actually went to my mother's door?'

'Why?'

'Well, I heard that Sharpe-Harding sometimes uses a firm of enquiry agents called Leigh-Sampson to do that sort of work for them.'

'Where did you hear that, Miss Dahami?' he asked.

The way he said my name made me realise I might have made a mistake. I got up. 'Coffee?' I offered brightly.

'No, thanks.' Ed looked annoyed.

I said, 'I can't remember where I heard it.'

'Could it have been at the Palatine Estate, night before last? When someone, not a million miles away, called us out to investigate your kidnapping? Where nothing you described about the interior of the building you were supposedly held in was found, and where hundreds of potential witnesses had disappeared without a trace?'

'I expect so,' I said, throwing a help-me glance at Hannah, who was serenely contemplating her beautiful but threadbare Persian rug.

'You see,' Ed continued, recognising that I wasn't going to expand on my answer, 'That wasn't my particular call-out. Nor was the next one when an extremely sick young woman disappeared from the Royal Free. And funnily enough I was in my kip last night when a certain someone was involved in a traffic incident on Lyttleton Road. See, I've got other cases to work on but this week your name has come up in so many bulletins I find myself wondering if you're accident prone or an attention-seeker. Care to explain?'

'Not really,' I said after a long pause while Ed waited with exaggerated patience. 'I think I got in with a bad crowd. Usually, I'm not that interesting.'

'I should hope not.' The detective sergeant eyed my broken arm and bruised face with a sarcastic leer. 'You understand, don't you, that we can't act without evidence and witnesses?'

Titus stirred. 'I was witness to the incident last night. I gave statement and descriptions.'

'Which will be followed up in due course,' Ed said in his pompous cop-speak voice. 'But like I say, not my case.'

'Then follow up the Leigh-Sampson tip,' I said. 'And someone should find out what happened to Mark Kirkby, rugby football star of the London Scorpions who was also at this imaginary reception that didn't happen night before last.'

'*The* Mark Kirkby?' Ed was instantly transformed from cynical old cop into keen sports fan half his age. Hero worship, it seems, takes years off a man. I recognised the look: I'd seen it on Jake's face very recently.

'Yeah, him,' I said crossly. 'He seemed to be Garth Harding's protégé.' I would've said 'candidate' but I was now too tired and too cautious. Although I hadn't mentioned Lazaro by name I knew he would think I was betraying him as surely as if I'd stuck up Wanted posters all over London.

'How do you know?' Ed asked.

'He told me Mr Harding was sponsoring him in the Tuareg Trek Trial.'

'You actually know Mark Kirkby? You've spoken to him?'

'Ask my flatmate and her boyfriend. I know you all think I'm an attention-seeking fantasist, but they saw him too.' I was pissed off with Ed for only coming to life as a sports fan. 'However, you say it isn't your case. Your case was just the murder of a middle-aged Jewish woman – unsolved and shelved.'

'Look,' DS Richardson said, bristling, 'no one saw anything; no one heard anything and the perp didn't leave any clues. The case is open and will be reviewed regularly, but there's bugger all I can do without clues.'

'Take it easy, Ed,' I said, happy to have got a rise out of him but frustrated to the point of gnawing a chair leg. I got up. 'I need a pain killer. I'm hurting.'

As I left, followed closely by my canine shadows, I heard Hannah murmuring in a deceptively sweet voice, 'Detective Sergeant, are you interested in hearing a unifying theory?'

In the kitchen I flexed my fingers and rolled my shoulders trying to ease the tension without disturbing the broken bone. I took a couple of pills and stood at Hannah's kitchen sink holding the cold water glass against my swollen cheek. I didn't want to hear Hannah's theories about games of dominance and submission anymore. Games I could never win because I'd already lost. Amy was right – I was a born loser.

I refilled the dogs' water bowls in the utility room and watched them drink. They were sloppy drinkers – they splashed water all over the paper I'd put down for them. I dried their muzzles with an old dish towel. They stole it and wrestled with it for a couple of minutes until they tore it in half and proudly carried the two halves with them into the living room. I was glad someone was having fun. I surely wasn't.

Back in the living room I found that Titus had taken my place on the sofa leaving me with the spindly chair next to Richardson who was saying, 'Yes Mrs David, I hear what you're saying, but I'm afraid we ain't interested in what consenting adults do in private.'

'Seema did not consent,' Hannah said.

'I'll take your word for it,' he said without looking at me.

Up to a point his scepticism was well founded, because up to a point I *had* consented – although I still didn't know what I'd consented to. But I wished he'd just sling his hook. Everything, every mysterious, strange, beautiful, ghastly thing that had happened in the past week turned to dross when faced with the banality of police procedure. Detective Sergeant Edward Richardson was reducing my living, baffling experiences to fit the clichéd, commonplace world he was familiar with.

Was I a fool or a romantic?

I sat on Hannah's antique chair barely listening to the rational arguing with the hackneyed, and wished I was with Beau and Bro on Hampstead Heath, where Keats himself had walked, watching the two creatures who, because they weren't human, really knew how to love and to enjoy every free moment.

I realised too that it was Friday again. What if, a week ago, I had picked up the phone and said 'Shabbat Shalom' to my mother and then gone to supper with her? What if my duty as a daughter had come before my guerrilla gardening? What if there'd been no one for Pasqual to find at the roundabout?

What if I had not been beguiled by dreams of a Moonlight Garden or the Garden of Earthly Delights? I could've said, 'Sorry, not interested, I've got a boyfriend and I don't speak to strangers however handsome they are.' I didn't say that. I *was* interested and I *do* speak to strangers. It's in my nature. I didn't have a boyfriend, true, but no one had told me that yet. Illusions, delusions – I was, it seemed, a sucker for both.

TWENTY-THREE

It wasn't exactly raining. I sat in my room at Frank Farm, hundreds of miles from London, making pen and ink studies of unfurling bracken. This was my temporary refuge until my arm healed sufficiently to allow me to drive. At the moment the Exe Valley was shrouded in a heavy mist that was neither rain nor fog and the bracken and ferns were jewelled with minute drops of water.

Ashley Frank isn't crazy about bracken. It poisons cattle, harbours sheep ticks and is invasive enough to edge out heather and bilberries. But it is old, old, old: there are fossil brackens that are fifty-five million years old.

My drawings start very naturalistic and slowly evolve into abstractions of narrow triangles. Each frond is an isosceles triangle made up of triangles, serrated in turn by more triangles.

My mother is lying on the East side of Hoop Lane Jewish cemetery, so far without a gravestone and without benefit of greenery, even ancient bracken. These are the horizontal burials for desert people on the East side. The West side, where there is grass and the gravestones are upright, is far more recognisable to the English.

The service was in Hebrew which I read in English translation. When I struggled to follow the sixteenth psalm I wished I'd paid proper attention in Hebrew lessons. 'I will not pour out libations of blood... ' I mouthed silently, and, 'You will not abandon me to the realm of the dead.' Who could I possibly be thinking of when reading lines like that? Not my poor old mother, that's for sure. And at last, 'You make known to me the path of life.' How I wished that was true.

Afterwards Hannah and I took stones to place on my father's grave. Even here, among my dead family, I felt out of place and alienated. What was the point of respecting the traditions if you didn't believe in god? If Hannah had no problem why should I? But I did.

The Prayer Hall at Hoop Lane was filled with people who knew my mother better than I did, who were connected to her more closely than I was. They could pray for her. I couldn't. They could both praise god and mourn his absence in a single famous prayer. Not me. God, for me, has always been absent.

At that moment I felt like a young shrub cut off at the roots and left to die alone. I had condemned her for having buried my sweet-natured, rational father, against his wishes, in the traditional way. But on the day of *her* burial I was glad to know where he was and put stones on his grave. At that moment Lazaro went far, far away even though it wasn't half a mile from the place when I'd first met him. Had he chosen the Italian Bar for it's proximity to the Jewish burial ground? Was he *so* devious and addicted to metaphors?

Neither Amy nor Jake came to the funeral. They didn't come to eat bread and eggs at Mira Joseph's house afterwards either. It was too soon for Mother's house, now my house, to be clean enough for sitting Shiva. In any case, no one wanted to go there. Everyone stared at it as they filed into Mira's. It was an unlucky house now. It would take a lot to lift the curse. I would not enter it myself until I knew the specialist cleaners had finished. That was something else I would have to sort out when I got back to London; like making sure Amy was absolutely gone from my flat. Maybe I'd have a specialist cleaning job done there too.

She texted me a week ago: she wrote, 'Are we really going to leave it like this?' I didn't reply. She didn't know where I was and I was glad. Jake sent three texts: 'I still love you', 'I miss you', and, 'Who'd have thought the hardest part would be losing my gardening buddy?' I didn't reply to him either. I wanted them both gone and dead to me. But of course they weren't. It would take years, I thought, to get over that loss.

Meanwhile I was spending a month in the country on the edge of Exmoor. I was drawing and painting and playing with the dogs. When he saw them, Ashley nearly evicted me before he'd even shown me my room. But I demonstrated how gentle and tractable they were. And I promised that they wouldn't chase wild sheep or Exmoor ponies and that his poultry would be safe too. So he let us stay.

I made promises about them but I was only just beginning to tell them apart. Beau, I decided was the eldest. He was just a little broader in the chest and just a shade faster than Bro. But Bro was the trickster who hid my hairbrush and made sure I only had one lonely bedroom slipper. Beau was above such puppyish pastimes.

Meanwhile I was discovering that Ashley was more a conservationist than a farmer. He makes a good part of his living by offering specialist guest accommodation to people who were interested in the Farm Without Harm movement. I was learning a lot from him. In fact I would've been half in love with him already if it weren't for his wife and family.

It was a lovely family, close, humorous and self-supporting. Well, that's what I saw, looking in from my position outside it. I was only a paying guest. And that month I was battling with self-pity. I don't think it was depression because I could still immerse myself in work and explore the river valley and the surrounding moors with the dogs. I went everywhere with two dogs and a drawing book. My clothes were speckled with paint and my fingers were blackened by ink and charcoal.

'Sorry Mother,' I whispered. 'Whatever I try to do well dirties my hands.' I couldn't say Qaddish for her; I could only apologise for the things that used to annoy her – the things I would never have apologised for when she was alive.

Dirty hands were a theme. Because of them I did not wear Lazaro's ring except on a chain round my neck. I tried to think clearly about him; I tried not to think about him at all. But he was present in all my drawing and painting. He had taught me something profound about art and the natural world. I just didn't yet know what it was. But I was sure I'd emerge from this period of mourning a different sort of gardener – maybe even a different sort of woman. I hoped so. I was pissed off with the old me who put up with constant criticism, untrustworthy friends and my own superficiality.

I thought with shame about how my callous disregard for Jake's dignity had been exposed at the horrible Palatine Estate competition. If that was how I felt I should never have hooked up with him. Without all the expectations and complications sex dumps into a relationship he could has been a valued friend. With them, he'd been an undervalued boyfriend.

What was the 'He'll Do For Now' game all about anyway? It was two ignorant teenage girls pretending to be cynical, pretending not to be ignorant, pretending not to care, and pretending we were not searching for love and acceptance. It was a juvenile attitude that became fossilised over years of misuse. We'd been stuck in the past, Amy and I. Our habitual friendship, she dominant, me submissive, had stuck as well. She was the pretty blonde for whom all doors opened, while I trailed behind, convinced I was only welcome because the blonde vouched for me.

Hannah's observation that she was jealous of me was unthinkable. I was jealous of her – that was the agreement we'd settled on when we were five – when, now I came to think of it, she was a natural blonde – when my mother, dragging a comb painfully through my tangled mop would habitually say, 'Why can't you have hair like Amy's?'

A relationship forged in kindergarten had never been re-examined. Left to itself it rotted like a fallen apple, and neither Amy nor I noticed. Or it wasn't in our interests to notice.

I wondered if I'd ever be more than a paying guest to the Franks. I drew their house, yard and barn. I drew the children digging up the last of the Jerusalem artichokes to feed to the pigs. I drew the pigs. Mrs Frank wanted the drawing of her house and I gave it to her. Currying favour again, I thought dismally, trying to buy acceptance. All the same she thought of me as a real artist. I told her I was a gardener and we had long discussions about whether or not the microclimate in the valley would allow her to espalier a Comice pear tree along the south facing wall of the house. I thought on the whole it was worth a shot and she made me promise to come back in the winter to help.

Right now my arm wasn't quite strong enough to dig. And because I'd given my usual clients the numbers of a few alternative helpers to fill in while I was away I expected to find I'd lost a lot of business when I got back. Who'd want a one-armed gardener?

'Everyone,' Hannah assured me. But I didn't believe her.

'You're young,' she said. 'The break could've been a lot worse. Keep up the exercises and you'll be as good as new. Are you sleeping? I think you need a lot of rest.'

'It shouldn't take a month to get over a week,' I grumbled.

'First you have to *want* to get over it,' she said. 'That's what takes the time.' She was talking about Lazaro as if he was a disease I could fight; as if will-power would somehow close the gulf that separated what I knew from what I felt.

Sometimes I thought, 'Well everyone knows that love conquers all, including common sense and self-preservation.' That was a lazy thought that let me off the hook. Sometimes I thought about what he said to me and how he spoke, as if I was valuable to him and our connection was precious. Then I thought, 'How could anyone who said he loved me mean me harm?' And I remembered the pretty words spoken between Jake and me during the year when he was humping Amy as well as me. And I thought, 'Don't be so effing naïve – turds use pretty words too.'

But Lazaro had taught me something about beauty and its

place in my life. It should be central, and it should be the compass that would always guide me. The lesson was a gift independent of the theft he'd committed when he took my love and allowed me to feel valuable to him. The lesson was everything. If Hannah was right my value to him would probably have depended on my death. I was only a convenience – a tool to be used for his own ambition.

Then, early one morning a few days before I was due to leave the farm, I found out something appalling. I was having breakfast with the family. It was porridge mixed with sweet bilberries gathered from the upland by the children, and served with cream Lara Frank made from the milk of her own cows. Ashley was already out and about so I took his newspaper. As usual it fell open at the sports section and there I saw a picture of Mark Kirkby. He was at the apex of an astonishing leap – at full stretch, the finger tips of his right hand just making contact with the ball. His red-gold hair shone under stadium lights and his blue eyes were concentrated and joyful.

The headline read, 'Tragic Death of a Rising Star'.

Tears burned my eyes. I read that Mark, so recently called up to join the England squad, had died suddenly in the dressing room after playing in a league match for the London Scorpions. A team-mate reported that he simply fell down as he was coming out of the shower. 'We all thought he was kidding us. We were waiting for him to get up and laugh. He was the fittest guy on the team. We're all too shocked to believe it yet.'

'He'd had a spectacular season,' said Scorpion coach Will Fellows. 'We'd just renewed his contract. A great team player, he'll be sorely missed. Our hearts go out to his family and girlfriend.'

The team doctor said it was too soon to speculate but Mark's sudden death had all the signs of a catastrophic cerebral accident like a stroke or an aneurism.

'Why is she crying,' asked Lara Frank's youngest. The children stared at me with morbid fascination. A grownup, especially one who sometimes gave them drawing lessons on rainy afternoons, doesn't cry.

'Eat your porridge,' ordered Lara. She handed me a handful of kitchen paper and refilled my mug.

Eventually I blew my nose and explained, 'I just found out a friend of mine died. It's the sort of thing that makes a person cry.' I'd grown fond of the three curious, energetic kids and didn't want to worry them. They responded by telling me how much they'd cried when a fox killed their oldest hen, and the moment passed. It was a good thing that sometime in the last month I had stopped crying bloody tears and I hardly ever had a nosebleed.

I looked at my phone. I knew Hannah would call. And ten minutes later she did.

'How's everything in paradise?' she began cautiously.

'It's alright, I've seen the paper,' I replied.

'Good,' she said with a relief familiar to anyone averse to giving bad news. 'So, what do you think?'

'It's hard to think. I keep seeing him and his amazing tattoos. He was so bursting with juice.'

'What about the mysterious dietary supplement?' she persisted. 'You know, don't you, that the Detective Sergeant wants a word?'

'He'll have to wait till I get back,' I said. 'I haven't heard from him and anyway I don't know anything that isn't hearsay. Also, as Mark said himself, there was nothing in the supplement that showed up when he was drugs tested. And professional athletes are tested all the time.'

'Then his recent superb performances might have been caused by a placebo effect?'

'Hannah!' I almost laughed. 'Have you been watching the rugby on telly?'

'Maybe a little,' she said huffily. 'It's a brutal, mindless game, but there are occasional moments of stunning grace. And your friend Mark certainly provided more than his fair share of those.'

I too had watched some of Mark's games on the Franks' TV. I was silent for a few moments.

Hannah said, 'If the supplement was harmless I wonder why it was a secret. But I wonder as well if in fact there was *no* active ingredient, and Garth Harding was demonstrating that his control of Mark's mind, and therefore his improved performance, was superior to Lazaro's control of yours. You were *actually* given a Class A substance.'

'We don't *actually* know anything,' I said.

'Except that you tested positive for opioids and Mark died very suddenly and unexpectedly. I wonder if he told his girlfriend what he told you. And I wonder if Harding, Sharpe or Lazaro suspect that he told you something that would incriminate them.'

I had the old sensation of falling through icy air I thought I'd put behind me. 'Are you saying that he'd served his purpose in helping Garth Harding win the effing contest? And that he'd become disposable? Are you telling me you think I'm still in danger?'

'I talked to Titus in the Netherlands before ringing you.' She sounded energised. 'He said we should watch for news of an accident to Mark's girlfriend – what was her name?'

'Cat-Lynne.'

'Cat-Lynne. And he asked me to convey to you the warning that maybe you should be discreet when you speak to the police.' It was a suggestion I was to act on in the future.

Hannah enjoyed enumerating possibilities and weighing one against another. I always tired before she did, and after we'd hung up I lay on my bed to think for half an hour. The dogs prowled restlessly, taking it in turn to nudge me and remind me it was time we tramped the moor in search of enemies. We'd never found any but my wonderful hounds hugely enjoyed the search.

My safety depended on them. But unfortunately their safety depended on me. I'd taken precautions before I left London. A vet had removed the chips from their ears and discovered two more under the scruffs of their necks. She replaced them with ones that merely had my phone number on them. No one from the Palatine Estate could track them, or me through them. That was a decision, though logical, which caused me heartache. Because of course the abject side of my nature wanted Lazaro to be able to find me. I promised myself I would not go looking for him. But if *he* searched *me* out and happened to find me...

Happily, my concern for Beau and Bro trumped my pitiful fantasies. And it was this concern that sent me out into some rare sunshine to look for Ashley.

———◆———

Ashley suggested that I should visit his friend Ollie in Taunton. So we all went two days later – six of us rammed into the Franks' twenty-five year old Land Rover.

Ollie, well placed in the heart of a popular tourist destination, hired out and sold caravans, campervans, mobile homes and RVs.

The children, it turned out, adored Ollie and his parking lot. They had thousands of acres of the most beautiful countryside to roam and play in but they were fascinated by small-space living. They went wild in Ollie's trailer park, scampering from one tiny home to another searching out concealed cupboards and foldaway beds while the grownups drank cider in Ollie's office and discussed my options.

In the end he decided that what would suit me and London best would be a second hand low-profile coach-built motor home he happened to have for sale. It was not much longer than the gardening van I'd totalled on the Lyttleton Road, but it had a double bed, a tiny kitchen, an even tinier shower and a cassette toilet. There was enough room for a mattress on the floor for the Beaus and overhead storage space for clothes and tools.

I was almost as excited by the cunning use of space as the children were. It would be my interim home while I sold both my flat and my mother's home. It was a midget house on wheels that no one could find but me. I could live safely until I found out if anyone was looking for me. The dogs would protect it and me, and I could protect them by being elusive. Catch me if you can, I thought.

Ollie took me out for a test drive but there was really no need; I was accustomed to a big vehicle. He was impressed by my ability to parallel park it. I told him about trying to find parking spaces in London, so he admired my fortitude too. I admired his deep growly laugh. Something about him woke me up. Maybe it was his admiration. Or maybe it was because he was friends with the Franks who I'd come to respect and trust.

We exchanged phone numbers and WhatsApp addresses. But as he lived in the West Country and I was going back to London in a couple of days I didn't expect anything to come of it. It was nice to be asked though.

———✦———

Spring was very late that year. There was precious little sun and even when it showed its face there was no warmth in it. My clients seemed depressed and out of ideas. I potted up seedlings on Mr Sorkin's patio: corn, courgettes and mangetout peas. He allowed me space for Hannah's Persian Carpet zinnias. While I was getting my hands dirty he watched TV. But unusually, he called me in to share his outrage at a news item. There, on the screen, was the terrifying sight of vast acres of burning Amazon rain forest. Unable to believe such stupidity, he said, 'And so the earth fries.' He buried his head in his hands, shaking with fury.

That same day two new clients, the Elias sisters, wept and showed me a site online where someone was selling, for £9-99, t-shirts celebrating the execution of a Polish Jew in Auschwitz. They couldn't look at my plans for their tiny front patch after that and re-booked me for the next day. Insanity was boiling up in the world.

That night I was just cold, not lonely. I slept cuddled up with the dogs for warmth. They were big and strong, but they couldn't protect me from my own mind. And towards morning I had a dream that echoed Mr Sorkin's fury and the Elias sisters' grief. I was standing in the dark corner of a hospital ward. Three masked men walked in. They stopped at a bed close to me. Someone said, 'This one is damaged. She's scheduled for disposal.' Another man stepped forward and scooped a woman out of her bed as if she weighed no more than a baby. The 'baby' was Kim. Her head lolled back showing me her ravaged, hairy face. Her hands too were covered with hair and pustules. The man said, 'She smells like a dog.' I wanted to help but my feet wouldn't move and I was afraid that she would turn into one of my hounds. But as the men walked away carrying their gruesome burden Lazaro said, 'The pit awaits, but don't be jealous: it isn't your turn yet.'

I woke up sweating with fear and outrage, and because I couldn't go back to sleep I drove to the traffic island in North Kilburn where Jake and I had made our guerrilla garden. It was the first time I'd been there since I got back from the country. I didn't want to think about Jake, but it was time to tidy up the garden. There was, waiting for me, enough rubbish to fill a bin bag – sweet wrappers, crisp packets, beer cans, plastic bottles, plastic bags, plastic, plastic and more plastic. I cleaned the plot and dead-headed the daffodils and tulips.

There was hardly any traffic so I let the Beaus out to stretch their legs too, and we made a circuit of the roundabout while I tried to decide what I'd plant next, or whether it'd be better to cut my losses and abandon the site altogether.

While I stood, pondering, the moon suddenly emerged from behind soapy clouds. It was a waning three-quarter moon bright enough to show me that, astonishingly, the *Papaver somniferum* I'd planted over six weeks ago were poking tiny green shoots out of the ground. The Green Man was rising from his winter grave, fingertips first. Opium poppies were showing the way. I didn't know whether to be jubilant or horrified. I thought, without thinking, if I can grow opium in North London, would there be any need for opiods?

I started to shake and raised my hand to touch the ring I still wore round my neck. It was as cold as ice. I shivered. Without warning the temperature dropped close to freezing. The darkness scraped my face like a rough blanket.

As in my dream I found my feet stuck to the roadside. Beau and Bro stirred uneasily. One of them raised his muzzle to the sky and howled. The moon hid its face and immediately I could move again. I sprinted to the house on wheels, chasing the dogs who were much quicker than I. We scrambled in and I turned on the engine and started to drive – anywhere, but as far from the traffic island as fast as I could. Then I stopped.

The hair on my neck was still pricking. The hair along the dogs' backs was erect. I didn't think I could drive safely – even on quiet roads.

My mind was crammed with images of dead Mark Kirkby and Kim who had not been seen or heard of again. I thought of all my unanswered questions – the ones Hannah and Titus thought were blown away by their bright, germ-free rationality. Everything, from snow to bloody tears had passed under their scientific gaze and come out explained into nothingness. Except my terrified love.

If there was nothing to fear, why was I so frightened?

If Lazaro was a pervert and sadist, why was I still obsessed with him? Why, in spite of everything I could not forgive him for, was I still tangled up with him like a fly in a spider's web?

I tried to think about forgiveness but found that it was impossible to forgive what I could still remember. My mind sagged under the weight of things I couldn't forget, even that I *should* not forget – like the burning rainforest and Auschwitz. Did I, like those incredible examples of human inhumanity, require eternal vigilance?

Dawn was breaking. Beau and Bro twitched in their sleep and I rubbed my sleepless eyes with hands that still trembled. 'Explain away fear, Hannah,' I said out loud.

Then suddenly I knew, just *knew*, he was calling me. How in hell did he know where I was? Was it because at last I'd come out at night after weeks of avoiding the dark? Explain that, Hannah.

Or was it the ring? The voice of reason unreasonably said, 'There's a tracking device in the ring. He can find you whenever you're in range.'

'But why would he want to?' I cried aloud, making the dogs flick their ears.

'Because you're easy,' a voice replied. It wasn't Hannah's voice, but it could have been Jake's or Amy's. 'You're a sucker for any sign of affection and approval.'

I looked down. Both my hands were clasped around the ring. 'I'm protecting it,' I whispered in disgust. 'I'm still keeping secrets – his secrets.'

I didn't bother to unclasp my hands. I simply wrenched the ring off my neck, chain and all. I felt the gold bite into my neck and knew there would be an angry mark in the morning. Maybe even a life-long scar.

I let the dogs out of the van. They were still edgy and trotted close beside me as I walked back to the roundabout. They were scared too but I was certain they would protect me. They were the only creatures I'd seen who could perturb Lazaro. That was another unanswered question: how could I adore to the point of self-destruction someone who hated dogs?

'I can't,' I said forcefully. 'I mustn't.'

Beau and Bro stood guard while I dug a hole and buried the ring among the shoots of the young opium poppies.

I found myself weeping while I worked because illogically I

felt as if I was burying my dreams. But when I wiped my eyes on my earth-stained sleeve I saw no trace of blood.

'Is it over?' I asked the dogs as I tamped down the earth over the token of Lazaro's love. But I couldn't suppress the ripple of fear as Beau, Bro and I sprinted back to my home on wheels.

'You can't conquer unreasonable fear,' I told them as we scrambled back into the motor home and I started the engine. 'You can only ignore it.' I started to drive south. I wanted to put running water between me and Lazaro so I made for Lambeth Bridge. I thought I was acting on an ancient superstition.

As I drove I asked myself, 'How could a Jew be an atheist, and how can an atheist be superstitious?'

Nothing made sense. It hadn't since the night I met a handsome old guy in the Italian Bar and Grill on the eve of Shabbat.

ABOUT THE AUTHOR

LIZA CODY is the award-winning author of many novels and short stories. Her Anna Lee series introduced the professional female private detective to British mystery fiction. It was adapted for television and broadcast in the UK and US. Cody's groundbreaking Bucket Nut Trilogy featured professional wrestler, Eva Wylie. Other novels include Rift, Gimme More, Ballad of a Dead Nobody, Miss Terry, Lady Bag and Crocodiles and Good Intentions (the sequel to Lady Bag.) Her novels have been widely translated. In 2019 she won the Radio Bremen Krimipreis.

Cody's short stories have been published in many magazines and anthologies. A collection of her first seventeen appeared in the widely praised Lucky Dip and other stories.

Liza Cody was born in London and most of her work is set there. Her career before she began writing was mostly in the visual arts. Currently she lives in Bath. Her informative website can be found at www.LizaCody.com which includes her occasional blog. You can also follow LizaCody on twitter.

Lightning Source UK Ltd.
Milton Keynes UK
UKHW010801220920
370318UK00001B/31

9 781663 205025